The Descent

ALSO BY MATT BROLLY

Detective Louise Blackwell series:

The Crossing

Lynch and Rose series:

The Controller

DCI Lambert series:

Dead Eyed

Dead Lucky

Dead Embers

Dead Time

Dead Water

Zero

The Descent

MATT BROLLY

THOMAS & MERCER

Text copyright © 2020 by Matt Brolly
All rights reserved.

No part of this book may be reproduced, or stored in a retrieval system, or transmitted in any form or by any means, electronic, mechanical, photocopying, recording, or otherwise, without express written permission of the publisher.

Published by Thomas & Mercer, Seattle

www.apub.com

Amazon, the Amazon logo, and Thomas & Mercer are trademarks of Amazon.com, Inc., or its affiliates.

ISBN-13: 9781542017008
ISBN-10: 1542017009

Cover design by Tom Sanderson

Printed in the United States of America

For Claire Louise Webber

Prologue

The elevation of Saint Nicholas' Church in Uphill gave the group an unparalleled view of Weston-super-Mare and the surrounding coastline. In the distance stood the promontory of Brean Down, and closer still the outline of Uphill Church and the mouth of the River Axe. Directly below, beneath the sheer drop of the cliff top, was the marina centre or, as some locals called it, the dead boat yard.

Amy Carlisle pulled the light fabric of her coat tightly around her. The day's residual heat had dissipated in the last hour and their small bonfire was doing little to warm her. She'd received the message at midnight after spending several nights in her bedsit waiting for news from Jay.

From her spot on the dry grass of the churchyard, Amy glanced at Jay, trying not to make it look obvious. He was older than everyone else in the group and certainly more relaxed. There was an easiness to his long-limbed body; a sense of grace that belonged to a dancer. He sat on the other side of the fire, his arms wrapped around Claire. This in itself didn't mean Claire would be chosen tonight, but if last month's events were anything to go by then she would be the one. The thought brought with it a mixture of jealousy and relief. Amy's time would come, but sitting here overlooking the town with its glittering lights, the sea for once at full tide, she began to doubt herself. Such hesitation lasted only seconds. She only had to think back to the bedsit – somehow always cold despite the intense heat of the last few days – and her reasons for being here, for her resolve to return.

As Amy gazed towards Jay, she caught a look from Megan. Megan was the newest member of the group, and in the glow of the fire she looked impossibly young. Amy offered her a smile and Megan came and sat down next to her. 'I'm glad you're here,' said Megan.

Jay had found Megan six weeks ago. At the last meeting he'd asked Amy to look after her – as he did with all the new women – and since then they'd made regular contact in the private online group. Megan was in her late twenties and had been sleeping rough in Bristol. She'd told Amy that Jay had found her a place but as they weren't allowed to meet outside of the group gatherings, she hadn't told her where. 'I'm glad you're here too,' said Amy, as Megan moved in close, her skin ripe with sweat and body spray.

'I hope he chooses me,' said Megan.

'You may have to be patient.'

Megan laid her head on Amy's shoulder. In her past life, Amy would have resented the personal intrusion but she welcomed it now, the feel of Megan's body as light as air as Jay stood and began circulating among the group, offering its members cups of the tea he'd been boiling over the campfire.

The tea was called Ayahuasca. Jay had first given her the tea that first night in Kewstoke, where she'd been sleeping on the beach. She'd been reckless then, figuring she had nothing to lose. The dose had been small but with Jay's guidance she'd experienced something she hadn't believed possible. When she'd come round she thought she'd been away for hours, but only minutes had passed.

'Do you see?' Jay had said, and at that moment everything had become that little bit clearer.

Jay hunkered between Amy and Megan. 'I'm glad to see you are both getting on so well,' he said, smiling as he handed them the tea.

Amy had so much she wanted to say but remained silent as she took the drink, her only response her embarrassed smile.

Under Jay's instruction, they all drank the cooling tea. Ayahuasca contained the mind-altering drug DMT and although the dose Jay gave them was small, it wasn't long before Amy felt its effect. Warmth spread through her as her body began to vibrate. She closed her eyes, present but far away, as her mind whirled with images of shapes and geometries. It wasn't the same as taking the full dose of DMT. It was a glimpse, and when she came to minutes later she wanted to experience more. She saw the same desire in the other members of the group, Megan gazing up at her, her hazel eyes open wide in wonder as she returned.

A hush grew over the group as Jay stood. Amy loved and hated these moments, as one by one the group explained their reasons for being there. It was painful hearing everyone's stories but the tea made it easier. When it came to her turn, she told her story without embarrassment, grateful that Megan was sitting next to her.

'Aiden was a beautiful baby. You know sometimes they're ugly? That sounds horrible I know,' said Amy, to a murmur of laughter from the group. 'But it's true. Some babies just aren't very good-looking. They're wrinkly and scrunched up as if they haven't formed properly. But Aiden wasn't like that. He was complete from that moment I first held him. He had a shock of red hair, this perfect little tuft. And when I held him, he looked straight at me and I could tell at that very second he knew who I was. I can't really explain it, though I do have a better idea now thanks to Jay, but it was as if at that moment he could see me completely. Does that make sense?'

The group responded, positive and encouraging, and Amy felt Megan's hand stretch towards her.

'Well, that was what it felt like to me. He could see me completely and I welcomed that analysis. It bonded us in a way that could never be taken away. And although I knew he would never remember that moment, it would always be part of him and that gave me some comfort.

'They took him later that day. That was part of the deal. I was too young. I had no money, no family, no home to offer him. They were a lovely couple and I don't blame them for what happened. They couldn't have children of their own and had so much love to offer. I didn't tell them I'd called him Aiden and they didn't ask.

'Did I cry when they took him away? Of course I did. But I knew we had that connection. He'd seen me and I'd seen him. I was part of him now and no one would ever be able to take that away from me.'

Jay put his arm around her and she eased into him. He knew what was coming and she was grateful for the comfort. The first time she'd spoken in front of the group, he'd told her that she didn't need to continue, but she'd battled through and would do the same now.

'I never saw him again. I knew where he lived but it would have destroyed me to see him. And it wouldn't have been fair on him or his new parents.' Amy paused, her mouth dry. Taking a deep breath, she continued.

'I only found out about it by chance. Can you believe that?' she said, tears stinging her cold skin. 'I read about it in *The Mercury*, in the memorial section. If I hadn't decided to go to the library that day, I may never have found out. I may have thought he was still alive even now.'

Megan trembled next to her as she continued. 'It's okay, Megan,' said Amy. 'Little Aiden passed away just before his fourth birthday. He had a heart defect I never knew about. His parents did their very best for him. I know that.'

4

Amy grabbed Megan's hand as Jay held her tighter. 'Of course I was completely destroyed. It didn't matter that I hadn't seen him since the day he was born. He was my little boy and always would be.

'I made the mistake of trying to speak to his parents. The mother in particular wouldn't understand. She was consumed by grief, I understand that now, but when she told me that Finley – the name they'd given little Aiden – wasn't my son, it was like she'd stabbed me in the heart.

'In truth I wasn't in a great place when I found out. I was already drinking and using. My life was shit and stayed that way until I met Jay.'

Another murmur of approval went around the group, Jay holding her even tighter. 'I'd thought of taking my life before but had lacked the courage. Part of me thought it would be a betrayal to Aiden's life but that was cowardice speaking.'

Amy paused again and glanced at Megan who, despite having heard the story before, was consumed by tears. 'I'll admit too that I was very dubious when Jay tried to introduce me to DMT. I'd tried practically everything by that point and I didn't believe his claims. How wrong I was,' she said, to a chorus of laughter.

'I'd like to thank Jay for showing me that something waits for us, that Aiden isn't lost. I have experienced him on my journeys there and I can't wait to be with him again. You see, he branded my soul that very first second he looked at me and I know, I just know, he is there waiting.'

Jay held her for a few more seconds, as the group processed what they'd been told, before moving to Claire.

Claire smiled. 'I'm ready,' she said, as Jay placed his arms around her.

Amy had chatted to the other woman on numerous occasions. She was in her thirties, had been in and out of hostels for the last ten years. Her lank black hair swayed behind her and when she smiled at Jay she revealed a number of missing teeth.

'This is your choice,' said Jay, his voice soothing, the sound flowing over the distant rattle of the sea.

'I'm ready,' said Claire, and Amy could see in her eyes and toothless grin that she was telling the truth.

Chapter One

DI Louise Blackwell parked up and ran to the school, her progress momentarily blocked by the thick metallic gate. Emily was waiting for her in the school office, her face peering out from the window like a prisoner. A lone teacher frowned as she buzzed Louise into the school building.

'Louise Blackwell, Emily's aunt. I'm sorry it's taken so long for me to get here, I've driven from Weston.' Louise looked over at Emily, who sat cross-legged, arms folded, on one of the chairs. Her niece didn't smile back. Her face turned down and sullen, she appeared to be on the verge of tears.

'I'm sure you'll be hearing more from the school tomorrow,' said the teacher, holding the door open for her. 'Goodbye, Emily, see you tomorrow,' she added, as Emily slouched through the door.

'Hi, darling,' said Louise. 'I'm sorry I took so long getting here. Shall we go for something to eat?'

Emily looked at her shoes, swaying on the spot. 'Where's Daddy?'

Louise crouched down so she was at eye level. She'd received the call at the station. Her brother, Paul, hadn't picked his daughter up from school forty minutes ago. She'd called her parents, who lived close by, but the call had gone straight to answerphone so she'd been forced to make the journey up the M5 from Weston. Emily was a tough cookie but her eyes were red, a lone tear escaping down the left side of her face. Louise considered lying but Emily deserved more. 'I'm sure he's fine, but he couldn't make it in time.'

'Is he drunk again?'

Louise grabbed the girl close to her, devastated by the question that aged her niece beyond her five years. 'I'm sure he's okay, darling.' The girl's body trembled in her arms, and not for the first time Louise wished she'd been able to protect her better from this, from everything that had happened to her in her short life.

This wasn't the first time Paul had done this. Emily's mother, Dianne, had died three years ago after a short struggle with cancer. The swiftness of events had surprised everyone and naturally Paul had been hit hardest. The drinking only started to get out of hand in the last year and Louise had thought he'd got a hold over it in the last six months, but the trouble had started again three weeks ago, on the anniversary of Dianne's death.

Louise blamed herself for letting it reach this stage, but that didn't absolve her brother of responsibility. She wanted to find him, to tell him exactly what she thought of his actions, but couldn't do so with Emily in tow.

In the car she phoned her parents again.

'Hi, Lou,' said her mother. 'I'm sorry, Dad and I have been out and have only just received the messages.'

Louise bit her tongue, wanting to ask why their mobiles hadn't been switched on. 'I've got Emily,' she said. 'We're going for something to eat.'

'Hi, Emily.'

'Hi, Grandma.'

Louise pulled over so she could take her mother off speakerphone. She stepped outside, gently shutting the car door. 'You need to go and see Paul.'

'Dad's already on his way.'

'This can't go on, Mum,' said Louise under her breath, fighting back her own tears.

'I know, darling, I know. Bring Emily over to us after you've eaten. I have some of her school clothes here so she can stay with us for the time being.'

They were always finding temporary solutions for Paul's problem. He refused all offers of help, was in complete denial of his situation. He'd been a devoted husband and his time with Dianne had been the happiest Louise had ever seen him. He'd doted on Emily when she was born, and although his love for her hadn't disappeared following his wife's death, it was as if his daughter's presence was a constant reminder of the woman he'd lost. Louise was convinced he would never purposely harm Emily, but he didn't understand the damage he was already causing her.

Louise took her niece to Pizza Express. She didn't push the girl, gave her space as they sat in silence. Her father sent her a text to tell her he'd found Paul back at his flat. He'd been out cold, but was responding now. Louise told Emily her dad was okay, omitting the details, and the girl smiled briefly, a tendril of hot cheese spilling from her mouth. What could Louise say to her? Despite her earlier question about whether Paul was drunk, she was too young to be told her father needed help, that he only behaved this way because of what had happened to her mother. She'd already endured too much. Again, Louise was overcome with the desire to grab the girl and take her away from all this.

Louise declined dessert as Emily ate an ice-cream sundae. 'You're going to stay at Grandma's tonight. Is that okay?'

Emily nodded. 'Daddy's sick, isn't he?' she said.

Louise didn't know if the girl was making a general statement on her father's hangover, or his mental state in general, but wasn't going to ask for elaboration. 'He'll be okay, but best if you stay there for the time being. It's fun at Grandma's, isn't it?'

'Are you going to stay, too?' asked Emily, looking hopeful, and genuinely happy for the first time since Louise had picked her up from school.

◆ ◆ ◆

Back at her parents', Emily ran into the opening arms of her grandmother. Louise's mother glanced at Louise as she held tight on to Emily. Her eyes were heavy as if she hadn't been sleeping. 'Dad's inside,' she said.

Louise's father was pacing the living room. A stocky, powerful man now in his late sixties, Danny Blackwell was the sweetest man she'd ever met. She'd idolised him as a child, possibly to the detriment of all her future relationships. She'd yet to meet a man who could live up to his standards, even though she knew the comparison was not really a fair one; knew it was possibly a way of protecting herself, preventing her from fully having to commit to someone else.

Louise rarely saw her father angry but there was no hiding it now. 'How was he?' she asked.

Her father stopped pacing. He'd been totally oblivious to her arrival and looked at her, momentarily confused. 'I couldn't get a word of sense out of him. He stank of alcohol. He mumbled something about a Tuesday morning club at the local pub, and there was a half-empty bottle of whisky on the table. I dragged him into a cold bath but he hardly stirred. I know he's had it hard, Louise, but he's a selfish little bastard. How the hell can he do that to Emily?'

'I know, Dad. I know.'

'What can I do? I don't know what I can do to help.' Her dad collapsed on to the sofa, engaged in a fierce battle to contain his emotions.

'Granddad,' said Emily, running into the room.

Louise's father wiped his eyes as Emily ran towards him. 'Sweetie,' he said, holding his hands out to embrace his granddaughter.

Louise returned to the kitchen and put on the kettle.

'I suppose it would be bad form if I had something stronger?' said her mum, raising her eyebrows.

'Mum,' said Louise, shaking her head. Her mother had always had a dark sense of humour and was usually the first to defuse any difficult situation.

They drank tea together, smiling at the sound of Emily playing with her grandfather, each avoiding discussing the situation. 'How's the seaside?' asked her mother.

'Better now the warm weather has arrived.'

'Any juicy cases?'

She only asked out of politeness. She'd always been supportive of Louise's role in the police, and was proud of her, but she didn't really want to hear any details; didn't want to face the reality of Louise's work.

'I need to get back soon but we need to discuss what happened today. You know the school are within their rights to call in social services? Imagine if they visit Paul now? Emily could go into care, Mum.' Louise felt her emotions getting the better of her, and marvelled at the way her brother could cause so much distress in his absence.

Her mother smiled. Outwardly, nothing ever appeared to affect her but Louise knew she carried the burden of everything that happened to her family. She'd been the strong one during the last weeks of Dianne's life, and the traumatic aftermath. She'd kept the family together for years as Paul descended into alcoholism. Louise rarely acknowledged it, but she was lucky to have two such great role models for parents. 'Your father and I have been discussing the matter and we've decided that we're going to look after Emily for the next few months over the summer holiday period.' Her words were defiant, suggesting Louise shouldn't argue.

'Have you discussed this with Paul?'

'Not yet.'

'I don't think he's going to agree, Mum.'

'He won't have a choice. Like you said, sooner or later social services are going to get involved and even your brother isn't stupid enough to risk losing Emily.' Her mother moved towards her, reached for her hand. 'Look, I don't mean that. Your brother's not stupid, far from it, but he's not in a position to help himself at the moment. I'll speak to him and explain it's for the best. Hopefully, it will be the kick up the bum he needs. We've told him we'll get him help and we'll tell him again tomorrow.' She closed her eyes, inhaling deeply through her nostrils. 'He's killing himself, Lou. Your big brother is killing himself and we need to help him.'

'Oh, Mum,' said Louise, grabbing her mother, disturbed by the lightness of her body as she caught the familiar scent of lavender on her neck.

Her mother pushed her away gently, embarrassed. 'Will you—'

'I'll do everything I can, Mum. I'll try and get here every weekend, and can help out at evenings.'

'What do you think we get up to?' said her mother, smiling. 'You think your dad and I are out partying every night?'

'You're not?' said Louise, feigning mock surprise.

'Thank you for your offer and we'll take you up on it when needed, but I was going to ask if you would speak to Paul. Not tonight, but sometime in the next few days. Tell him you stand by our decision, and try to get him to get some help.'

Louise doubted her brother would listen to what she had to say but agreed anyway.

'Right,' said her mother, clasping her hands together as if everything was now all right with the world. 'You better get going. You probably have lots of work to do and I have a little lady I need to get to bed.'

Chapter Two

Louise thought about little else other than Paul and Emily as she drove back to Weston. She recalled the day Paul and Dianne announced that Dianne had cancer. The subtle change that immediately became evident in her sister-in-law's posture, the aged way she moved. Even so, Dianne's rapid deterioration over the following weeks came as a shock to everyone. The next time Louise saw her she'd been in her hospital bed, her body wasting away before her eyes. They spoke about Emily, Dianne thanking Louise for being a presence in her daughter's life, Louise making unnecessary promises about looking after the child. That had been the day Louise first saw the change in Paul – the hardening in his eyes, a defiance and desperation he'd never recovered from.

Though the change in him was unwelcome, it hadn't come as a surprise. Louise had experienced this kind of thing with him before. As a child, Paul had been a kind and caring older brother, and although there had been the usual sibling falling outs, they'd always got on well. At times, and she hated admitting it, Paul had been her best friend. A wave of melancholy always hit her as she thought about how that friendship was gradually eroded. It was a natural part of growing up, but it still stung her to remember Paul hitting his teenage years and eventually leaving her behind.

In retrospect, it had all started then. He must have been fifteen or sixteen when he'd started drinking. Initially, Louise's parents hadn't been that concerned – he wasn't the only teenager drinking cheap white cider in the local park – but Louise had hated the change in him. He became sullen and withdrawn, hanging out with new people at school. When he did talk to her he was short and impatient and the young Louise had felt somehow to blame, as if she was responsible for the change in him.

It was only when Paul started developing more sophisticated habits that her parents began to share her concerns. One infamous holiday – Paul's last with them – was never mentioned at family gatherings. They'd been in Cornwall when Louise's father had found some speed in Paul's pockets. She'd never seen her father lose his temper in such a way. Paul had just received some disappointing results in his A-levels and the atmosphere following the discovery had been so bad that they'd all travelled home that day.

A few weeks later, Paul left for polytechnic. He'd hugged Louise goodbye before he'd left but their relationship had already been changed irrevocably. The poly did little more than provide three years of partying for her brother; a way of life he continued after leaving and starting a dead-end job in telesales.

He would probably still be living that same life if it hadn't been for Dianne. The change had been immediate, his drinking eased and the drugs ceased. Louise began to see the return of the kind and caring boy Paul had once been. It had been wonderful to see, and by the time Emily was born Louise had long since stopped worrying about him.

Louise had hoped that Emily would have kept Paul grounded when Dianne passed, but maybe they'd underestimated the influence Dianne had had on him. He'd tried, Louise knew that, but without Dianne there was nothing to stop him returning to his old ways.

Louise left the motorway, driving past a tide of cars leaving the seaside town, the tourists and day trippers for once having enjoyed a day baked in sun. The police station's office manager, Simone, had taken the call from the school and was no doubt offering her opinion as to why Louise had to leave in such a hurry, and Louise had no desire to face the questioning glances and sly asides.

Although she'd lived in Weston for over two years now, Louise had managed to keep her private life – what existed of it – separate from her colleagues at work. It was an open secret that she'd been forced to move to the seaside town. Prior to that she'd been working in MIT, the major investigation team based out of headquarters in Portishead. Following an investigation where she'd shot an unarmed man – albeit a vindictive serial killer by the name of Max Walton – she'd been offered a take-it-or-leave-it move. She'd been unable to hide her resentment at the time and this, in part, had hampered her integration. Things had improved over the last seven months following a successful murder investigation, but Louise was still an outsider to the small group of officers in Weston.

Back in her small bungalow in Worle, on the outskirts of Weston, Louise ate her dinner for one in front of the television. As she chewed brown, indefinable meat, she glanced at the shadow covering half of the living-room wall. Eight months ago, photographs had littered every inch of the cream-coloured wall. Although they'd not made for pleasant viewing – they were mainly photos of victims of a brutal killer dubbed by the press as the Pensioner Killer – they'd given Louise a grim purpose. Since that time, her role as detective inspector of Weston's small CID department had been as uneventful as the town itself. Her most recent success had been the arrest of a small group of marijuana dealers working in the Bournville estate, an investigation she wouldn't have even touched when she'd been part of MIT.

She placed her plate in a dishwasher she activated once a week at most and went to bed. Out of habit she checked her phone before sleeping, half expecting an unwelcome text from her old colleague in Bristol. She tried to sleep, her thoughts returning again and again to her brother and niece.

Paul's drinking hadn't resumed immediately after Dianne's death. For a period, he'd carried on as normal. Louise had admired him at that point, the way he'd been a solid presence for Emily who'd only half understood what had been happening. Then one Sunday lunchtime he'd failed to turn up for a family get-together. Louise had driven to his flat and found him asleep on the sofa, an empty vodka bottle by his side while Emily sat on an armchair watching television. They should have done something about it then, got him help immediately, but they'd let the problem fester. Now, Louise worried they would never be able to help him.

She awoke at 5.30 a.m. with a jolt. There was no point trying to return to sleep. She put on a pot of coffee before showering, changing afterwards in a semi-trance. When she managed to take the first welcome slurp of caffeine, her phone pinged. 'Be careful what you wish for,' she mumbled to herself, as she read the message.

Twenty minutes later, Louise parked up at the Uphill Marina though 'marina' was a stretch. Although the area technically linked to the sea, it only did so at times of high tide via the meandering tributaries of the River Axe. Most of the time the place was a dumping ground for old boats. Derelict and abandoned vessels fought for space in the mud plains above sea level, Louise doubting that any of them would feel water against their hulls again.

Louise followed the line of officers to the cordoned-off area at the foot of a sheer cliff drop where a white scene-of-crime tent had been erected. Above them, the ruined church of Saint Nicholas glistened in the sun like a perfect image from a picture postcard.

The body of a young woman had been discovered earlier that morning by the owner of the marina café who'd gone for a short walk before opening up. At first, Giles Lawson had thought the shape at the foot of the cliff was a bag of discarded rubbish. Only as he approached the bundle did he realise it was the twisted body of the deceased.

Lawson explained as much to Louise outside the SOCO tent where the scene-of-crime officers and the county pathologist, Stephen Dempsey, were examining the corpse. Tears welled in the café-owner's eyes as he recalled finding the body. 'I've never seen a dead person before,' he said.

Louise had some sympathy for the man, recalling the first dead body she'd found on the job. She'd vomited on that occasion and would have shared the story with the man if she'd thought it would help him. Instead, she handed the man over to one of the uniformed officers and donned the white SOCO uniform before heading into the tent.

Stepping into the confined space, Louise fought the nag of claustrophobia as she moved towards the twisted body. The woman had landed face down. She'd been photographed and the scene recorded by video and she had now been moved on to her back so the remains of her face were showing. Louise's breath was hot against her protective mask as she fought the rising nausea. A SOCO was busy photographing the pulpy mess of the woman's face, the flash of her camera illuminating the inside of the tent as if stopping time.

'Ma'am, we found this,' said one of the other SOCOs, handing Louise a purse protected by a small plastic bag. 'We have a name from an NI card but no photo ID.' The SOCO glanced at the mangled face of the woman as if suggesting that the photo ID wouldn't have made much difference.

'What's her name?' asked Louise.

The SOCO's eyes were glued on the woman, as if he was trying to make sense of the misshapen form. 'Claire Smedley, ma'am.'

'Thank you,' said Louise.

At that second, whatever her protestations about the humdrum nature of her current job, Louise wanted nothing more than to escape the tent, to be far away from the unfortunate soul inches from her feet. The smell and cloying atmosphere brought back so many bad memories that it would be easy to turn and run. Instead, she knelt down next to the pathologist.

Dempsey was wearing a mask but she saw his smile in the breakout of laughter lines around his eyes. In her first weeks in Weston, Louise had spent the night with Dempsey. She'd made worse mistakes but what she regretted most was the impact it had on their professional relationship, however hard Dempsey pretended to shrug it off.

'I think we may have ourselves another jumper,' said Dempsey, by way of greeting.

Louise wasn't sure if this revelation was a source of relief or frustration. Six weeks ago a twenty-eight-old, Victoria Warrington, had fallen from a cliff in Brean Down. Victoria had lived alone in a grungy shared flat in a tower block in Oldmixon. They'd yet to have a coroner verdict but everything pointed to a verdict of death by suicide. Although suicides were far from uncommon in the small seaside town, the method and the similarities between the two women were possibly a concern. 'No sign of a struggle?' said Louise.

'Not that I can see at present. As she fell, she did place her right arm in front of her face. I can't see any defence wounds aside from that but of course we will know more later.'

'We'll need a tox report as soon as possible,' said Louise.

'Okay,' said Dempsey, hesitating for a second as if he wanted to say something to her, before returning to the corpse.

Outside the tent, Louise was stopped by DS Thomas Ireland. 'What kept you?' she said, the hot air of the morning giving little respite from the heat of the tent.

Thomas grinned and Louise looked away, chiding herself for her emotional response to seeing him. Thomas was the closest thing to a friend she had at the office and in her weaker moments she would admit to thoughts of their relationship developing beyond the professional. In the past, such thoughts were mere idle fantasy but after a turbulent year, Thomas and his wife had decided to apply for a divorce. The separation shouldn't have changed any-thing between Thomas and Louise, and she imagined it was mainly in her mind, but occasionally she noticed the odd glance from him. Nothing could come of it. For one, Thomas reported to her and she wasn't about to embark on an affair with a soon-to-be divorced man. Furthermore, Weston station – and the town itself for that matter – was not a place for secrets. Louise had enough problems fitting in as it was without being known as the chief who slept with her staff.

'We have a name,' she said, hiding her embarrassment while Thomas gazed at her nonplussed.

'Do you want me to run it?'

Louise had wanted to check on the young woman herself, but handed Thomas the plastic covering with Claire's ID within. 'Let me know when you find a family member. I'd like to be there.'

As Thomas turned to leave, Louise told herself to get a grip. She gave him five minutes before leaving the car park on foot. It wasn't even 9 a.m. but the sun was already high in the cloudless sky. She loved Weston on days like these, however few and far between they were. The light changed the town. Instead of highlighting its blemishes it somehow hid them, its rays distorting the scenery into a perfect vision. Even the air tasted different, the smell of the distant sea enticing rather than repelling.

Louise walked around the corner and began the steep climb up the hill to the ruined church, surprised to see a small herd of cows in the field next to the entrance. The ascent made her breathless, her legs like lead by the time she reached the summit. *When did I get so out of shape?* she thought, promising herself she would start running again when she next had a spare moment.

From her position, the seafront of Weston-super-Mare curved to her right, both the piers – the Grand and the old derelict Birnbeck Pier – protruding into the mud bed where the sea would be later in the day. Further out, the mound of rock known as Steep Holm jutted out from the murky sea. Louise would never be able to view the small island again without recalling the events that unfolded there late the previous year when she'd searched for the Pensioner Killer. Absently, she touched the small scar on her arm that would forever link her to that place.

Instead of a tent, the SOCOs had cordoned off an area close to the cliff edge, by the wall of the church's graveyard facing Brean Down and the muddy mouth of the River Axe. The area was still being worked but one of the SOCOs left the barrier tape to speak to her. As she pulled the mask from her mouth, Louise recognised her as Janice Sutton whom she'd worked with numerous times in Bristol.

'Hot one,' said the SOCO. 'How are things with you, Louise? Haven't seen you since that nasty business last year.'

'Good to see you, Janice. I thought you'd stopped covering this patch.'

'You know me, go where I'm needed. Not sure we have much for you at the moment. The ground is so dry that we're struggling for footprints,' said the SOCO, glancing down at a small thicket of grass sprouting from the ground which was mainly sand and dry mud. 'As you can see there was a small campfire,' she added, pointing to a burnt pile of sticks. 'I would guess from last night. We're going through that area, usual procedure.'

'Any sign of a struggle?'

The SOCO shrugged as if it hadn't occurred to her that this was anything but a suicide. 'Impossible to tell at the moment. No blood at the scene so far.'

Janice pointed to a man in full SOCO uniform hovering by the edge of the cliff. 'That's where we estimated she fell from. Best you don't come in for the time being,' she added, glancing down at Louise's shoes.

'It could have been an accident?'

'I guess so. As you can see, there is a sheer drop just over the side of the wall. I imagine Dempsey will give you more insight into that. I guess, in the dark, maybe she was pissed, could have been an accident.'

Louise rubbed the back of her head, not knowing what was worse: choosing to jump or falling accidentally.

Chapter Three

Amy finished mopping the floor of the café before leaving for the day. Keith, the café owner, scowled as he handed her a small share of the day's tips in a brown envelope as if he was doing her a favour. He hung on tight to the envelope as she reached for it. 'Don't spend it all at once,' he said, clearly enjoying her struggle.

Amy lowered her eyes, and Keith's grip loosened. She wasn't a violent person but at that moment Amy wished only the worst for her obese boss, whose eyes ran up and down her body as she pulled off the grotty maroon apron she used for cleaning.

'Don't be late tomorrow,' he warned, his tongue darting between his bulbous and cracked lips.

Amy left without answering, her mood improving as she stepped into the sunshine. It was early afternoon and she took the short walk from Keith's greasy café to Grove Park. Nothing waited for her at home, save for the same damp grey walls of her bedsit. She passed the playhouse at the bottom of the high street, dropping a fifty-pence piece into the chipped bowl of a homeless man and his dog.

The park was a fantasy. Walking around the rows of perfectly arranged flowers, and up the incline through the woodland area, Amy could almost believe this was her life. She pictured a small detached house at the top of the hill, overlooking the only town she'd ever known. What simple joy it would be to cross the road every morning and step into this green wonderland, if for only a time. It wouldn't solve everything but it would be better than her current alternative.

At the top of the hill she took a seat on a park bench, receiving a sigh of exasperation from the pensioner already sitting there. Wishing she'd brought a book with her, Amy stared out at the town. The sea was in, the reflection of the cloudless sky masking its usual brown colour. She followed the coastline as far as she could see but was unable to make out the area where she'd been last night. The memory came with a sting of melancholy. Claire had hugged everyone goodbye before Jay injected her with the full dose of DMT. The group had watched, guarding her, as she'd gone to that other place, and hand in hand with Jay she'd walked to the edge of the cliff, where she'd let go of Jay's hand and continued walking.

Although she felt happy for the other woman, Amy had stopped watching at that point. The Ayahuasca tea still rushing her blood, she'd looked away as Claire made that final leap, humming to herself so she didn't hear the thud of Claire's body landing below. She'd turned back – sensing the intake of breath from the group as Jay gazed over the cliff edge and confirmed that Claire had moved on – and felt Megan's hand in hers as everyone started hugging and kissing, celebrating Claire's life and her journey to the new place where she was now safe and happy.

Before meeting Jay, she would never have conceived that someone taking their life would be a positive thing. Yes, she'd felt the pull before, but her desire to take her life was a means to end her sadness. Now she believed it was more a beginning than an ending. She'd never fallen for the con trick of religion, and had been dubious when Jay had first suggested she try DMT. However, what he'd shown her surpassed all fantasy. She'd not only seen, but she'd experienced the wider universe. Callous as it might sound, she was pleased Claire had taken her life, that she'd made it to that other plane of existence. She hoped to be there one day soon.

She regretted not taking Megan's phone number or address. She wanted to see her now even though it was forbidden. Their interaction was restricted to the online group. Jay knew best and Amy respected that, but still she wished she could see Megan and share the strange empty feeling she had from last night's events.

Sighing, she stood and took the walk along the Bristol Road back to her bedsit in Milton, wondering if Claire's body had been discovered yet.

◆　◆　◆

The same dusty rank smell reached Amy's nostrils as she opened the front door of her block of flats. The odour was caught forever in the carpet and the greying wallpaper that peeled from the walls in tiny patches, like skin exposed too much to the sun. Amy's bedsit was little more than a glorified room, though it did at least have its own bathroom with a small kitchenette. She knew most of the building's occupants by sight, though there was nothing approaching a community between the tenants. Beyond perfunctory nods and greetings, everyone kept to themselves, all lost in their secret lives.

From the small fridge that took up half the kitchen counter, Amy took out eggs and a handful of vegetables for her omelette. She heated a pan of water – her makeshift kettle – and threw the eggs, onion and tomatoes into the frying pan. The resulting mess was more scrambled eggs than omelette but her appetite had been sated from lunch at work, the one benefit of working for that ogre.

She sat with her dinner on her lap, watching random YouTube clips on her laptop. She couldn't concentrate, her mind elsewhere. She didn't know if it was pity or jealousy she felt for Claire, and that uncertainty scared her.

When she'd first met Jay, everything had seemed so clear. Absently, she rubbed her left wrist where he'd touched her on that first night. It hadn't felt like an intrusion, the feel of his skin and his kind words soothing her in a way she'd never before experienced. She didn't believe in love at first sight but there had been a connection she hadn't believed possible. He'd talked to her, his dark eyes never leaving hers, and it was as if he'd known her all her life. She hardly had to explain the traumas of her life, her absent father and drug-addicted mother, her years in and out of care homes where she'd suffered such abuse that living alone was a distant dream, her life's only ambition. And when she'd told him about Aiden, he'd listened intently and offered only comfort, not judgement.

Jay knew her more than she knew herself. He'd listened and understood and the few precious days they'd spent together over the ensuing months were the best of Amy's life.

She didn't get to see him alone any more and she'd come to accept that. His mission was too important. She'd seen him work his magic on the others and was proud of the way he'd helped so many people, even if it ate into the time they shared together.

It could have been her last night – Claire had only joined the group two months ago – and although she still wanted that, she'd had to look away as Claire leapt from the cliff edge. She'd caught Jay's glance at that moment and feared she might have upset him until he offered her his secret smile. That one simple gesture made the world make sense again. She didn't doubt him; it was the physicality she'd turned away from: the visceral crunch of bones as Claire landed, the blood and momentary pain before she moved beyond this plane.

The eggs, although sprinkled liberally with salt and pepper, tasted of nothing. The rubbery texture left a vacant taste in Amy's mouth. She forced the food down as there was nothing else in her room to eat. How she wished for more of the tea Jay had given her last night. It wasn't quite the same as the full hit Claire received – Amy had only received that pleasure the once – but it never failed to centre her. With Jay's encouragement she'd learnt to decipher the messages the drug sent to her: the interconnection between the realities, the promise of something else, something better. She'd felt part of a bigger universe last night, an existence beyond the meagre solitude of her bedsit, and she wanted that again now.

Switching off YouTube, she went through the laborious process of connecting to the chat room. Jay had set up the precautions to keep their conversations private, but the route was so cumbersome that sometimes she didn't bother.

Ten minutes later, bouncing from one IP address to the other with a Wi-Fi signal that was little better than an old dial-up connection, she reached the private group. A sense of warmth came over her as she saw the green light next to Megan's avatar and the three flashing dots meaning she was typing out a message.

> *Hi honey, I've been waiting for you to get online. Everything ok?*

Amy closed her eyes and sank into her chair. It was surprising how connected she felt at that moment, as if Megan was sitting in the room with her. She replied, others joining in the conversation. They spoke in the code Jay had taught them, never revealing where they'd been last night or what they'd seen. Amy would have liked to talk alone with Megan but was content to share her with the group. Everyone was contending, in their own way, with what had happened last night and being in a group was beneficial to most.

It was only when she scrolled down the list of names that she noticed Claire's name had already been deleted from the list.

Chapter Four

Louise had been inside enough churches in the past year to last a lifetime, though she'd never visited the ruined cliff-side church of Saint Nicholas before. She peered in through the locked gates of the building and up through the hole where the roof had once been, as a man wearing a dog collar approached her with a set of keys.

'Tristan Reeves,' said the man. 'I'm the reverend of Uphill Church, and caretaker of this fine building. I was told I was needed.'

The vicar looked pale, the hand holding the keys shaking as Louise explained what had happened last night. He was a tall, bespectacled man, with a well-spoken, nondescript accent that suggested he was an outsider.

'How old was she?' he asked, his voice wavering.

Louise pictured the pile of bones and flesh they'd found at the bottom of the cliff. 'In her thirties. We believe her name is Claire Smedley. Would she happen to be one of your parishioners?'

'I don't believe so. Do you have a picture of her? You realise we no longer perform services here?' he added.

Louise had read the notice on the board, though the lack of roof was a bit of a giveaway. 'I'll get one to you as soon as we have some positive identification. So you get a lot of tourists here?'

'Yes. Obviously it's a beautiful setting and the church has some considerable history. We open the gates at selected times so people can see the interior.'

'We believe there was a campfire here last night, to the rear of the church. Would you know anything about that?'

'Sometimes kids get together up here, away from prying eyes. We often have to clean up after them. Lot of discarded alcohol cans and bottles, that sort of thing, but I only get here once a week at most. We have a caretaker who checks out the place at weekends. I can give you his details if you like.'

Louise took the caretaker's details and thanked the cleric. The SOCOs had finished their work on the area and Janice allowed her inside the barrier tape. Louise was not one for heights and tentatively climbed over the high stone wall separating the graveyard from the cliff edge. There was a patch of grass, six or seven metres before the drop. She bent to the ground, glad to have Janice behind her as she peered over the edge. The drop was sheer, the landing place now the white SOCO tent.

Louise returned to the wall and climbed back over, pleased to be on the right side of the barrier. She tried to gauge how someone could be desperate enough to step over the edge – it would take an incredible amount of courage to make those few steps – but knew it was pointless trying to see things from the jumper's point of view. Unless you were in a place where you were overwhelmed, maybe from events in your life or from depression or related mental illness, then it was impossible to conceive of what went on in the mind of someone ready to take their own life.

Not that Louise didn't have experience. As a probationary officer, she had worked in the Clifton area of Bristol. One of Bristol's enduring landmarks was the Clifton Suspension Bridge that spanned the River Avon. It had seemed like every day she'd been called to Isambard Brunel's masterpiece, either to try and talk a jumper down or help with someone who had fallen. Often it was a cry for attention, a desperate need for human interaction. Louise considered some of her greatest achievements the times she'd rescued someone from the bridge and arranged for further help. Each jumper always had a different tale: a lost loved one, an addiction that had got out of hand, an incurable illness, a depression that had finally got the best of them.

The parallels to Paul were obvious and a shiver of concern passed through Louise as she contemplated the same thing happening to her brother. It wasn't mere fanciful thinking. Paul's illness was not solely his alcohol addiction. Understandably, Dianne's death had changed him. Although they'd sought out help for him, her memory consumed him. The alcohol was a by-product of that despair, but it was also a disease within him that Dianne's death had exacerbated. It staggered Louise to admit it, but it wasn't a reach to imagine him taking his own life.

From Uphill, Louise made the trip to the new headquarters via the town centre. Days like this reminded her of the family day trips they'd made as children to Weston. Until much later in life, Louise had always equated Weston with the sunshine. She'd made happy journeys sitting in the back of the car with Paul as they'd taken the short drive from Bristol. They'd had picnics on the beach, walked the pier, and had sometimes been allowed to visit the Tropicana, the town's now defunct open-air swimming pool. It was sad to think that version of Paul, the pale-skinned carefree young boy, was gone forever. Yet, however much she wished she could take away his pain, she had to think about Emily and what this was doing to her. She wanted to grab her brother and tell him to pull himself together, but as the woman lying under the white tent in Uphill proved: life was rarely that simple.

She reached the new station fifteen minutes later. The grey, purpose-built building was set on a grim industrial estate in Worle. Although more convenient for her, she lamented the move from Winterstoke Road, which was a few hundred metres from the seafront. The new building was isolated and so devoid of character that Louise felt she could be working anywhere in the country.

The gentle hum of the air conditioner greeted her as she was buzzed into the CID department on the second floor. Although soulless, the new offices offered better facilities and she wouldn't miss the smell of the last building – an underlying stink of body odour and heated food that she could summon to her nostrils by thought alone.

She stopped by Thomas's desk and asked for an update. She hadn't noticed earlier, but he looked drawn, his eyes heavy with dark bags. He'd asked not to be quizzed about the on-going divorce, yet Louise felt she was somehow failing him; as if her own complicated feelings were preventing her from being there properly for him. Thankfully, he rescued her by speaking.

'We have a confirmed name and address for the jumper. Claire Smedley. She has a flat in Kewstoke. She was orphaned as a child, lived in and out of the care system. I have an address for an old foster parent but she left their care when she was thirteen.'

Louise took the address from him. 'Everything okay, Tom? You look a bit peaky.'

'Yeah, just a bit tired. I'm staying at my parents' while . . . well, you know. I feel like a bloody teenager again.'

'How's Noah?'

Noah was Thomas's four-year-old. 'He's good. Doesn't really understand what's going on obviously. I still get to see him every other day so that's good,' said Thomas, sounding as if it was anything but.

'I'm here for you if you need to talk,' said Louise, hating the inadequacy of the words as they left her mouth.

'Thanks, Louise, I appreciate it. Do you want some company?' Louise must have looked blank because he added, 'The address. Claire Smedley's place.'

'Yes. That would be good.'

They sat in companionable silence as Louise took the old toll road to Kewstoke. She liked this hidden part of Weston, the narrow winding roads and remote houses. It was like entering the past, and when she had time she would always drive this way into Weston's town centre. At the small village, she took the winding road to Sand Bay. As the name suggested, the place was a beachfront sharing the same channel of water as its more illustrious neighbour up the coast. Louise preferred it here. The seafront was less garish and the small bay was much quieter, even though it offered a beach and views that to Louise's mind surpassed Weston's.

Louise tried hard to focus on the case, but her thoughts kept slipping to Emily. She told herself she was being hysterical, but seeing Claire's body at the foot of the cliff had only deepened her concern for her niece.

Like Claire, Emily was now an orphan of sorts. Fortunately, Emily still had a loving family surrounding her but it was too easy to picture her in Claire's place. She still knew little about Claire's history, but she was almost certain that the loss of her parents at a young age had contributed one way or another to her being in a position where taking her life felt like the only answer. It wasn't that far a stretch to imagine Emily going down the same road if they weren't careful.

'You with us?' said Thomas.

Louise took a deep breath. 'Sorry, I was miles away.'

Claire's bedsit was off the seafront, at the end of a narrow lane above a tyre garage. A man in blue overalls stopped what he was doing as Louise and Thomas left the car. As he walked towards them, he wiped his greasy hands across his chest. 'DS Ireland?' he asked Thomas, his accent a thick West Country drawl.

'Mr Applebee. Thank you for meeting us.'

'I live here, don't I?'

A short, stout man, his rotund stomach pushing through the fabric of his overall, Applebee suited his name. He was the owner of the bedsits above the garage. Thomas had made contact with him earlier and explained what had happened to Claire.

'This is my colleague, DI Blackwell. Would you mind showing us to Claire's flat?'

Applebee grunted, his eyes not reaching Louise's as he looked her up and down. 'Suppose so,' he muttered, walking back towards the garage.

Inside, a battered Fiat Punto hung precariously on a hydraulic lift. It was missing its tyres and was so rusted that Louise doubted it would ever see the road again. 'Good little runner if you're interested,' said Applebee, taking a set of keys off a rusting key hook. 'Through here,' he said, opening a side door that led to a dimly lit staircase.

'How many flats are there here?' asked Thomas as they ascended the stairs, Louise fighting the smells of nicotine and urine in the stairwell.

'Four, though only three are let. Only two now, I suppose. More trouble than they're worth sometimes. Here,' said Applebee, opening a door covered in chipped paint. 'Whatever state the place is in has nothing to do with me.'

Coldness hit Louise as she walked through the threshold. It permeated the room despite the glare of sunshine leaking through the opaque curtains. Calling the place a flat was a misnomer of the highest order. It was a room with a small single bed and a cheap plastic garden table that held a kettle and toaster.

'Not supposed to cook in here,' said Applebee, as Louise ran her fingers over the grease-sodden table top.

'Where did she cook?'

'There's a shared kitchen.'

'And a shared bathroom, I presume?'

Applebee sensed the disdain in her voice and ignored her. Louise opened the window, allowing fresh air to filter into the room. *No one should have to live like this*, she thought. Claire appeared to have no possessions beyond the few clothes in a chest of drawers and those littering the floor.

Thomas bent down next to the single bed. 'There's a power cable here. For a laptop.'

Louise glanced at Applebee, unable to hide her accusing eyes. 'Have you been in here recently, Mr Applebee?'

'No,' said Applebee, a little too vehemently.

'So if we did a search of this place we're not going to find Claire's laptop?'

'What the hell are you on about? He phoned me a couple of hours ago,' he said, pointing to Thomas, 'and I've been working on the cars ever since. I never go in these rooms unless I have to.'

Louise could well believe that. 'That laptop could have some vital evidence for us. If you know where it is, now would be a great time to tell us.'

'I have no idea. I've seen her on a laptop. Huge, monstrous thing like something out of the eighties. Even if I'd been so inclined, that machine wouldn't have been worth anything.'

Louise ripped the duvet off the bed. Everything in the room seemed coated in a film of dust. 'Did she have a phone?'

'I have a number for her so I presume so.'

No phone had been found on the body or at the scene. 'What about an Internet connection. You provide that?'

'There is a small fee. They share the Wi-Fi code.'

'Very generous. We'll need details of that.'

'Whatever. Can I get back to my cars now?'

'A girl has died, Mr Applebee,' said Louise.

'Don't I bloody know it? What am I going to do with all this shit now, and who's going to pay her bloody rent?'

Louise's skin tingled, heat prickling her body. She looked over at Thomas, who shook his head. 'Thank you, Mr Applebee,' she said. 'You've been very helpful.'

Chapter Five

DCI Robertson summoned Louise into his office the second she returned. Her boss was about as enthusiastic about the move to the new building as Louise. His office was half the size of his last one and overlooked the grey tarmac of the station's car park. Like her, Robertson was an outsider. Originally from Glasgow, he retained a thick accent despite spending over half his life south of the border.

'That girl, Claire Smedley? We've confirmed death by suicide?' he asked, as Louise sat opposite him.

'Everything points to it at the moment though we've only managed to speak to one person to have met her before. There are signs of a small gathering last night by the church. An extinguished bonfire, some empty bottles.'

'It could have been an accident then?' said Robertson, momentarily buoyed by the thought before remembering they were discussing a young woman's life. Lowering his tone to a guttural drawl, he said, 'Maybe there was a group there, she slipped, and they got spooked and dispersed?'

'We're going through all the usual processes to find out who was there. Unfortunately there are no cameras by the church though we're running through CCTV images from the marina.'

Robertson leant back in his chair, nodding to himself as if weighing up the possibilities of it being an accident.

'You've considered the similarities with Victoria Warrington?' said Louise.

Robertson stopped rocking as if she'd sworn at him. 'I don't want this to be another suicide, Louise,' he said.

'I'm not sure if that's our decision, Iain.' The comment was unnecessary and she regretted saying it.

'You know what the press will do with this information, don't you?'

'Create something that isn't there?' said Louise.

'That's hardly the point. The town is still recovering from that psycho Simmons,' said Robertson, referencing the Pensioner Killer.

'The town doesn't seem to be suffering at all. From what I've been told bookings are up, the place has never been busier.'

'You know as well as I do that's a smokescreen. We were big news for a few weeks in the winter and that spiked the curiosity of a few voyeuristic arseholes. Once this summer is over we'll be back to normal. I'm on about the residents. The ones who lived through all that shit. Don't underestimate the psychological damage that sort of thing can have on a community like this.'

'You don't have to preach to me, Iain,' said Louise, irked. Of the two of them, she had far more experience of dealing with violent crime and its aftermath. But he had a point. She'd noticed a subtle change to the town. It was difficult to pinpoint exactly. The place felt quieter, especially at night, as if a sense of unease had permeated its way into the populace. Robertson was right: the last thing they needed was another tragedy and a linked suicide could be just that.

It was different to her time in Bristol. The suspension bridge had long been used as a suicide destination, a gruesome fact connecting it with similar spots worldwide. Sad as it was, they'd expected it to happen there. Suicide was a tragic reality of life, common enough to be accepted without much fanfare and the incidents at the bridge rarely troubled the news.

However, if Claire's death was a suicide then the similarities between her and Victoria would strike alarm within the town, coincidence or not.

'I understand your concern, Iain, but if Claire has died by suicide then that's something we'll have to face. Yes, the death of two young women both falling from great heights would be a terrible coincidence but we can stop it becoming a drama,' said Louise, doubting her words.

'I take it we don't have a note yet?'

By this time after Victoria's death, the investigation had all but been wrapped up. A note had been found in the house she shared with six other people in Oldmixon. She'd apologised for not telling her housemates first, and told them not to worry about her as she was going to a better place.

It was because of this that after leaving Claire's bedsit, Louise had cordoned off the whole building while a team of uniformed officers scoured every inch of the place, much to Applebee's chagrin. She'd heard one of the uniformed officers suggest it was a little over the top and that officer had found out exactly her opinion on that matter, much to the man's embarrassment. Louise wanted Claire's life to matter and finding a note was the first step towards that goal. 'If there's a note, we'll find it,' she said.

The cold atmosphere of the open-plan office didn't prove conducive to working. At MIT, an officer of her rank would never have dealt directly with such an incident and even now she wondered if she was giving it too much of her time. Robertson's concerns withstanding, chances were Claire's death was another unfortunate incident. Nothing suggested the deaths were linked beyond the similarities in ages and the method of death, so why was she obsessing over it?

A quick glance over her open cases revealed the answer: a spate of low-level burglaries in Winscombe, sightings of a drug dealer loitering outside a secondary school, a case of GBH in a town centre nightclub that was already with the Crown Prosecution Service. Louise had wanted more from her career. Worse still, she'd once had it and it had been taken from her.

Forty minutes later, Louise had left the office and was walking up the steep banks of Brean Down. There was a hint of cloud and Louise fought a stiff breeze as she stumbled up the incline. A colony of seagulls circled above her head. They moved as if caught in the air currents, falling and rising, their wings appearing not to move.

Louise caught her breath as she reached the summit. Brean Down was the closest part of the mainland to Steep Holm, and the island was more defined from her vantage point. She gazed across the bay, imposing her own bad memories on the rock of land she'd last visited late last year. A high-pitched squall tore her from her reverie, as a seagull swooped down towards a young boy nearby who was carrying a sandwich. The boy screeched – half in terror, half in delight at the game – as his mother shooed the bird away. Louise smiled at the mother, who rolled her eyes, suggesting the boy was to blame as much as the seagulls.

Twenty yards from where they stood was the spot where Victoria Warrington had taken her life. At the exact place where she'd jumped, a middle-aged man in shorts and T-shirt was being dragged along by a Rottweiler. The dog was having the time of its life, tail wagging, tongue lolling, as the man struggled to keep him under control. The dog's leash was stretched to breaking point as the man's flip-flops slid on the grass, the joyous pair oblivious to the tragedy that had occurred on that very same spot a few weeks ago.

Louise gazed down at the jagged rocks, the drop much steeper than in Uphill. It felt wrong to compare the two sites. Had Victoria known what waited for her in the darkness, the pointed tip of the slick rocks that had all but ripped her skull from her torso? Her death would have been instant, but Louise wondered, as she had in Uphill, if Victoria had experienced a split second of unimaginable pain as she'd struck the rocks.

An hour later and they would have missed her body completely. An old couple had discovered the body on a morning stroll and called it in before the sea came in and took the body. It had meant that the SOCOs had little chance to examine the scene, the seawater wiping all traces of evidence minutes after they arrived and took the corpse away.

From there the case had been straightforward. The suicide note was found at Victoria's flat, another young life no longer prepared to accept what the world had to offer.

Louise wasn't sure why she was here, only that it felt right, respectful even to visit the site today. She'd attended Victoria's funeral, dismayed to be the only other person there aside from the undertakers and officials. It wasn't her job, wasn't possible to give more than a passing thought to people she dealt with on a daily basis. In her time, one way or another, she'd presided over so many deaths that if she carried them with her she wouldn't be able to function. Yet it had dismayed her to think that Victoria's memory would not live on after that moment when her body was rolled into the cremation chamber; dismayed her now to think that the memory of Claire Smedley would fall victim to the same fate.

Louise looked away as her mind played tricks on her – the memory of Victoria's broken body on the rocks, replaced by a vision of Emily in the same situation. She hurried down the stone pathway as if she could outrun the image. She was breathless by the time she reached the bottom. Getting her breath back, she ordered a take-away coffee from the small café. Paul called as she walked across the gravel car park. She let her phone ring until she reached the car, answering it as she leant against the driver's door.

'Paul.'

'Was it your idea to let Mum and Dad take Emily?' he said, by way of greeting.

Louise considered hanging up. There was no talking to him when he was like this but she was so agitated at the moment that she welcomed the ensuing argument. 'We could have let her sleep on the streets if that would have made you happier?'

'Don't be ridiculous. They had no right to take her.'

'Can you even hear yourself, Paul? You were too drunk to collect your daughter from school. Too drunk. Dad couldn't even rouse you when he went to see you. Can't you understand that?'

The line went silent and she was about to hang up when Paul said, 'I made a mistake.'

Louise placed her coffee on the roof of her car. The car park faced the mud blanket that was currently the Bristol Channel. It was hard to accept that at times the sea would reach the high sea walls. 'You made a mistake?' she hissed down the phone. 'There are mistakes, then there's goddamn irresponsibility. You realise if I'd been working I'd be forced to get social services involved in this? I'm surprised the school haven't got them involved already.'

'Oh, fuck them.'

'Jesus, are you drunk now?'

'No.'

'Paul, you have to get yourself sorted. If not for you then for your daughter. You're going to lose her, Paul.' Louise hesitated, not wanting to bring his wife into the conversation as he always clammed up at the mention of her name. 'You think this is what Dianne would have wanted?'

'Don't,' said Paul, his voice unsteady.

'It's been three years now. I'm not saying you have to stop grieving, Paul, but you have to sort your life out for Emily. We can get you some help, you just have to be willing to accept it.'

'It was just a mistake, Lou.'

Louise rubbed her forehead. 'How many mistakes do you want, Paul?'

'It won't happen again.'

Louise didn't believe a word her brother said. 'That's not good enough, Paul. You need help.'

'I'm not going to any bloody counsellor, Lou. They don't know what the hell they're talking about.'

'We'll find the best help for you. I've told you that. You just have to let us help you.'

'I'm taking Emily back tonight.'

Louise looked away from her phone, her jaw muscles clenched tight. 'Listen, Paul, do not even try to take Emily tonight. No one is going to stop you seeing her but it is for the best if she stays at Mum and Dad's for the time being.'

'I'm taking her.'

'Paul, if you try to take her back then I will be getting the authorities involved, do you hear me?'

He was beyond hearing. 'You'd do that to your own brother?'

'I would do it to protect Emily.'

'Well, fuck you, sis.'

Louise hung up. She understood his behaviour to a point – he was an addict now, always had been, and had suffered a tragedy many people would struggle to move past – but why couldn't he think of Emily? It was the last thing she needed at the moment.

She tried to turn her thoughts back to the case as she drove off. It would be easy to forget about Claire Smedley. Already she sensed everyone moving on. Yes, it was a tragedy but occasionally terrible things happened. As long as procedure was met, Louise wouldn't need to get any more involved in the case. The coroner's report was a foregone conclusion and soon Claire would be a statistic, another of the small percentage who took their lives every year in the UK.

But Louise couldn't leave it at that. She recalled the dingy room where Claire lived and something that had been bugging her sub-consciously all day began to reveal itself.

She needed to pay Claire's landlord another visit.

Chapter Six

The town-centre traffic was at gridlock. The day was ending, the cars parked on the beach – a bizarre allowance particular to the town – leaving the ramp in single file as Louise edged along the seafront. It was only late afternoon but already groups of revellers were out preparing for the night ahead. A group of shirtless young men marched along the promenade chanting songs, a large plastic container of a light-brown liquid being passed between them. They stopped as a hen party – dressed in fluorescent pink – crossed their path. It took a few seconds for the lewd comments to start, Louise laughing at the look of shock on the boys' faces as the women harangued them for a few seconds. As the hen party proceeded to the beach, the boys moved on in silence. Louise shuddered to think what might happen if the same situation was replayed in a few hours' time when the boys' courage had risen.

To her right was the Kalimera, a Greek restaurant she'd used to visit every morning before work. She missed the solitude of that place, the early mornings drinking coffee before a deserted seascape. She even missed the surliness of the restaurant owner, Georgina, who'd treated her with latent hostility on her visits. Louise hadn't been able to justify her daily jaunt to the restaurant since the station move and had yet to find a suitable alternative. Maybe if she left thirty minutes earlier tomorrow she could make a quick pit-stop.

Traffic was still snail-like as she headed along the front towards Marine Lake. She tried her best to ignore the lump of rock in the distance, her hand rubbing the healed wound on her arm from her last visit there. She'd set off on that night from this very spot by the Lake. She could still taste the saltwater; feel the coldness on her skin as the dinghy had cut through the darkness. It felt like yesterday and she realised she would always link this section of the town with that night.

She was not the only one taking the scenic route out of town. The toll road, past Birnbeck Pier – the old pier, as it was known to locals – was slow moving as the tourists returned to their caravan parks and rented beach homes for the night. Louise thought about Victoria's suicide note, the lack of people at her funeral. In the summer Weston was a place of transition, the populace changing on a weekly basis. In the winter, Weston could be a desolate place. It reminded Louise of a nightclub once the lights were switched off at the end of the night, the illusion of the glittery lights destroyed by grim reality. With summer departed, Weston became that empty nightclub: cold and drab without the revelry of the departed tourists. It was too easy to see how Victoria and Claire would suffer in such an environment. They were on the fringes of the town, not part of the summer crowds and invisible to the town folk in the winter months.

A car horn blared at her as Louise took a side road towards Sand Bay. The driver gesticulated wildly at her as he edged along the toll road, his car brimming with children. Louise ignored him and continued towards Claire Smedley's old residence.

Applebee was outside working on a car, the uniformed team having departed. He was wearing a vest now. Louise imagined it had once been white but it was so covered in grease and oil that she couldn't be sure.

'Back so soon?' said Applebee, wiping his hands on a cloth dirtier than his vest. He grinned, Louise seeing nothing pleasant in the gesture. She imagined what Claire had thought of him, at the thought of having to walk through his garage every time she wanted to go home.

Louise moved towards the man. His heavy breathing was audible, his brow moist with perspiration. She'd felt he'd been lying this morning and was now convinced. She decided to try a half-truth herself. 'Something was missing from Claire's room this morning,' she said.

'Oh really?' said Applebee, wiping his hands again with the dirty rag. 'Your colleagues didn't seem to think so. They've gone through every inch of her place.'

Louise came close to arresting him at that point. She knew what he'd done but decided there was an easier way. 'We believe Claire's death might be part of an on-going investigation. Any cooperation you could give us at this moment would be greatly appreciated.'

'I don't know what you mean,' said Applebee, wiping his hands vigorously as if trying to destroy evidence.

'Let's say for instance that Claire left something in your care, something for safekeeping as she went out. No one would think any less of you for forgetting about that, Mr Applebee. A laptop maybe?'

Applebee wiped his brow with the dirty rag, his eyes squinting against the sun. Louise saw his brain ticking over, finally concluding that he'd been offered a chance. 'Now that you mention it, she did leave something with me. I was going to call you when I'd finished the car. In all the chaos today I completely forgot about it.'

'I understand,' said Louise, crossing her arms.

She followed him inside where he withdrew the laptop from a cubbyhole. 'Place it down on the counter,' said Louise, all pretence of goodwill vanishing as she used gloves to put the laptop in a protective container. 'Was there anything else? A note perhaps.'

Applebee shook his head and from the look of fear in his eyes she knew that this time he was telling the truth.

◆ ◆ ◆

The CID office was deserted, except for the figure of DS Greg Farrell busy working on his laptop, the fluorescent lights reflecting off the gleam of his slicked-back hair. Farrell was a rising star in the department. He was young and hungry for success, and although Louise admired his energy they sometimes clashed when his determination was superseded by his arrogance. In a way they were kindred spirits. Neither of them really wanted to be in Weston. Farrell wanted bigger and better and was working his way towards it, whereas Louise wanted a return to the type of role that had been taken from her.

'Hey, boss, didn't see you there,' said Farrell, looking up from his screen as Louise sat behind her desk.

'You're working late,' said Louise.

Farrell grinned. The gesture used to annoy her. More smirk than smile, she'd always thought he was trying to undermine her, but now she'd grown to accept it as being part of him. 'That set of break-ins over in Worlebury. Need to collate all these witness reports. Not exactly the high end of investigative work but what are you going to do. What are you working on?'

'The suicide in Uphill.'

Farrell frowned but the lightness in his eyes didn't fully dissipate. 'Tania Elliot asked about that today. Says she was going to call you.'

Tania Elliot was the town's celebrity journalist. Following the Pensioner Killer case, she'd made a name for herself selling the story nationwide. She currently worked for the *Bristol Post* but was ever present in the affairs of the town. 'I've a missed call from her. It can stay missed for now,' said Louise, pulling on a set of protective gloves from inside the desk drawer.

As Applebee had suggested, Claire Smedley's laptop was a brick of a machine. Louise wanted a quick look before she sent it to the IT department in Portishead tomorrow. The machine groaned into life as she pressed the on switch, the fan immediately on overdrive. Farrell glanced up at the noise, smiling before returning to his work.

The home screen was scattered with tens of icons. Louise was surprised to see a link to MySpace, having believed the social-media site no longer functioned. She clicked on the icon, Claire's email and password stored automatically on the site. Nothing except a lone picture of Weston's Grand Pier from ten years ago came up on her profile. Louise searched on the more popular social-media sites but couldn't find any more profiles for the woman. The tech team would be able to do a more thorough search and if there was something on the machine they would find it.

The laptop was struggling, the fan whining as if something was broken within. Not wanting to risk breaking it, Louise was about to close the machine when she noticed an icon for an open-source word-processing application. She didn't have to scroll down far on the recent files to find what she was looking for. There was only one file, and it was simply titled: Goodbye.

Chapter Seven

Amy spent the next three hours switching back and forth from the group chat to YouTube and the free-to-air television channels on her laptop. She took some comfort in having the group chat open. It wasn't quite like being alone. Each new message played at the bottom of the screen as she watched a comedy show on iPlayer. You were supposed to have a TV licence to watch the shows but no one had ever checked on her. If they did she would plead ignorance, hoping her lack of television would prove good mitigation.

The messages were pretty random. Some of the group were prone to speaking in platitudes. There was much shallow thought and comment about the pointlessness of life and mumblings about what lay beyond. Most of it was the sort of nonsense you got from people who were high, as Amy imagined most of the group were. Yet, like her, they had all experienced something that set their drug talk apart – Jay had recruited them.

It had taken weeks for Jay to reveal himself to her. She'd known by the second or third time they met that their relationship was something out of the ordinary. Yes, of course, she fancied him. It was almost impossible not to. He was the archetypal tall, dark stranger, the embodiment of her fantasies. She'd wanted to be with him from the first time she'd set eyes on him but somehow he transcended the physical. She would have given herself to him then, as she would now, but although they'd held hands and held each other close, Jay had never made a play for her. She understood his elusiveness was part of his charm, why in part she craved him, but there was so much more to it than that. She'd never met anyone like him. He knew things no one else knew. He'd travelled the world, seen things she could only dream of seeing.

He'd told her early on about his visit to the Peruvian Amazonian rainforest and how it had changed his life. At first she hadn't understood as he'd recounted his visit, the days and nights with the indigenous people, and when he'd told her about first trying the drug it sounded like the worst thing in the world.

'I have to tell you the full story so you understand,' he'd said, before proceeding to tell her about the next night when he'd had his vision.

From anyone else she would have been incredulous. She'd done enough drugs in her time, had experienced enough outlandish trips to spot a fellow user, but the raw emotion in his voice made her listen. She'd heard about DMT before but had never tried it. She'd put anything beyond the occasional spliff behind her. She'd heard similar tales about self-revelation before but it had never attracted her. Yet the way Jay spoke about it made it sound like something else, something life-changing. He told her about the other worlds he'd experienced, his now iron-clad belief that something else waited for them beyond the confines of this world. 'And I can prove it to you,' he'd said, and she'd believed him.

She was about to switch off the laptop when a note from Megan popped up on the screen. A conversation had been rumbling on for the last thirty minutes about the changing seasons that she'd all but ignored beyond saying her favourite season was the spring. She'd waited to see if Megan would respond to that but she hadn't commented until now:

I'm a summer girl myself. I like nothing more than long walks in the park on a summer morning. The light in Ashcombe Park has to be seen to be believed.

Amy felt her heart beat in her chest. Ashcombe Park was less than half a mile from her house. Had Megan meant this message for her? Jay continually warned them not to meet offline. He'd stressed it even more after Claire's passing on. He was rarely present in the chats but they knew he was watching. It was a risk on Megan's part but already four of the group had said how much they loved summer mornings, oblivious to the possibility of a hidden message. Amy didn't respond, didn't want to risk anyone knowing she'd taken the message in. Instead, she wished everyone a good night before logging off. She didn't need to be in work the following day until the afternoon. What better way to spend the morning than a visit to Ashcombe Park?

Amy woke with a headache at 6 a.m. She'd struggled to get to sleep, her mind consumed with thoughts of seeing Megan. She wasn't sure why the thought so excited her. In truth, she hardly knew the woman. Maybe it was simply the thought of speaking to someone other than Keith and the same customers she saw every day at the café.

After a breakfast of stale toast and tea, she left her building to the welcome glow of morning sunshine. It had been a long time since she'd approached a day with such anticipation. Not since her time with Jay had a day been so full of possibility. On the nights where they were summoned there was no time for anticipation. They were usually given a day's notice at most, her body so full of adrenaline that she was rarely able to appreciate the time for what it was. She savoured that feeling now as she walked along the Milton Road to the park. She hadn't been there since she was a child when a group of them would bunk off school, changing venue each time as if anyone really cared they were absent.

Amy walked along the stretch of grass that used to hold a pitch and putt course, smiling as she reached the playground area, remembering the sulky teenager she'd once been. Dressed in the hideous brown school uniform, she'd sat on the swings with the other truants smoking cigarette after cigarette, rarely inhaling, thinking she'd looked so cool. Now there she was alone on the swings, no cigarettes to her name, wearing tatty jogging bottoms and an oversized T-shirt, waiting for someone who probably had no intention of visiting the park that morning.

The overhanging branches of the trees blocked the sun. Amy folded her arms together for warmth. She wished she'd engaged Megan more on the group chat last night. The park was a huge area and if her note had been a coded message, chances were high they would still miss each other. At the rear of the park, a teenage boy rode up on a bicycle, stopping short as he noticed Amy on the swings. He stared at her as if she was a phantom. He looked too young to be threatening but she didn't like the way he looked through her.

With his eyes still on her Amy stepped off the swing, a familiar tension in her stomach. She tried not to rush but the panic had started to overcome her and, eyes focused on the ground, she ran straight into a second person who must have been standing behind her all the time.

Chapter Eight

It hadn't taken long for Louise to decipher the similarities between the two notes. Each told distressing stories about tragic lives, but it wasn't that which caught her attention. What made her stop and take note was the repetition of two lines in both notes:

> *There are other worlds than this*
> *Death is not the end*

She'd remembered the lines from Victoria's note. They'd struck her as odd then, out of sync with the rest of the note, and they jarred now. With little to be achieved last night, Louise had printed Claire's note and placed the laptop in the safe ready to be transferred to MIT. She recognised the second line – death is not the end – as the title of a Bob Dylan song. She'd downloaded the lyrics last night, and it was the first thing she'd looked at this morning on waking, her dreams troubled with images of Victoria's and Claire's broken bodies.

By the time she'd showered and breakfasted it was only 6.30 a.m. Mr Thornton, her monosyllabic neighbour, was waiting for her outside. The elderly man had an innate ability to always be taking out his rubbish at exactly the same time Louise left the house. She'd presumed the man was lonely but every time she tried to strike up a conversation with him he'd only offer a one-word answer. Undeterred, she tried again. 'Are you enjoying this lovely weather?' she asked, cringing at her mundanity.

'Too hot for me,' said Thornton, retreating indoors.

'I see,' said Louise, getting into the car. It was the opposite for her. She loved this weather, the way it not only changed the environment of the town but its inhabitants. It was an illusion, but a charmed one she was happy to fall for.

She took the back road out of Worle along the toll road, passing the turn for Sand Bay and Claire Smedley's old bedsit. The woman's note was on the seat beside her. It was incongruous to think of the hope in the final words. Again, her overworked imagination surprised her by a vision of the note, this time signed by Emily.

With her meeting with Robertson still ninety minutes away, she parked up on the seafront and walked across the road to the Kalimera. She hadn't visited the Greek restaurant since the move of the station and the reception from the owner, Georgina, was not warm. The statuesque woman lowered her head in greeting, her dark eyebrows pointing inwards as her eyes narrowed.

'Good to see you again, Georgina.'

'Coffee?'

Louise smiled. For the first year of visiting the restaurant, she hadn't even known the woman's name. Over time, they'd developed something of an understanding. Louise accepted her enigmatic behaviour for what it was and decided to apologise for her extended absence.

'You think I only open this place early on the off chance you will show up?' said Georgina, the hint of smile lines flourishing on her heavily made-up face.

Louise looked about her at the empty seats. 'I promise I'll try and visit more often,' she said, as Georgina turned her back to make the coffee.

Georgina brought the piping hot drink over to Louise's seat by the window five minutes later, surprising Louise by sitting next to her.

'Why do you open this place so early, I never asked before?'

'I can't sleep for more than three or four hours. I get here early and begin preparations. Why not open? You're not our only customer.'

The comment wasn't meant to be hostile and Louise welcomed the woman's company. When she'd first moved to Weston, the Kalimera had been her refuge. Sometimes she thought she'd only survived her time in the town due to the thirty minutes of quiet contemplation she spent there every morning before work.

'How is that handsome work colleague of yours?' asked Georgina.

Quiet though she was, the woman had great insight when it came to people. She'd noticed Louise's attraction to Thomas before Louise had really understood it. 'He's going through a divorce.'

A sly look crossed Georgina's face but she didn't comment. She was an old schoolfriend of Thomas's and knew he had a young child. Not that Louise had any plans to discuss the matter with her. Thomas was on the no-go list and would remain so for a long time. Things were complicated enough already.

Thinking of Thomas's little boy reminded her that she'd promised to see Emily that night. She hadn't had time yesterday to check in with her mum and was worried about how Emily was faring without her dad. 'I better be going,' she said, draining the remains of the coffee.

'I hope to see you before the end of the year,' said Georgina, deadpan, as Louise left.

The first wave of tourists was heading towards the seafront as Louise left the restaurant. The forecast was another day of heat and already a few cars were trailing on to the beach in readiness for the day to come. Louise felt nostalgic for her own childhood and days of promise by the seaside. She missed her brother from that time, his enthusiasm and relentless energy. She hated what had happened to him, and worse still his reaction to those events. Her mood was clouded further by thoughts of Claire Smedley. The sun highlighted the girl's wasted promise and Louise was motivated more than ever to find out what had driven her to her death.

Louise joined the commuters heading out of town to Bristol as she made her way to the station down Locking Road – with its Victorian brick buildings gleaming in the sun – towards Worle. As she entered the station's car park, her pulse quickened as she recognised the man sitting behind the steering wheel of a brand-new Mercedes saloon car. He was on his phone and hadn't noticed her. She parked up, hating the way her pulse was racing, and waited until he'd driven away.

The man was DCI Finch, currently lead detective from MIT in Portishead. They'd worked together as DIs at MIT before Louise was overlooked for promotion following an incident where she'd killed an unarmed man – Max Walton – who'd been responsible for the murders of tens of innocent people. Finch had told Louise that Walton was armed, a fact he'd denied during the hearing. Louise had never forgiven him for the lie and relations between them had only got worse after her move to Weston. It was as if the case against Louise, and Finch's promotion, had given him the freedom to be the man he truly was. He'd spent the next eighteen months trying to force Louise out of the police. He'd sent her anonymous texts on an almost daily basis, and during the last major case he'd tried to take over.

The atmosphere inside the station was muted as if everyone was preparing for the fallout from Finch's visit. As she entered the CID floor, Louise swore she could smell Finch's aftershave in the air. It made her eyes itch.

'Morning, Louise,' said Simone, the office manager.

Louise ignored the smirk on Simone's face as she headed straight for DCI Robertson's office. Robertson lifted his hand as Louise entered without knocking, as if to warn her off before she spoke.

'What was he doing here?' said Louise.

'Who?'

'Don't give me that, Iain. You bloody well know who. I just saw Finch in the car park. Is this why we couldn't meet until eight thirty?'

'Sit down, Louise. Of course it isn't. DCI Finch called this morning. I suggested he come in early, partly in the hope that you wouldn't see each other. I thought we were over all these petty games now, Louise.'

Louise's eyes widened. Robertson knew the story, and in general had proved to be very supportive, so the comment surprised her. 'He tried to get me framed so he could take my promotion, Iain,' she said, incredulous.

'You have to let it go. That was what, nearly three years ago now?'

'I'll never let it go, Iain. I think you know that.'

Robertson bit his lip, his head bobbing up and down. 'You're going to have to accept that you will run into him now and again. Do you not think I have enemies down here? I went to a conference the other week in Avonmouth and I swear if I'd had a gun there was a good fifteen or twenty officers I'd have happily killed.' Robertson paused, lost in thought. 'With no remorse,' he added.

Louise leant back in her chair. Robertson had a way of defusing situations and some of the tension left her. 'Why was he here though?' She hadn't even told Robertson about Claire Smedley's suicide note yet, so Finch's appearance couldn't be attributed to that.

Robertson squirmed in his seat as if the truth were worse. 'He wants to borrow DS Farrell.'

'Borrow?'

'They have a couple of officers on maternity leave and there is an organised crime case they're short-handed on. I think it will be good for him.'

'Finch or Farrell?'

'We're not exactly snowed under at the moment and Farrell has been doing good work.'

Louise couldn't argue. Although she didn't want to lose him, she agreed that Farrell could use the experience. 'He probably won't come back, you know that?'

'Why would he give up all this?' said Robertson, holding his arms out wide. 'Anyway, you wanted to see me?'

Louise didn't prolong the argument even though she was convinced Finch was manipulating them. There would be many able replacements at Bristol CID so there was no need for Finch to take one of her team. Finch was beyond petty. It wasn't enough for him that he'd destroyed Louise's career. It irked him that she was still surviving, that she was proving a success here in Weston. For his own perverted reasons, he wouldn't stop until she'd left the force; if he was prepared to stop at all. Trying to forget Finch, she showed Robertson the printout from Claire Smedley's suicide note, the DCI's face draining of colour as Louise highlighted the two lines that matched Victoria Warrington's note.

'Could this be a coincidence? I don't want to sound facetious but I imagine "death is not the end" has appeared on a suicide note before.'

'I'm not saying it hasn't,' said Louise, not sharing her boss's surety. 'But we have to consider this is something more than coincidence.'

'Do we have anything suggesting that they knew each other?'

'Nothing yet, not that we've been looking that hard. We need to upgrade this, Iain, to serious crime.'

'You don't think it's suicide?'

'I'm not saying that. But whether this is suicide or something else, I'm worried that this might not be the last death we have to investigate.'

Chapter Nine

Amy fought a vague dizziness as she turned to face whoever was standing behind her. She'd been in such positions before, had been forced to succumb to unwanted advances on too many occasions in her childhood. She retreated into herself as the figure spoke to her.

'Amy?'

She opened her eyes, a wave of relief surging through her as she saw Megan. Amy put her arms around her, sensing at first a surprised tension in Megan's body, then a softening as she returned the embrace. Amy realised she was crying as she pulled back.

'Amy, what is it?' said Megan, her voice so full of concern.

It should have been comforting, but Megan's alarm made her feel even worse. She started shaking, her sobs racking her body.

In the distance, the teenager pedalled away up the hill. In retrospect it had been ridiculous to see him as a threat. 'I'm sorry, Megan, I'm a bit on edge at the moment.'

'That's okay, honey. I'm the same way. With what happened to Claire . . .'

They weren't supposed to ever speak about the group's activities outside the forums or their occasional gatherings, though they weren't supposed to be meeting each other at all. Megan was right, of course. However much she believed in Jay, it was only natural that the death of a friend would weigh heavily on her. She'd felt the same way about Victoria. She'd been so pleased for her, envious even, yet a cold melancholy had come over Amy that lasted for weeks after her passing. At least it explained her jangled nerves. 'I can't believe you're here,' she said, as if Megan hadn't spoken about the other night's events.

'You understood my message,' said Megan, smiling. Her happiness made her look younger and that in turn made Amy smile.

'I wasn't sure it was a message for me but here I am.'

'I know we're not supposed to meet but I needed to be with someone. The group chat is great but sometimes I feel isolated. Do you know what I mean?'

Amy placed her hand on Megan's shoulder, feeling the hard ridge of bone, embarrassed by her earlier display of emotion. 'Jay doesn't need to know. As long as we're careful, what harm can it do?'

They walked up the hill together, a lightness to Amy's footsteps that she hadn't experienced for some time. The park was still deserted and for a brief time it was as if the place was their personal garden. Megan began running, her thin figure eating up the ground, her long hair streaming behind her, giggling as she went; Amy followed, breaking into a run as she became caught up in the moment. Together they sprinted the remaining yards to the top of the park. By the time they reached the summit, Amy was out of breath. She bent over on her knees, trying to suck in air, her lungs bursting, yet she couldn't wipe the smile from her face.

Megan offered her a cigarette as they walked along the Bristol Road. They had no destination in mind, Amy welcoming the freedom of just walking.

'Do you think Jay read my message?' asked Megan as they stopped by a bus shelter, their view of the Bristol Channel and the mud-sea glistening in the high sunshine.

Although he rarely commented on the forum Jay was omnipresent. During their gathering when Victoria had passed over, he'd reprimanded three of the members for talking about DMT on the message board. At that moment the sweet, loving man she knew, the only one she could talk to, had disappeared. His replacement was edged with a darkness she hadn't seen in him before, a hush descending over the group as the three members visibly trembled before him. The darkness lasted an instant, replaced by Jay's benevolent smile as he reiterated the risks they were taking. 'They won't understand,' he'd told the group. 'They'll try to stop us. We have to be mindful, over the coming weeks and months especially.'

Amy feared seeing that side of Jay again but kept her concerns to herself. 'As long as we don't tell anyone else, we'll be fine,' she told Megan.

They walked through Grove Park into town. It was a risk but Amy had never seen Jay in the centre before. She didn't know where he lived but she got the impression it was far out of town. He had an old camper van he drove to the meetings; she'd been inside once but he'd never invited her to stay anywhere.

They crossed the bridge at Knightstone that separated the channel from Marine Lake. At high tide, the seawater submerged the crossing and even now it lapped at the rocks surrounding the walkway. They stopped and gazed towards the horizon as if daring the rising tide. 'I saw him with Claire,' said Megan, her gaze still towards the sea and the two islands – Flat Holm and Steep Holm – that rose from the brown water.

'Saw who?'

'Jay.'

Amy's stomach fluttered. 'What do you mean, Megan?'

'He was with her on that night, when she, you know . . .'

'We all were.'

'I arrived before everyone else. They arrived together in his van. They were holding hands.'

It was ridiculous to be jealous about a dead girl, yet Amy felt that familiar ache.

'She knew it was going to be her time,' said Megan, warming to her theme.

'You don't know that, Megan.'

'I talked to Lisa. She said before Victoria died she'd spent the night with Jay.'

Amy breathed in the sea air as next to them on the path two seagulls battled over a scrap piece of food. Megan's words pained her but she accepted them. She recognised the ache in her friend's voice, the jealousy so clear in her features. The rest of the group liked to talk among themselves. At times, Amy felt like a mother hen. She was the oldest, and she wondered if that was why Jay had yet to let her go. 'We're all so lucky to have found one another, Megan. It will be our time soon. We have to be patient.'

This appeared to placate Megan, the worry easing from her face, her gaze lowering to the seawater that had begun trickling on to the path. Together, they broke into a run to the opposite end, screaming with delight as they raced the incoming sea.

Breathless again, Amy hugged Megan goodbye. 'I have to get to work,' she said, noticing the frailty of Megan's frame.

'See you tomorrow? In the park?'

'It will have to be in the afternoon. Three p.m. okay?'

'See you then,' said Megan.

Chapter Ten

Louise spoke to Farrell that afternoon. He'd been present for the morning briefing on Claire Smedley and Victoria Warrington but she hadn't allocated him any duties on the case. They were sitting in one of the interview rooms, Farrell opposite her like a suspect. 'So you're leaving us for the big city?' said Louise.

Farrell lacked some of his usual spark – lines cracked the skin under his eyes and his hair looked brittle and haywire – but his familiar smirk was present. 'Appears so. Listen, Louise, I wanted you to know that I didn't ask to be moved. DCI Finch approached me. He remembered how I'd helped out on the Pensioner Killer case. I just thought, you know, it is MIT.'

'Stop your rambling, Greg,' said Louise, gently, putting the young DS at ease. 'It's a good opportunity for you. I just wanted to speak to you before you went. You need to make sure you don't waste the opportunity. It would be sad to see you leave here permanently but if it's right for you then no one will get in your way from this station.'

'Thanks, boss, that means a lot.'

Louise hesitated. Farrell knew about her time in MIT, how it was Finch's word against hers that had led her to being moved to Weston. She wanted to warn him about Finch, while not wanting to come across as being unprofessional. Chances were Farrell would end up working closely with Finch and she didn't want Finch to know that he'd got to her. 'I have no grandiose words for you, Greg, other than be careful.'

'I understand, boss,' said Farrell, his eyes narrowing.

In the past, they'd briefly discussed what had happened to Louise when she'd been working with Finch, and Farrell had seen first-hand what Finch could do to a team during an investigation.

'Just be careful who you trust.'

'Ma'am,' said Farrell, as Louise left the room.

Louise had reopened the investigation into Victoria Warrington's death. It was now being treated as a suspicious death and being investigated in tandem with Claire Smedley. A separate incident room had been set up in a room adjacent to the main CID office. The day had been spent investigating the backgrounds of the two women but they'd yet to find anything suggesting they knew each other. Claire's landlord, Mr Applebee, had been called in for questioning as had Victoria's former landlord. Already, the investigation felt loose and Louise could tell some of the team were not fully committed to its necessity yet. The only connection was the two notes, and she conceded the two matching lines could be coincidental.

Louise's phone rang as she returned to her desk. It was her mother. Louise had texted her earlier when she realised she was going to have to work late. 'Hi, Mum. Sorry I can't see Emily tonight.'

'Hi, Lou. Don't worry, she'll get over it. That's not why I'm calling. Are you busy?'

'Always, but I can chat. Anything the matter?' Her mother fell silent and Louise's first thought was that she was calling about Paul. 'What's he done?' she asked.

'He tried to pick Emily up from school yesterday. Your dad was there and they had a bit of an argument.'

'Jesus, I'd only just spoken to him. What happened?'

'Your dad told him in no uncertain terms that Emily was coming with him.'

'And she did?'

Her mother paused. 'Yes, but I'm worried he might do the same again today.'

'Christ, Mum, why didn't you tell me about this yesterday?'

'I didn't want to worry you.'

Louise laughed to herself. Telling her now when she was unable to help was the most worrying thing she could do. 'I'm not going to be able to get there today, Mum, I have too much on.'

'I wasn't suggesting you should,' said her mum, sounding impatient.

'What's the matter, Mum?'

'Oh, I don't know. You said you've spoken to Paul?'

'Yes.'

'And how was he?'

'Belligerent, unresponsive. Paul, basically.'

'What are we going to do, Lou?'

Louise clutched her phone. 'Look, I'll come over on the weekend. I'll try and spend some time with Emily to give you a break and we can make a plan about what we're going to do next.'

'Okay, darling, that sounds good.'

'Okay, Mum, bye.' Louise ran her fingers through her hair, her scalp dry and itchy. She had no idea what type of plan they were going to put together. The only person who could solve the situation was Paul, and he was hell-bent on destroying himself and his family. She would get him help if he would take it but he wasn't at that stage yet. Maybe the incident with Dad would shake him up, make him realise how close he was to losing Emily. Maybe it was simply too late.

Louise looked around the office, concerned that one of her colleagues might have overheard her conversation. It wasn't like her to drag her personal life into work and she didn't want anyone to accuse her of a lack of focus.

On her laptop she loaded pictures of Claire Smedley and Victoria Warrington. She hated thinking this way but as she stared at the images of the two women, she began to imagine them as they would have been at Emily's age. She played over the countless scenarios that could lead from a happy childhood to taking your life as an adult. Emily's mother was dead, and her father was a selfish alcoholic. It wasn't a great leap of imagination to picture her niece's life unravelling like those of the two unfortunate women.

Louise shut the screen, more determined than ever to solve the reasons behind Claire's and Victoria's deaths; as if understanding the reasons behind the tragedies could somehow prevent it from happening one day to Emily.

Chapter Eleven

Four men dressed in loud shorts and wife-beaters had been hassling Amy ever since they'd arrived that morning. The smell of alcohol was pungent in the air as she placed the fried breakfasts on the table. 'Thanks, love,' said one of their number – a thickly muscled skinhead – in a broad Black Country accent, as he placed his hand around Amy's waist.

Amy slipped from the grip, her gaze moving to Keith, who was behind the counter smiling at the scene.

'I didn't think they were shy down here,' said the skinhead.

Amy was used to such inappropriate attention. The café was a beacon to such men, who were drawn to Keith as if sensing a kindred spirit. As Amy returned to make coffee for a lone male smoking outside, Keith moved over to the group of lads. Instead of reprimanding them, he appeared to make a joke, the laughter fading as Amy walked past them.

'Cheer up, love, may not happen,' said the skinhead.

'It never will with that attitude,' said Keith, prompting more laughter from his new-found audience.

Amy paused by the door. It was taking all her strength not to turn around and launch the coffee into her boss's face. A time would come soon when she would do just that, but for now she needed the job so she opened the door and placed the coffee on the outside table, the customer ignoring her as if the drink had appeared out of thin air.

Keith stopped her in the back office two hours later as she was about to leave. 'That guy wasn't wrong, you know, earlier,' he said. As usual, Keith was too close. Grease and sweat coated his body, his breath stale with instant coffee and egg sandwiches. Amy breathed through her mouth as the room shrunk in size. 'You really could do with cheering up,' continued Keith.

Why did men think they had the right to comment on her demeanour? She'd heard the same mantra all her life, ever since she was a little girl: men telling her to smile, to sit up straight, to behave. She would have told Keith exactly what she thought about his theory, and his new sleazy buddies, but for now she was more concerned about the close confines of the room and the exit blocked by Keith's considerable bulk.

'I may have something that would cheer you up,' said Keith, stepping closer so Amy could see the sweat clinging to the chest hairs sprouting up from under his chef's apron.

Another sentiment she'd heard too many times before. 'I'm going home, Keith. Are my wages ready?'

Keith's breathing deepened. He didn't answer, just swayed on the spot as if embroiled in some internal monologue. 'Out by the counter,' he said, eventually, not moving.

Amy was forced to squeeze by him. She would have sworn he was actually salivating but didn't want to concentrate on his face as she quickened her pace out of the room. Snatching the brown envelope, she left the café already dreading her return.

She'd never welcomed the cool sea breeze more in her life. Refusing to allow Keith to make her cry, she walked the back streets to the seafront and along to Marine Lake. She wanted to see Megan but she'd managed to get herself some part-time work at a holiday camp in Brean Down. They'd met often since that morning in

Ashcombe Park. It was such a novelty having someone to share things with and she was surprised by how much she felt Megan's absence.

At the man-made lake, Amy took off her shoes and bathed her legs in the brown seawater. Although Saturday was generally known as changeover day, the area was alive with holidaymakers. Children were building dams and sandcastles while their parents lazed on sun loungers, smoking and staring at their phones.

The sight of the happy children brought memories of Aiden. He'd be a teenager now and she could picture him playing with the other children in the sand. Amy lay down, the coarse sand trickling through her hair and down her back, the sun heating her skin. Jay had been the first person she'd spoken to about Aiden in years and it was with his help that she'd been able to share her pain with the group. She wondered when she would next get that opportunity.

She was content to stay with the holidaymakers for the time being. She headed inland to buy an ice cream – much cheaper from the supermarket than the seafront outlets – and returned to the promenade before it melted. She laughed at the sight of a full-figured woman in a tight bikini waterskiing in between the moored boats. It didn't look safe – the line dragging her was fit to snap in half, and she skied within inches of the fishing and rowing boats – but the woman was so caught up in the action of skimming the sea that she had no other care. Amy envied her focus, wishing she could be so lost in an activity that nothing else mattered. She followed her path as if she was the one on the skis, almost dropping her ice cream in laughter when the slack gave on the rope and the woman careered head first into the sea only to be rescued by the pilot of the motorboat, a perfect smile on her face.

Ice cream finished, Amy crossed the road and took the carved stone steps down on to the beach. She removed her shoes, already brimming with sand, and walked along the beach towards the

Grand Pier. The smell of the sea kindled conflicting memories in her mind. She recalled coming here as a child – paddling in the sea, even once riding the donkeys, but her childhood had not been a joyful one and it was difficult to believe she'd ever been happy here. Yet the seawater made her feel something akin to happiness. The recent memory of her confrontation with the four tourists and Keith was now a distant pain as she walked along the shore. Every now and then, the water would lap at her toes and she allowed the coldness to envelop her feet. She wished Megan could be here to share this with her. Amy imagined her dashing in and out of the water, and wanted nothing more at that moment than to see her friend filled with laughter.

Under the pier a flock of seagulls were fighting over some carrion. Amy moved towards the commotion, the sudden change in temperature sending goosebumps down her spine. The seagulls' prey was the remains of a pigeon, its dull, tattered feathers giving away its identity. As soon as she stepped away the seagulls returned, all the more frenzied for being denied their prize.

Amy ran across to the other side, pleased to be back in the sunshine and away from the netherworld of the pier's underside.

She skipped back on to the promenade. She didn't want to blow her meagre wage packet on the first day but the pier only cost a pound to enter and she could enjoy the spectacle – the buzzing lights and electronic beeps of the arcade machines, the restless energy of the excited children. It was only as she reached the seafront that she stopped, crouching down on to her haunches as if she'd committed a crime.

There, by the pier entrance, was Jay. And he wasn't alone.

Chapter Twelve

In her role as a detective, Louise didn't have weekends. Technically she could choose not to work but reality nearly always got in the way. Even now as she made the short journey from Worle to her parents' house in Bristol she felt guilty for not being at the station. She'd spent the majority of the last two days working on the suicide case, the investigation becoming increasingly frustrating. So far, very little linked Victoria and Claire. Although both local to the West Country, they'd attended different schools and had come from different upbringings. Claire had lived in the care system from the age of thirteen whereas Victoria had lived with her mother until she passed away when Victoria was nineteen. They'd conducted door-to-door searches of the women's neighbourhoods but at present the only thing linking the two victims was the similarities of their suicide notes. Even the tox reports had been a bust, the only common factor a trace of marijuana in both sets of bloodstreams. Louise had requested further testing but it would be at least another week before those results came back.

She took the A370. She preferred the route to the monotony of the M5 and enjoyed the winds and turns as she drove through the small villages separating Weston from the big city.

Emily was waiting for her. As Louise pulled into her parents' drive, she saw her niece's face pushed up against the glass of the living-room window and by the time she'd left the car Emily was already out of the front door. Louise hunched down and Emily jumped into her arms. 'My goodness, you're getting big,' said Louise, as her niece gripped her as if already trying to stop her leaving. Although very affectionate, Emily had yet to learn how to express her emotions verbally but the length of the hug, and the force behind it, told Louise everything she needed to know about the way the girl was feeling. 'Come on, let's get in,' said Louise, prising the girl's fingers from her.

'Grandma's making pancakes,' said Emily, skipping down the hallway.

'Is she now? I don't remember having pancakes when I was a child.'

'Grandchildren get treats, not children,' said Emily. She sounded pleased with the fact, but Louise noted the damning verdict on parenthood; made somehow worse by her niece's youth.

Inside, her mother was flipping pancakes at the stove, her father drinking coffee and reading the Saturday papers. She kissed them both on the cheek, a wave of nostalgia hitting her as she sat at the kitchen table.

'How are you, sweetheart?' asked her father, putting down the paper.

'Tired.'

'You work too hard.'

'Tell me about it.'

'Here we go,' said her mother, placing the American-style pancakes on to the table. 'Batch one.'

Her father rubbed his hands together. 'Pass the maple syrup, Emily.'

No one spoke about the missing member of the family as they talked. Paul was supposed to be taking Emily out in the afternoon and Louise hoped he'd recovered from the hangover she presumed he had by then.

Her niece was so easy to read. Her smile came and went as she ate her second batch of pancakes as if her mind was in constant turmoil. Louise wasn't sure she would ever be able to forgive Paul for putting her through this. 'Get changed,' said Louise, once they'd finished. 'We can go to the park if you like?'

Emily's face lit up and she skipped upstairs.

'When did you last speak to Paul?' asked Louise, once she was out of earshot.

'Yesterday,' said her mum.

'How was he?'

'He didn't sound on best form but he promised he would be on time today.'

Louise filled the dishwasher, noticing the tiredness in her mother's eyes as the sun pierced the kitchen window. 'Has he said anything more about Emily living here?'

'He asked when he could take her back. Said he had a fight with you on the phone.'

'What did you say?'

'We said we'd talk to him about it when he arrived,' said her father, pouring himself some more coffee.

'I'm not sure talking is enough at the moment,' said Louise.

'What do you suggest?' asked her mother.

'He needs to know this is serious.'

Her mother sat down on one of the kitchen chairs, groaning with the exertion. 'He told us what you said.'

'What did you want me to say to him?' asked Louise, hating the defensive tone to her voice.

'Even if Emily could live with us full-time, think about what that would do to her. It would be like losing two parents.'

'Mum, I don't expect that to happen but Paul has to realise it's a possibility. The threat of losing Emily is the only thing we have to make him change his ways. We can get him some help but he needs to want it. If losing Emily is the threat he needs to take action, then that is what we have to do.'

73

'I don't want to leave Daddy.'

Louise cursed under her breath as Emily walked into the kitchen, head hung low.

'You shouldn't eavesdrop,' said Louise's mother.

'I don't want to leave Daddy,' repeated Emily, tears welling in her eyes as she stood rigid in front of them.

Louise's father grabbed the girl and pulled her towards him just as she broke into tears. 'No one wants you to leave your daddy,' he said, his own eyes reddening.

'I'm sorry, Emily,' said Louise, walking over to her niece. 'You know your daddy isn't very well at the moment.'

'He misses Mummy,' said the girl, through sobs.

'I know, darling, we all do. We want to help your daddy get through this and we can do that together as a family. Shall we go to the park now?'

Emily frowned and kissed her granddad before getting her coat from the hallway.

'Are you going to be able to stay so we can all speak to Paul together?' asked her mother, her voice lowered so Emily couldn't hear.

Louise looked away. 'I need to get back, Mum. I shouldn't even be here now.'

'It's the weekend.'

'I know, Mum. I might be able to shoot over this evening but I need to go in an hour.'

'Okay. I understand,' said her mum, though it was clear from her body language that she didn't.

The park at the end of the road was the same one Louise had played in as a child; a happy memory of playing there with Paul came to her mind, only to be ruined by a latter recollection of seeing him, years later, with his friends, smoking and drinking, mortifying her by telling her to go home.

Emily was still downbeat as they walked the perimeter towards the tennis courts. 'Fancy going on the swings?' said Louise.

Her niece frowned as if the question was ridiculous and Louise saw a glimpse into the teenager that Emily would one day become. Louise held her hands up. 'Just a suggestion.'

'A bad one,' said Emily, with a hint of humour.

'So what do you want to do?'

'We can just walk.'

It was the best idea Louise had heard in a long time.

They must have walked four laps of the park before returning home, Emily holding her hand for the last two. They walked almost in silence, both enjoying the stillness of the crisp air and the simplicity of being in one another's company.

As they approached her parents' driveway, Emily stopped and looked up at her. There was such sadness in her eyes it was all Louise could do not to turn away.

'What is it, sweetie?'

Emily paused, her face full of concentration. 'Do you love Daddy still?'

'Oh, silly billy, of course I do.' Louise hunched down and wrapped the girl up. 'Everyone still loves your daddy. We care about him so much, that's why we want to make him well again.'

Louise waited for as long as she could at the house before leaving. She had an afternoon appointment with one of the tech-heads in Portishead and couldn't risk being late, but it was so hard leaving Emily, even with her parents looking after her. The girl gave her such mournful looks that Louise wanted to drop everything and stay with her. Stuck in traffic on the A369 she would have called Paul but couldn't face another argument. She would have to trust that he would do the right thing, and she would do everything in her power to help make that happen.

Chapter Thirteen

The Avon and Somerset Police Headquarters was a purpose-built building in Portishead on the outskirts of Bristol. It was like a slightly dated, but larger version of the new station in Weston. One of the tech team Louise used to work with at MIT, Simon Coulson, owed her a favour and had agreed to escalate the examination of Claire's laptop. He'd completed the job late last night and suggested she meet him that afternoon.

Louise hated coming back there. Her positive associations with the place had been destroyed by memories of the Walton case and its fallout. She refused to be cowed by Finch – if he was there so be it, they were supposedly part of the same team – but she was still relieved to reach the IT department without running into anyone she knew.

'I come bearing gifts,' she said to Coulson who, as usual, was hidden behind a screen. She placed the coffee and croissants on his desk, yet it was a couple of moments before he looked up.

'Louise, good to see you,' he said, struggling to make eye contact.

Coulson had the pale, blotchy skin of someone who sat in front of glaring computer screens too much. The whites of his eyes were crossed with lines of red and Louise wondered how often he went outside. 'Good to see you too, Simon. I imagine this isn't really your weather,' said Louise, nodding at the sunshine outside the office.

'You know me. The weather can't affect you when you're inside.'

Part of her envied Coulson's obsession. He lived for his computer work and would be sitting behind a laptop somewhere even if he wasn't being paid. He could be sociable company when he wanted – he had a dry sense of humour, and wasn't afraid to speak out when necessary – but Louise was sure he didn't have much of a life beyond his work. She guessed that was why he was there working now; the irony that she was as well was not lost on her.

'So what do you have for me?' she asked, taking a bite of one of the croissants.

The change in Coulson's face was so obvious it made Louise smile. It was as if he'd been switched on, his eyes animated and full of wonder as he pulled two laptops from a desk drawer. 'Old machines. This one was recovered from Victoria Warrington's home,' he said, handing her one of the machines still in its protective bag. 'Identical machines. I was surprised with what I found and I have to admit I almost didn't find anything,' he added, his enthusiasm stopping him from getting to the point.

'What did you find, Simon?'

'Oh yes, sorry. Here,' he said, pointing to some screen shots on his laptop. 'I had to go quite deep into the system to find this. Quite a clever piece of kit. You see, the user will enter an IP address on the search bar here to access their chosen page but the software automatically destroys the history of the address both in the page's history and the system itself. It's similar to how users access the so-called dark web but this is quite sophisticated, especially for machines this dated.'

'So what were they trying to access?'

'That's the thing, I have no idea. There is an Internet history, normal stuff, social media, porn and whatnot, but I can't tell when or if this software was used.'

'Any ideas?'

'As I said, some dark-web shit. The user probably used the software to access an encrypted site where they could connect with other users. Maybe to buy and sell stuff.'

'And you found this on both the laptops?'

'Yes, exactly the same software.'

'Could it be coincidence?'

Coulson snorted. 'No way. This isn't standard stuff – this is custom-made by someone who really knows what they're doing. The users were either in contact with each other or a third party.'

'Is there anything else you can do?'

'There's a department in the Met that specialises in this sort of thing, they might be able to help. I'll get the laptops to them. I've already left a note to see if they've come across this specific software before as it is a new one to me and isn't on our database.'

'Thanks, Simon. What are you up to for the rest of the weekend?'

'Probably stay here and catch up with some work. You?'

Louise shrugged. 'Looks like work for me as well,' she said, just as DCI Finch entered the room.

She smelled his aftershave before she turned to look at him, the same citric scent he always wore. It repulsed her to think she'd once liked the aroma.

'Louise, what a pleasure. I was told you were back at your old stomping ground,' said Finch, emphasising old as if Louise had forgotten she no longer worked at the station.

Louise fought the rush of adrenaline. Coulson had returned to his computer screen and was trying to be invisible.

'I was just leaving,' said Louise.

'I'll walk you out,' said Finch, smiling.

It shamed her to think she'd once liked that smile, when all she wanted to do now was rip it from his face. To Coulson's credit, he looked up to check Louise was happy with Finch's suggestion. 'Thanks for your help, Simon,' she said, nodding as Finch held the door open for her.

Not for the first time, Louise wondered if Finch had some kind of tracking device installed on her phone. He used to send her anonymous texts when she was alone, often when falling to sleep, and now here he was. It was a paranoid line of thought and she hated that Finch made her think that way. She didn't engage him in conversation, forcing herself to keep her pace steady through the winding corridors, when what she really wanted to do was get out of there as soon as she could.

'Your man is working out very well here,' said Finch, still smiling.

'Farrell's a good officer.'

'Your best, I'd say.'

The walls of the corridors felt narrower than Louise remembered, and despite the relative safety of being in a police station it still unnerved her to be alone with Finch. It wasn't that he scared her, but more that she was worried about what she would do if she had to endure being in his proximity much longer. By the smug look on his face, she was sure Finch understood this. He wanted her to make a mistake, to say or do something that would make her look unprofessional, but she wasn't going to give him the satisfaction.

'What did you want with Coulson?' he asked, clearly disappointed at her lack of response.

'What do you think? He works in IT, figure it out.'

'Specifically?'

'Why don't you ask him yourself, Timothy, I'm sure you will as soon as I've left.'

Finch grimaced at the full pronunciation of his first name. 'I didn't know we were in the habit of keeping things from one another, Louise.'

'There's a lot of things you don't know, Tim. Nothing changes, I guess,' said Louise, buzzing through the glass doors to the car park.

'Be seeing you,' shouted Finch, as she walked over to the car.

Louise kept her pace steady, ignoring Finch's glare as she opened the car door and sat down, letting out a long breath in place of a scream.

She wanted nothing more than to take the short route back to Bristol and to spend the rest of the day with Emily and her family. Although she'd felt sorry for Coulson and his lonely obsession, the mirror to her own life was all too clear. Whereas the majority of her team were enjoying the weekend off, here she was, as alone as Coulson, working when she could be doing anything. She'd been the same at MIT, but occasionally she wondered why she used up so much energy to the detriment of everything else. She couldn't deny that she still had the urge to prove herself. It was hard to concede, but the fallout with Finch had dented her confidence. However unfairly she'd been treated, she was now viewed with suspicion both by headquarters and in Weston. It wasn't hyperbole to suggest that many people would be pleased if she left the force. It would be the easy choice to make. Her skills were transferable and she'd already had offers of better-paid jobs with much more sociable hours. But she wasn't about to be dictated to by others. She'd worked damn hard to get to her rank, and although her present location was far from ideal she could still make a difference and if that meant lots of lonely hours of unpaid overtime then so be it.

Coulson had promised to email her all the details he'd uncovered so she headed back to Weston. She'd been right to escalate Victoria's and Claire's deaths to suspicious, but being right gave her no comfort. The simplest explanation was that they were in contact with each other on some form of suicide forum. Louise had come across such groups, many quite open on the Internet, during her time in Clifton. At first they'd felt alien to her, strange dark places where people discussed different ways of ending their lives. Yet the longer she dwelt in the discussion boards, the more commonplace it felt. These were just normal people enduring abnormal times. Judgement was frowned upon and the community was nearly always supportive. No one advocated that people take their own lives and there were always links to counselling and support networks. Louise imagined the places saved hundreds of lives every year.

With the new knowledge regarding the matching laptops and software, Louise was convinced a definitive link between the two women would be discovered in the coming weeks. It was tragic they'd had to take such a final decision but there was a small comfort in knowing they probably had each other to discuss their options with before they died.

Louise's immediate concern now was whether or not the two women had been in conversation with other like-minded individuals. The thought of further suicides was a concern and although she fought it, Louise's mind returned to thoughts of Emily.

The rational part of her brain told her it was inevitable that she would make comparisons with the childhoods of the dead women and what was currently happening to Emily, but she hated the way her personal and professional life was merging. The look on Emily's face when she'd asked if Louise still loved Paul haunted her, and was affecting the way she viewed the case. It was as if her mind was wandering beyond her control at the moment, and thoughts of an older version of Emily signing up to a suicide website and sharing her despair with online strangers accompanied her all the way home.

The heat was draining her of energy, and Louise was pleased not to see Mr Thornton as she pulled into the drive, her small-talk limit exhausted for the day. She poured herself a pint of water and sat in the shelter of the bungalow's living room looking out into her miniscule paved garden area. There was no sound coming from any of the other bungalows. The area was a retirement village in all but name. Louise pictured a street full of lonely old people, huddled in their living rooms much as she was doing now. She appreciated the peace but feared she was growing old before her time. Before moving to Weston she'd lived in a flat around the corner from Clifton Village in Bristol with its bustling bars and restaurants. Her little bungalow was so far removed from that flat that she might as well have been in a different country, never mind the twenty miles that separated the two places.

The thought prompted her into work. From her holdall, she took out pictures of Victoria Warrington and Claire Smedley and pinned them on the empty panel on the living-room wall. Underneath she added printouts of both suicide notes. She drew a line between the two and wrote the word 'software' beneath. Maybe she was giving the case too much attention but she wanted these two lives to matter. With everything that was going on with her own life at the moment, it felt more important than ever. Aside from the suicide notes and their living conditions, she still knew so little about either victim. So far the only person who'd had any on-going contact with Claire Smedley was her landlord, Applebee. Louise refused to believe he was her sole human contact. There had been a bonfire at the scene of her death, signs that other people had been in the area either during or close to the time that her life had ended. Louise had to find them, credence had to be given to Claire's life.

Louise spent the next few hours researching suicide forums on the Internet for signs of activity, of mentions of Victoria and Claire. The vast majority of people were anonymous as was to be expected but there was the odd mention of the two women; although not named, the deaths in Weston were referenced.

It was dark by the time Louise shut the laptop. She made herself a sandwich and watched a mindless sci-fi film on ITV before getting ready for bed. In the darkness of her bedroom, she listened to the distant sound of cars travelling on the motorway, her thoughts alternating between her niece and brother, Victoria and Claire, and what was still unknown.

Chapter Fourteen

Amy fought the ache of jealousy. She had no claim on Jay. They hadn't so much as kissed and she'd seen him so many times surrounded by other women. Why, then, was it so hard seeing him alone with another woman now?

The woman's name was Sally and she'd been part of the group since before Amy had joined. She was short and stocky, her hair a black mop that appeared to have a mind of its own. Amy had spoken to her a number of times at the meetings and she'd always been friendly and welcoming. She wasn't Amy's enemy, and it was wrong to see her that way. Amy remembered what Megan had said about seeing Claire arriving with Jay on the night she'd jumped, and the rumours that Victoria had been sleeping with Jay before she'd passed over. Did this mean Sally would be next?

She watched from a distance as Jay bought them both ice cream, the swirling white kind, from the kiosk at the foot of the pier. Even from her spying position, she'd never seen Sally look happier as they walked off together along the pier.

Could she risk following them? If Jay saw her, he would know she'd been following him, even if she hadn't initially intended to do so. And what would she achieve from watching them together? Reluctantly she remained where she was, watching from the entrance of the pier – as tourists rushed by her smiling and oblivious to her feelings – until the two figures faded out of sight.

As she passed by the ice cream vendor who had served Jay, it crossed Amy's mind that Jay might know she was meeting up with Megan. Was this a way of punishing them? She thought Jay was above such things, but then they'd never tested him in such a way before. She sat on the sea wall and stared at the pier, waiting for the pair to return. Jay could be trusted, that much she knew. She'd never trusted anyone else more in her life. It sounded ludicrous, especially to someone as cynical as she was, but from that first meeting she could tell he understood her. It was so easy to tell him everything. It was as if he knew it all already. Even when she'd come to tell him about Aiden, he'd known. 'I can see the loss in your eyes,' he'd said, prompting her to cry for the first time in years.

So what if he was with Sally now?

She walked past the row of amusement arcades towards the high street. Sally had issues of her own and it wasn't fair to limit the help Jay could offer. He would do right by Sally as he'd done right by her. He'd taught her that jealousy was an empty emotion, had shown her that what lay beyond this world was free of such petty concerns. Let Sally be with him for now. Her time would come.

But as she walked up Grove Park, the smell of cut grass carrying on the air and making her sneeze, Amy kept thinking of Sally and Jay together. Everywhere she looked, happy couples and groups of smiling people enjoyed the sunshine. It was as if she was the only person alone in the whole town. Normally this didn't bother her, was more of a pleasure than a burden, but knowing it could have been her on the pier with Jay served to highlight her isolation. At one point she'd even considered catching a bus to Brean to surprise Megan at work but she had no idea what shifts she was working.

In the end, it was a relief to get back to the bedsit. She switched on the radio, losing herself in the inane tunes for a time as she lay on the bed with the curtains shut. At moments like this, she wanted to see the photos hidden under the bed but she usually resisted. The last time she'd viewed them had been the day she'd placed them in the box, a few weeks after reading the newspaper report. She only had three of them and although she could picture each in exact detail, she knew she didn't have the strength to hold them in her hands.

After blasting her ready meal in the microwave she pulled the curtains apart, determined not to hide from the world completely. Once again, she told herself Jay had important work to do and it was selfish to be jealous of his actions, yet she panged for that time when they'd first met.

It had been at least a month into their time together before he'd given her a hit of DMT. It had been the diluted version they shared in the tea. It had given her a pleasant high and hinted at what was to come. At Jay's prompting she'd been prepared for the suggestion of something else, of a consciousness beyond their corporeal world. It wasn't the first hallucinogenic she'd taken and she'd been relaxed with Jay so the trip had been a positive one. He'd promised her the real thing would take her so much further and although he hadn't come out and said it, there was a suggestion of something miraculous waiting for her.

It was weeks later when he'd injected her. She hated needles and had been anxious the whole morning but he'd insisted it was the most controlled way to administer it. He'd given her the tea first and when it came time for the injection she'd been more relaxed. He'd been so calming that she'd actually watched the needle pierce her flesh, before closing her eyes as her life changed forever.

She remembered that period as one of the happiest in her life. Jay was hers and they'd meet at least twice a week. He'd helped set her up at the bedsit and together they'd found the job at the café. The group had been smaller then and when they met they only drank the tea together. She thought that was what was really bothering her. Sally had been part of the group from the beginning, so she'd already gone through the time of being Jay's focus. It seemed unfair that she was back as the centre of his attention.

The message appeared on the screen of Amy's laptop at 9 p.m. Megan had yet to sign in and Amy hadn't paid the group much attention. The laptop always played a little noise when Jay messaged, a three-chord beep that prompted a visceral reaction from Amy, as if he were in the room.

As she read the message she began to understand. They were to meet again this Thursday even though it wasn't the end of the month. It was a new location, in the woods close to Worlebury. At that moment, Amy felt she was the only person who knew who would be next.

She wondered if Sally knew too.

Chapter Fifteen

Within minutes of getting into the car on Monday morning, Louise abandoned her resolution to visit the Kalimera every day. She needed to get to the station. Although she'd spent the best part of Sunday continuing her research into the online suicide groups, she was restless to continue working on the suspicious death cases.

The uniformed officer behind the desk in the main entrance ignored her as she entered the building, and kept his head down as he buzzed her in through the security door.

Upstairs, the CID department was empty except for Simone. 'I forget to ask you, is everything okay with your niece?' said the woman, as Louise approached the incident room.

Louise stopped dead. She wasn't even aware that Simone knew about Emily.

The confusion must have been evident on her face as Simone added, 'From when the school called the other day.'

'Oh, that was just a misunderstanding,' said Louise, opening the glass divide to the incident room, keen not to prolong the conversation.

Louise had checked in with her parents yesterday. Paul had come over for lunch on the Saturday. He'd been hungover but hadn't drunk anything and had left early evening without any fuss. This week was the last of the school year. Her mother had said

Emily had cried when Paul left but was happy to remain at their house for now. Yet, after her last telephone conversation with her brother, she wondered if it had all been a show for her parents; if Paul was playing the perfect dad until they allowed Emily to return to him with no fuss.

With a deep sigh, Louise ran through her investigation handbook. Nearly everything that could be done had been. Now it was a waiting game. The extended forensic tests she'd requested could come through any day, and there was no ETA for the specialised IT department at the Met. If a junior officer had been working on the case she would have told them to put it to one side for the time being, so why was she finding it so hard to do just that? She stared at the photos of Victoria and Claire on the wall – a replica of the incident board in her bungalow – before deciding to take her own advice.

Sometimes it was best to step away, even for a few hours, and return with a fresh focus. Simone offered her a false smile as Louise returned to her desk in the outer office to check through the outstanding cases. Once again, she marvelled at the difference between current cases and her old caseload in the MIT. Maybe that explained her obsession over the suspicious deaths. When it competed with a set of house burglaries and reports of marijuana dealers hanging around outside secondary schools, it was hard not to take an over-keen interest.

One by one, the rest of the team filed into the office. Thomas stopped by her desk and asked how she was. He looked a bit better than he had the other day, as if he'd got some sleep. 'How's Noah?' she asked.

'He's good. I got to see him all weekend,' said Thomas, explaining the change in his humour. He hovered by the desk as if he wanted to say something more before moving off.

It was a strange type of torture being cooped up on a day like this. The air conditioning kept the temperature constant but the sunshine tormented Louise through the windows. She read every outstanding case in the department, reassigning a couple of Farrell's files. Such was the monotony of her work, she didn't balk when Simone put a call through to her from the editor of the local paper, *The Mercury*.

Dominic Garrett was a Falstaffian character she'd met on a handful of occasions. Each time had been at a bar or a function and she'd never seen the man without a drink in his hand. A terrible gossip, Garrett was probably the best-connected person in the town. She couldn't recall him calling her directly before and seconds into the conversation she regretted picking up the phone.

'Ah, Inspector Blackwell, so good to hear your voice, how the devil are you?'

His patter was too constant to be an act. He lived every second as if he were in a play, projecting his voice even though he was on the telephone. She pictured him speaking in a crowded bar, its occupants falling silent as he spoke. 'I'm very well, Mr Garrett. How are you?'

'Now, now, we're not going to have to go through that again, are we?' he replied, rekindling an old conversation they'd once had.

'Sorry, I forgot. Dominic, how are you?' said Louise, playing along.

'I am splendid, Inspector. It's the first day of the week, the sun is shining, and I am about to leave the office. That's why I'm calling you in fact. I was wondering if you would care to join me in a spot of lunch with a former employee of mine?'

'I'm intrigued, Dominic, but I am a bit busy at the moment.'

'Don't you even want to know who would be joining us?'

'If I was to guess, I'd say Tania Elliot.'

'Splendid, I guess that's why you're the inspector.'

It didn't take much deduction. She'd been avoiding Tania's calls since Claire's body had been discovered but was surprised that the journalist would go to such lengths to see her. 'What's it about, Dominic?'

'Exciting times, Inspector. Ms Elliot is working on another extended feature. You know how it is, she's had a taste of the limelight and now she wants more.'

'And this involves me how?'

'Oh come, Inspector. Those two poor unfortunate souls who took their own lives.'

'What about them?'

'I'll let young Tania tell you more. She has a theory about how their deaths are linked.'

Louise let out a long sigh. 'Where and when?'

Louise parked in the shopping centre car park just off the seafront. As she cut through the Sovereign Centre into the pedestrian-zoned high street she was struck by a sense of déjà vu, as if walking past the same faces and hearing the same noises – the endless whispering chatter, the squawking of the seagulls above. Despite the infiltration of holidaymakers that would almost double at the end of the week when the schools kicked out, Louise felt the smallness of the seaside town at that moment. The high street had seen better days. She remembered how busy it had been as a child, the wonder of walking down its street free from the threat of cars. There had been a coffee shop then, not the chain offering that was there now, but an actual coffee shop selling coffee beans. The smell of the place had been alien to her and made her occasional visits more exotic. Now the street was tired, the shabby storefronts overrun with pop-up shops selling mobile-phone accessories and remaindered books.

Dominic Garrett was waiting for her in the bar area of the Royal Oak Hotel. A wide smile formed on his face as Louise approached, his rich baritone welcoming her with, 'Inspector Blackwell, what a treat. You'll remember Tania Elliot. Unfortunately no longer on our payroll but forever connected to our humble little paper.'

Louise held her hand out to the journalist. Tania was a different woman to the one she'd come to know over the last couple of years. Gone was the *faux* confidence that must have used up all her energy each time they met. In its place was the relaxed demeanour of someone who'd been recognised for their efforts. She even dressed differently, in a sharp business suit adorned with expensive-looking accessories around her neck and wrist. 'Good to see you, Louise,' she said, her tone neutral as if she was doing Louise a favour by being there.

Garrett ordered drinks for them, Louise surprised when the editor chose a glass of sparkling water for himself. 'I've gone from the "it's six somewhere in the world" to the "not before six" drinking routine,' he explained. 'It's done nothing for my waistline but I have a clearer head during the day.'

The lack of alcohol didn't affect the editor's personality. His presence had taken over the bar. On the way to the table he stopped to talk to different groups of people on three occasions, shaking hands and making jokes.

'Is there anyone you don't know?' asked Louise, as they took a seat overlooking a patio garden area.

'I think there is a family in Worlebury I've yet to meet,' he said, groaning from the exertion of taking his seat.

'So how can I help you both?' said Louise, the question centred on the journalist who'd so far kept quiet.

Tania glanced at Garrett before retrieving a piece of paper from her handbag and placing it in front of Louise without speaking.

Louise eyed the pair before unfolding the paper, preparing herself not to give anything away. She gave a cursory glance at it before speaking. 'I guess it would be pointless asking where you got this from?'

The paper was a copy of the two suicide notes from Victoria Warrington and Claire Smedley. Tania had underlined the matching lines. 'Care to comment?' asked Tania.

'Beyond stating that this is evidence and you shouldn't have it, no.'

'It was sent in from an anonymous source.'

Louise wasn't sure what troubled her most. That the journalist had the note, or that someone in her team had leaked the messages.

'It would appear we may be on the verge of a suicide pandemic,' said Garrett, wincing as he sipped his sparkling water.

'That's quite hyperbolic even for you, Mr Garrett.'

'Pandemics have to start somewhere,' said Garrett.

'You'll recall what happened in Bridgend?' said Tania.

Louise rolled her eyes. The journalist could obviously smell a story. A few years ago, a group of young adults had killed themselves in the small mining town of Bridgend in South Wales. The total deaths came to twenty-six over a two-year period. Louise's team at MIT had been called in to advise on the tragedy. No clear connection had ever been discovered for the suicides. All but one of the young adults had taken their lives by hanging. 'I think it's too early to be making comparisons to Bridgend, Tania. Suicide pacts between two people are not uncommon. These two women could have agreed to kill themselves. That is the theory we're working on at present. Suggesting anything else at this stage would be highly irresponsible.'

'Did the two women know each other?'

Louise had dreaded the question even though she'd expected it. 'I can't confirm or deny that. This is an on-going investigation.'

Tania raised her eyebrows at Garrett, the three of them understanding Louise's response. Garrett drank again, his displeasure at the lack of alcohol all too evident on his face. 'I would agree that publishing anything at this stage would be unprofessional. Maybe we can reach an agreement?' said Garrett.

'An agreement?'

'I don't publish anything for now. In return, you give me a heads up on any developments before anyone else,' said Tania.

It sounded like the journalist wanted there to be more deaths. Louise stopped short of saying as much and agreed in principle. It meant very little. Louise had no intention of updating the journalist beyond possibly answering her calls on an occasional basis. But for now, it would be much better for the story to stay out of the press. It could prompt others to take their lives and Louise was happy to make such an agreement for the time being to stop that from happening.

Chapter Sixteen

Amy visited Ashcombe Park every morning that week. She knew Megan wouldn't be there – she'd told everyone about her mind-numbing shifts at the holiday camp on the group chat – but it still gave Amy some comfort to make the daily jaunts. She was desperate to tell someone about Jay and Sally. The knowledge was a burden. Amy's dreams were besieged with images of Sally falling to her death and she needed someone to tell her that this was okay, that it was what Sally wanted.

It was now Thursday, the day of the ceremony. She'd been at the park for over an hour, sitting on the swings enjoying the isolation. She had to be at work in fifty minutes. The thought made her want to stay on the swings that much longer. She pushed herself off, moving higher into the air. As she rose and fell, she kept her gaze upwards so all she could see was the trees on a canvas of misty grey sky. Each time she reached the zenith she considered letting go of the taut chains to see if she would ascend into the clouds or fall back to earth.

She was sweating by the time she dragged her feet across the ground to stop the swing. She pictured Aiden as a toddler, smiling as she pushed him on the swings. The fact that the images were pure imagination didn't diminish their impact. She'd missed out on such simple joys but that didn't mean that was the end of it. Jay had shown her that and, despite the tears trailing down her hastily made-up face, she believed him.

Work was quiet. Tomorrow was the last day of the school year in most places so everywhere was preparing for the onslaught of additional holidaymakers. Keith had hired a new girl to help out for the season. Nicole was a nineteen-year-old who'd just completed her first year of study at Swansea University. She was a quiet, frail thing, and already Amy had caught Keith glancing at her. Amy checked the rota for the coming weeks. Fortunately, the season promised to be so busy that there wasn't a time when Nicole would be alone with the café owner, but that didn't mean she would be out of his reach.

Amy walked Nicole to the bus stop after their shift. She was more talkative away from the café and told Amy about her Materials Engineering course at university. It didn't make much sense to Amy but it cheered her to see the girl so animated.

'I know you don't need me to tell you this but keep an eye on Keith,' said Amy, once the girl had stopped talking.

'Is he a bit of a letch?' said Nicole, with a snarl. 'I had a feeling. I was surprised how hard it was to get a job this summer. Everywhere decent was full up. No offence,' added Nicole quickly.

Amy laughed. 'No offence taken.' She wanted to warn Nicole that Keith was more than a letch. She had no proof but was sure the man was dangerous. 'I hope you don't mind me saying this but if you can find something else you should take it.'

'That bad?' said Nicole, as her bus arrived.

Amy shrugged. 'See you tomorrow.'

'Bye,' said Nicole, stepping awkwardly on to the bus.

As Amy walked back through town she regretted being so forthright with Nicole. It would be the last thing she needed to hear on her first day in work. She should have waited, at least allowed her to get her first pay packet before scaring her off. At least she would be at work nearly every day over the next four weeks. It shouldn't be this way, but she would be able to keep an eye on the girl and hopefully something else would come up for Nicole in the meantime.

A nervous anticipation ran through her as she prepared for the evening. She was too excited to eat much but forced half a Spanish omelette down with a glass of milk. She always got this way before the ceremonies, and the feeling had intensified each time since that night in Brean when Victoria had jumped. Before then, her nervous energy had focused on seeing Jay again. And although that was still the case, and in truth she couldn't wait to see him, she was also looking forward to seeing Megan again. But there was more to it than that. If her theory was correct, then Sally would be the one jumping tonight.

The knowledge conflicted her. It was why they were all part of the group. Jay, with the help of the DMT, had shown them that something better waited beyond the confines of this world. She wouldn't have believed it before, would have dismissed it as nonsense, wishful thinking, but Jay had shown her. Why then did she want to warn Sally? Surely Jay would have told her, had prepared her as he always promised he would.

Amy put it down to nerves. She'd never known in advance who would be chosen so this had freaked her out. It would all be okay. She had faith in Jay. He knew what he was doing and seeing him together with Sally earlier in the week didn't change anything.

She washed, the grease from the café taking numerous scrubs to come clean from her skin, and reapplied her make-up. Since she was a teenager she'd never gone outside without it. There was no vanity to it. She wore it as a means of protection. The make-up was a mask she hid behind, so she could be anyone she wanted.

The heat from the day was unrelenting. The sky was still pitted with occasional clouds, but this somehow only served to make it hotter. Before heading off, Amy stood in the shade at the front of the flats and tried to control her breathing. Her body hummed in expectancy, and she fought the trickle of sweat forming at her temple. She stayed that way for fifteen minutes, allowing the cool of the shade to lower her pulse and body temperature.

The meeting point was three hundred yards into the woodland area from the car park along the toll road. Still early, Amy made slow progress to the rendezvous point, her eyes darting nervously on the lookout for Megan or other members of the group.

A group of men, teenagers most probably, whistled to her as she made her way along Milton Hill. Amy smiled at them when she wanted to raise her middle finger. Chances were they meant nothing by it but it didn't excuse their behaviour, leering over a lone female when they were in a group fuelled by testosterone. One of them looked uncomfortable. He raised his hand as if in apology; somehow, Amy despised him the most.

The temperature dropped as she made the steep climb to the car park. The darkening clouds threatened rain and she realised she was completely unprepared for such an eventuality. A hush descended as she entered the car park area, as if the birds and the rest of the woodland wildlife were preparing for the storm. She recognised Jay's camper van, one of only three vehicles in the car park, and her heart skipped involuntarily as she stepped on to the green trail, into the heart of the woodland.

Trying to control a mounting panic – she enjoyed being alone, but this isolation was unnerving – Amy stepped along the dried footpath and hurried forwards until she saw the group gathered by a large sycamore tree.

Jay welcomed her with a big smile and a hug, and it was all she could do not to cry. 'Could we pick somewhere a little less creepy next time?' she asked, as he pulled her close. She could have stayed this way forever, despite the eyes of the other group members boring into her. She closed her eyes to banish their gaze, savouring the smell of Jay's neck and the heat from his skin, until he gently pulled away.

Amy caught Sally's glance as she took a step backwards. She looked different to the time Amy had seen her with Jay by the pier. Amy couldn't quite pinpoint it but the woman appeared older, wiser even, as ridiculous as that sounded. Sally looked completely at ease and wasn't troubled by Jay embracing her. Amy was sure now that Sally knew it was her turn tonight; Amy hoped she would be as calm when her time came.

Megan was the last to arrive fifteen minutes later. Amy fought her own ridiculous jealousy as Jay embraced her, his dark eyes closing as he held her tight.

'I was scared I wasn't going to make it in time,' Megan whispered to Amy, as they made their way through the woods. 'I had to pretend to be sick to get off my shift.'

No one had ever dared miss a ceremony before. It went beyond a fear of missing out. Each occasion could be the night they were chosen. Although it was now apparent to Amy that Sally would be next, everyone else was under the illusion that it could still be their turn.

The trek went further and further into woodlands, Jay walking forwards without a map until a clearing appeared and they made their way across the toll road and through more woodland until they reached the cliff edge. A general murmur of approval spread through the group as they set up camp. Soon they were sitting around a campfire, Megan snuggled close into Amy like before. It felt even more right this evening, and Amy wanted to share what she knew about Sally, but there wasn't time.

Jay stood, his features lit by the glow of the fire. Behind him the sky had darkened. The clouds had vanished and a bank of stars winked down on them. Jay took the pot from the fire and allowed it to cool.

One by one he went around the group and offered them the Ayahuasca tea. Despite knowing it was Sally's turn tonight, Amy experienced a flutter of doubt as Jay moved towards her as if he was going to single her out. 'For you,' he said, handing her the tea. Amy took the drink, all her doubts obliterated by Jay's melodic voice, and drank it in one. She was used to the acrid odour now, the dank taste of the earthy tea that had repelled her the first time she'd tried it.

The physical world slipped from her immediately as she travelled through a long vortex tunnel to the place she called the waiting room. Although it had four walls, the word 'room' was a stretch. Amy felt as if she was floating and beyond the confines of the room she knew Aiden was waiting. She didn't break through this time – the tea wasn't strong enough – but she was aware of the other dimensions as her body thrummed with an overwhelming sensation.

Jay was waiting for her when she returned. A couple of the others were still in the process. Across from her, her figure flickering in and out of the shadows from the fire, Sally had already returned. She looked serene as if she'd made her peace with this world.

One by one they told their stories. It hurt Amy every time but it was important. Cathartic, Jay had called it. It had taken her some time to understand what he'd meant but she understood now. It was okay to cry and she did so as she told the group again about Aiden.

As Megan placed her arm around her when she struggled with the last part of her tale, Amy noticed a look from Jay. It had only been a flicker, a subtle change in his features. It was as if he was jealous of the attention she was receiving from her friend. She'd never seen that look from him before and concluded she was probably reading too much into it. She didn't have time to dwell as Megan took her turn to speak.

Megan's story never got any easier to hear. It was staggering how together she was after what had happened to her. The abuse had started at a tragically early age. It went on for over two years before Megan was taken from her mother and stepfather but it hadn't stopped there. Megan still blamed herself for what happened in the ensuing years. She told the group now, tears streaming from her face, about how she was passed from body to body in her various care homes. The shocking mistreatment went beyond even what Amy had experienced. Megan crept closer into Amy's embrace – her body too frail, like a pile of twigs – as she spoke, and again Amy saw Jay noticing. He'd caught her looking this time and smiled, as if encouraging her to care for her friend; it despaired her to think in such a way but Amy wasn't convinced the gesture was genuine.

Jay stood to thank everyone else for speaking. From his bag he took out the cloth drawstring bag, and prepared the syringe. One time he'd shown the group how the shaman he'd met in Peru had taught him to smoke the vine; and how he'd discovered through trial and error how the dose could be controlled better with the syringe.

The chanting began as Jay walked behind them, touching their shoulders as if testing they were ready. Amy joined in with the recital, the words 'death is not the end' falling from her lips, but for the first time ever she began to question the ritual. If Jay had already picked Sally, then why all the pretence?

Twice he stopped by a different member of the group and lingered, only to move on as the chants increased in tempo until the words stopped making sense, becoming simply a rhythmic noise.

And then he stood behind Sally and the chanting stopped.

Sally was remarkably poised, almost devoid of emotion, as she unrolled her sleeve. Like Amy, she would have taken DMT before with Jay. Even so, there was something sordid about using a needle. It reminded Amy of the portrayal of addicts on-screen, but Jay was so precise it was like watching a doctor in action. Sally took a quick glance at the assembled group and nodded to Jay.

She was gone within seconds.

Amy knew what the other woman was experiencing. It was incomparable to the tea. Amy had enjoyed glimpses of what DMT offered before she'd taken that first proper hit but she hadn't been prepared for what had followed. She'd heard stories of DMT – the disassociation of mind and body, the confidence many users shared that what they experienced was real and not a trick of the mind – but had doubted the validity of such statements. She'd learnt over the years that drink and drugs could make you believe in anything. She'd made so many resolutions while high, thought she'd come to some form of understanding, but her resolution changed after that first full dose of DMT.

With Jay's assistance, the DMT had guided her to something beyond her comprehension. More importantly, the impact hadn't faded after time. It hadn't been an effect, it had happened. Like so many people who'd used the drug, it was almost impossible to put what happened into words. To say she'd travelled to another reality was inadequate. She'd experienced something. She wanted to call it love but that too was insufficient. It was more complete than that. And although she didn't have the words to express the feeling she'd experienced, Jay had been right. She'd had a glimpse of eternity and

102

within that eternity she'd sensed Aiden waiting for her. From that moment onwards it was all she could think about.

It was thirty minutes before Sally came round. The group took turns embracing her. The vibrations from her body shook through Amy as she briefly held the woman in her arms. She saw certainty in her eyes as Jay led her off into the thicket at the back of the camp.

The drop was steeper than in Uphill. Jagged rocks pointed upwards at the foot of the cliff surrounded by dense woodland. As Jay walked Sally further away from them, the group started chanting 'Death is not end' – only this time Amy held back.

Sally didn't hesitate. Smiling, she stepped into the void. Amy turned away as the crash of her landing caused a flock of birds to rise into the air. Silence ripped through the congregation, the chanting cut off mid-sentence. They stood, motionless, contemplating Sally's departure, until one of the group, Beatrice, shone her torch down into the valley and broke the calm with a loud shriek.

'What is it?' asked Amy.

Beatrice handed her the torch. Shaking, she said, 'I don't think she's dead.'

Chapter Seventeen

The school playground was awash with tired parents and hyperactive children. When Emily saw Louise she broke into a full sprint. 'Aunty Louise,' she said, jumping into her outstretched arms.

'As it's the last day of term we thought we'd surprise you,' said Louise's mother, who was standing next to her father.

Emily hugged Louise but her smile faded. The hurt and confusion Louise saw in the girl's eyes was unbearable. 'Daddy is coming to see you tomorrow,' she said.

Emily studied her as if confused, as if searching for a hint that Louise wasn't telling the truth. Louise maintained her smile, internally cursing her brother once more, and involuntarily let out a sigh when eventually Emily nodded, seemingly satisfied with her statement.

The local pizza restaurant was already filling up with families by the time they finished the short walk from the school gates. Louise was exhausted just being there, the excited energy from the schoolchildren palpable. It made her wonder if she would ever be ready to have children of her own. She loved Emily with every inch of her being but that love was made easier by knowing she wasn't ultimately responsible for her. Her father had used to joke with Paul and Dianne that the joy of being a grandparent was being able to give the children back at the end of the day. It wasn't a joke he'd made recently.

Back at her parents' house, with Emily up in her room drawing, Louise asked after her brother. She hadn't spoken to him since their argument on the phone.

'I really don't know,' said her mum. 'I thought things were going fine, then on Tuesday he didn't come over as he was supposed to. We called and called but no response. Dad didn't even go round to see if he was okay, we just presumed he was either out drinking or at home drinking. He sent us a text message yesterday lunchtime apologising. Said he would take Emily out for the day tomorrow. I'm worrying we made a mistake taking Emily from him. Instead of getting him to buck his ideas up it looks like we've been giving him the freedom he wanted.'

'Paul loves Emily, Mum.'

'No one is saying he doesn't, Louise.' There was a hint of ice in her mother's words, as if Louise was to blame for her brother's actions.

'Has he asked when he can have Emily back?'

'He hasn't asked since last week and that concerns me.'

'I'll come over tomorrow and speak to him, how's that?'

'That would be good, thank you.'

Louise had technically finished work for the day but checked her emails as she walked with Emily to the park. The week had been a bust. The extended blood tests had come back negative save for some traces of cocaine found in Claire Smedley, and the specialised IT division in the Met hadn't been back in contact with her about the laptops.

She took Emily to the playground. Watching her dart from activity to activity helped keep Louise's mind off her worries for a brief time. It was difficult to accept she'd just finished her first year in school. She remembered the day she was born, how fragile Emily had felt when she held her for the first time. So much had happened since then. They'd lost Dianne, Louise had lost her job, and now Paul was changing into something he might never recover from. The only constant was Emily. Louise felt a surge of such profound love for the girl that she almost started crying thinking about everything she'd endured in her short life.

'Come on,' she said as Emily jumped from the swings, landing awkwardly.

They walked back hand in hand. 'I'm going on holiday,' said Emily, as a message pinged on Louise's phone.

'I know. You're on holiday,' said Louise, distracted by the urgent message.

She called the office as Emily knocked on her grandparents' front door. Louise's mother opened the door, Louise pointing to her phone as she headed towards her car. 'Simone, it's DI Blackwell.'

'Hi, Louise. There's been another body, I'm afraid.'

Louise made the mistake of taking the M5, fearing the back roads would be busy. The motorway was gridlocked with motorists thinking they'd head to their holiday spots in Devon and Cornwall a day early. Outside Nailsea, Louise activated the lights on her unmarked car and pulled into the hard shoulder.

The details Simone had given her were minimal but were enough to suggest a possible link to the other deaths. The body of a young woman had been washed up at the foot of the rocks by the Kewstoke toll road. A small party of tourists had discovered her that afternoon, her body close to shore. The tide was due to reach its highest point at 9.13 p.m. and Louise didn't know at this stage if the water would reach the body. The SOCOs had been despatched but she wanted to see the body before it was moved.

She left the motorway at Worle and took the back roads. The toll road had been cordoned off just after the turning for Kewstoke. She wound down her window and spoke to one of the uniformed officers, PC Hughes. 'Where should I be heading?' she asked.

'We have two camps set up, ma'am. One at the top of the road and one down by the shore. The body is proving hard to reach,' said Hughes.

Louise took the turning towards the shore. She reached the beach area to see the surreal sight of the white-suited SOCOs trailing across the jagged rocks. The pathologist, Dempsey, was changing into the protective outfit as she left the car. Louise looked at her watch. It was 7.15 p.m. 'We haven't got long, Stephen,' she said.

'Tell me about it. You coming over? I could do with a hand,' he said, looking at the two bags on the ground.

Louise nodded and changed into the suit she always carried with her. Despite the hour and covering of cloud, the air was humid. 'Lead the way,' she said, through her mask, as Dempsey headed towards the rock where the body waited for them.

The sea was ominously close. Without the sun's reflection, it was a blanket of brown getting nearer with every passing second. Louise's footing slipped as she looked outwards, her knee jarring on one of the slick grey rocks.

'You okay?' asked Dempsey.

'Fine. Keep going.'

The journey was harder than she'd anticipated. It took them over ten minutes to reach the rudimentary boundary set up by the SOCOs. Her former colleague from Bristol, Janice Sutton, was waiting at the foot of jagged rocks where the woman had fallen. 'I know. What are the chances?' said Janice, as Dempsey moved past her to where the team of forensic experts were working.

'What are we looking at?' said Louise.

Janice handed her an evidence bag. 'Young woman again. We've actually got a photo ID this time.'

Although she had her gloves on, Louise didn't open the bag. She could see the woman's driving licence through the plastic. Sally Kennedy aged twenty-eight.

'We'll need to verify that naturally. Unfortunately there has been a lot of damage to her face. The hair is quite distinctive though so I think it's a match.'

Louise glanced at the photograph of a smiling woman with thick, wiry black hair. 'You know we're up against time?'

'I think we were lucky actually. Depending on how long she's been there, she would have only missed the low tide this morning by a few metres.'

To Louise's left, two bodies dressed in white scrambled down the cliff side. 'There's a ledge at the top where she fell from,' said Janice. 'We have a team up there now.'

Louise followed the path taken by Dempsey. A pair of officers were photographing and videoing the scene. Louise didn't want to impose but it felt necessary to see the body in situ.

She glanced around the side of Dempsey, who was now examining the corpse, his work expedited by the oncoming tide. A twist of Sally's thick hair was slicked back against the rock, matted with blood. She was turned on to her left side but the right side must have impacted with something on her descent as its features were all but missing.

'Another jumper,' said Dempsey, through his mask.

Louise's opinion of Dempsey was complicated, her feelings clouded by the drunken one-night stand she'd had with the man when she'd first moved to Weston. For a period, everything he'd said had antagonised her. It was only after she'd come to realise that he possibly had feelings for her, and that she hadn't treated him as kindly as she could have, that her thoughts had softened. Yet, she was annoyed by his certainty, his hand still in contact with the young dead woman.

He turned to look at her, his brow furrowing.

'What is it, Stephen?'

'It would appear the time of death may have been some minutes after she fell.'

Chapter Eighteen

From the beach in Sand Bay, Amy and Megan watched the white uniforms swarm across the beach to Sally's body. They'd come close to calling the police earlier, knowing the sea would probably reach Sally's body at high tide. It had been a relief of sorts when they'd spotted the group of tourists finding the body earlier that afternoon.

Beatrice had been correct, the fall hadn't immediately killed Sally. When Amy had shone the torch on her last night, they'd seen the smallest of movements – Sally's final shallow breaths. Amy had kept the torch steady as others in the group began to panic. It had felt right to keep the light on her, to watch her depart. There had been no way to help beyond jumping into the void after her. Amy had glanced at Jay and the indecision in his eyes had unnerved her.

'Everyone needs to go. Go straight home and do not talk to anyone,' he said eventually.

He'd taken the torch from Amy then. 'She's gone,' he said, under his breath. Amy had taken a last look at Sally and it had looked as if she'd finally stopped breathing.

'She might be in pain,' said Amy.

'She's gone, no one could survive that,' said Jay, as everyone began leaving.

In the end, she'd believed him. Megan pulled at her arm, leading her back through the woods. Megan had stayed the night and they'd left first thing, catching the bus to Sand Bay.

Jay would have been furious if he'd known. He'd always warned them never to return to the site of the departed. They'd avoided walking into the woods and hadn't even seen Sally's body, but Amy had determined Sally's location from their vantage point in Sand Bay and together they'd watched the sea approaching that morning, the water not quite reaching the rocks, and had stayed there ever since.

'I've got something for you,' said Megan, who was rocking on the spot, her thin arms wrapped around her legs. 'I was going to give it to you last night but after everything . . .'

Amy dragged her eyes away from the distant sight of the white-uniformed police officers. 'A phone?' she said, glancing at the old-style mobile phone in Megan's hand.

'Take it. I got it off one of the guys at the theme park. It's completely wiped and I bought you a pay-as-you-go SIM card from the shop. Now we can stay in contact with each other.'

Amy didn't know what to say. She took the phone and hugged Megan.

'Do you think we should go now?' asked Megan, once Amy had let go of her.

'Can we wait? I just want to see that they have her.'

They hadn't really spoken about what had happened last night. Amy had surprised herself by falling straight to sleep when they'd got back to hers and when she'd told Megan she wanted to see Sally that morning, her friend had agreed without comment. Amy couldn't quite pinpoint what was troubling her. The only real difference between Sally's death and Victoria's and Claire's was the fact that Sally hadn't died instantly. No one had been prepared for such an eventuality. In retrospect, her panic had been the most natural response. She hated the thought of Sally being in pain, even if it had only been for a few minutes.

The team of white-suited police officers recovered the body with seconds to spare. At one point, Amy thought they were going to pull the body by wires up the cliff side but if that had been the plan it was abandoned. Amy's stomach rumbled in complaint as four of the officers carried the black body-bag back across the rocks. This last indignity was the hardest to bear. Amy hadn't considered what happened to the bodies once they'd been discovered. She'd been contented with the knowledge that they'd moved on beyond the pain of this world. Watching Sally being carried like a bag of rubbish made her question everything, Jay included.

Last night, she'd seen a side of his personality she'd never experienced before: the hint of jealousy as he'd watched her with Megan, and the indecision in his eyes at Sally still being alive. Maybe it was paranoia, but until that point she'd seen Jay as being almost infallible. It was natural for her to feel doubtful after what had happened, but what if Jay wasn't everything she'd made him out to be? It was selfish thinking this way, especially now as Sally was being hauled into the back of the ambulance, but Jay had promised her it would be painless. But it hadn't been painless for Sally, and what if the same happened to her?

Megan grabbed her hand as if in response to her thoughts. 'I need to go,' she said, gently. 'I can't miss another shift.'

Amy had called in sick that morning. She'd left a message and although she'd face Keith's vitriol tomorrow, she didn't care. He would never be able to find someone like her to do the job, especially for such meagre pay. Her real concern had been leaving Nicole with him for the day.

Hand in hand with Megan, Amy headed to the bus stop on the seafront in Sand Bay. It was so beautiful that for a second Amy forgot why they were there. She tried to hold on to the moment but visions of Sally alone at the foot of the cliff destroyed it. Everything faded so fast and as the bus took them back to Weston – past the blinking lights of the emergency services on the toll road – Amy forced herself to cling on to her belief in Jay. He was human after all. How was he to know that Sally would survive the fall? It had only lasted seconds and his reaction had been a human one.

Amy had seen what lay beyond. Jay had shown her and he would lead her there. If she had to endure a few moments of pain to get to that place, to be with Aiden again, then so be it.

Chapter Nineteen

Like ghosts – their white suits glowing in the moonlit darkness – they carried the body across the rocks to the waiting ambulance. Louise had gone ahead, the rising sea threatening to trap her.

The SOCOs placed the body in the back of the ambulance, the silent flashing light a solemn siren. Louise had already tracked Sally Kennedy's address to a caravan park in Winscombe. A team had been sent over there now. Louise already knew what to expect, a laptop and a suicide note, and had prompted the team to search for those first.

As the ambulance took the body away, Louise thought about what Dempsey had told her. The fact that Sally had lived for a few minutes after her fall shouldn't have bothered her but it did. Louise wondered if the young woman had been conscious for those few minutes as she'd bled out.

Had she regretted her actions, or tried to call out for help? Or had she just wished harder for death to claim her?

Louise had little doubt now that the three suicides were linked. If nothing else, it proved that her instinct to mark Claire's and Victoria's deaths as suspicious was correct. The case had definition now, especially with the software link. Something must connect the three women and if she could find out what then she would be a step nearer to working out the question that was bothering her so much: why?

Louise was about to head towards Sally's caravan park when another vehicle entered the car park. Louise wasn't surprised to see the journalist Tania Elliot park up and walk towards her, her narrow face framed by her bobbed haircut. 'Inspector,' she said, her notebook held in her hand like a weapon.

'It's been too long, Tania. How are you?' said Louise.

Tania chuckled at Louise's sarcasm and at that moment Louise felt they could have once been friends. 'I'm sorry it's taken this to bring us together,' said the journalist, gesturing around her as if their location was to blame. 'I believe there was another jumper?'

Louise wanted to dismiss the woman but after their meeting she knew it was important to keep her on side. A report on three linked suicides would be devastating and it was vital to delay the inevitable story for as long as possible. 'It looks like there was another suicide but I can't confirm anything yet. I remember our conversation, Tania. I promised I would keep you updated and I will.'

'Do you have a name for the deceased?'

'We believe so but we can't confirm that yet.'

'Do you think the death is linked to Claire Smedley and Victoria Warrington?'

'Listen, Tania, you know as well as I do that it's too early to speculate on that. We've only just put the poor woman into a body-bag.'

'This is the third woman to take their life by jumping from a cliff, surely it's not a coincidence, Inspector?'

Louise took a deep breath, her lungs filling with the sea air. 'We've discussed this. I can't make a comment yet, Tania, but as soon as I have something concrete I will let you know. If you publish any supposition based on this, you will jeopardise the investigation.'

Tania kept on talking as if she hadn't heard. 'Do you think this will be the last suicide, Inspector Blackwell?'

'Off the record, Tania?'

'Of course.'

'I don't honestly know but I'm sure you wouldn't want the blood of anyone else on your hands, would you?'

'That's a bit melodramatic.'

'Is it? We need to find out what links these women, why they've jumped. What we don't need is to create a panic, or worse put ideas in vulnerable people's minds.'

'This is my job, Inspector.'

'I understand, Tania, but I am asking you to wait.'

'Will you tell me as soon as you've confirmed the name of the victim?'

Louise fought her growing rage but agreed.

'And if you find a note?'

'We'll need to process it but I'll let you know before anyone else.'

'I can sit on it for one more day but I can't risk anyone getting hold of the story.'

'I understand. You need to be the first and you will,' said Louise, unable and unwilling to hide the disdain in her voice.

Thomas was at the address they had for Sally and was coordinating the search of her home. From the outside, Sally's caravan appeared to be abandoned. It was not fixed like the majority of the caravans on the park, more the old-fashioned trailer type. Oblong in shape, its shell was a rusted brown, the whole thing balanced precariously on two flat tyres and piles of bricks.

'We've spoken to the owners of the park,' said Thomas. 'Apparently, Sally did odd jobs on site and was allowed to keep her caravan here in return.'

'Is this even legal?' said Louise, stepping inside. The interior made Louise's bungalow look palatial. There were two rooms. One for living and sleeping in, and a small cupboard-like area that would once have been a toilet.

'It's connected to the mains but isn't plumbed,' said Thomas. 'The owners said she used the block of showers and was allowed to use the kitchen area but rarely did.'

Louise should have been shocked at the way Sally lived but she'd seen much worse in her time. At least Sally had a place she could have called home. 'Have you found a laptop?'

'There was a note attached to it,' he said, handing her the plastic-covered sheet.

Any remaining doubt faded as she read the note. This time there was no life story, just the two lines that had formed a perverse earworm in Louise's mind:

> *There are other worlds than this*
> *Death is not the end*

After almost not discovering Claire's laptop, the fact that Sally's note had been taped to her laptop felt deliberate. The mistake at Claire's flat withstanding, it seemed important to all three women that their notes were discovered.

'Have we found anything else of significance?'

'Just these,' said Thomas, handing her a second bag with a number of paper tokens.

Louise recognised them as the paper vouchers the machines in the amusement arcades spat out in lieu of actual prizes. The vouchers could be collected to purchase prizes in the gift shops in the arcades. It was a perfect scam, the cost of playing the games far outweighing the cost of the prizes. It was nothing new. Louise had collected similar vouchers herself as a child on her day visits to the town. She'd once saved up her tokens over two summers and purchased a toy, a little plastic man with a makeshift parachute attached to its back. Paul had one too and together they'd launched their little men over the edge of the pier. Louise could still picture her awe as the wind carried them out towards the mud, a year's worth of anticipation gone in seconds.

'They look recent,' said Thomas, glancing at the roll of tokens.

'We know where they're from yet?'

Thomas flipped one of the tokens over. In the dim light of the caravan Louise read the small print: Property of the Grand Pier.

Chapter Twenty

Louise was at the seafront the following morning by 6 a.m. After a number of calls, the weekend operations manager at the Grand Pier had agreed to meet her and Thomas at 7 a.m. She'd told Thomas to meet her at the pier, so she went to the Kalimera alone.

Georgina served her coffee in silence. Where once she'd felt the owner simply didn't like her, Louise now thought she was sulking with her for not returning sooner. 'How's business?' she asked, as Georgina placed the coffee on the counter.

'Look about you,' said Georgina, pointing to the empty restaurant.

'It's generally empty. I rarely see anyone else here this time of the morning.'

'That's not the point,' said Georgina, turning her back and walking off to the kitchen.

Louise could have done without the restaurant owner's histrionics but she was smiling as she took her coffee to the window seat with its view of the seafront. The place always gave her a sense of calm, and Georgina had only responded that way because she'd missed seeing her. Again, she promised herself to visit the place more often as she flicked through her notes.

She'd left the caravan park after midnight last night. She'd pushed the team to work to their limit. Together they'd searched every inch of Sally's meagre home. Louise recovered a battered address book and had instructed her team to get into the office early that morning to go through every number and address. She wanted to find someone who knew Sally apart from the owner of the caravan park, and somewhere there had to be a link between her and the other two dead women.

Louise fidgeted in her seat, restless for 7 a.m. to arrive. Having to work to other people's timetables was part of the job that frustrated her. She wanted everything sorted that moment and would have gladly met the operations manager last night, whatever the hour.

Leaving payment on the counter, Georgina still absent, Louise headed across the road to the seafront. With the schools breaking up yesterday, today would be one of the busiest of the season. It was already warm and the familiar smells of the sea and the fresh cut grass on the lawns opposite the front made Louise nostalgic for her childhood. On her day visits with Paul, the Grand Pier had been a kind of holy grail. They'd enjoyed playing on the beach, and to a lesser extent in the muddy sea, but their daily goal had been to spend some time on the pier with its lights and noise, its endless possibilities.

It was still ten minutes to seven, the main entrance to the pier locked shut. Although she'd agreed to meet the operations manager at the entrance, Louise squeezed through the side gate where a group of men dressed in cleaning overalls were making their way up the walkway of the pier.

The concession stores near the entrance were boarded up and in the early morning the place felt like a ghost town, the illusion it created when open destroyed. A man in an ill-fitting grey suit walked over to her as she leant against one of the shutters. 'DI Blackwell?' he said.

Louise showed the man her warrant card.

'Stephan Daly,' he said. 'I'm the ops manager here this weekend.'

Daly had the unhealthy pallor of a smoker. Louise glanced at his fingers, her hunch confirmed by the yellow nicotine-stained skin. There was a slight tremor to his hands and she wondered if he was nervous of meeting her or was seeking his next nicotine hit. Louise showed him the roll of paper tokens. 'These are from here?' she said.

'Clearly,' said Daly, pointing at the Grand Pier insignia.

'We're looking to find video evidence of the person who won these tokens. Would you be able to tell me which machine they come from?'

Thomas arrived as she was speaking, checking his watch to make sure he wasn't late. Louise introduced him to Daly. 'I was just asking Mr Daly which machine the tokens came from.'

'I'm afraid it's impossible to say. We use the same tokens on practically every machine. All I can say is that they were probably won this month. We tend to change the colour of the tokens every few weeks,' said Daly.

'Which machines give out these tokens?' asked Louise.

'There are a number of them located in the main building. I can show you if you like?'

'Lead the way.'

'I hate these places,' said Thomas under his breath, as they walked along the promenade behind Daly.

'You're just getting old,' said Louise, though she felt the same way. Like everything in the town, the pier had changed beyond recognition since Louise was a child. She felt it as she gazed at the wooden boards beneath her feet. As a child she'd been able to glance at the mud, and occasionally the sea, between the gaps in the boards. The mild threat of danger had excited her then, but now the gaps were sealed shut. Nothing could live up to the excitement she'd felt as a child, but even the main body of the pier appeared soulless. There had been something chaotic about the pier in the past with its funhouse and ghost train. Now everything was a little too clinical, a fact compounded by the lack of people inside.

Not all the machines were switched on yet but there were enough flashing lights and electronic noises to give the place a hazy, distorted feel.

'We start here,' said Daly, pointing to a roulette-type machine.

'So you spend money, and receive this in exchange?'

'If you win.'

Daly walked them through the pier, stopping at different types of machines. Louise remembered one of them – a skittle alley game with its scoring hoops – from her childhood. 'So what are these tokens worth?' said Louise, remembering the green plastic man she'd sent parachuting from the end of the pier.

'Players can redeem the vouchers in the shop.'

Some things never changed. The shop displayed the same low-quality prizes she remembered as a child. For a thousand tokens you could get a cheap-looking cuddly toy, no bigger than the size of her palm. Behind the counter was an electronic device worth ten thousand tokens.

'You would need to spend a fortune to win one of those,' said Thomas.

Daly shrugged his shoulders as if Thomas's comment was irrelevant.

'So who counts all the tickets?' asked Louise.

Daly pointed to a machine inside the shop. 'You put them in there and it counts them for you.'

'Are there any more machines that issue these tickets?' asked Louise.

'There are a couple at the entrance to the pier as well.'

Louise looked up at the cameras spread throughout the hall. 'Everything is videoed?' she asked.

'Yes, we have quite a comprehensive monitoring system.'

'Okay, we're going to need all the video surveillance on these machines for the last month.'

'The last month? You're talking hundreds, no, thousands of hours of footage.'

Louise showed Daly a picture of Sally. 'This young woman died and it looks like one of the last things she did was visit this place. I want to find out who she visited here with. We'll start with Thursday's footage and work back from there. Does that work for you, Mr Daly?'

Daly's face reddened from the reprimand. 'I can get them over to you this morning,' he said.

'We need to speak to all the employees,' said Louise to Thomas, as Daly headed off to the office. 'Daly is right about the hours of images. Let's see if we can find someone who saw Sally in the last week or so.'

If Thomas thought the request for the CCTV was going overboard he kept it hidden. 'I'll get some uniforms down here,' he said.

'Let me know as soon as Daly has the footage ready. I'll get a team together at the office to start going through it,' said Louise, hoping the job wouldn't be as difficult as it sounded.

It was after lunch before the first files arrived from Daly. Louise had called in Simon Coulson and was surprised when he'd agreed to set up the screening team in Weston. Together with a team of five uniformed officers Louise had managed to recruit, they'd taken over the incident room.

'Even at triple speed it's going to take us hours to get through all these,' said Coulson under his breath before giving his instructions out to the rest of the team. 'Pause your screen as soon as you feel yourself getting tired. All it takes is one lapse and we may miss what we're looking for,' he told the officers, who looked less than pleased to be inside staring at grainy images on their screens.

'Do we have any more images of Sally?' asked Coulson, once they'd started. 'I've scanned her details and can run the CCTV images through facial-recognition software but we could do with something a bit clearer. The more images you can find of her the better.'

'I'll see what I can do but at the moment we only have the driver's licence and the photos taken at the scene.'

'Okay, leave it with me,' said Coulson, returning to his desk. Louise was impressed with the change in the man. It was like seeing a different person. He'd taken charge of the situation, and was so much more animated than the time she'd seen him in Portishead.

'I think he's sweet on you,' came a voice from behind her.

Louise turned to see Simone. She frowned. Louise was in no mood for small talk with the office manager. 'Simon is a diligent professional, Simone. We should all strive to act like him,' she said, walking off to her own desk.

Thomas returned in the afternoon. 'No one remembers seeing Sally,' he said. 'I'm not that surprised either. By the time I left, the pier was a madhouse. I've never seen it so busy. I never really liked the place but I can't stand it now.'

Thomas had lived in Weston all his life so Louise was surprised. 'You must have liked it as a child?'

'Not really. My parents didn't have much money so when we went all we got to do was look at everyone else enjoying themselves.'

'Poor you,' said Louise. 'Remind me when this is all over and I'll treat you to go on the bumper cars.'

'You're on.'

Louise looked back at her laptop as her skin flushed. 'I was going to say, Tom. If you need to get back to see Noah that's not a problem.'

'That's okay. Becky has him this week so I'm a free agent.'

Louise did her best to ignore the implied message – meant or not – and returned to her screen without comment.

More officers joined the team scouring the CCTV images. News of the suicides had spread through the station and Louise was proud of the way both her team and the uniformed officers had rallied around to help. With her own stretch of video stream to view she knew first-hand how tedious the job could be.

As twilight approached outside she rewarded the team by ordering take out. She acknowledged the cheers of approval, pleased that a common goal was uniting everyone. Indian was the prevailing choice and soon the office was awash with plastic containers and the smell of spicy food. Louise was about to take a mouthful of prawn biryani when her phone buzzed.

'Hi, Mum, everything okay?' she said, her mouth watering as she waited for her to answer. 'Mum?' she repeated, only now remembering she'd promised to pop over and speak to Paul the last time she'd talked to her mother.

The silence began to panic her and she asked again more urgently. 'Mum, what is it?'

It was her father who spoke eventually. 'Sorry, Lou. It's Dad. We have a bit of a situation here.'

'For God's sake, Dad, what is it?'

'We're probably overreacting but Paul took Emily out today and he hasn't returned yet. He was supposed to be back this afternoon. He isn't answering his phone. I've just been round to his flat. I let myself in but there was no one there.'

Chapter Twenty-One

Louise's parents were not the kind of people to jump to conclusions. They were correct to be worried, and they wouldn't have contacted her if they hadn't been convinced it was necessary. Leaving Thomas in charge, Louise headed for the car. She wasn't panicked, more annoyed with Paul for letting this happen. Yet, as she drove to his house in Bristol, her mind kept playing out worst-case scenarios. Passing a smashed car on the A370, she recalled the numerous RTAs – road traffic accidents – she'd attended over the years, the terrible injuries she'd seen and the countless lives lost. Immediately she thought about Paul driving under the influence. She would have trusted him never to do so, especially with Emily, but considering his recent behaviour it wasn't beyond a possibility. She played out other scenarios in between leaving messages on Paul's answerphone. Paul in the pub somewhere with Emily, too out of it to look at his phone or to look after his daughter; Paul unconscious in the car, Emily confused and alone trying to wake her daddy. Could he really be that selfish? He'd done some pretty lousy things since Dianne's death but that would be unforgivable.

Her father was waiting for her in Paul's flat. He'd let himself in and was searching the place for clues as if he was a SOCO. He couldn't hide his worry for his only granddaughter. It was written all over his face, in the lines carved deep into his forehead and around his eyes. What was harder for Louise to see was the disappointment. Her father wasn't one for over-elaborate displays of emotion. He was a tall, stoic man. Gentle and caring, but reserved. To see his helplessness made her feel guilty, as if it were her and not Paul who'd failed the family.

Putting on her police voice she told him not to worry, that Paul was probably running late and his phone had run out of battery. It was way too early to panic. If someone had called this into the station they wouldn't have sent anyone out yet to deal with it. Emily was Paul's legal responsibility and had only been out with her for a few hours. Yet, she shared his concern. Paul had promised to bring her back on time and with what had happened recently, that he hadn't done so was a concern.

She took a look around the flat, not sure what she was looking for. 'Where did he say he was taking her?' she asked her father.

'They were going into town to do some shopping, then to the cinema over in Cribbs Causeway.'

'Do you know what they were watching?'

'I think it was the new Spiderman. Mum will know, I'll check.'

The sound of concerned hope in her father's voice was distressing to hear. Chances were Paul would walk through the door any minute, but still she went through everything in his room. She called him again, swearing under her breath into his voicemail as her father returned.

'Mum says it was Spiderman. The four-twenty showing. Paul said he would come straight to us afterwards. This is the last straw, Lou.'

Louise went to her father, his body tensing as she held him. 'Come on, let's go back home. We shouldn't leave Mum alone,' she said.

From her car, Louise took a chance and called one of her former colleagues from the MIT. She wanted someone to check on recent hospital admissions and RTAs but didn't want anyone from Weston knowing her business – she could already hear Simone's fake concern on hearing that Louise's only niece had gone missing.

As well as working with Louise at MIT, DI Tracey Pugh had been seconded to assist her in Weston during the Pensioner Killer case. Tracey was the only member of her old MIT team still left in Finch's department. Finch had purged the rest of the team mainly by getting them transferred out of the area. Although Tracey worked for Finch, Louise trusted her and she was pleased when Tracey answered. 'I thought you'd be out on the town on a Saturday night,' said Louise.

'Chance would be a fine thing. I'm still at the bloody office with one of your blokes.'

Louise was momentarily confused, thinking she'd meant Finch before remembering Farrell was working there. 'How's he getting on?' asked Louise, more for politeness than anything else.

'Hard worker, I'll give him that. So why are you calling this late?'

Louise explained the situation. Tracey was something of a family friend. Emily loved her and Tracey knew all about Paul. 'Don't worry about a thing. I'm on it. I'll check the database and get on to the hospitals. You go see your mum.'

Louise let out a long sigh as if she'd been holding her breath ever since her parents had called. 'Thanks, Tracey. Can we keep this between ourselves?'

'Do you need to ask? Go see your family. I'm sure he'll turn up any minute but I'll let you know if I hear anything.'

She felt more relaxed knowing Tracey was on the case. It was hard being on the other side of the fence. She'd always been able to empathise with people in similar situations, but now it was happening to her she began to feel more deeply the worry that a missing person could cause. If there was any news, Tracey would find it and her friend was probably right. Paul would most likely arrive sometime soon, contrite and ready to face the full force of his family's anger.

Louise's mother was not having such a rational approach to the situation. She was drinking heavily from a wine glass filled to the brim. 'I should never have let him go,' she said to Louise, in welcome.

Louise hugged her mum and eased the glass from her hand. 'I know it's a worry but he's only been gone a few hours. He could have broken down. I've asked Tracey to look into it. She knows they went to the cinema earlier and she'll check up on everything.'

Louise stopped short of mentioning hospitals and RTAs. She put on the radio, desperate for anything to break the cloying silence. As she poured herself a glass of wine she remembered what had been bugging her ever since her parents called. She took a drink, the wine rich and tangy, and closed her eyes. How could she have been so stupid? 'I just remembered something,' she told her parents, hating the expectancy in their wide eyes. 'Emily told me she was going on holiday when I saw her yesterday. I dismissed it at the time as I thought she was talking about breaking up from school. What if she meant she was going on holiday with Paul?'

'Do you think Paul would have told Emily that and not us?' said her father.

'To be honest, I hope that's what he's done. It would be a bloody relief. At least we would know they're together,' said her mother, looking around for her glass of wine.

'I should have asked what she meant,' said Louise. 'I was distracted by a text message.'

'Don't be silly. It's not your fault, Louise,' said her father. 'It's only one person's bloody fault and he'll find out about it when he gets home,' he added, his tone souring.

Despite their reassurances, Louise still felt responsible. After persuading her parents to go to bed, she sat up in the living room with a second glass of wine. It was typical of Paul to do this, make her feel guilty for something that was evidently his fault.

She finished the glass and took her laptop to her old bedroom. It was redecorated now, the walls a neutral cream colour, but it always felt like a regression staying the night. There was no point sitting there worrying when she could be working, yet she felt guilty as she opened her laptop and downloaded a file of the CCTV footage from the Grand Pier. Thomas was still at the station with the team and it felt necessary to make her contribution.

Watching the sped-up images of people coming and going – placing coins into the machines and winning their tokens – was having a hypnotic effect. For all she knew, Sally could have been hiding just out of shot and even if they did spot her would it help? Louise wasn't sure why finding the footage of her was important. Deep down, she guessed, was the hope that Sally hadn't been alone and that whoever she'd been with would be next to take their life. Louise was desperate to stop that from happening so she continued watching until her eyes could no longer take it and she fell asleep, her dreams plagued by tourists walking in triple speed along the pier and off the end into the waiting sea.

Chapter Twenty-Two

Amy kept looking at her phone during her shift. She only had the one number in it, and knew the adage that a watched phone never rang, but still she glanced at it every time she had a second to herself. Not that there was much opportunity. Nicole had turned up late and hungover, and had been less than useless all morning. Keith had been watching her with mounting hostility as she made error after error serving the subdued Sunday morning crowd.

'Everything okay?' Amy asked the girl as she placed an order of coffees on a tray for her. She could smell the alcohol on her skin and the sweet perfume she'd tried to mask it with.

'Long night,' said Nicole, her hands trembling as she took the tray over to a crowd of teenage girls who didn't look much better.

'You need to sort her out,' said Keith, looking up from the grill at Amy.

Since when has it been my responsibility to look after the staff? she thought, walking away before she said something she might regret.

The mistakes continued and after Nicole dropped a pot of tea, the scalding water just missing one of the customers, Keith summoned her to the back area of the café. Amy finished taking a payment and followed them.

'This doesn't concern you,' said Keith, who was standing with his hands on his hips, his stomach stretching his striped apron to breaking point.

'Can we do this later?' said Amy. 'It's rammed out there and I'd rather not be alone.'

Nicole was facing Keith, her thin shoulders hunched as if cowering. Keith wasn't one to hide his emotions and his cartoon-like scowl was comical in its severity. 'Get back to work, both of you,' he said, spittle falling from his lips.

'Thank you,' said Nicole, moving past her, her forehead lined with sweat.

'Just try and concentrate. See if we can get through the rest of the shift without any more accidents,' said Amy, following Nicole out and leaving Keith alone in the back office to fume.

Amy decided to stay late until Nicole's shift was over. She didn't know why she'd become so overprotective of her colleague. Nicole wasn't the first young woman to work at the café and she wouldn't be the last, so why was she taking such an interest in her? She guessed it had to do with events outside of work. The last two days had been draining, and she couldn't get the image of Sally, alone in the darkness, her body broken but still breathing, out of her mind. Had she still been conscious? The thought was unbearable. It diminished everything they'd done together; worse still, it was beginning to make her doubt Jay.

She helped Nicole clean up and walked her out of the café before Keith had a chance to stop and reprimand her.

'Thanks for staying. I owe you one,' said Nicole, once they were outside.

'You can't give him the chance to have a go at you,' said Amy. 'If you come to work in such a state again, I won't be able to help you.'

131

'I know. Things got a bit out of hand last night. I shouldn't have come to work really. I need the money more than ever now though.'

'How come?'

'Spent all of my wages last night,' said Nicole, with a knowing shrug.

Amy saw herself in the girl. She'd been just the same at her age, though things had soon unravelled. Maybe that was why she felt so protective. She had a chance to stop Nicole making the same mistakes she'd made. Nicole had the kind of opportunities Amy had never had, and could do something with her life.

'Go and get some rest,' said Amy, as Nicole's bus arrived. Hearing herself, she thought she sounded like a parent. The thought clouded her with melancholy, bringing with it memories of Aiden. She checked her phone again and considered calling Megan even though she would still be working.

Megan had responded differently to Sally's death. Amy had been grateful she'd accompanied her to the beach. In the kindest way possible, Megan had reminded her of their goals, the reasons they'd gone to the woods that night. Sally had found her way and Megan had reminded Amy that she'd gone to a better place. And although Amy had agreed, she wished she could have articulated better what was troubling her; if only she could fully understand it herself.

Unable to face logging on to the group chat, Amy went to bed early, checking her phone once before falling into a dreamless sleep.

She rose early the next morning and walked into town. Her shift was later that day so she took the opportunity to visit the central library. She loved the musty smell of the old building and although she wasn't much of a reader any more, there was something powerful about the potential of the books; the hundreds of different worlds on offer to the curious.

In the reference library, she scanned the newspapers, looking for a report on Sally's death. *The Mercury* wouldn't be out until Friday and the death seemingly wasn't of enough importance to make the nationals. It wasn't surprising really. People took their own lives all the time and unless it was a celebrity or someone of import then it rarely made the news. Her best chance was waiting for later that afternoon when the *Bristol Post* would be published. With the amount of police at the scene the other evening, they had to print some sort of story. Amy wasn't sure what she wanted to read, she just wanted someone to tell her that Sally hadn't suffered.

Nicole was on much better form during her shift. With the worst of the hangover dissipated, she was like a different person, flitting from table to table without a care. Keith left her alone, engrossed in the back pages of his tabloid newspaper in between bursts on the grill, and the day passed without incident.

At the end of the shift, Amy walked Nicole to her bus stop. Again her actions were like that of a parent's and this time the thought made her smile.

As they approached the stop, Nicole paused. 'It's my day off tomorrow. Can I buy you an ice cream to celebrate?'

Amy was taken aback by Nicole's suggestion. 'You don't need to do that,' she said.

Nicole grimaced. 'I think I do. I was in a terrible state yesterday. If it wasn't for you I'm not sure I could have managed. And you stuck up for me in front of Keith. That couldn't have been easy.'

'Don't you worry about him. Okay, if you insist. An ice cream would be perfect and I know just the place.'

Amy walked her to the small supermarket and they took their ice creams over to Marine Lake. The sea was out and the man-made lake looked like a gigantic puddle. A group of children were making sandcastles, but without the sea, and the sky being peppered with clouds despite the heat, the place wasn't as busy as the last few days. They sat with their backs against the sea wall, Amy savouring the sickly sweetness of her ice cream. She'd sat there so many times alone that it was a bit surreal coming here with Nicole so soon after spending time with Megan. The two were completely different. She felt like she'd known Megan for years even though their relationship was in its infancy, and she felt much more maternal to the young woman with her now.

'I didn't tell you the full story about Saturday night,' said Nicole, biting down on her ice cream and looking away.

'What did you get up to then?' said Amy. 'Don't tell me, there was a boy involved.'

Nicole laughed, a hint of nervousness in the gesture. 'That was partly why I felt so bad. I stayed over in Bristol and had to rush back first thing to change then get to work. My parents still aren't speaking to me.'

'Was he worth it?'

'I think so. He messaged me this morning.'

Amy enjoyed the girl's happiness. There was something innocent about the way she talked, and Amy didn't want to dispel that notion by finding out any specific details about her life. 'You be careful,' she said.

'You sound just like my mum,' said Nicole.

Amy blushed. She wondered if her mum would have warned her about boys had she still been in her life. Maybe if she'd had that sort of influence, Amy wouldn't have got herself into so much trouble. She regretted the thought as soon as it arrived. It felt like a betrayal of Aiden, and that was the only pure thing ever to happen to her. 'You just be careful,' repeated Amy, this time wagging her finger.

Megan called her as she walked Nicole back to the bus stop. It was the first time she'd heard the phone ring. She had no idea how to change the volume that must have been set to maximum, the digital ringing tone causing a number of bystanders to look her way.

'You going to grab that?' said Nicole.

Amy fumbled with the phone, eventually locating the green answer button. 'Hello,' she said.

'Amy,' came Megan's high-pitched voice. She sounded different, excited to the point of hysteria. 'I'm so glad you answered. I need to see you. Now.'

'Okay, okay. Is everything all right?'

'Yes, I just need to see you. Can you get to the park?'

'Yes, I can but tell me what it is.'

'In an hour?'

Amy laughed. 'Sure, if that's what you want.'

'Wonderful, I'll see you then,' said Megan, hanging up.

After leaving Nicole at the bus stop, Amy walked along the Bristol Road to Ashcombe Park. Despite the darkening clouds, it was hotter than ever, the air so heavy she could feel the moisture against her skin. Her ice cream with Nicole and Megan's excited call had buoyed her spirits and she'd almost forgotten about the other night, until she saw the pile of newspapers in a newsagent's front window. The headlines didn't mention anything about Sally, and Amy considered leaving the newspaper for the day to focus on the positive things in her life while she still had such things to consider. In the end, curiosity got the better of her and she bought a paper and took it to the playground area where she'd agreed to meet Megan.

In the late afternoon there was a much different feel to the place. The playground was swamped with screaming toddlers, and hyperactive juniors running around in unpredictable patterns. Amy took a seat on one of the benches, trying not to feel conspicuous, and searched through the paper.

She was surprised to find the story buried halfway in the newspaper. Sally's death was only given a few lines and there was no mention of her name. She was just a body that had been found near the rocks on the road out of Weston. As Amy closed the paper, it occurred to her that Sally might not have had any identification with her. She didn't know that much about the woman beyond the stories of her life that she'd discussed at the ceremonies. Like so many of them, she was an orphan of sorts. Her mother had died when Sally was a young child and her biological father had wanted nothing to do with her. Aside from that, Amy knew very little about her. She didn't know where she lived, the only time she'd seen her out of the group sessions was the day she'd seen her in Weston with Jay. She wasn't sure why the thought of Sally being unidentified traumatised her so. She was at peace now, and those who were important to her – Jay and the rest of the group – knew she'd moved to a better place. Yet, it felt wrong for her to go that way, as a nameless body. Somehow, Amy would have to let the authorities know her real identity.

The feel of flesh over her eyes banished the thought. 'Megan,' she said, smelling the faint aroma of her friend's perfume.

'What a guess,' said Megan, taking her hands away.

The manic happiness Amy had sensed over the phone was even more evident. Megan's face was ablaze, the joy visible in her wide eyes and wider smile, even in the vibrancy of her skin. Megan's hands were moving, seemingly of their own accord, and instead of speaking she flung her arms around Amy.

'What is it?' asked Amy, sharing Megan's joy.

Megan held on a bit longer before pulling back. When she did so there were tears in her eyes. 'It's so wonderful, Amy, I can't believe it.'

'Are you going to make me squeeze the information from you?' Amy was smiling but a nagging feeling had crept into her stomach as she'd realised the one thing that could make her friend this happy.

'He came to see me today. Jay,' said Megan, as if the very thought was impossible.

'That's great,' said Amy, her stomach now tight.

'He wants to see me tomorrow. I think I'm going to be next.'

Chapter Twenty-Three

On Monday morning, Louise drove to the Kalimera in a daze. Sleeping at home hadn't been any better than staying at her parents'. Her mind had been in a constant swirl, oscillating between the suicide case and her concern over Emily and Paul. Her fears had fed into her dreams; the bodies she'd discovered being replaced by haunting images of Emily and Paul, and her mother and father.

Sunday had been another day of CCTV checking and double-checking. The work was slow and painful and it was all too easy to miss something. Simon Coulson had volunteered his services again and run his facial-recognition software on the files they'd received from the Grand Pier but they were no nearer to spotting Sally than they had been when they started.

Louise was grateful that Tracey had agreed to meet so early. She was waiting for her at the Kalimera, chatting away to Georgina as if they were long-lost friends. 'What time do you call this?' said Tracey, wiping the tangled weave of her dark hair from her cheek.

It was so good to see her friend's welcoming face. That smile had got her through some tough times and already her positivity was rubbing off on Louise.

'Here,' said Georgina, placing a freshly brewed Americano on the counter.

'Thank you,' said Louise, surprised by the gesture. 'You haven't told her anything, have you?' she asked Tracey, when they were sitting alone by the window.

'What do you take me for?' said Tracey, feigning hurt. 'Just like old times, eh?'

Tracey had been seconded to Weston for a few weeks last year. In that short time she'd made the place her own. She had an easy way with people that Louise envied. Her absence had been felt when she'd returned to Portishead, but Louise doubted anyone would feel the same way about her if she ever left. 'We might have a vacancy now if you fancy it?'

'You may be right. I think Finch likes young Mr Farrell.'

The conversation stalled at Finch's name. He was Tracey's boss but it still struck a nerve hearing his name out loud. He hadn't sent Louise a text since the day she'd seen him at HQ but he'd been on her mind. 'Thanks for coming over, especially so early.'

'I thought I'd catch a bit of the sunshine on my day off. Though typically the weather is like this,' said Tracey, pointing to the grey sky.

'It's good to see you, anyway.'

'You too,' said Tracey, holding her coffee cup up. 'Cheers.'

They talked for a time about Bristol and Farrell's introduction into MIT. 'I haven't told him yet about Paul and Emily,' said Tracey, bringing the conversation around to the reason for her being there.

'I appreciate that. I trust him. I think,' said Louise, after a little thought. 'Obviously the less people who know the better at the moment.'

'No one in Weston knows?'

'Not yet.'

Tracey frowned. 'We could escalate it. If you're really worried.'

Louise's coffee was bitter and still a little too hot. 'I'm worried but I don't think that's enough to escalate it. It's my parents I feel for. My guess is that Paul is just being a dick, proving to us that he can do what he wants and that he can look after Emily.'

'Some way of proving that.'

'He doesn't think straight any more, that's part of the problem. I just wish I hadn't been so stupid. Emily had said she was going on holiday. I should have known he would plan something like this.'

'Don't do that.'

'What?'

'Blame yourself. That is exactly what he wants you to do. He's the one being irresponsible. Dangerously so.'

Tracey was right. Her brother had done some stupid things in his time but this was a new low. And things could get worse. If he didn't contact them soon then she would be forced to take it further. Parental responsibility or not, this was not the way to raise his daughter and if it became official then trouble would be heading his way. 'You're right. He's going to be in for a hell of a time when he gets back,' she said.

Tracey offered to come to the station to help with the CCTV images but Louise refused. 'Enjoy your day off,' she told her before agreeing to meet her for dinner later if time allowed.

Despite meeting Tracey for coffee, she was still the first one into the office. She put on the coffee machine before checking the incident room was set up. As the coffee brewed, she looked through the incident book, checking the additions from yesterday. A new entry had been listed with the contents recovered from Sally's caravan. Louise clicked on the link and was about to run through it when a booming Scottish voice made her jump. 'Louise, my office now.'

Louise poured a coffee before heading to DCI Robertson's office. 'I didn't know you were in, sir,' she said, sitting down.

Robertson stared at her with stoic intensity. 'Anything you'd like to tell me?' he asked, a printout in front of him.

Louise couldn't recall him being this serious in a long time. 'Sir?'

Robertson shoved the papers towards her. 'Can you tell me what the hell I'm looking at?'

Before her was a roster of names and numbers. It was a list of overtime accumulated over the weekend. Louise lowered her eyes. Despite being the senior investigating officer on the case, she should have received permission from Robertson for any unauthorised overtime. Her first thought was to justify her mistake by blaming the speed of the investigation and the fact that she hadn't seen Robertson since Friday, but that would have been an error. She'd made a mistake – a significant one judging by the surprisingly high numbers on the sheet – and had to take responsibility. Unfortunately, she knew a simple sorry wouldn't suffice.

'I've fucked up.'

'Too damn right you have. I have to justify these figures and from what I can tell there is little or no justification for all these wasted man hours.'

Robertson appeared to be biting his hand, and Louise swallowed the inappropriate laugh building in her throat. 'How long do you intend going on with all this?' he said, gesturing to the outer office.

'We've only gone back four days,' said Louise.

'Only four days? What exactly is it you're hoping to find?'

There was little she could say to ease the situation. Louise had been asking herself that same question non-stop over the weekend. The truth was they still knew very little about Sally. Like Victoria and Claire, Sally had lived her life as if invisible. 'I know it's not much to go on but if we get an image of her at the pier with some-one, we might be able to get some answers. Maybe stop it happening to another woman.'

Robertson frowned. In his gruff way, he'd always been supportive to Louise since she'd moved to Weston. He rarely interfered in her work, respecting the experience she brought with her. 'You haven't done yourself any favours here, Louise. There's already a lot of noise about this investigation, and an increased wage bill will only make things that much harder for you,' he said.

'Noise?'

'Don't be flippant, you know what I mean. Three suicides in seven weeks. Three almost identical notes. There's concern this is going to get worse and when I'm asked what we're doing, I don't like to say we're staring at computer screens all day, pissing money up the wall.'

'But isn't that modern police work, sir?'

Robertson scratched the back of his head. She couldn't tell if the look on his face was a grin or a grimace. 'This is the last day of overtime.'

'How about a replacement for Farrell?'

'Sure, I'll just magic up a new CID officer for you,' said Robertson, with his Glaswegian slur.

'We could get him back?'

'Don't push it, Inspector. Now, if there isn't anything else?'

Louise slumped back to her desk. She was grateful the rest of the team had yet to arrive. In conversation with Robertson, she'd half tried to play the mistake off, but in reality it was a devastating error, one that someone of her experience should never have made. She had to concede that her constant worry about Paul and Emily had seeped into her work. For Louise, that was unacceptable. However traumatic her personal life had been in the past, she'd always been able to remain focused at work. She'd had no option. Given her history with Finch, and her effective demotion to Weston, she was always being watched. A slip like this could cost her everything, and now she would have the added burden of Robertson on her case.

She started to question herself. The CCTV footage was a long shot. Even if they did pinpoint the time Sally had visited the pier, chances were it wouldn't tell them much. Either way, her conversation with Robertson had struck a chord. It reiterated how isolated Claire, Victoria, and now Sally, had been in Weston. In the summer especially, the illusion that everyone was having a great time was hard to get past. Yet these three women had lived a life of obscurity with no family or friends, at least none that were evident. It made Louise question her own complaints about her place in the town. She had family and friends nearby and the occasional pangs of loneliness were nothing in comparison to what the three dead women had experienced.

Louise watched the rest of the team filter into work, checking for signs that they knew about her mistake. It was only when Thomas stopped by her desk that she realised she was acting paranoid. Despite having worked all weekend, he was looking good. Freshly shaven, there was a lightness to his eyes that she hadn't seen in a long time. 'We back in front of those screens again, boss?' he asked.

'Yes,' said Louise, as certain as she could be that there was no double meaning to his question. 'And stop calling me "boss".'

'I only do it to make you look good, boss.'

'I don't need your help on that account. Today is the last day though. Robbo is pulling the plug so let's find something?'

'Cracking idea,' said Thomas, walking off to the incident room.

Trying to forget her earlier error, Louise pulled up an inventory of belongings gathered from Sally's caravan. One particular article – listed as 'a green cuddly toy' – caught her attention. She couldn't recall seeing such an item at the caravan so she uploaded the image on to her screen. She zoomed in on the image of a very cheap-looking dinosaur toy.

She hadn't seen it at Sally's caravan but she was sure she'd seen the toy somewhere before.

◆　◆　◆

Leaving Thomas in charge, she drove to the town centre, parking in the Sovereign Centre. The small precinct was busy and she had to park on the top level. It seemed the cloudy skies had encouraged the holidaymakers to leave the beach behind. They covered the pier like ants and when Louise reached the far end, the noise of people combined with the constant electronic trill of the machines made her want to turn back.

She persevered, battling her way through the hordes of tourists until she reached the token-exchange shop. A group of giggling teenage girls holding lines of tokens from the machines were looking at the shelves of tat on offer, working out what they could get.

And on the lower shelf, Louise found what she was looking for: the green dinosaur, identical to the one recovered from Sally's caravan, available for a mere five hundred tokens.

She snapped the image on her phone and waited for the giggling teenagers to disperse before speaking to the young man behind the counter. He didn't look out of his teens, but his neck was covered in a number of intertwined tattoos. A spike stuck out from his eyebrow, and his left ear had a flesh tunnel that extended his earlobe. His look, and her unavoidable response to it, made her feel old. She couldn't understand why he would do it to himself and could tell by the way he looked at her that he had little concern as to her thoughts on his appearance.

To save time she showed him her warrant card. The teen's response was so non-committal it was laughable. 'Do you keep a record of the gifts you give away?'

The young man took some time to weigh up the question. 'They're registered on the till,' he said finally, his voice a surprisingly deep baritone.

'Would you be able to get me a list of when a specific product was purchased?'

'What do you mean?' he said.

'Is your operation manager, Stephan Daly, in?' said Louise, growing impatient. The teen shrugged and Louise leant across the counter. 'I suggest you find out,' she said, causing the boy to back away and bump his head on the shelf behind him.

It took another forty minutes for Louise to get what she wanted, a printout of every exchange of the green dinosaur in the last month. Although surprised by the number – forty-eight people had somehow thought it prudent to get the toy – she was impressed with the printout that listed the exact day and time of exchanges.

She scanned the images on to her file and sent them to Thomas. By the time she returned to the station, they already had a match for Sally.

Chapter Twenty-Four

Thomas played her the two-minute footage of Sally at the shop counter the second Louise returned to the station. Sally appeared as excited as a child as she looked at the goods on offer. But her excitement wasn't what interested Louise. It was the person with her.

'We're focusing on the images from that day, going through them now,' said Thomas, as Louise watched the video again.

The image was surprisingly good quality and Louise was able to focus on Sally's companion and get a decent image of the man. 'This is who we're after,' she said.

'I've already sent it to Coulson. He's making it a priority,' said Thomas.

Louise looked again at Sally's companion. He was much taller, and leaner, than Sally. He had classic good looks – dark hair, large doleful eyes, and full lips that formed into a smile as Sally chose the silly green dinosaur. But when Sally wasn't looking at him the smile vanished. Its replacement was a concentrated detachment. Louise had seen the same look on impatient parents after they'd humoured their child over something that didn't really interest them. Only with this man the change was more profound. In Sally's gaze, his body shape changed. His shoulders relaxed as his smile seemed to filter through him. But out of her eye line his body tensed, his back straightened as his face went blank. 'You seeing this?' said Louise, as she replayed the video for Thomas.

'He doesn't look that pleased to be there,' said Thomas.

Louise let the video play out. Sally grabbed her toy and the pair walked out of frame. 'And she doesn't look like someone who wants to end her life,' said Louise. 'I realise this is an oversimplification,' she added, as Thomas went to speak.

'No, I was thinking the same thing. This is only two days before she took her life. I guess there's no guessing her mental state at this point but something happened to trigger her actions.'

'Such as?'

'He dumped her? That's if they were seeing each other.'

Louise had been thinking the same thing. It was depressing to think that the smiling woman in the video would take her own life because of this man but it wasn't beyond the realms of possibility. 'That wouldn't explain why Claire and Victoria took their lives. Why they all had the same lines on their suicide notes.'

One of the uniformed officers had located further footage of the pair. This time they were hand in hand, walking back along the pier, Sally holding the dinosaur to her chest with her free hand. 'This is our sole priority for the moment,' she told the assembled team. 'I want to know who this man is and I want to speak to him as soon as humanly possible.'

Back at her desk, Louise tried to call Paul again. After the fallout with Robertson, the very act made her feel guilty, but the thought of Emily was a constant nagging ache in the pit of her stomach that she couldn't ignore. Her instinct told her she was fine with her father – whatever his current mental state – but she was desperate to hear news of her niece. She swore under her breath as the call went straight to answerphone. In her peripheral vision she noticed Simone had stopped dead in her tracks and was trying to eavesdrop.

'Help you, Simone?' she said, slamming the phone down and turning to face the office manager.

Simone shrugged her shoulders, as if she had no idea what Louise was talking about, and walked away without speaking.

Was Simone relaying her actions to Robertson? She dismissed the notion as quickly as it had arrived, dismayed by the creeping paranoia of her thoughts.

Her afternoon was spent trawling through video images of Sally and the mystery man. It was important not to get ahead of herself, and there was a danger of reading too much into the situation, but the scene by the shop wasn't the only sign of the man's duplicity. Maybe it was simply a character trait, but she noticed the blankness of his face as they walked along the pier, and in a second video they'd recovered of the pair playing the machines; it made the changes in his demeanour when Sally looked at him all the more fake.

She was growing frustrated with the lack of progress in the case and at that moment wanted to be anywhere but in the sterile office environment. She envied Tracey her day off and would have loved to have been spending time with her friend rather than going over and over the same thing. Experience told her she must. It was clear to her that something was amiss and the only way to discover the anomaly was to keep working.

Try as she might, she found it impossible to ignore her mistake regarding the unauthorised overtime.

Every time her thoughts drifted to Paul and Emily, she tried to force them back on to the case. The conflict only served to make her feel that she wasn't giving either situation the attention it deserved.

'Call for you, Louise,' said Simone, distracting her.

'Hi, DI Blackwell, this is Dr Alice Everson from FIU in London.' The Forensic Investigation Unit was a specialised division of the Met. At Louise's insistence, Portishead had sent forensic samples from the Claire Smedley and Victoria Warrington scenes for testing. 'We've had an interesting match on the samples you sent us. Nothing in the blood, but we found something in both hair samples. We've been running a new programme on psychedelics and we discovered traces of DMT in both women.'

DMT wasn't something Louise had come across that often before. 'I have a rudimentary grasp of how DMT works, Dr Everson. We're talking along the lines of LSD, mushrooms?'

'Yes and no. Recreational DMT users usually smoke it. Depending on the dose, it can give a very strong hallucinogenic response.'

'Could it affect their mental state in any way?'

'Aside from hallucinating?'

Louise explained what had happened to Claire and Victoria. She wanted to know if the drug could have made them take their own lives.

'Well, depending on the dose, and it is hard to ascertain that from these samples, their mental state would be greatly affected. However, we're not talking about someone taking an acid trip and believing they can fly. DMT can kick in almost immediately, depending on how it is taken, and is very intense. It's unlikely they would be able to do that much under its influence. The trip may not last long but during that time the recipient would usually be pretty much incapacitated.'

'Could it promote suicidal tendencies?'

'It's possible. It may depend on what it's mixed with. However, there were no traces of drugs or alcohol in Ms Smedley's blood sample. I believe there has been another death?'

News spreads fast, thought Louise. 'That's correct.'

'I think it is unlikely then. Maybe in an isolated incident but the chances of it causing three people to commit suicide are slim. Of course, you would have to analyse outside factors such as the person's mental health. I can send through details on the drug. It's quite an interesting proposition. Lots of anecdotal evidence about shared visions. Not sure it will help your investigation. A very important factor to consider is the setting where these women took the drug. The effect of psychedelics is greatly influenced by where the user takes it and who they take it with.'

'So they could have a bad trip if they're in a bad setting.'

'Very much so. If they're taking it under duress, or in extreme circumstances, or with people they don't know or trust then it can make a dramatic difference.'

'How quick could you analyse the blood and hair from the third woman?'

'Send it for my attention and I'll make it a priority.'

Louise thanked the doctor and hung up. She was about to start searching online for more on the drug when she noticed Simone loitering near her desk again.

'Sorry, I was waiting for you to finish your call,' said Simone.

'What is it, Simone?'

'You have a visitor.'

There was a hint of a smile on the office manager's face and Louise's first thought was Finch. Unwilling to hide her impatience she asked, 'Who is it?'

'That journalist. Tania Elliot. Said you would want to speak to her. I've put her in interview room two. Shall I tell her to go?'

Although it was bad practice for the journalist to visit the station uninvited, after her last meeting with Tania it felt prudent to hear what the journalist had to say. 'I'll be there in five minutes,' she told Simone, turning her attention back to her screen.

Ten minutes later, Louise entered interview room two. Tania was sitting behind the desk drinking tea and didn't stand as Louise came into the room. Louise didn't bother with any pleasantries. It was an unwritten rule that journalists didn't approach officers at their workplace and Louise wasn't about to apologise for keeping Tania waiting. 'What can I do for you, Tania?' she said, her voice laden with disinterest as she sat down opposite her.

'Courtesy visit,' said Tania. 'We're running a story in the *Post* tomorrow evening. I thought you may like to comment.'

Tania eased two sheets of paper face down over to Louise. 'What's the article about?' said Louise.

'I think you know. I'll need your comment by tomorrow morning at the latest unless you want to speak to me now?' Tania tilted her head in question and Louise considered kicking her out of the office. She turned the sheets over, the title of the article screaming out at her:

Suicide Epidemic Sweeps the Seaside

Chapter Twenty-Five

Louise lowered her eyes, fighting her rising pulse. 'You are fucking kidding me, Tania?'

The journalist remained neutral and Louise was thankful for her response – even a hint of a smirk could have provoked Louise into responding in a way she would later regret.

'Please read the article.'

Louise caught her breath. She wanted to throw Tania out of the station but curiosity got the better of her. 'This is pure sensationalism,' she said, once she'd finished. Tania had correctly linked the three suicides, but the knowing tone of the piece aggravated Louise.

'Three suicides in just over six weeks. Do you agree they're linked, Inspector Blackwell?'

'I'm not on record with you, Tania.'

'I've seen the first two suicide notes. Was there a note for Sally?' said Tania, ignoring her.

'I thought we agreed this could do more harm than good?'

'I think that was your conclusion. Maybe this article will alert people. Make them keep a closer eye on their loved ones.'

Louise wasn't sure any of the three women had had loved ones but wasn't about to tell Tania that. 'I can't stop you publishing this, Tania, but if there are any copycat suicides then you'll have something to think about.'

'Do you think the three suicides are linked, Inspector, and if so how?'

'You can go through the normal procedures if you want anything from me. I'm not sure why you're here.'

'I told you, professional courtesy. I don't want to make an enemy of you, Louise. I have a job to do as well as you do. I appreciated the time you gave me during the Pensioner Killer case and I wanted to repay the favour.'

Louise had experienced both sides of the press. Sometimes, they could be an asset but during the Walton case – which had ultimately seen her leave the MIT – she'd suffered at their hands. She felt as if she'd been tried by the papers without a trial. Naturally this had left her with a distinct lack of trust for all journalists, and reading Tania's article wasn't changing her mind. 'Well, thanks for the heads up. I'll speak to the PR department and they'll be in contact if necessary,' she said, leaving the interview room.

'Don't let that happen again,' she said to Simone, emailing the article to the internal PR department before shutting down her computer for the day. Had she made another mistake? She could have kept a closer eye on Tania following their meeting, could have enlisted Dominic Garrett's help to stop this from happening. But second-guessing herself wasn't helping anything. She grabbed her phone and checked for any news from Paul before leaving the station.

It was a relief to be outside, despite the cloying heat. Reluctantly, she called Tracey and cancelled their get-together. She couldn't face a night of socialising, even with someone as easy-going as her friend. But she didn't want to be alone either, so she joined the snake-like line of cars leaving Worle and headed towards the M5 and her parents' house.

She arrived an hour later, much of her journey spent stationary by Cribbs Causeway. The dark mood of her parents appeared to have manifested itself in the house. They sat in the living room, shrouded in a cloak of shadow, her mother drinking wine again. The irony wasn't lost on Louise, but she didn't try to take the drink from her. 'Tracey is working on it. I've just spoken to her and she'll let us know if there is any sighting. No one matching Paul or Emily's description has been admitted to hospital in the last seventy-two hours. I'm sure he's taken her away somewhere and it's just his selfish way of punishing us.'

Her mother shuddered at the mention of the hospital and took a swig from her wine glass. Louise exchanged a look with her father but neither made a comment.

Louise made the three of them pasta and together they pretended to watch the evening television. When her mother went to open a new bottle of wine, her father stopped her and made them tea. As the kettle boiled, her mother's phone rang. 'It's him,' she said, her skin losing all of its colour.

Her father grabbed the phone before Louise could get to it. 'Paul,' he said, his voice more hopeful than angry.

Louise studied her father for his response and fought back tears as his body relaxed. 'What the hell are you playing at, son? Is Emily okay?'

'Put it on speaker, Dad,' said Louise.

'Fine,' said Paul, as her father placed him on speakerphone.

Her mother crying, Louise took the phone from her father. 'Where the hell are you, Paul?' she said, her anger taking over now the shock of relief had dissipated.

'I'm not going to tell you that.'

'Where is Emily?'

'Sleeping.'

'You need to get back here tomorrow, Paul. Do you have any idea what you've put us through?'

'Don't give me your sanctimonious shit,' said Paul, his words running together.

'You've been drinking?'

'Yes, I've been drinking. So what?'

'You need to bring her back tomorrow, Paul, I'm warning you.'

'Or what? I'm Emily's dad. That's something you all seem to forget.' He was screaming now and Louise feared he would hang up.

Understanding, her father took the phone back from her. 'Listen, son, we just want the best for you and Emily. Please come back. We can sort this out. We all love you.'

Louise heard the sound of her brother fighting back tears as she moved over to hold her mother. *You selfish bastard*, she thought, at the same time overcome with sisterly empathy. It was hard to stay angry with him. Dianne's death had slowly destroyed Paul and no one knew how to help him.

She heard him sobbing as he said, 'I'll be back before the end of the week.'

'Paul, Paul?' screamed her father. But the line had gone dead.

Chapter Twenty-Six

Amy couldn't concentrate at work. She moved through the day in a void, serving faceless customers on autopilot. The café had always been a dreadful place to work but it was worse than ever today. The grease lingered in the air. It coated her skin and hair, invaded her lungs and body. She wanted to scrub herself clean, inside and out. She was tired of the mindless drudgery of her day, of Keith in his grime-soaked vest, barking orders and not even trying to hide his lusting over Nicole.

'Are you okay?' asked Nicole. They were wiping the outside tables, a hint of rain in the air.

'Just a bit knackered.'

Megan had stayed the night. They'd shared a bed to begin with but Megan had been so restless and over-excited about her meeting with Jay, that Amy had moved to the sofa. Even so, she hadn't been able to sleep.

At first, Megan's excitement had been contagious. Amy was genuinely happy for her friend, still was, but the actuality of what her meeting with Jay meant soon began to trouble her. It wasn't just jealousy. Yes, her stomach fluttered at the thought of Megan seeing Jay without her, but she'd learnt long ago that Jay was not hers alone.

The lesson had been a hard one to learn. She'd known from the beginning that there had been others – Jay's work was too important to be limited – but she still recalled the night she'd been introduced to the rest of the group with a sense of horror. They'd been lovely of course but that hadn't stopped the feeling of panic as Jay introduced her. Part of her had thought – at least hoped – that it wasn't true, that Jay was all hers, and seeing everyone else had been a shock.

She'd seen the same look on Claire's face when she'd been introduced – the last of Jay's disciples, his group now complete – some months later: the confusion and panic, the dawning realisation that things would now forever be different. Yet, although the twang of jealousy at sharing Jay had never fully dissipated, it had faded. It was special and important being part of Jay's work. Amy was part of something much bigger than herself and it was selfish and irresponsible to question it. So why then had Megan's news affected her so?

She should be feeling good for her friend and had pretended to be so last night. Megan had suffered more than most in her group and she deserved to be with Jay, deserved the opportunity to move on to that special place Jay had shown them. And truly, Amy didn't begrudge her that.

It finally dawned on her that it wasn't Megan's imminent death that was worrying her; it was that with Megan gone, she would once again be left alone.

On her walk home she considered calling Megan but refrained. Jay had been picking her up at lunchtime so Megan would have switched her phone off. Not that she would have answered. Megan wouldn't risk Jay finding out they were in contact with each other outside the group.

Amy bought the early edition of the *Post* and took it to their spot in Ashcombe Park. The threat of rain had subsided and for once she enjoyed the noise of the children rampaging through the playground. She took a seat and found a small article about Sally buried within the paper. The article hadn't even stated how Sally had died. She still wasn't named and again Amy considered calling the police, finding the thought of Sally fading from the world with no one knowing unbearable.

As Amy shut the paper, it occurred to her that at some point soon she would be reading a similar article about Megan. Some of the parents glanced over at her uncomfortably as she burst into tears.

Chapter Twenty-Seven

When Louise's phone pinged just as she was going to sleep, she'd been surprised to see DCI Robertson's name flash on the screen, her intrigue soon turning to dismay when she read the message summoning her into work for a 7 a.m. meeting.

She had stayed overnight at her parents' house again, creeping out in the early morning while they were still asleep. They'd all stayed up late, opening another bottle of wine. Louise had drunk with them – more to stop her mum from drinking than anything else – and regretted it now, a dry mouth and a faint throbbing in her head her reward for overindulgence.

She was in and out of her bungalow to shower and change within minutes and reached the station just as Robertson arrived. He was carrying two cups of coffee and handed her one before buzzing them in. She thanked him but he didn't respond as she followed him silently to his office, wondering if another reprimand was coming her way.

One thing Robertson couldn't be accused of was holding grudges. He wasn't one for games and he got straight to the point. 'I had a lovely chat with the assistant chief last night.'

Louise sucked in a breath. The unauthorised overtime had been a simple mistake and she was surprised it had got as far as the assistant chief constable.

'He asked me if I knew anything about this,' said Robertson, pushing a printout of Tania Elliot's proposed newspaper report towards her.

At first it was a relief that the overtime was no longer an issue, but when Louise looked down that relief turned to dismay. She'd sent the report to the PR team but hadn't cc'd in Robertson. 'I didn't think I needed to run this by you, Iain.'

'Oh no?'

'It was late and I presumed PR would deal with it.' It was normal procedure but in retrospect it would have made sense to include Robertson, especially after the debacle with the overtime.

'They dealt with it all right. They sent it to Morley in a panic, and now all the shit in the world has been let loose.'

Louise shook her head. Yes, the article could potentially cause some issues but she was senior enough not to have to run everything by Robertson. No doubt Morley had seen her name on the report and had decided to make an issue where there wasn't one.

Assistant Chief Constable Morley had presided over her departure from the major investigation team. If he'd had his way she would have been dismissed for what happened during the Walton case. The man was firmly on Finch's side and had given him both a promotion to DCI and a free rein to completely overhaul the MIT. Louise was sure Morley had expected her to resign. The move to Weston had been as good as a dismissal, but she'd stuck it out and ever since he'd been waiting for her to slip up.

'I don't know what you want me to say, Iain. The article is factual enough. It is the third suicide and the notes are almost identical.'

'She doesn't mention the latest note though?' said Robertson.

'No, that hasn't been leaked to her yet,' said Louise, regretting her defiance as soon as she spoke.

Robertson leant back, rubbing his hand over his mouth and down his chin. 'Jesus Christ, Louise, one crisis at a time.'

They sat for a while in silence, Louise studying Robertson, who was gazing at his office ceiling as if an answer lay there. 'Aside from these notes, do we have anything linking the three women?' he asked.

'We have the software on the first two women's computers,' said Louise, before showing him the CCTV image of Sally's male companion. 'This was taken two days before we found her body.'

'Do we have a name for him?'

'Not yet. There's one more thing.' She told him about her chat with Dr Everson, and the DMT that had been found in the hair samples of Victoria and Claire.

Robertson breathed out, his cheeks inflating then deflating. 'The last thing this town needs is another drug story. Does the journalist know about this yet?'

'No, only me and Dr Everson.'

'Let's leave it like that for now, shall we?' Robertson leant back. 'Is there nothing you can do to stop this Elliot woman from running this story?'

'Save from arresting her, no.'

'I don't know why she doesn't just fuck off to London. Why she has to hang around here bothering us is beyond me. You can't sweet-talk her into postponing, or get Garrett to have a word with her?'

'I don't like it any more than you, Iain, but to be fair to her she has sat on the story.'

Robertson was about to speak when both of their phones pinged in unison. Louise looked down at her message as Robertson's phone began to ring. It seemed Tania Elliot wasn't content to wait for the story to hit the evening paper. It had already reached one of the national tabloids.

◆ ◆ ◆

It was annoying, but not surprising, how quickly resources could be found when the assistant chief constable took an interest in a case. By the afternoon, the office was overrun with officers, all concerns about overtime vanished. The suicide case was now the only priority and Robertson – who had been summoned to Portishead without Louise to see Morley – had cancelled all leave. The three images of the dead women had been blown up and moved out of the incident room to the CID department where they took centre stage with the photofit of Sally's companion from the pier.

New searches were being conducted at the homes of Victoria, Claire and Sally and at one point, Louise noticed Claire's old landlord Mr Applebee being led to an interview room by one of the junior officers. Simon Coulson appeared to have taken up residence in Weston. He was heading the digital campaign and was trying to uncover a link between the three women online. The women's laptops were now allegedly something of a priority at the specialised department at the Met.

Despite all the activity they still knew relatively little. Nothing beyond the shared software, the three suicide notes and the hair samples from Victoria and Claire connected the women. They'd never worked or lived together, yet everything pointed to a connection.

Louise's phone had been off the hook with requests from media outlets. She could hear the journalists sharpening their pencils. The town was already trending on social media, and when Simone placed a later edition of a tabloid newspaper on her desk Louise knew the attention was only going to increase. The paper had gone with the headline:

Suicide by Sea

Experience told Louise that she now had two options: resent the involvement of the press, or use them for her own ends. She chose the latter, calling Tania before she could change her mind.

'Hi, Louise,' said the journalist, as if nothing out of the ordinary had happened between them that day.

Louise could have punished Tania and gone straight to the nationals, but felt it better to have her on her side at that point. 'I have an image I need circulating. A man, possibly one of the last people to have seen Sally Kennedy alive. Do you think you could get it into the later edition of the *Post* tonight?'

Louise thought she could hear Tania sitting up straight on the other end of the line. 'Can you email it over now? I'll do my best. Thanks, Louise, I appreciate this.'

Louise hung up, wondering how much the journalist's appreciation was worth.

Thomas was standing by her desk as she did so. 'Boss, I might have something. I've managed to locate Sally's father. Goes by a different surname, and he's not on the birth certificate, but we have a record of him from social services at the time Sally was put into care. Works in a warehouse over in Nailsea.'

'Let me send this and I'll be right with you.'

Louise let Thomas drive, checking on a message from Tracey as he weaved through the afternoon traffic. Louise had told her about Paul's call last night and Tracey was wondering if Louise wanted her to continue the search. Louise would have called her but didn't want to get Thomas involved. Although she trusted him, she couldn't take the risk that news about Paul and Emily would spread. She could just picture the satisfied smirk on Simone's face at the knowledge that Louise couldn't even look after her own family properly. She sent a text back:

I'll keep trying his phone. Leave it for the time being x

At least we know they're safe x, replied Tracey.

Tracey was right, but that didn't make it any easier. She had to consider Paul's frame of mind. He'd been stupid enough to take Emily away without telling anyone, so what was to stop him doing it again? From what she understood, Dianne's life insurance had paid off the flat and provided him with a lump sum. And although he'd managed to drink a fair share of that, she imagined there was still some money left.

The factory was in an industrial estate on the outskirts of Nailsea, a more run-down version of the isolated area where their new police station was situated. Thomas had called ahead and the man they wished to speak to was waiting in the reception area.

'David Lancaster,' said the man, as Thomas introduced them.

Lancaster was a giant of a man. He had to stoop under the doorframe as he led them to a small office area. It was hard to imagine that he was the father of Sally who'd been tiny in comparison to him. 'What's this about?' asked the man, his voice a deep West Country slur.

'It's about your daughter: Sally Kennedy,' said Thomas.

The man squinted. His face was like a giant slab of concrete, his jaw and forehead over prominent. 'Sally isn't my daughter,' he said, after a pause.

Thomas looked at Louise and handed Lancaster a print of the social services letter. The man scrutinised it. 'Oh, this. I just put my name down as the father as it seemed the easiest thing to do. Angela was already pregnant when I met her. Angela was a piece of work. When she died there was no one to look after Sally so I went to the council. What else could I do?' said Lancaster, his oversized jaw thrust out at them in defiance.

'I'm afraid we have some bad news. Sally was found dead earlier this week. We believe she may have taken her own life.'

Lancaster frowned. Louise couldn't tell if he was upset. 'Didn't you consider looking after her?' she asked, when he didn't respond.

'What the hell do I know about looking after children? I only put my name on the form to help out Angela. Sally was four years old when Angela died. I didn't even know her that well. I didn't even live with them. It was an on-off sort of thing. She was better off without me. Better off without her mother that was for sure.'

'Did you keep in contact?'

'With Sally?' The man scratched his head and Louise saw a hint of regret in his eyes. 'I ran into her once. Last year. She had no idea who I was. I wasn't even going to speak to her, only recognised her because she looked so much like her mother.'

'You spoke to her though?'

The man shrugged. 'Yes. I told her I knew her mum and she was interested about that. I bought her a cup of tea and told her what I remembered, missing out the bad shit. Of which there was a lot.'

'Sally's mum, Angela, she took her own life as well?' asked Louise.

'She was a selfish . . .' Lancaster stopped himself. 'I almost didn't tell Sally that but I did in the end.'

'Didn't she already know?' asked Thomas.

'No. They'd kept it from her. Not that it bothered her. She started coming out with all this weird shit about one world, everything being connected. I didn't know what the hell she was going on about.'

'Do you think she may have been taking anything?' asked Louise.

'Drugs? Well, she sure as hell sounded high. And now that you've told me she did the same thing as her mother then it doesn't surprise me.'

They showed him the picture of Sally's companion at the pier but Lancaster didn't recognise him.

'Can I go now?' he asked, as if news of Sally's death meant nothing beyond a minor inconvenience.

◆ ◆ ◆

Back in the car, Thomas appeared to be in a sullen mood. His eyes were focused on the road as if he expected something to jump out in front of him. Louise had seen it all in her time in the police but the callousness she was sometimes forced to witness never ceased to amaze and dishearten her. At one point, Lancaster had been a surrogate parent of sorts to Sally. The fact that he couldn't muster even a hint of empathy for her death and the life she'd been forced to lead, puzzled Louise to the point of anger. Despite herself, she considered the parallels between Lancaster and her brother, regretting the comparison as soon as she'd made it. Paul had been making mistakes of late but no one could question his love for his daughter. Where Lancaster had abandoned Sally after his partner had died, Paul had clung on to Emily. He thought he was making the right decisions and it was wrong of her to associate the two men.

'It's Noah's birthday soon,' said Thomas, breaking the silence.

Louise was thankful for the chance to discuss something more positive. 'Already?' she said, stopping short of repeating the cliché about children growing so fast. 'You having a party?'

'Yep, jelly and ice cream and all that sort of stuff. Though it's more hummus and wraps nowadays.'

'How are things with Rebecca?'

'Better. I mean, we're not going to be getting back together but we manage not to shout at each other every time we meet. Funnily enough, I feel I see Noah more now that we are separated. Rebecca gets some time off as well so she's more relaxed. Shame we couldn't work that sort of system when we were together.'

Of all the officers at the station, the last one she'd imagined succumbing to a police divorce was Thomas. She'd seen so many police officers go through it. With the unpredictable hours, it was a wonder how anyone in their profession survived outside relationships. In fact, some of the most successful relationships she'd seen had been police marrying police. It sounded hackneyed, but there was a certain mindset to being in the force and often being in the profession was the only true way to understand. He'd always seemed so together, but such things were notoriously impossible to predict.

'Things like this do make me wonder whether I'm making the right decision though,' said Thomas.

'What do you mean?'

'These poor women. They all come from broken families. Maybe if Sally hadn't had such a bastard stepdad like Lancaster, her life would have turned out different. What if I'm risking the same happening to Noah? He might not understand now but as he grows older he could come to resent me.'

'It's not the same, Thomas, you know that. He's got two parents who love him. Sally didn't have anyone.'

Louise wanted to tell him how she had the same worries about Emily. Her niece would have to grow up without a mother, and at present with an alcoholic father. If anyone could understand it would be Thomas but she couldn't bring herself to confide in him. She needed to remain professional, to avoid all distractions.

Thomas looked embarrassed by his revelation and didn't look at her. 'Yeah, maybe. Anyway, how's your little niece? Haven't seen her for a while,' he said.

'She's fine,' said Louise, taking a sharp intake of breath.

'You'll need to bring her into the station one day.'

'I will,' said Louise, her attention diverted by something she'd seen on the forecourt of a garage. 'Go back to that petrol station, will you,' she said.

Thomas did a U-turn and parked up in the forecourt of the petrol station. It seemed Tania had been working hard. The billboard for the *Post* had a picture of Sally's companion on it under the headline:

Local Man Wanted for Questioning

Louise bought two copies of the paper and returned to the car.

'We're going to get all the crazies on the phone now,' said Thomas, pointing to the helpline number in Tania's article that linked directly to the station.

Louise gazed at the photo of Sally's companion. The image had been lifted from the CCTV footage but was well defined. 'I'm fine with that as long as it leads us to find out who this man is,' she said.

Chapter Twenty-Eight

Calls relating to the *Post* article had already started coming in by the time they returned to the station. A small pile of notes waited on Louise's desk for her to action, and she feared the reaction to the photograph would lead to more work than the small station could handle. Dr Alice Everson from the Met had called, so Louise turned her attention to that first, giving the pile of slips to Thomas.

The call to London went straight through. 'Sorry I missed your call earlier, Dr Everson,' said Louise.

'No problem. We ran some tests on your third woman, Sally Kennedy, and found an almost identical trace amount of DMT in her hair samples. You can draw your own conclusions but these results would suggest she'd taken a similar amount of DMT as Claire Smedley and Victoria Warrington.'

'Okay, I'm not sure if I wanted to hear that or not.'

'Yes,' said Everson, as if distracted by something. 'Yes, here we are. I'm glad you called actually. I was discussing your case with a colleague. He doesn't work in the police but has an interest in psychedelic drugs and in particular DMT. He's currently running a clinical trial on DMT in London. He'd be interested in talking to you. He's at a conference at Exeter University and said he would be happy to meet you to discuss further. That's not too far from you, is it? His name is Dr Mark Forrest.'

'No, that would be great,' said Louise, taking the contact details before hanging up. She managed to catch Forrest just before he was about to leave and arranged to meet him the following morning.

Before leaving for the day, she checked in with Thomas, who'd been coordinating the telephone hotline since their return from Nailsea. 'We have a few names but no two are the same so far,' he told her.

She considered asking if he wanted to go for a drink but the day had drained her. She wanted to get back to eat and shower, to get a full night's sleep for once. She hesitated a bit too long.

'Everything okay, boss?' asked Thomas.

Louise shook her head. 'Sorry, miles away. And stop calling me "boss",' she added, walking away.

At home she called her mother while boiling some ravioli. Despite the drama of the last few days, Paul's phone call had placated her parents somewhat. Her mother sounded lucid, close to her usual self. 'His phone is still off but I suppose he doesn't want us tracing him,' she told Louise.

Louise didn't like the way her mother made excuses for Paul, but she was content for now that he had called. The next two weeks would be hard on everyone but even Paul wouldn't be selfish enough not to call again. 'How's Dad?' she asked.

'You know him. He's gone all silent now. I'm worried about what will happen when they come back but for now I'm happy they're both safe.'

'You'll call as soon as he contacts you again?'

'Of course.'

'Okay, Mum. Sleep well,' said Louise, hanging up.

Louise had tried tracking Paul's phone on her find-a-phone app but didn't have any login details for him. She'd considered asking Coulson for help but doubted there was much he could do at that moment and she didn't want anyone else involved. However, she already had a mental list of where Paul could have taken Emily. She'd ruled out the first possibility – Weston – but there were other options. If she had to guess, she would say he'd gone somewhere in Cornwall. They'd spent summer holidays in the county, and Paul and Dianne had taken Emily there on a couple of occasions when she'd been a baby. Louise wasn't about to start a county-wide search for her brother just yet, but should it come to that she would at least have a head start.

A picture of Sally's companion flashed up on her television screen as she ate her dinner. Louise closed her eyes as the news-reader repeated the emergency number, wondering if among the nuisance calls they would strike gold.

Despite her earlier promise to herself, she didn't go straight to bed. Pouring herself a decent measure of vodka from the bottle she kept in the freezer, she updated her files, still reeling from the headline she'd read earlier: Suicide on Sea.

The drink had an immediate effect, the tension melting away as the alcohol seeped into her bloodstream. She stood, wobbling slightly as she drew a line connecting the images of the three women on the crime board. Beneath it she wrote DMT and connected that to the image of Sally's companion, Mr X.

Chapter Twenty-Nine

Joy was painted on Megan's face. It was visible in the loose way her limbs moved as she walked across the street to greet Amy as she left work. Although Amy felt a tang of envy, she couldn't begrudge her friend. She could tell Megan wanted to tell her everything there and then. She was about to speak when Amy introduced Nicole, who'd been standing behind her as if using Amy for protection.

'Oh, hi,' said Megan, with a look of confusion.

'We were going to get an ice cream,' said Amy.

Megan's features hardened and she didn't respond.

'That's okay, I'm feeling tired,' said Nicole. 'Why don't you two go and I'll see you tomorrow.'

The tension was obvious in Megan's body and Amy wondered what had come over her friend. 'Okay, Nicole, if you're sure.'

'I'm sure. I'll see you tomorrow. Nice to meet you,' said Nicole.

Megan raised her head, something akin to a grunt escaping her mouth. Amy stared at her as Nicole walked away.

'What?' asked Megan.

'That was a bit rude.'

'I'm sorry, it was. I just need to tell you about last night and I couldn't with her there. Please apologise to her for me tomorrow,' said Megan, the lightness in her eyes returning.

They walked towards the pier, then down on to the sand. The sea was halfway in, the white foam dissolving as it broke on to the shore. Megan skipped along by the side of Amy, trying to say everything at once. Amy found herself tuning out, her senses focusing on the light sea breeze, the hint of salt in the air, the tingle on her exposed skin from the sun.

'We took it again. Together,' said Megan, as they walked behind the old building where the Tropicana water park had once been.

The words filtered through to Amy and she stopped walking. 'DMT?' she said.

Megan nodded three or four times, as excited as a child. 'It was a full dose, like when . . .' She stopped, still smiling, as she referenced the others who'd passed over.

'He injected you?'

'Yes.'

'And Jay took it as well?'

Megan's eyes were wide in amazement. 'He took it first,' she said. 'I sat with him. He looked so serene. He talked to them and told me they were waiting again.'

'And were they?'

Megan started crying. 'Yes. It was even clearer than when I smoked it. They held my hand and showed me. I truly understand now, Amy. They're waiting for me. I know something better is waiting for me, isn't that incredible?'

Amy hugged her friend. 'They' had different names. 'The guardians', 'the entities', 'the guides', 'the aliens'. Amy had been sceptical when Jay had first told her about the drug, about what she could expect. She'd done pretty much everything by then, except thankfully stopping short of injecting herself. She'd certainly taken her share of psychedelics – mushrooms, LSD, among others – and the one thing she'd known was that no two trips were the same. She'd experienced such different reactions herself, and had seen the wildly varying effect the drugs had on others. She knew more than one person who'd taken things too far, who'd been permanently affected by taking them. When Jay had met her she'd been off them for years. She'd heard about DMT, yes, but it had never been widely available so she'd never taken it.

She'd laughed when Jay told her about the guardians. She'd heard rumours but when it was said aloud it sounded ludicrous.

'It's well documented,' Jay had said, amused by her humour. 'Thousands of people over the world have had the same experience. How could everyone be having the same trip?'

He told her about his time in Peru, how he'd joined an extreme-travel group and spent months with two Amazonian tribes where he'd eventually taken part in the Ayahuasca ceremony. 'It is life to them. They are still connected, we,' he'd said, pointing to the build-up of street lights and office buildings, 'have lost our way.'

He'd given her some books to read and she'd agreed with much of what he'd told her, yet she was still doubtful up until that day he'd let her take the drug properly. He'd taken her camping, a remote spot he knew on the Brean peninsula. He'd given her little tastes before but that had been the first time he'd offered to inject her.

The thought of using a needle had troubled her, she'd seen the fallout from shared needles in her past, but Jay had been meticulous about safety. He'd never forced her. The choice was hers to make. When she'd agreed he'd acted as a counsellor, his words soothing and guiding, as the DMT hit her bloodstream. He'd told her what she could expect – the sense of floating, the swirling geometries, the waiting room and the guardians – and although not exactly as she'd imagined, his predictions had come true.

The memory of what happened next had never faded. She'd heard enough drug tales over the years, had experienced moments where she'd felt connected beyond anything in her normal life, but this eclipsed everything. The world dissolved and she became part of something else. It was more a feeling than a sight, a blurring of colour and sound. She felt it within her and knew – at the time and afterwards – that it was real. The two guardians were in the floating waiting room. They didn't speak but explained to her that they'd been waiting for her to break through, and as they led her into a maze of colour and shapes she began to see the outline of two figures.

She hadn't needed to explain what had happened to Jay. He'd known. And although Amy was naturally suspicious of most things, she'd believed in the power of the drug from that moment onwards. Her belief was only cemented from the testimonies from everyone else in their little group, Megan included, who'd experienced such similar reactions.

And when Jay had told her that one day she could leave this world and go to that special place, she hadn't been scared, she'd been desperate to go.

'What happened afterwards?' said Amy, hating the hint of jealousy in her voice.

'We stayed the night together,' said Megan, blushing.

Amy had never slept with Jay. They'd never discussed the reasons why and she knew he hadn't slept with the others; at least until it became their turn to move on.

Amy was unable to control the rapid beat of her heart. 'Does this mean . . . ?' she asked Megan, who was staring at her with a look of such serenity that it was difficult to hold her gaze.

'This weekend. Jay will be messaging us all soon. He asked me to leave something,' said Megan, handing her a piece of paper.

Amy unfolded the note, both of them crying as she read about Megan's life. Amy took her friend's hand. 'I'll miss you,' she said.

Megan grabbed her tightly. 'Death is not the end. I'll be waiting for you.'

Chapter Thirty

Louise called Dr Forrest first thing in the morning. Although she would have liked to see the man face to face, a journey to Exeter felt extreme for what could amount to nothing more than a lecture on drug-taking, and there was too much to do at the station.

The doctor was understanding. 'That's fine, how can I help?' he said.

Louise was surprised by the high-pitched tone of his voice, disappointed by her own preconceptions. 'Dr Everson mentioned to you that traces of DMT have been found in the three suicide victims in our town in the last few weeks?'

'Yes, a very tragic situation,' said Forrest.

'Is there anything in your research that would link the taking of DMT to suicide?'

'Not specifically,' said the doctor.

'What can you tell me?' she asked.

'What is your understanding of DMT?' asked Forrest.

'From my discussions with Dr Everson, I know the basics. I know that it is a hallucinogenic.'

Forrest cleared his throat, a squeaking sound passing through Louise's earpiece. 'I understand. I will confess, Inspector, I have been giving your case some thought since Dr Everson brought it to my attention. What piqued my interest was the suicide notes. This idea of a connectedness, another world. I can email some literature on the subject. There has been some interesting long-term analysis of DMT and this idea of another world, or a parallel universe has been prevalent. A particular quirk has been the feeling in many subjects that what they have experienced has been real.'

'In what way?'

'Well, the usual hindsight response after taking a hallucinogenic, LSD for example, is an acceptance that the experience was essentially a chemical trick of the mind. However, many users of DMT contend that their experience was a real one, that the drug transported them to another world or plane of existence. Furthermore, they tend to be able to recall the experience in greater detail even many months after taking the drug. And then there are the guardians.'

'Guardians?'

'Many of the volunteers in DMT trials claimed to have been met by guardians in these parallel worlds. They can take many forms – my particular favourite is the description by Terence McKenna, who called them "self-transforming machine elves" – but they do seem to be a constant as an experience to many who take the drug.'

'This sounds like the stuff of science fiction,' said Louise.

'Doesn't it just? As yet, we don't know for sure why users have such similar experiences. The nature of researching such phenomena makes it very difficult to quantify. However, some users of DMT often become convinced of the existence of an afterlife. I am only speculating of course but maybe this was a factor in the decision of the women to take their lives. Fascinating though. Another possible avenue you may wish to explore would be the connection between DMT and NDEs.'

'Again, you'll have to elaborate, Dr Forrest.'

'Apologies, I can get caught up in the jargon. NDEs are near-death experiences. I'm sure you've heard of those. Many patients who technically die, maybe undergoing cardiac arrest during an operation, often claim to see things like a light at the end of the tunnel, or have an out-of-body experience where they see themselves on the hospital bed. Again, we have no real explanation for this, but there are certain consistencies between the recollections of NDEs and those who have taken DMT. Perhaps this might give a hint as to the motivation of these three women. Fascinating stuff, isn't it?'

Louise didn't comment on the man's fascination and bit her tongue rather than reiterate that three women were dead. Certainly the link to near-death experiences was of interest. If the DMT had somehow convinced the women of an afterlife, it could be a motivating reason for them to take their own lives. 'Coming back to these guardians, I still find it inconceivable that everyone who takes the drug sees the same thing.'

'Not everyone of course, and I would argue it's not exactly the same thing, as these so-called guardians have different appearances. Furthermore, the most extensive clinical research so far conducted used sixty participants and only half of those reported experiencing a different plane of existence and encounter with a guardian. Obviously, the very fact that the subjects are taking a highly hallucinogenic drug makes the findings difficult to interpret. Many volunteers were unable to fully describe what they saw, and then there is the possibility of habitual influence.'

'By which you mean . . . ?'

'In a layman's term, what the subject experienced could arguably be influenced by other factors including their surroundings and the people they were with when they took the drug. And of course, you would have to consider the purity of the drug itself. There are countless possible derivatives and the drug could be mixed with other narcotics.'

'What you're saying is that people who are given DMT could be prompted to see specific things.'

'I am saying that is open to debate but certainly the scene and setting is pivotal to the hallucinogenic experience. You wouldn't want to take any psychedelic in the wrong frame of mind or in an extreme situation. The commonality of the guardians is still something that is yet to be fully explained. But yes, it is conceivable that a user could, to a certain extent, be open to the possibility of suggestion. I'll send you some literature. Please keep me informed and I'd be happy to help further.'

Louise hung up and drank her third coffee of the day. She checked on her parents before leaving for work, unsurprised that Paul hadn't called.

She thought about her conversation with Dr Forrest as she made her way to the station. All the talk of other worlds, guardians and aliens, and near-death experiences made her feel like she was still dreaming. That she'd heard such explanations from a renowned scientist, on the recommendation of a Met specialist, made it all the more confusing.

A rainstorm greeted her as she reached the police station. It was as if summer was over, gone in a few glorious days. A grey sky hung low over the station. The car park was already full and Louise sensed the heightened activity as she entered the main entrance. She wasn't sure what everyone was working towards. Was it finding out why the three women had taken their lives? Or was the station fighting the inevitable feeling that there would be more suicides?

She scrolled through the new pile of notes waiting for her on her desk, the lists of sightings of Sally's companion with follow-up information. She logged on to see twice as many emails waiting for her including an email from Dr Forrest with the literature he'd promised. Louise wasn't sure she had the heart to tell the team that the case had something to do with little green men just yet, but she clicked on the links anyway.

Louise was no scientist but she didn't see anything comprehensive in the articles she read. There appeared to be a lot of conjecture though Forrest had been right about the constant reference to guardians. At the moment the information was more harmful and confusing than helpful, and she was glad when Thomas placed a coffee cup on her desk.

'Boss.'

'Thank you, I need this,' said Louise, drinking the coffee as if it were quenching her thirst.

'Thought you'd like to know, we have something of a lead for our mysterious man. Three callers have given the same name for him. Jay Chappell. May I?' said Thomas, looking at her keypad.

'Sure.'

Thomas loaded Facebook and located a profile for Jay Chappell. His page hadn't been updated in over a year but the blurred profile picture was a good match for Sally's companion. 'We have an address in Newport, Wales. Local CID are on their way now.'

'Never let it be said the press aren't helpful,' said Louise.

'There's more. Not sure what it means but Coulson has found some online groups that Chappell is a member of. I'll send you the links over. Some weird, other-world shit.'

Louise's chest tightened. 'Can you be more specific than "other-world shit"?'

Thomas laughed. 'Sorry, that is a bit vague. Here,' he said, touching her arm as he typed on her keyboard again. 'Something to do with the Peruvian rainforest. Some tribe he went to visit.'

'That is something,' said Louise, scanning the information. She'd seen enough coincidences in her time not to get carried away but as she read about Chappell's foray into the rainforest, and his testimony about Ayahuasca, the DMT tea, she found it hard not to get her hopes up.

However, she was still surprised when an hour later Simone led the man into the office.

Chapter Thirty-One

A collective hush descended over the room as Louise walked over to Simone.

'This is Jay Chappell. He's just been processed by the front desk,' said Simone.

'I saw my picture in the paper last night,' said Chappell. He was taller than he'd appeared on-screen, at least 6'2". He was smiling at her. Not in an unkind way, more like he was amused to be finding himself at the station.

'DI Louise Blackwell. Thank you for coming here. Simone, please find an interview room for Mr Chappell. That's if you're okay answering a few questions?'

'Of course, however I can help.'

'I wish the job was always this easy,' said Thomas, as Louise returned to get her notebook.

'I'll interview him alone. You watch from the video link, see if you spot anything,' said Louise. 'Get Coulson there as well. Make sure it's being recorded properly.'

Chappell stood as she entered interview room three, a glass of water in front of him.

'Thanks again for coming to see us so soon, Mr Chappell. It must have been a bit of a shock seeing yourself in the papers.'

'It was but not as much as seeing the news about Sally. And you can call me Jay.' The early amusement had faded from the man's eyes, replaced by a studious seriousness.

Louise explained the formalities, offering Chappell legal representation if he felt it necessary while trying to sound as light as possible about their conversation.

Chappell waved the suggestion away. 'No, I know why you wanted to speak to me. I was with Sally the other day not long before she . . .' His hesitation seemed genuine, his eyes watering as his words faltered.

'Could you tell me what your relationship was to Sally Kennedy?'

Chappell sniffed, pulling a handkerchief from his pocket. 'Sorry,' he said. 'I've known her for some years. We're good friends, though I don't see her as often as I would like.'

'You were holding hands on the pier,' said Louise, keeping her tone light as if her comment didn't really mean anything.

The man shrugged. He had an intense way of looking at her, his eyes never leaving hers. Louise imagined most people would find his gaze unnerving, or flattering, depending on their viewpoint. 'Friends can hold hands can't they?'

'Of course. So how did you know Sally?'

'We go way back. I met her years ago now.'

'She looked like she was having a wonderful time on the pier.'

Chappell lowered his gaze. 'She was. That's why I don't understand why she did it.'

'When was the last time you saw her, Jay?'

'It was that day. We took a bus home to her place. I dropped her off there then went home.'

'To Newport?'

Louise noted the flicker of hesitation in the man. His eyes narrowed and he paused before answering. 'I don't live in Newport any longer.'

'Oh no?'

'No, I live here – well, Berrow, to be precise. I can give you the address.'

'Thank you,' said Louise, handing him her notebook and pen.

She studied him as he wrote down his details. His classical good looks were even more evident in the flesh. He had a very easy way about him, a confidence that was quite rare in the intensity of a police interview. He smiled as he handed her the notebook and she noticed what looked like scar tissue around his neck. 'I know this must be difficult for you to answer, but did Sally say or do anything that would suggest she wanted to take her own life?'

Chappell kept eye contact with Louise as he considered the question. 'She seemed happy when she was with me, but she suffered, Inspector Blackwell.'

'Suffered, how?'

'You've seen where she lived?'

Louise nodded, keeping silent to allow Chappell to speak.

'Her life was blighted with trauma after trauma. She was prone to mood swings. Sorry, that isn't quite right. I'm underplaying it. It was more than mere mood swings. She suffered with depression. It would come and go. I am surprised and devastated that this happened, don't get me wrong, but sadly it's not a complete shock.'

'Did she say anything to you during your day together?'

'No, as I said she was having a great time,' he said, echoing Louise's previous description as if mimicking her. 'That's the thing with depression. It can come on like that,' he continued. Louise was drawn to the movement of his fingers snapping together, the noise echoing in the room.

Louise blinked before asking Chappell if he knew Victoria Warrington and Claire Smedley.

The man was slick, she had to give him that. He barely reacted. 'No, sorry. I read the article. They're the other women who took their lives?'

'Did Sally mention them?' said Louise.

'No, of course not.'

Louise pursed her lips, fighting the urge to look away from Chappell's intense gaze. 'Can you tell me about your time in the Amazon?' she asked.

He reacted this time, a small crease forming on his forehead. 'You really did want to speak to me didn't you?'

The question had changed the dynamic of the interview and Louise knew she had to be careful not to lose him now. 'We were just trying to locate you, Jay. It made for some very interesting reading. You took Ayahuasca when you were there?'

A flicker of unease came and went on the man's face. 'You're not going to lock me up for that are you?' said Chappell, smiling. 'It was a foreign country, personal use and all that.'

Louise matched his smile. 'Quite a thing though?'

'You can only imagine. It changed my life.'

'I think it changed Sally's life too,' said Louise. It was a risk, but everything about Chappell's reactions up to this point had been so perfect that she felt the need to try and throw him off guard.

She couldn't tell for sure if it worked. He shrugged. 'What do you mean?'

'Traces of DMT were found in Sally's body.'

Chappell's mouth opened slightly as if he was about to ask a question.

'We don't normally check for such things as you may know?' said Louise.

Chappell's frown was laced with anger. 'How would I know that?'

Sensing the interview was turning, Louise said, 'Would you mind if we took your fingerprints and DNA sample, Mr Chappell? It's just procedure.'

Louise saw a hint of derision in Chappell as he answered. 'I only came in to help out and now you're treating me like I've done something wrong.'

Louise got to her feet. 'As I said, Mr Chappell, purely procedural.'

Chapter Thirty-Two

Thomas took Chappell to be processed. The hints of anger and derision Louise had sensed in him at the end of the interview had vanished. He seemed eager to help and went along with Thomas with a smile. Louise didn't know what to make of the man, but his reaction to her question about DMT had been revealing. He'd taken it as a personal affront, as if by asking the question she'd somehow offended him. It was the switch in behaviour that intrigued her. Prior to that he'd been the perfect interviewee, calm and respectable if a little overconfident. His anger suggested his earlier performance might have been a front. The reveal of DMT being found in Sally's body had rattled Chappell and Louise was convinced he was holding something back from them.

Two missed calls were waiting for her as she returned to her desk: one from her mother, the other from the journalist, Tania Elliot. She called her mother first, not bothering with the answerphone messages. 'Everything okay, Mum?'

'Didn't you listen to my message?'

'No, I thought it would be quicker to call.'

'Oh,' said her mother, as if the thought was ludicrous. 'Anyway, we received a postcard today. From Emily.'

Louise tensed. 'Where is it from?'

'The picture is the beach at Sennen. The postmark says Cornwall.'

Sennen was a beautiful area in Cornwall. As a family, they'd spent an eventful holiday there once when Louise was twelve. It had been their last real enjoyable time together, being the year before her father had found drugs in Paul's pocket. It had been a rare Cornwall summer – perfect sunshine and no rain. Paul appeared to be retreating into the past, trying to recapture something of an earlier happiness with his daughter. 'What did Emily say?'

'You know, nothing much. Having a great time and missing us. She's not about to put down that she's been kidnapped.'

'Oh, Mum, that's not necessary, is it?' The guilt at ignoring her niece's comment about going on holiday still haunted Louise, but the fact that Paul had called and had now sent a postcard was encouraging.

'Well,' said her mum, her anger palpable over the phone. 'Can you send someone down there?'

'To Cornwall?'

'Yes.'

'To do what?'

'Find them and bring them back of course.'

Louise understood how her mother felt but couldn't entertain such a course of action at that moment. 'I can't talk about it now,' she said, looking round the room for a sight of Simone. 'But I don't think we need to do that just yet. I'm sure he'll phone again soon and we can discuss it with him.'

The line went silent and Louise heard the distant sound of her mother sobbing. 'It'll be okay, Mum. He's called, and sent the postcard. He's not exactly hiding from us, is he?' She was whispering now, her hand gripping the handset tight.

'I'll call you tonight, Lou.'

'Okay, Mum. Bye.'

Louise rubbed her forehead. For what felt like the hundredth time that month, she silently cursed her brother before reminding herself that the postcard was a positive thing. Self-conscious, she looked around the office. Try as she might, she couldn't prevent her private life leaking into her work. The last thing she needed now was for Robertson to think she was too focused on a family matter to fully give her attention to the case. The conflict was leading to mistakes. She'd messed up the overtime, but she'd also missed Emily telling her she was going on holiday. She had to straighten herself out, to get her focus back. She could deal with both things but she had to separate them. For now, her focus had to be on her work.

'He's gone,' said Thomas, returning.

'You watched the interview?'

'Yes. He didn't like it when you mentioned the DMT. It has to be more than a coincidence? He's been to the rainforest and tried this Ayahuasca, and three women kill themselves with traces of the drug in their blood.'

'It's our job to prove it's not a coincidence,' said Louise, but in truth she didn't know what it all meant yet. They could connect Chappell to Sally, and Chappell had all but confessed he'd taken the same drug at some point. However, the man had attended the station of his own accord and had been helpful. Taking the drug for personal use wasn't in itself a crime in Peru. Maybe if he'd sold it to Sally and the others, and they could somehow prove they'd taken their lives because of the drug, they might have a case – a reason to pursue Chappell further – but at the moment that was, at best, supposition.

She could already hear Robertson's thoughts, and those of the assistant chief. Without a direct link, these types of cases were almost impossible to pursue. The main issue was ascertaining the state of mind of the person who'd taken their life. All they had to go on at present was the suicide notes, and now the anecdotal evidence from Chappell of Sally's depression. If Louise went to Robertson now and tried to present Chappell as a suspect in the suspicious death of the three women he would laugh her out of his office.

But something was off. Hunches and feelings had no place in police work but Louise understood motivation and people's characters. The link of the suicide notes and the DMT was enough to keep her interest in Chappell high. He was hiding something, and she owed it to the three women to keep going and find out what it was.

The focus of her briefing later that afternoon was all on Jay Chappell. 'We need to find out everything we can about this man. I mean everything from the past to the present. Thomas, I need you to focus on this DMT link. Simon, how long do we have you from HQ?'

'As long as necessary, as far as I'm aware,' said Coulson.

'I know it's a lot of work but can we trawl through the CCTV images once more. All we need is to link Chappell to Claire or Victoria.'

Without Farrell, the team suddenly felt understaffed. It was the nature of a CID department in such a small station. If DCI Robertson ever returned from his meeting with Morley, she intended to request Farrell's return – once, that was, she'd worked out how she would explain her current line of investigation.

While the light was still good, Louise decided to revisit the three suicide sites. She wanted to explore the spaces again, now she had the connection between the DMT and Jay Chappell fresh in her mind. As she drove to Saint Nicholas' Church, she fought her growing frustration with the case. Everything was so intangible. There was a risk she was making a mistake; that she was looking for something that didn't exist. It was beyond question that the three women were linked in one way or another but it didn't mean anything more than that. Presumption could kill any investigation and her focus had to be on facts. She could argue for now that Chappell had an interest in DMT and the drug was found in the women's hair, but that couldn't commit her to that line of investigation indefinitely.

Rain started falling as she walked the steep incline to the church where Claire Smedley had taken her life. The graveyard was desolate, Louise's view of the coast hampered by a growing blanket of mist. It seemed incredible how recently they'd discovered remains of a small campfire among these very same tombstones. Louise climbed over the stone wall at the perimeter. Her back to the wall, she admired the stunning view of the Brean peninsula in the hazy distance.

Following Sally's death there had been more press attention on Claire's suicide; more attention than she'd ever experienced in her life. Louise thought about the woman's dingy bedsit, and the obese landlord, Applebee, and how easy it could have been to dismiss her case as just another lonely person's cry for help. Had she really been so despondent that she could only see one way out? And had the DMT aided her in that decision? Had, for that matter, Jay Chappell influenced her in some way? Maybe if she hadn't seen that glimpse of anger and resentment in Chappell, she wouldn't be thinking along those lines, but she just couldn't get him out of her mind.

A scratching noise distracted her attention and Louise looked over the wall to glimpse two hares scrambling across the graveyard. She pushed herself back over the wall, her hand slipping on the algae-covered top. Drained of energy, she considered how easy it would be to go home, to sleep off the tiring day and bad weather, but revisiting the locations where Victoria and Sally lost their lives seemed more important now than ever.

Back in the car, she switched on the heater to deaden the wet chill on her skin. She was about to leave for the second part of her pilgrimage – Brean Down where Victoria had died – when her phone rang. 'Tracey, everything okay?'

'Hi, Lou. Yes, all good. Nothing to worry about but I thought you should know. There has been a spate of house burglaries recently in Knowle. I was just going through the list when I realised one of the homes broken into belongs to your brother.'

Chapter Thirty-Three

Megan had spent the night again. As before, Megan had fallen into a peaceful sleep while Amy tossed and turned, slipping in and out of troubled dreams she could no longer recall.

Megan's happiness hadn't faded in the morning, the same serene look on her face as she kissed Amy goodbye on the cheek. Some of Megan's good cheer rubbed off on Amy, chipping away at the edges of her concern until she thought everything might work out okay. A feeling that was dashed seconds into retrieving last night's *Post* from the paper-recycling unit outside the block of flats.

Amy did a double take, her heart hammering so fiercely in her chest it was audible to her, as she viewed Jay's photograph. Her hands were shaking and she clenched the newspaper tightly as a neighbour left by the front door and grunted a morning greeting.

Jay was wanted for questioning in connection with the suspicious death of Sally Kennedy. A second, smaller photograph showed Jay on the pier with Sally on the same day Amy had seen them together. Amy rubbed her eyes, wondering if this was really happening. There was a phone number in the article and for one desperate second she considered calling it.

And tell them what? *That you saw Jay and Sally together? That you were there the night Sally took DMT and walked through the woods to her death? That you sat on the beach with Megan and waited for someone to discover Sally's body before it was taken to sea, while never quite knowing for sure if she was dead or not?*

She threw the paper back in with the recycling and walked away, trying to contain her panic as the threat of tears welled inside her.

She thought about nothing else during work, managing to ignore Keith's constant barracking of her and Nicole. Someone would recognise Jay. No one from the group would identify him but someone in the town would know him. The thought made her realise how little she truly knew about Jay. She didn't even know if he had a job, though he'd once managed to fund himself a trip to the Amazon and was always well presented. And what would happen when he was identified? She hadn't thought about the criminal aspect to their work before. Victoria, Claire and Sally had all wanted to end their lives but Amy was sure the authorities wouldn't view their deaths in such a sympathetic way, especially when they found out the rest of the group had watched. She presumed there was some form of duty to try and stop people taking their own lives. Was she being selfish to think that way? Maybe they had done something wrong, maybe she should call the number after all and stop it happening to Megan?

'Is everything okay?' asked Nicole, as they stood waiting at the stop for Nicole's bus home. 'You've hardly said a word all day.'

'Just tired,' said Amy, which wasn't a complete lie.

'Have you ever thought about opening your own place?'

Amy's mind was so full of conflicting thoughts and images of Jay and the others that the question barely registered. 'Huh?' she said.

'Your own café? You run that place as it is. All you'd need would be a cook and you'd be set.'

Nicole's innocent optimism diverted Amy from her despondency. 'I'm afraid I'd need a bit more than that. My own place for a start.'

'You could get a business loan.'

Amy laughed. 'They don't give business loans to someone like me.'

Nicole frowned. 'I could help. I'm studying business, and my parents—'

Amy cut her off. 'I think this is a conversation for another day,' she said. Despite her recent reservations about Jay and the group, her future was already planned out. She didn't want a place in this world and had made her peace with that. Her belief that Aiden was waiting for her was unwavering. She would have explained it to Nicole but she would never understand.

To her relief, Nicole's bus arrived before they could speak further. 'Have a think about it,' said Nicole, climbing the steps.

Amy smiled and turned away.

She kept checking her phone as she walked home, even though the only person in her contact list would be at work until midnight. She bought the *Bristol Post* from the newsagent close to her flats and had skimmed through it three times by the time she got home. It was as if yesterday's paper had been a hoax, the story reduced to an eight-line article deep into the paper. There was no picture, only a mention that police were looking to talk to the person last seen with Sally.

She showered in the bathroom, her body jittery as if she'd drunk too much coffee. After cooking pasta with shop-bought sauce, she logged into the group chat desperate for some answers but it was deserted, no one had logged in since last night. She closed the connection quickly, fearing she'd somehow made a mistake; that the chat room was being monitored and the police would be knocking on her door at any second.

However, when the doorbell rang thirty minutes later it wasn't the police waiting outside for her.

Chapter Thirty-Four

Tracey was standing outside Paul's ground-floor flat. She smiled shyly on seeing Louise as if somehow the break-in was her fault. Louise examined a hole in the front window, surprised the pane of glass hadn't collapsed.

'They threw something from the inside,' said Tracey. 'They broke in through the front door. Looks like they just kicked the lock through.'

'When do we think it happened?'

'Last night probably. One of the locals reported the broken window this morning after seeing the front door was ajar.'

A cold draught welcomed Louise as she prised open the front door. She'd walked down this very same corridor hundreds of times before, Emily running towards her to jump into her arms. It had only been a few days since the girl had left, and Louise had to remind herself she'd only gone on holiday, but with the shattered lock on the door a place that usually felt welcoming was now bleak and desolate. Photographs of Paul, Emily and Dianne filled the walls. It hurt to look at them, particularly Paul; it was as if the carefree, smiling man captured in the images no longer existed.

She prepared herself as she entered the living room. She'd attended break-ins as a matter of course over the years. To those involved, the invasion was the most traumatic thing in the world, and Louise had soon learnt how important it was to disassociate herself from the emotions such break-ins aroused. It was the only professional way to cope and as she viewed the scene – the sofa torn and upended, the dark patch of wallpaper where the television had once been – she tried to do so with a dispassionate eye. *This was just another house burglary,* she told herself, probably some chancer kids who'd seen Paul and Emily leave for a holiday. But as she moved through the flat, her resolve faded. In Emily's room, she sat on her niece's bed holding one of the torn paperbacks that had been scattered around the room. Thankfully Tracey had remained downstairs and couldn't see her hand shaking as she flicked through the book. Heat rose through her body as she pictured the strangers ransacking Emily's room, her despair turning to anger as she gripped the book tight and thought about what she would do to those responsible.

The pattern was repeated throughout the rest of the flat. Every room was upturned but little had been taken beyond the missing television. Louise understood that it wasn't what was missing that affected the victims of house burglary. It was the intrusion. She'd known countless families who'd been forced to relocate following break-ins, unable to live in a place where others had invaded.

'We think it's part of a spree. There have been a few other break-ins in the area,' said Tracey, who was waiting for her in the kitchen.

'They don't seem to have taken much, though they've turned the place upside down,' said Louise.

Tracey shrugged. They both knew there was no explaining the actions of those responsible. Louise was worried she was looking for something that wasn't there, but the whole enterprise felt wrong as if the burglars had taken the television just for show.

'You're thinking this could be linked to Paul and Emily leaving, aren't you?' said Tracey.

'Now why would you think something like that?' said Louise, with a joyless grin.

'I can understand it, Lou, but think about it. Imagine you were investigating this yourself. It's just coincidence. Your brother's behaving like an idiot, yes, but there's nothing more beyond that. This is just kids having some idiotic fun. You wouldn't give it a second thought if it wasn't Paul's flat.'

Louise knew she was right. 'You can shoot off. I need to call a locksmith.'

'I can stay, help you tidy.'

'No, you're fine. I'll get the place secure and then come back tomorrow.'

Tracey hesitated before giving her a quick hug goodbye. 'You know where I am,' she said.

With nothing else on offer, Louise made herself black instant coffee as she began to straighten up the kitchen. Tracey had been right of course but she still couldn't shake the feeling that the break-in was linked to Paul disappearing.

She winced as she drank the tasteless coffee; another thing to blame Paul for. Who drank instant coffee any more? As she emptied spilt cereal into the bin, she told herself her brother was to blame for everything. The place would never have been burgled if he hadn't left with Emily, and Louise and her parents wouldn't have to be enduring this kind of half-life waiting for them to return.

The tidy-up job was harder than anticipated, her energy fading as she went from room to room straightening things up as best as possible. She would have to tell her parents at some point but couldn't face burdening them with this just yet. She would have to come back tomorrow. She blamed Paul again for the inconvenience.

She had better things to do than tidy up after him – something she felt she'd been doing for too long.

Louise made one last tour of the flat before leaving. She considered compiling a list of things that were missing, but didn't get beyond the television. Paul would know better but nothing obvious had been taken.

She ventured into Paul's room last. The smell reminded her of his room as a teenager, the slight fungal tang of body odour in the trapped air. She had to wonder if the burglars had been in the room at all, or if the clothes and empty pizza boxes scattered across the floor had been there all along.

She checked the bedside table and found one of Paul's old iPhones. She knew the names of some of Paul's friends but didn't have any of their numbers. If she could open his address book she might be able to speak to someone who knew what the hell was going on with her brother's life, and that could hopefully bring her one step closer to finding Emily.

Chapter Thirty-Five

After a brief search, Louise found a charger for the phone. It was an old phone and Paul hadn't protected it with a pass lock. As she called Paul's old acquaintances – so far none of them had seen Paul since Dianne's death – Louise flitted from murderous thoughts about her brother to the on-going case back in Weston. An image of Jay Chappell filtered into her mind, her skin prickling with heat as she recalled speaking to him earlier that day. He'd been processed now, his DNA and fingerprints would already be in Portishead waiting to be cross referenced. If they could only link him with either Claire or Victoria, there might be something to talk to him about again.

Louise was surprised by the intensity of her feelings that thought aroused in her. It would be days before the DNA and fingerprints results came back – at the moment Chappell was technically a non-suspect to a non-crime so there would be no rush at HQ – and Louise knew she was approaching hunch territory, but she was convinced they were not finished with the man just yet.

She got lucky on the sixth call. One of Paul's old school friends, John Everett. Everett had been at Paul and Dianne's wedding. He'd been pissed before the speeches had started, his behaviour rapidly deteriorating during the evening. She couldn't recall Paul speaking about him much since the marriage, and she hadn't given him another thought since that day.

'Who's this?'

'John, this is Louise Blackwell. Paul's sister.'

The line went silent and Louise thought Everett had hung up on her. 'Oh, Louise,' he said, eventually. His response was elongated as if he was taking meticulous care over each word.

'Hi, how are you?'

'Good,' he said, the answer sounding as if it were a question.

'I was wondering if you could help me. Paul's not answering his phone and I'm trying to locate him.'

'Oh.'

It was clear Everett had been drinking, clear too that he knew something. 'John?'

'I don't really know nothing, Louise, I'm sorry.'

'That doesn't really clarify things, John. Where are you? It would be good to catch up. To have a drink.' She'd seen the way he'd looked at her during Paul's wedding, and the occasional time they'd both been out together with Paul in the past, and tried to play up to the attraction.

She could hear him thinking on the other end of the line. The quick, shallow breaths as he contemplated why she wanted to speak to him. 'That be great,' he said, slurring the words. 'Tomorrow night?'

'I'd like a drink now, John. Where are you?'

Again, a hesitation in his voice. He knew she was in the police and his hesitancy made her wonder if he was hiding something from her. 'Tomorrow would be better . . .'

'It's a one-off offer, John.'

That got his attention. 'Okay, I can meet you at the Commercial Rooms. In an hour?'

'Okay, John, that would be great.'

She felt a little sorry for Everett, as she grabbed her keys. The Commercial Rooms was a bar in the centre of Bristol, a world away from the local dives he would normally drink at in south Bristol. He was either trying to impress her, or hoping no one would see them together.

She spotted him immediately. He radiated insecurity, standing at the bar nursing a full pint of bitter, scoping the crowd as if everyone was a threat. 'John?' she asked, as she reached the bar.

Everett had been at school with Paul but looked at least a decade older than her brother. His career in alcohol consumption had started earlier than Paul's and had continued long after Paul had given up his old ways and moved in with Dianne. It showed in Everett's features: the dank greasy hair, the skin sagging from his skeletal face, the bump of his stomach that seemed incongruous on his scrawny body. His hand was shaking as he reached for an imaginary cigarette. 'Good to see you, Louise,' he murmured.

As she ordered a sparkling water, and another drink for Everett, she searched for something in the man's features, anything to reconcile him with the young man he'd once been, but came up empty. He was so far removed from the man she'd known, it was like seeing a completely different person. She closed her eyes, drowning out the noise of the bar, and hoped it wasn't too late for Paul and that he could retain what Everett had lost.

'You seen much of Paul recently?' she asked, once they'd finished exchanging pleasantries. She smiled at Everett, trying to get him to relax.

He was almost too easy to read. His eyes gave him away as he pretended to think about the question. 'We have a drink now and then,' he said, downplaying his answer.

So Everett was one of Paul's enablers. She couldn't blame him specifically. It was obviously a symbiotic association. She'd seen countless examples of such relationships in every early-opening bar in the city. When Paul had failed to pick up Emily from school the other week, he'd spent all day drinking in the local bar. She pictured him with Everett, sharing war stories as they drank their cheap booze.

'He's been drinking a lot recently?'

'Depends what you count as a lot,' said Everett, with a hint of defiance.

'Enough say to forget to pick up his daughter from school?'

Everett's pale face blossomed into a patchwork of red blotches. 'I heard about that,' he said, eyes downcast.

'Have you spoken to him in the last few days?'

Everett shook his head.

'John, look at me. This is important.'

Everett looked up. Louise wondered what his state of mind was like at that moment, what incoherent thoughts were running through his head. 'I've called him a few times but his phone is switched off,' she said.

Louise drummed her fingers on the bar counter. Everett had always been kind to her at school. She'd been a few years younger than him but he'd never been mean, never teased her for being Paul's younger sister. If anything, he'd treated her as if she were grown up and she'd never forgotten that. She decided to trust him now, hoping that part of the original him still existed. 'Do you know that Paul's taken Emily away?'

'What do you mean, taken her away?'

'They've gone on holiday, but Paul didn't tell anyone, and we don't know where he is.'

'So?'

'What do you mean, so?'

'She's his daughter, isn't she?'

'She is, John, but that isn't the point. Paul has a network of support. We all look after Emily. It isn't like him to just take off like that. We're worried about him. We're worried about Emily, John.'

Everett buried his mouth into his drink. He looked on the verge of tears.

'You knew he was going away, didn't you, John?'

'I told him not to go. Or at least not to take Emily.'

'Why would he go without Emily?' said Louise.

Everett shook his head, his gaze focused on his nearly empty glass. 'I promised,' he murmured into his drink.

'You need to think about Emily, John. Paul is not in the right frame of mind. You must know that, John.'

Everett couldn't look at her. His neck muscles tensed as if it was taking effort to keep his head upright. 'Paul's in trouble,' he said. 'He owes some money to people you shouldn't owe money to.'

Chapter Thirty-Six

Amy peered through the window at the figure in the courtyard. As if he knew he was being viewed, Jay glanced up at her. He waved, Amy's body shaking in reaction. 'I'll be down just now,' she said.

Amy wished he'd warned her that he would be coming over. He'd only ever been to her place the once, on the day she'd moved in. She'd been ashamed of the place then but it was even worse now. Her clothes were scattered throughout the room and the air inside was dank and cloying. She recoiled from her reflection in the mirror, the grease from the café in her shiny hair and patchy skin. She wanted to take a shower, to scrub herself clean but couldn't leave him waiting. She hurried into a change of clothes, disrobing from her grey jogging bottoms and T-shirt into jeans and a black vest.

She made herself walk down the stairs when every nerve in her body told her to run. Despite her recent doubts, she was so desperate to see him.

She took in five deep breaths before opening the communal front door but was still speechless when he smiled at her. 'Amy, I am so pleased to see you,' he said, pulling her close.

She savoured his warmth, the smell of his skin, and the timbre of the heartbeat in his chest. As it always did, his presence made her forget about everything else. She could quite easily have stayed this way forever. 'Can we talk?' he said, his deep rich voice vibrating through her bones.

'My place is a mess,' said Amy, as Jay eased away from her.

His smile told her none of that mattered. He reached for her hand. 'Show me the way,' he said.

Amy felt his eyes on her as she climbed the steps to her bedsit. She held on to Jay's hand as she led him upwards but it was as if somehow he was guiding her, his grip strong. 'I'm sorry, if I'd known you were visiting . . .' she muttered, as she showed him into her room.

Jay placed his finger to his lips. 'None of this matters,' he told her, as he sat down on the wooden chair by the side of her beaten old bed settee.

'No,' said Amy, agreeing as a matter of course.

She didn't ask him if he wanted a drink or anything to eat. Instead, she took a seat on the settee as close to him as possible. He was slightly higher up on the chair, and it created the impression that he was looking down on her. It wasn't a bad thing. She liked gazing up towards his smile and she rested her hands on his knees as she waited for him to speak.

'Have you seen the newspapers?' he asked, taking her hands.

She could never lie to him, yet she couldn't hold his gaze as she nodded.

'I imagine you were worried?'

Amy fought the emotions that the simple question evoked. She was always worried about one thing or another, but something about the concern in Jay's voice as he asked her made her want to cry. Had she come close to doubting him? It seemed absurd now. He'd shown her things. Demonstrated, physically demonstrated, that something waited for her beyond this mundane way of living. Yes, she'd been concerned and she revealed herself by burying her head in Jay's lap, as the tears she'd been holding in for an eternity were released.

Jay murmured comforting words as he stroked her hair. If she could have passed on now she would have accepted exiting the world in this manner; the combination of his soothing words, and the way he ran his fingers through her hair to her scalp, made her want to close her eyes and fade away.

'We're so close,' he whispered and she agreed. 'But we need to be careful now.'

Reluctantly, Amy pulled herself up from his lap and wiped her eyes clear. 'What do you mean?'

'I've closed the online group. We can't risk it at the moment.'

Amy blinked. 'Can't risk what?'

'I went to speak to the police today. There's nothing to worry about but we can't risk them interfering with our work. We're going to meet tomorrow evening. I'm telling everyone personally.'

Amy struggled to breathe. She understood she wasn't the only one. She'd struggled with her jealousy on seeing Jay with Sally, and then latterly hearing about Megan's day – and night – with him. But she'd hoped that this visit had been special to her. To hear that it wasn't, that he was simply making the rounds, hurt her more than she could have imagined. She wanted to know the order he'd seen everyone in. Was she the first or the last person he'd called on?

As if reading her concerns, Jay reached for her hand again. She tried to pull it away but he held her tight. 'You are so special to me, Amy, you must know that. Your time will come but it has to be right. You have to be ready to see Aiden again.'

Jay relaxed his grip and Amy allowed her hands to be held. The mention of Aiden was enough to banish her doubts before they had time to fully materialise. Did he know that Megan had told her about their time together? She would be surprised if he didn't. He knew everything about her, about all of them; had done so from the day she'd met him.

He gave her directions for the meeting place the following evening. She wanted to ask if it was to be Megan's turn but the question would be an act of betrayal so she just smiled and agreed to see him there.

An emptiness crept over her as she walked Jay back down the staircase. She wanted him to stay but he was needed elsewhere. 'I'll see you tomorrow,' he said, kissing the tears from her cheeks.

'Tomorrow,' she said, reluctantly allowing him to prise himself free of her embrace.

Chapter Thirty-Seven

Louise took the decision to drive to Cornwall at 5 a.m. after waking in the dark and being unable to get back to sleep. She waited until eight to call Sergeant Joslyn Merrick in the small harbour town of St Ives, by which time she was already deep into the county.

It was now nine thirty and she was sitting in a chain coffee shop adjacent to a supermarket on the outskirts of St Ives. Joslyn sat opposite, next to her daughter who was busy drawing pictures on a sketch pad, a pair of bulky earphones isolating her from the conversation.

'Thanks for agreeing to meet with me,' said Louise.

'I didn't really have much option, did I?' said Joslyn, with a hint of a Cornish accent. 'What did you plan to do if I hadn't answered?' she added, with a grin.

'I wasn't thinking that far ahead. Would have probably grabbed myself a cream tea then headed home.'

Joslyn laughed and her daughter looked up before returning to her drawing. 'Just remember, jam before cream on the scones.'

'How could I forget?'

Louise had first met Joslyn during the Pensioner Killer case and they'd remained in contact since. Joslyn was married with two children and from what Louise could tell seemed to all but run the small police station in St Ives.

After meeting with Everett, Louise had grown concerned that Paul's visit to Cornwall wasn't what he'd claimed it to be. Everett had told her about Paul's financial difficulty. It seemed the insurance money he'd received after Dianne's death had all but gone following three years of life with only occasional work and a vigorous drinking habit. Louise had heard of the Manning family Paul had allegedly borrowed money from. They were a two-bit crime family based in Bristol, but not small-scale enough not to pose a threat to those who'd wronged them. She wasn't sure what troubled her most about the situation. That Paul had done something so stupid, or that she'd been so blinkered to his situation that she hadn't found out about it.

Joslyn listened patiently as Louise explained. The woman was a few years older than Louise and had probably dealt with hundreds of missing-person cases over the years. She didn't rush to judge once Louise was finished, when it could have been easy for her to dismiss Louise's concern in an instant.

'You don't strike me as one to jump to rash conclusions,' she said. 'I can only imagine what it must have been like for your brother, for all of you, to lose your sister-in-law. Obviously, you know what I would tell you if you were a civilian?'

'That's why I've come to you directly, Joslyn. I don't want this to go official.'

'I have to ask though. Do you really think Emily is in danger?'

'Whatever my misgivings about Paul, I know he would never let anything happen to Emily.'

Joslyn glanced at her daughter whose attention was fixed on her drawing pad. 'That's not what I asked you, Louise.'

Louise took a deep breath. She was usually so quick at analysing situations but with Paul and Emily her mind became fuzzy. 'I don't know the extent of what Paul owes the Manning family. That is my next call. I don't believe they have the resources, or probably even the will, to try and track Paul to Cornwall. So at the moment, no, I don't believe Emily is in danger.' Louise considered her own words, wondering if they'd sounded a little too forced.

She pulled the Sennen postcard from her bag and gave it to Joslyn. 'I realise this doesn't narrow the search down but the postmark is from Penzance. We used to come to this area as children. I've put together a list of the places we stayed, the beaches we visited as a family.'

Joslyn squinted in concentration as she read the list. She'd been impressed with the woman from the first time she'd met her, and admired the way she seemed to juggle a family life with the pressures of being a sergeant in the police. She wondered how much further her career could have progressed if she'd been stationed somewhere more populated; if, like Louise, she didn't have an immediate family.

'You've driven through this county of ours?' said Joslyn.

'I know it's a huge ask. A huge task.'

It was Joslyn's turn to sigh. 'I'm not back into work until later this week but I can get someone to start calling the campsites and caravan parks. We can start with this list and develop from there. As a matter of fact, I have just the man in mind to do the job,' she added, with a smile. 'Is there anyone in the county that he might be staying with?'

Louise had grilled Everett on the very same question. 'I don't think so. We have no relations or friends in the region that I'm aware of.'

'Present company excluded of course,' said Joslyn, with a pretend frown.

'Thank you, Joslyn, I really do appreciate it.'

'You're welcome. Right, you,' she said, taking the earphones off her daughter. 'We better get going. Best not to be late for Nana Boswell.'

The sea was visible as Louise exited the car park, the water an enticing turquoise-blue. She couldn't remember the last time she'd had a proper holiday. She'd had leave but hadn't gone away for longer than a weekend since her time at MIT. She vowed then to take a holiday when this was all over. She would arrange a family holiday with her parents, with Paul and Emily. She realised she'd taken things for granted; how, prior to Dianne's death, Louise had the perfect family but never appreciated it. Even when Paul started drinking, she'd let it slide when she should have intervened much earlier. The signs had been there all along but she'd let him continue destroying his life, as if she thought one day Paul would simply stop; would find a solution on his own and turn his life around. Well, that would change when he was back. She would insist he found support and would help him rectify whatever mess he'd got himself into with the Mannings.

She cut back through the neighbouring beach town of Hayle, on the lookout for somewhere to buy a quick snack. Rounding the corner of the main street, her breath caught as she saw the distant figure of a man hand in hand with a young girl who looked to be Emily's age. She blinked, her heart beating so fast she thought she would have to stop driving.

Controlling her breathing, she kept her eyes focused on the pair, who'd just turned the corner into a supermarket car park. She smacked the steering wheel as the traffic edged forward, the car in front of her stopping to let a vehicle out from the side road. 'Come on,' she screamed, pointlessly, at the driver, before taking the corner a little too fast into the supermarket.

Something akin to melancholy hit her as she saw parent and child still hand in hand, walking into the supermarket. Her breathing spiked then slowed as they disappeared out of sight. She couldn't believe her own foolishness. How could she have thought, even for a second, that the two figures were Paul and Emily?

Realising the car had stalled, taking up three parking spaces, she restarted the engine and left towards the A30. She tried to divert her attention from Emily and Paul by focusing on the case. She felt guilty for doing so, yet equally guilty for not having her full attention on her work.

The surprise of Jay Chappell having walked into the station of his own accord still worried her. She couldn't quite pinpoint why. Obviously, his motive for visiting the station couldn't have been completely selfless. He'd had his picture printed in the newspaper so it made sense for him to clear his name but there had been a sense of arrogance, both in his dramatic arrival and the way he'd answered her questions as if he were untouchable. She was used to facing arrogance, people so sure of themselves that they thought they were smarter, better even, than the officers questioning them. Somehow, Chappell transcended this. She'd seen an unwavering confidence in him that she'd rarely encountered, a type of self-belief that couldn't be faked. What it all meant, she didn't know, but there was something Chappell was hiding.

She called Thomas for updates. At her request, he'd been looking further into Chappell's background but had little to report. He didn't ask where she'd been and she didn't offer an explanation, though part of her wanted to share. She hadn't even told her parents of her jaunt to Cornwall and the only people who currently knew about Paul's problems with the Mannings were Louise, Everett and Joslyn.

Perhaps it should have bothered her more that she had no one to confide in, but there was always Tracey. She would tell her friend about the Mannings when she returned, despite only having the say of one of Paul's alcoholic mates as evidence.

The threat of sleep encroached as she made slow progress back up the M5. She buzzed her window down and let the cold wind invigorate her. She would have stopped for another coffee but felt guilty enough already for being absent from Weston.

◆ ◆ ◆

It was early afternoon before she reached the station. She was greeted with the usual wall of silence, the paranoid part of her suggesting that everyone knew about Paul and Emily and where she'd been that morning. Simone gave her one of her antagonising looks as she entered the office. It was amazing how much emotion the woman could muster on to her face. She looked at once disappointed but knowing and Louise turned away from her before she was forced to say something.

A long list of emails awaited her attention and she stared at the screen in the hope they would disappear. Tania Elliot had left two messages for her at reception which she'd followed up by email. Louise ignored the emails and began checking the updates on Jay Chappell.

Unfortunately, as Thomas had earlier suggested, they still had little information about the man. The preliminaries had been covered – tax records, places of employment, school history, old addresses – but little else had been discovered about him so far. Was she taking the wrong approach to the case? It was possible her thoughts were muddled by her brother's situation, yet all she could think about was Chappell. She shut her laptop, unable to concentrate, and left the office to get some fresh air.

Thirty minutes later she found herself pulling up outside Chappell's home in Berrow, wondering why she was there at all. Like her, Chappell lived in a bungalow, only his was a detached property at least three times the size of hers. It was painted a dirty white and surrounded by a lawn, more dried mud than grass.

She moved towards the front door before she knew what she was doing and rang the bell, hoping, or presuming, inspiration would strike if Chappell answered the door. The chime of the door-bell rang from within but no one answered. She peered through the small window in the front door, her view obscured by the frosted glass. She had no good reason to be there but couldn't drag herself away. Moving to the windows, she tried to see between the cracks of the blinds but no light reached the interior of the house as if Chappell was trying to hide something. She smiled to herself at the thought – recognising the presumption and paranoia – and stopped short of jumping over the back fence to see if she could spot anything in the garden.

It seemed she'd been just in time. As she walked back to the car, a vehicle came up the driveway. Louise stood her ground as the driver's door opened and Jay Chappell got out.

Chapter Thirty-Eight

Louise saw the smile before she took in the man himself, the light momentarily distorting Chappell's face, making his toothy grin the first discernible thing she saw. 'Inspector,' he said, his features coming into focus as he broke through the glare. 'What a pleasant surprise.'

Louise glanced down to see his hand was held out for her to shake. She let it hang there, Chappell maintaining eye contact with a ferocious intent. 'Mr Chappell, I'm glad you're back. I have some more questions to ask you.'

Chappell eventually dropped his hand. 'Of course,' he said, surprising her. 'How can I help?'

'Shall we go inside?' said Louise.

Chappell smirked, mocking her. 'Forgive me, Inspector, but you've plastered my face over the newspapers, given me the indignity of having my fingerprints and DNA taken, and now you would like to enter my house uninvited. Please don't take it personally, but I think I'd rather have our conversation here, outside.'

Louise considered suggesting they return to the station but he would be under no compulsion to do so, and would know as much. 'I understand,' said Louise. 'Maybe we should leave it until next time.'

The smile returned to Chappell's face, charging the glint in his eyes. 'There's going to be a next time?'

'Oh, I imagine so, Mr Chappell.'

Chappell didn't move, a strange enigmatic look forming on his face that she couldn't quite look away from. 'What the hell,' he said, breaking the spell with a sweep of his hands. 'I'm a bit busy but I could spare you a few minutes. Why don't you come in?'

Louise considered calling in her position but didn't want to alert Chappell to her concerns, and her GPS signal would track her if necessary. 'Thank you,' she said, following Chappell up the small pathway to the front door.

Chappell led her to a living-room area with cream walls, and a filthy-looking sky-blue carpet that looked as if it hadn't been cleaned in decades. The room contained a wicker sofa and arm-chair, the only other object being the floor-to-ceiling bookcase overflowing with titles. Normally, the sight of a good bookcase would endear Louise to someone but endearment wasn't something she was feeling now.

'I don't really have much use for material things,' said Chappell, by way of explanation. 'Give me a chair and a book and I am happy.' They were both standing in the middle of the room. It was becoming a struggle to maintain eye contact with Chappell, such was the unwavering intensity in his eyes, but Louise wouldn't be the first to look away. 'Where are my manners,' said Chappell, his eyes still on her. 'May I get you a drink?'

'I'm fine, thank you.'

'Then please, take a seat.'

Louise took the lone armchair, the dust visible as she sunk into the ancient springs poking up through the thin cloth exterior. Although she wanted to know more about Chappell, she hadn't prepared anything specific to ask him. The questions she wanted answered – did you drug Sally, Claire and Victoria – couldn't so easily be asked.

'Go ahead,' said Chappell, sitting on the sofa opposite.

For a moment, Louise didn't know who was in charge. The situation had the feel of an interview and at the moment she felt like the interviewee. She shook the notion away. 'Thank you for coming in to see us yesterday, it really helped to speed things up.'

'My pleasure.'

'As I mentioned during our last conversation we have found traces of DMT in the hair samples of not only Sally, but the other two women who took their lives.'

Chappell seemed more prepared for the question than last time. Louise didn't notice any spark of anger, only weariness as he answered. 'I think I answered your questions last time,' he said, his eyes never leaving hers, his voice a low rumbling baritone.

'Fascinating stuff,' said Louise, changing her approach, trying to take Chappell out of his comfort zone.

Chappell's eyebrows narrowed as if he were confused by the comment.

'The DMT drug,' Louise prompted.

'Yes.'

'You've taken it?'

'I believe we've ascertained that.'

Louise leant in towards him. 'What's it like?'

Chappell mirrored her, interlinking his hands as he shifted forward. 'Now there's a question.'

'I've been reading up on it,' she said.

'And what conclusions did you reach?'

He seemed genuinely interested so she kept the conversation going. 'I'd never really encountered it before. I'd heard of it but I didn't know about the research that has gone into it, especially about the shared hallucinations.'

Chappell's face was fascinating to watch. The lines on his forehead creased as he thought about what she had to say. 'Have you read *The God Principle*?'

'No, my research has been mainly online based.'

Chappell stood and walked to the bookcase. 'Here,' he said, returning with a well-worn paperback. 'This is a diary of sorts, written by a shaman from the Peruvian Amazonian rainforest. Obviously, it was transcribed but I think it's a true representation.' Chappell sounded defensive as he handed her the copy. 'A friend gave this to me when I was in the sixth form. It changed everything for me.'

For the first time since he'd turned up at the station, Louise caught a glimpse of the true Jay Chappell. Beyond the charismatic and reserved exterior lurked the enthusiasm and passion of a giddy schoolboy. Louise flicked through the book as Chappell smiled at her. 'You can borrow it,' he beamed.

'Thank you,' said Louise. 'So it was this,' she said, holding up the book, 'that led to your trip to the Amazon?'

'I'm not going to incriminate myself here, am I?'

'It's not illegal to take the drug in a foreign country, Mr Chappell.'

'And here?'

'I'm not going to arrest you for whatever drugs you've taken for personal use in the past. I think we both know that.'

Chappell regained some of his earlier composure. He leant back in his seat. 'I tried to source it in this country and after a few mishaps I managed to take it.'

Louise nodded, encouraging him to continue.

'If you've never taken it, you wouldn't understand but that first time – the first proper time – was a revelation. The things you may have read about, the separation of body, the sense of a wider world beyond our existence, the guardians, have to be experienced. I can't tell you more than you've read but maybe that will change your thinking,' he said, nodding towards the book.

He'd distracted himself, his composure slipping again. He shifted in his seat, his eyes still on her, as if trying to change his outward appearance.

'So why go all the way to Peru?' asked Louise, keen to keep him agitated.

Unfortunately, the question had the opposite effect. Chappell's back straightened, the knowing glint returning to his eye as he appeared to remember the rainforest. 'I needed a guide, needed to experience DMT in its purest form. I tried finding a shaman here but there are a lot of chancers out there.'

'A shaman?'

'I know, it sounds hippyish,' said Chappell with a pitying smile. 'But without a guide, you can't fully understand what you're experiencing. You need to be directed. The effect of psychedelics is to a certain extent determined by where you are, who you are with.'

The explanation reflected what Dr Forrest had told her. Louise wondered if the man was giving away more than he'd intended. 'And you found your spirit guide?'

Chappell became wistful. 'Yes, I did,' he said.

Ten minutes later, Louise sat in her car around the corner from Chappell's bungalow, flicking through the book he'd given her. The conversation had soured following the mention of his shaman. He'd gone quiet, his earlier verbosity disappearing until he'd become almost monosyllabic. Louise hadn't pushed about Victoria and Claire, knowing their conversation had reached a natural conclusion. The DMT found in the three women's samples was still too much of a coincidence for Louise, but she realised there would be a better time to push him further about that link.

She wasn't sure why she was still there, waiting for him as if he were about to lead her somewhere of import. It was hard to admit, but there was something about Chappell she found compelling. It was the way he held himself, his confidence, the deep conviction of his words. She could see why Sally had been taken with him and even when he'd lost himself with his talk of DMT, his enthusiasm had shown a positive side to him.

Louise would have stopped reading the book if it hadn't been so relevant. It was poorly written, something lost in the translation, but even the mention of the near-death experiences, spiritual awakenings and contact with 'them' in the opening chapter hadn't completely invoked her cynicism. She had no doubt the drug triggered such experiences but it was the shaman's certainty that these experiences were real that made her want to continue reading.

She grinned, imagining Robertson's scornful look if she even so much as showed him the book. It was pointless waiting here for Chappell to move with plenty to do back at the office. With a last look down the road, she closed the book and headed back to the station.

Chapter Thirty-Nine

The location of the ceremony had confused Amy, although the others seemed less concerned. After Jay had left yesterday she'd felt bereft. She'd wanted to call Megan but didn't know how to express herself. The conflicting feelings still rallied within her. The negative ones – the growing doubt, the fear about what would happen to Megan – were intensified by where Jay had told them to meet.

They were standing in the boat marina car park in Uphill. It felt wrong returning so close to the scene where Claire had died. The church of Saint Nicholas loomed from the darkness high above them, Claire's landing spot only metres from where they were huddled.

Without Megan and Jay they only numbered four. 'Jay told me where we are supposed to go,' said Beatrice. The youngest of the group, Beatrice was a flame-haired girl who always did her best to look presentable.

Amy resented the way she announced this message as if she were Jay's personal messenger. 'I thought we were supposed to meet here,' she said, hearing and hating the obvious jealousy in her words.

Amy felt worse about herself when Beatrice responded, her face downcast. 'I'm sorry, Amy. Jay thought it best if only one of us knew the actual location. He only told me because I was the last person he met.'

'What about Megan?' said Amy.

'Jay said she would arrive with him,' said Beatrice.

The group went quiet, each of them dealing in their own ways with what that meant.

'You better lead the way,' said Amy, placing her hand on Beatrice's shoulder to demonstrate she felt no animosity towards her.

Beatrice led them through the graveyard of boats, along the mud-caked River Axe that led to the Bristol Channel. Not that many of the boats looked like they were fit for sailing. Even those moored on the river looked as if they wouldn't last the journey through the meandering path to the sea.

Without Jay, the sense of wonder and anticipation Amy had felt walking through the woods in Worlebury was missing. Though that wasn't the only thing bothering her. Beatrice's declaration that Megan would be arriving with Jay cemented the fact that tonight would be Megan's turn to move on. She wanted to be happy for her friend – she knew this was what Megan wanted – but, selfishly, she wanted to keep Megan in her life. She considered asking Jay later if she could go with Megan. It would make everything so much easier, save her further days of unknowing without Megan in her life to help her through it.

But that was a fantasy. Jay would never allow it. She had to be prepared, had to be in the right frame of mind so she could fully let herself go. Jay had showed her that when she'd made her first trip. He'd told her what she should expect to see. They'd talked about slipping from the constraint of herself, and her body, and this was something that would be impossible for her in her current state.

Her foot slipped as they moved through the grassland towards the sea. Gradually, the boat yard eased into the background, as did the imposing view of the church on the hill. The sea air stung her dry lips as the smell of wood smoke drifted towards her.

Jay was already there, sitting by the small campfire with a beaming Megan. Amy had the same visceral reaction she always did on seeing Jay, her pulse spiking as heat spread through her. Seeing Megan with him intensified her feelings and despite all her reservations, she felt momentarily at peace. As if at that precise second, this location was the perfect place to be.

Megan stood and hugged her before turning her attention to everyone else in the group. 'Hi, Amy,' said Jay, taking his turn to embrace her, the comfort of his arms returning her to yesterday outside her block of flats. 'I'm so glad you're here,' he whispered in her ear.

She presumed he said that to everyone but still it soothed her to hear him use those words. His presence eased everyone. Amy saw it in the body language of her friends, the loosening of their limbs as Jay moved between them.

Their camp was situated at the beginning of the beach where the river and sea met. The tide was coming in but was still in the distance. With the campfire lit, the pot boiling, Jay invited everyone to sit.

Amy wanted to ask why they were here – on low ground, close to the edge of the shore with the sea rumbling in the distance – rather than high up. She studied Jay as he made the Ayahuasca tea. He seemed unconcerned, his concentration on his work, and by the time they'd all huddled in a circle around the fire she felt more at peace.

Jay blessed the Ayahuasca using the chants and incantations he'd learnt in the rainforest and one by one filled their bowls. Amy took hers without question, and as Jay held her gaze all her reservations faded away.

The sound of the sea increased as the drug hit her bloodstream. She thought she heard a whispering sound beneath the waves and it helped settle her. She heard Jay's deep voice soothing the group. 'Let yourself go,' he cooed. 'Move towards the waiting room and push through if you are able. You are safe. You are loved. Go to what is waiting for you, to your heaven.'

Amy felt light, insubstantial, as if she could fade into the damp sand beneath her. Everything was fine. Jay was right, everything was right. Her concern about Megan – about everything – faded as she travelled through the impossible geometries, her body humming in ecstasy.

When she returned, Jay smiled at her and there was such warmth and beauty in the gesture that Amy felt she could split into a million pieces. She'd been the first to return and for the briefest of times it was just her and Jay alone in the fading light.

'Was it beautiful?' he asked.

Amy could only smile, her mind still processing the journey the DMT had sent her on.

With the last of the group returning, they began to tell their stories. Just as they'd done before Sally's passing they each took turns explaining their reason for being there, Amy repeating the painful words she'd uttered so many times before.

'It's your turn now,' said Jay to Megan.

Megan held on to Amy as she told the group why she was there. The loneliness that had blighted her life since she was a child was a story they all shared but that didn't make it any easier to hear; and when Megan again recounted the horrendous abuse she'd suffered, Amy had to close her eyes and focus on something else.

The chanting began as soon as Megan finished speaking, Jay unrolling his cloth bag to reveal the single syringe. As he moved around the group, his hand finding Amy's shoulder and staying there for a surprising amount of time, Amy once again wondered why he was going through this pretence. He'd already decided it would be Megan, and when finally he rested on her she felt somehow cheated.

Amy moved towards Megan as Jay prepared it. 'Are you sure?' Amy said, hugging her tight.

It was all moving too fast. There were things she still wanted to tell Megan, but Jay was already next to her friend, injecting the DMT into her system as the group chant of 'death is not the end' reached fever point.

Megan's eyes widened then snapped shut. Her body twitched and she groaned, the DMT entering her system immediately.

Each of the group watched, mesmerised, their chanting falling to a low hum. Were they thinking about their own journeys like Amy? Amy could visualise what happened to her even if she couldn't quite put it into words. The heightened senses were not uncommon, but what made the DMT different was the reality of the trip. She still believed what had happened to her on DMT was real. She'd transcended this world and it didn't matter what others thought about that. Everyone in the group understood, and most importantly so did Jay.

He'd told them what they would see. Megan would be there now. Free from self, in another dimension, ready to move on. All that was left now was for her to leave her body behind.

The thought crashed Amy back into reality. They were on flat land. How would Jay help Megan through the final stage?

As if in response, Jay got to his feet. 'We're going to help Megan move on in a different way,' he said. 'She didn't like the idea of falling, so we will ease her into the next world in a different manner.'

Megan had never told Amy that she didn't like the idea of falling and Jay had told them all that it was a necessary part of the process. The sense of flying, or floating, in an endless space was part of the journey, and falling, he'd told Amy, eased the transition.

She bent down and held Megan's hand, a smile forming on her friend's face even though she was so far away at that point. 'You should look away,' said Jay, as he leant over Megan.

Amy held Megan's hand and looked at Jay.

'Please,' he mouthed.

The chanting increased in speed and volume as Amy looked away. Amy mouthed the words, but no sound left her lips. She felt Megan twitch and shake on the ground, the sound of the group frantic now. The high-pitched refrain – 'death is not the end, death is not the end' – pierced Amy's ears, as she turned back around to see Jay's hand over Megan's nose and mouth.

'Stop,' said Amy, but her words were caught in her throat, or drowned out by the chants, as Megan stopped moving and Jay let go.

The group stopped chanting. Amy thought she'd never experienced such profound silence before. Jay wrapped his arms around her. 'It's okay now, she's gone. She's where she needs to be,' he said, and Amy thought she believed him as his tears reached hers.

They took turns saying goodbye to Megan as Jay extinguished the fire. Somehow this was worse than when they'd left Sally at the foot of the cliffs. Jay had checked Megan's pulse and she was gone but it didn't feel right leaving her by the mud banks.

'The sea will be in soon,' she said to Jay.

Even in the darkness, she could see Jay's features. His eyes penetrating the shadows around him as he replied. 'The sea will take her, Amy. It's what she wanted.'

As Amy made her way home – the group going their separate ways once they reached the boat yard – she thought about what Jay had said, both about Megan not wanting to fall and her wanting to be taken out to sea. She hated doubting Jay – he'd shown her so much, had irrevocably changed her life for the better – but she couldn't stop wondering about whether he'd engineered the situation in his own interest. She could understand it if he had. He'd had to speak to the police, and another body at the foot of the cliffs would only lead to more interest in him. But she wished he'd been open about it rather than clouding the situation with mistruths.

Revellers were out in force through the town. The pubs were kicking out, locals and tourists alike heading for further drinking dens. It was hard to believe that Amy had once been part of this life. She'd rarely had the money to go clubbing, but she'd enjoyed the few times she'd managed to get out, minesweeping drinks or getting boys to buy one for her. She looked down at her drab clothing, her lank hair clinging to her skin. She would be laughed out of the nightclub queue before she even had the chance to reach the front.

She bought a bottle of wine from a late-night off-licence on Milton Road and headed back to her bedsit. The walls of her room seemed to close in on her as she unscrewed the bottle and drank, her body still groggy from the Ayahuasca.

She couldn't believe Megan was gone. She pictured her friend's body all alone on the mud banks and wondered if the sea had reached her yet. Megan had moved on to a better place but it didn't feel right leaving her there to be taken by the water.

Amy took another swig of the coppery wine, her head swimming. The walls were converging in on her now, edging closer with every second. She reached for her phone and looked at the last message Megan had sent her.

I need to see you

'I need to see you, too,' she said, before dialling another number.

'Hello, emergency services, what service would you like?'

Amy paused, her breath catching before she finally said, 'Police, please.'

Chapter Forty

The glare of blue emergency police lights illuminated the night as Louise rounded the corner into Uphill. They'd received the anonymous call just after midnight. She'd still been up, devouring the book Chappell had given her, and had made the journey in fifteen minutes.

The marina was already cordoned off. Behind the barriers, where she'd parked only the other day, two squad cars, one ambulance, and a fire engine battled for space. The uniformed officer recognised her car and let Louise through.

PC Hughes walked over to her as she got out of the car. 'You were the first responder?' she asked him.

'Yes, ma'am. I was with Stracky – Sergeant Strachan – ma'am, over by the Cineworld in Dolphin Square for chucking-out time when the call came in. The sarge is with the paramedics and fire service now, ma'am, trying to locate the body.'

'Have you heard this anonymous message?'

'No, ma'am. The details were relayed to us via dispatch.'

'Okay, can we see if someone can send me the message, please,' said Louise.

Thomas was standing by a line of derelict boats. They were all on stilts, waiting for repairs or restoration. His hair was unbrushed, his clothes rumpled. 'We got you out of bed, DS Ireland,' she said, in greeting.

'Something like that. Why are we here again?'

'Anonymous tip-off. A deceased woman left on the beach. Could be linked to the others.'

Thomas squinted as if trying to make sense of her words. 'What did the message say?'

'I only have the transcription at the moment. There seems to be a general reluctance to play me the message. Come on,' she said, walking to a second cordoned-off area. Another uniformed officer and two officers from the fire service were managing the police line. Louise recognised one of the men, Assistant Chief Fire Officer John McKee.

'John,' she said.

McKee was a rotund man; short in stature but loud of voice. 'Louise. I wouldn't advise either of you to go any further. We have a team out there now trying to locate this body. The sea is yet to hit full tide; when it does it will be pretty treacherous out there,' he said, his voice a rich Welsh tenor. He shone his torch along the meandering inlet of water that headed towards the Channel.

'We'll be okay,' said Louise, just as her radio sounded.

'Strachan here, ma'am. We've located the body. Deceased woman, late twenties or early thirties from what I can see.'

'Okay, keep the scene clean. I'm on my way.'

'That's the thing, ma'am. She's been left on the bank. It appears the sea is closing in. We're going to have to move her.'

'How soon?'

'This very second.'

Louise rubbed her eyes. 'Okay, keep as close to the scene as you can. Take photos if you're able. I'll be there now. Thomas, check where the SOCOs are; get them to the scene as soon as they arrive.'

The fire officer finished radioing his own team before saying, 'I'll lead the way.'

◆ ◆ ◆

McKee took a disparaging look at Louise's footwear as they moved past the last of the boats and on to the grassland. The seawater was fully in now, filling the meandering river. 'Let's hope we don't hit any mud,' he said.

'Let's,' said Louise, rolling her eyes as she followed the fire officer towards the glare of torches in the distance.

'We had no choice,' said Strachan, as she arrived at the scene. The body was a few feet from the seawater. 'She should be okay here,' he added, gazing over at the corpse.

Although the body had been moved, Louise was still careful not to contaminate the scene any more than necessary. The woman's eyes were closed, a serene look on her face. An unwelcome image flashed before Louise's eyes – Emily in place of the woman – which she banished with a furious shake of her head. 'Where did you find her?'

'She was in the Channel. Her back is caked in mud,' said Strachan, holding up his sludge-coated hands as if in evidence.

'Let's cordon this area and wait for the SOCOs. Any sign of what killed her?'

Strachan shook his head. 'From a cursory glance, no. No sign of blood or broken bones.'

Louise shone her torch around the surrounding area. It was hard to believe this was Weston. Despite the time of night, the heat was intense and there was a remoteness to the area only dashed when she looked to her right and saw the distant lights of the seafront, the pier poking out into the sea.

Although the location was close to where Claire Smedley had taken her life, nothing about the location matched the other three deaths. The nearest cliff was back at the marina, the same cliff Claire had fallen from. From what she could see, and what Strachan had told her, the deceased woman had not fallen to her death.

As she waited for the SOCOs to arrive, she thought back to Chappell. The relaxed way he'd been with her. Could he possibly have had a role to play in this? Louise had to concede that it seemed unlikely. If he'd been planning something he'd hidden the fact very well. However, she didn't believe it was beyond him. He had a peculiar sense of confidence she'd rarely encountered. She could imagine him inviting her into his house, talking to her about DMT, his trip to the Amazon, while all the time planning the night's events.

Not that she would give voice to her thoughts. She was already obsessing in a way that contradicted her training, making uncharacteristic mistakes. She shouldn't have visited Chappell earlier that day. But what if he was responsible? What if her turning up had prompted him to play a role in the woman's death?

The SOCOs arrived and she moved back towards the car park with the fire chief. 'This has been happening a lot recently, young women . . .' said McKee, as if needing to break the silence, his boots crunching on the dry ground next to the river.

There was no judgement in his words, only a weary recognition of the situation. He would be aware of the other cases, the three women who'd taken their own lives. It was easy, if a little lazy of thought, to presume this was a similar case. 'Let's hope this is a coincidence,' said Louise.

'I'm from South Wales, you know,' said McKee.

'You would never have guessed,' said Louise, deadpan.

'Family in Bridgend.'

Louise lowered her eyes as it dawned on her why he'd told her where he was from. 'Tragic thing,' she said.

'Bizarre. All those young folk taking their lives. You think it's happening here?'

Louise recalled Tania Elliot making the same connection. Whether or not the woman back along the shore was another suicide, it was hard to get away from the fact that something unusual was happening in the town. Maybe that was why she was obsessing over Chappell. Searching for an explanation that just wasn't there. 'I don't know, John. I hope this is just a sad coincidence.'

They looked at each other, both acknowledging that hope was often another word for wishful thinking.

'I've got it,' said Thomas, approaching them.

'I hope it's not contagious,' said McKee, walking off to the fire engine.

'Here,' said Thomas, handing Louise his phone. 'The anonymous call we received.'

Louise pressed the play button on his phone. After listening once, she pressed play again:

Police, how may I help you?
There's a body. You need to get it before the sea takes it away.
It's the body of my friend.
Can I take your name, please?
There isn't time. You must get there now.
Is your friend in danger?
It's Megan. She's dead.

The caller's voice was eerily calm. She went on to explain the location in detail before hanging up.

'We have a trace on this?'

'Only a number at present. Phone is switched off. I have someone back at the station calling. Coulson might be able to try and locate the caller. He's heading towards the station now.'

Louise listened to the message again. She placed the caller to be in her thirties though it was so difficult to tell with voice only. She closed her eyes as the woman spoke, picked up the laboured breathing behind her voice. It was as if she was forcing herself to stay calm. When she said, 'There isn't time', her words ran into each other, slurred as if she'd been drinking.

She handed the phone back to Thomas.

He gazed at her as if trying to read her mind. 'You look like you're about to do something.'

Louise ran both hands through her hair. A wave of tiredness came over her as she realised she hadn't thought about Emily or Paul since she'd arrived at the marina; or rather, she hadn't actively thought about them – they were always there, at the periphery of her thoughts, waiting to be dealt with.

'We could go and wake Jay Chappell up?' she said, more out of mischief than anything else.

Thomas shot her an enigmatic smile, too similar to the expression she'd seen on Chappell for her liking. 'I'm not sure that would be the best idea, do you, boss?'

Louise grimaced. 'If you're calling me "boss", you must really mean it.'

'It's just that—'

Louise stopped him. 'I know, I know.' Of course it was a bad idea. Chappell had attended the station voluntarily. At the moment, the only thing connecting him to the case was the footage of him with Sally at the pier. Louise had yet to include her visit to him yesterday on the case record, but a call in the middle of the night for something that could be wholly unrelated wouldn't be professional and could quite easily lead to a complaint. 'Why don't you go home and grab some sleep. Looks like we will have a long day tomorrow,' she said.

'Far be it for me to comment, but maybe you should, too . . . boss.'

Louise's eyes widened in mock outrage. 'Maybe you're right again,' she said, stifling a yawn.

Chapter Forty-One

It was after 3 a.m. by the time Louise reached her bungalow, and she'd barely managed to sleep when her phone rang at 6 a.m.

'Mum?' she said, shielding her eyes from the sunlight glaring through the bedroom window.

'Sorry to wake you, Lou.'

Louise sat up in bed, the events from last night, from the last few weeks, rushing at her. 'What is it, Mum? Is it Paul? Emily?' she asked, noting the high-pitched sound escaping her mouth as she said her niece's name.

'Everything's okay. Paul called last night.'

'What did he say, why didn't you call me?' It was too early, and she'd had too little sleep to deal with a cryptic conversation.

'He called to say that everything is okay. Emily is having a lovely time and they will be back next week. I didn't want to wake you last night, that's why I'm calling now.'

Louise stopped short of reminding her mother that it was 6 a.m. 'What time did he call?'

Her mother hesitated before answering. 'Just after midnight.'

'How did he sound?'

'He was fine.'

'Had he been drinking?'

Her mother clicked her tongue, as if somehow Louise was in the wrong for asking the question. 'He sounded a little slurred but I believe him, Lou.'

They both knew she wouldn't be calling if that was truly the case but Louise didn't push it. 'Did he say where he was?'

'No.'

'Did you ask?'

A sigh. 'Listen, Lou, I think maybe you should try him again. I think he'll listen to you.'

'I'll try, Mum,' said Louise, though she'd been calling her brother every day since he'd taken Emily away.

She showered and changed on automatic pilot, pouring a coffee to take with her to the station. Summer had vanished, its replacement a grey ocean of cloud hanging over the town in latent threat. Only the heat remained, her shirt clinging to her skin despite the early hour as she opened the car door. Soundlessly, she lifted her hand to Mr Thornton, who'd opened his front door in unison.

Leaning in to place her coffee in the cup holder, Louise stuck her head back out. 'Looks like rain,' she said to the elderly man.

Mr Thornton nodded and she was sure there was a hint of a smile on his lips as he retreated back inside.

The clouds threatened to break but held as she made the short drive to the station. She played the anonymous call on loop as she drove through the empty streets. Had the caller left the woman by the sea? Had she left her to die or had she been dead when she left? Did the caller know Jay Chappell, or were the deaths unrelated? Such questions rolled through Louise's head, each unanswerable at the present time.

As she parked up and walked to the office, Louise discovered she wasn't the only person searching for answers. 'DI Blackwell. Can you confirm another body was found close to Uphill Marina yesterday evening?' came the question, as soon as she'd left the car.

Louise looked up at the clouds as if some answers could be found there, before turning to face the person who'd asked the question. 'I can confirm a body was found near the marina, Tania, yes. As for it being "another" body—'

'Another suicide, Inspector.'

Louise closed her eyes, hoping that when she opened them the journalist would have disappeared. She was acutely aware of her body at that moment – the heaviness of each muscle, the joints of her bones, the roar of blood in her ears – as exhaustion threatened to engulf her. 'Print what you want,' she said, opening the station front door and pulling it shut before the journalist could follow her inside.

She was surprised to see Thomas already in the office. 'I thought you were getting some sleep,' she said to him, almost tearing the offered cup of coffee from his grip.

'I could say the same thing about you.'

'I couldn't sleep,' said Louise, though she felt if she lowered her eyes now she would do just that.

'Ditto. Dempsey has taken the body. Looks like we have a name,' said Thomas, pointing to the picture of the corpse he'd already posted to the crime board. 'Megan Davies. I've just finished a search on her. I have an address if you want to join me?'

'Inspector Blackwell, a word.' DCI Robertson's presence had been unknown to Louise, and the reverberation of his Glaswegian accent in the empty office permeated her bones like the sound of chalk on a blackboard.

'Robbo's in by the way,' said Thomas, walking back to his desk.

'Oh, thanks, DS Ireland,' said Louise, heading towards her boss's office.

'Another one?' said Robertson, before she had a chance to sit down.

The tension was palpable, her relationship with her superior strained ever since the overtime fiasco. It had to be resolved, and the only solution she could think of was giving him a result on the case. If she kept presenting him with issues then sooner or later he would assume she was simply repeating her behaviour from her time at MIT. If it reached that stage her position would be untenable. She only wished she had something more to offer him.

'Possibly. However, the manner of death is completely different to the others. We don't know if it's suicide at present. Could simply be accidental death.'

'Let's hope so, shall we.'

'Thanks for the pep talk, sir, but I really need to be getting on with some work. We think we have a positive identification and address for the woman.'

'You know what I'm doing after you've left this office.'

Louise could almost visualise the energy leaving her body.

Robertson's upper lip protruded as if he were holding back a frown. 'I'm going to call Assistant Chief Constable Morley.'

'Well, enjoy that.'

'Come on, Louise. A fourth body?'

'It's not as if I'm killing them, Iain.'

'Maybe not, but what do I have to tell Morley?'

'You could tell him there were over twenty suicides in Bridgend.'

'Are you fucking mad? I tell him that and this will go to HQ before I have the chance to hang up.'

Louise felt as if her whole time in Weston had been leading up to this conversation. Robertson had always supported her. He'd never come out and said it, but she was sure he believed what she'd told him about the Walton case. How Finch had lied, how Morley wanted her out of the force. She knew too that he had his own pressures. Morley thought of himself as some sort of media darling and hated nothing more than bad publicity. But something had to give.

'Do you ever wonder why we even have a CID department here, Iain?'

Robertson began shaking his head.

'I'm serious. What is the point, if every time we have an issue with a case Morley and the rest of HQ threaten to take it away from us?'

'You know it's not as simple as that, Louise.'

'Maybe not, but I don't want to have to fight Portishead every time I'm trying to do my job. Do you think MIT would have even bothered with this case? Because I'll tell you, they wouldn't have. At least not until Sally's death. And even then, I'm not sure. I was the one who found Claire Smedley's laptop. I found the connection between her and Victoria Warrington. Maybe tell Morley that.'

Robertson rubbed his brow as if he had something glued to it. 'This witness. Jay Chappell. Anything there?'

'Maybe,' said Louise, sighing.

Robertson glanced up at her and appeared to concede he'd lost the discussion. He opened his arms out. 'Fine, go,' he said.

Thomas drove them to the Brean Down holiday park where Megan Davies had lived. Louise snuck a glance at Thomas as he drove past the spot she'd stopped at yesterday, around the corner from Jay Chappell's house. She didn't know why she felt guilty. Beyond not having updated her report about her visit she hadn't done anything wrong. Maybe it was the way she'd surveyed the perimeter of the house, had toyed with the idea of breaking in to take a look at what Chappell was hiding, that bothered her.

The book he'd given her was in her bag. She wondered what Thomas would think of it. She promised herself to add it into the report once they'd done visiting Megan's home and tried to banish the feeling that she'd made another mistake by taking it. She'd almost finished it. Most of it was easy to dismiss. The translation was truly awful and much of the text featured abstract spiritual musings. What intrigued Louise was the detail the shaman recounted not only of his experiences on the drug, but those of his pupils. As Forrest suggested, there was a sense of a shared experience. The accounts discussed the so-called guides – some wildly described, alien and disturbing, others more human-like – that Dr Forrest had mentioned; and if it hadn't been for her discussion with Forrest, she would have dismissed the book out of hand. But what she had to consider was Chappell's reaction to the book. He'd told her it had changed his life and she had to unravel what exactly that meant.

The sun had yet to break through the blanket of cloud. Under the grey sky, the holiday resorts and beach shops looked woefully out of place. It made her wonder why people would travel to the area, with its unpredictable weather patterns and brown sea when there were so many better alternatives.

Not that the place wasn't without its beauty. As Thomas drove into a caravan park, Louise glanced over at Brean Down. Through a fug of mist, the promontory jutted out into the sea. A group of walkers in distinctive waterproofs were out for a morning hike, climbing the stone steps that from Louise's angle looked impossibly steep.

Thomas parked up. Louise had been in the same caravan park before with Farrell. That had been in winter, but she experienced the same feeling of bleakness when she stepped out of the car as she'd done in the colder months. With their identical doors all shut, the static caravans appeared empty, the park desolate.

As Thomas took a set of keys off the park's warden, Louise wondered how many more times she would have to go through this; how many more homes of deceased young women she would have to see before they got some understanding on what was happening.

'It's rented from the holiday park,' said the warden. 'They sometimes use it as overspill for their staff in busy periods.'

'Thank you. We'll get you if we need anything else,' said Louise, waiting for the warden to reluctantly walk away before opening the caravan door.

The interior was a great improvement on the derelict caravan where Sally had lived. Although dated, the furnishings were well maintained and the place had the feel of somewhere recently cleaned as if ready for new occupants. It wasn't until they reached the small bedroom cabin towards the rear that they even saw any of Megan's belongings. A neatly folded pile of clothes had been placed at the end of the bed, next to a toiletries bag.

'That's a bit strange,' said Thomas, pointing to the pink pillowcase and duvet cover, with its picture of a Disney princess on it.

'Comfort in childish things,' said Louise. She tried not to let Thomas see that she was looking away. Emily loved the character plastered over the duvet. She had at least three doll versions of the Disney princess, as well as the outfit. Louise's eyes began to moisten and she was forced to leave the caravan. Thankfully, Thomas didn't follow.

Louise pressed her back against the cold exterior of the caravan, the light breeze prickling her skin.

Megan had been twenty-eight. Louise pictured her alone in the caravan at night, wrapped in her childhood bedspread. Loneliness was a plague Louise understood. It had threatened to overwhelm her on occasions and it was something all four women appeared to have suffered from. Had this been what had driven Megan to take her life? The potential of one more night alone in the desolate caravan park, when the world was going by just down the road, too much for her to take?

Louise tried not to think of Emily alone as an adult, wrapped in the same childish comforters. It was frightening how easy it was to imagine something like this happening to her niece; not that she needed a reason, but the thought made her even more determined to find out what had happened to these unfortunate women.

Thomas looked towards her as she returned but didn't say anything. She wondered if he had the same concerns, if he was projecting current events on to fears about his son's future now he was getting divorced. It pained her to know that she would probably never know, that their relationship wasn't close enough to talk that intimately.

'Let's look for a note,' she said.

The search didn't last long, Megan's belongings easily found and processed. The note was folded neatly inside the small holdall in the wardrobe. It was longer than the others. Louise tried not to be diverted by the horrendous recollection of systematic abuse in the note, but promised herself that when this was all finished she would open a case investigating the accusations within. The note finished with the now-familiar refrain:

There are other worlds than this
Death is not the end

Louise placed the note in an evidence bag, and added the teddy bear from Megan's bed for processing.

'Old school,' said Thomas, retrieving a brick phone from under the mattress and handing it to Louise.

There was no pass code and Louise gained access to the phone with no trouble. Trying the address book, and recent calls, she realised there was only one contact on Megan's phone.

She didn't need to check to know it belonged to the anonymous caller from last night. They had a name now. Louise clicked on the phone number. 'Looks like we're looking for someone called Amy,' she said.

Chapter Forty-Two

From her fourth-floor window, Amy stuck her head out for something approaching the tenth time that day. The grey clouds looked out of place, as if they were hiding the sky, though they aptly reflected her mood. It was now 2 p.m. and she hadn't called the café to say she wasn't going to go into work today. Her phone was still switched off. She hadn't touched it since calling the police. The device was buried beneath a pile of unwashed clothes. But out of sight didn't mean out of mind. The phone – and the events surrounding her need to call the police – was all Amy could think about.

She oscillated from worrying that she'd made a mistake to needing to know what had happened to Megan, from concerns over whether she should have called to a desperation that she hadn't called in time. Were there messages waiting for her? Had the police taken her seriously? Had they recovered Megan's body in time?

She didn't know for sure why she'd called the police beyond the nagging feeling that it was wrong to let Megan's body be dragged out to sea and an uneasiness about the night's events.

Jay had never given any instruction on what would happen when they'd passed over, beyond the spiritual. Amy had assumed the body ceased to matter to him after that moment, a fact evidenced by the way he hadn't seemed overly concerned that Sally had momentarily survived her fall in Sand Bay. According to Jay, she'd already passed over to the next realm. Why, then, had he wanted Megan's body to be swept out to sea?

The only logical conclusion Amy could draw was that he didn't want the authorities to find her body. It was understandable considering he'd had his photograph in the paper and had been interviewed by the police. Yet it still felt wrong to Amy. She believed in Jay, still thought that her future lay in following Megan and the others as Jay had guided her, but it wasn't right for Megan to slip away unknown. Amy and the others from the group were Megan's only family, would have been the only people to have known she'd disappeared, had her body not been found. And for all Jay's talk about the body being a vessel, and her own brief experience of escaping from that prison, Amy didn't like the idea of Megan's body never being discovered.

But that wasn't what was really bothering her; at least, not just that. Hard as she tried not to dwell on it, she had to accept that Jay had killed Megan last night. He'd held her down and snuffed the life from her as Amy had uselessly held on to her hand. She told herself it was no different from before. Jay had guided Victoria, Claire and Sally to their deaths, had all but pushed them over the cliff edges. Why then did this feel so different? She wanted to believe she was reacting to the physicality of Megan dying. Jay had told them Megan hadn't wanted to fall, but hadn't there been an easier way of helping her into the next life?

Despite the clouds outside, it was repressively hot inside the flat. Amy considered going for a walk but couldn't face the day. Dressed in only her underwear, she huddled on the sofa and watched videos on her laptop. She did her best to avoid thinking about Megan. She should be happy for her friend but the manner of her death, and what happened afterwards, had dampened that euphoria. She tried to latch on to her own trip from last night but in the stark reality of existence, it was hard to grasp the sense of detachment, the fading of insecurities she'd felt after drinking the tea. If only she could go back there now, all her concerns over Megan, and Jay, would vanish. And as her doorbell rang, she thought maybe that time was going to come sooner rather than later.

She pulled on a T-shirt and stuck her head out of the window again, surprised when she didn't see Jay's familiar figure waiting for her.

'Nicole,' she called. 'What are you doing here?'

'I was checking you were alive,' shouted the girl.

'Wait, I'll buzz you up.'

Nicole was out of breath by the time she reached Amy's front door. She was pasty, her brow covered in sweat. 'Are you okay?' asked Amy, as she opened the door for her.

'Am I okay?' said Nicole. 'Where were you today? Keith is furious.'

Amy couldn't muster any concern for her boss. It was only her second-ever sick day. Keith would probably find a way to dock her pay but she could live with that. 'Did he send you?'

'No, of course not. I was worried about you. I found your address in the staff book.'

Amy blushed. Just hearing those words made her feel better. 'Sorry, Nicole. Thanks for coming over.'

'So?'

'Oh. I didn't feel so good this morning. My phone wasn't charged and I kept drifting in and out of sleep. I should have called in. Sorry.'

'You don't need to apologise to me. I'm just glad you're okay. Have you taken anything?'

Nicole's concern was plastered over her face and Amy did her best to reassure her. 'I'm fine. Must have been one of those twenty-four-hour things. I had some soup and bread earlier. I feel much better.'

Nicole stared at her, her eyes holding her gaze in a way that reminded Amy of Jay. 'What aren't you telling me?'

'Nothing. I'm fine,' said Amy, trying to convince herself. She'd only now remembered that Nicole had met Megan that one time. It was a shame Nicole hadn't had the chance to know the real Megan. Megan had acted out of character that day, and it was a shame that would be Nicole's only memory of her. Amy hoped Nicole's memories of her would be more positive.

She made some tea as Nicole opened the window. 'I confess, I have another reason for being here,' said Nicole, after a minute of comfortable silence.

Amy fought her initial panic, wondering if somehow the police had traced her call and gone to Nicole at the café. 'Oh yes, what's that?'

Nicole handed her a pamphlet. 'It's a free course being run by the library. Business Essentials. I thought perhaps we could go together. Find out what it takes to run a business.'

Amy smiled. The young woman's innocence and optimism was infectious. Working with Keith had yet to grind it out of her, and Amy was pleased she would soon be back at university. 'I'll take a look,' she said, 'but I could do with getting some sleep.'

Nicole couldn't mask the look of hurt. Amy would have loved her to stay, just being in her company had perked her up, but there was a danger for Nicole in being in her orbit. With her call to the police, and Jay being in the papers, she didn't want to risk Nicole being drawn into something she didn't deserve. It would be better for her not to know Amy at that moment.

'I'll look at it, Nicole,' repeated Amy, as she walked her to the front door of the bedsit.

'Sorry, I didn't mean to impinge in any way. It's just—'

'It's fine. I don't think I'll be opening my first Michelin-starred restaurant any time soon, but maybe this will be fun,' she said, waving the pamphlet in the air. 'We can talk tomorrow after work?'

This seemed to placate Nicole, who left with a smile on her face. Despite recent events, Amy was pleased to be alone once more and when there was a knock on the door ten minutes later she didn't answer it. As she hadn't heard the doorbell ring, she presumed it was one of her neighbours. Whoever it was they were persistent, and Amy shuffled towards the door after the third set of knocks.

She was surprised to see Nicole standing there when she opened the door, still smiling; however, that was nothing in comparison to the shock of seeing Jay standing behind her.

Chapter Forty-Three

The noise of the holiday camp leaked through the walls of the pre-fab hut they'd been given to conduct their interviews in. The sound of giddy youngsters, and the beeping of electronics from the arcade machines, while not as vociferous, reminded Louise of the noise she'd endured at the pier earlier in the week. They'd gone straight to the campsite after leaving Megan's caravan, keen to interview her former colleagues in the hope of finding out both more about her and the anonymous caller they now knew as Amy.

The morning hadn't gone well. It felt like they'd spoken to every monosyllabic teenager in the county, each with an almost identical story to tell: Megan kept herself to herself, and no, they'd never heard of anyone called Amy.

Before leaving for the station, Louise tried Amy's number again. 'Amy, this is Louise Blackwell. We found your name as the only contact on your friend Megan's phone. I know you're probably scared and it must be daunting coming forward to the police but please contact us. You can also speak to me directly if you feel you are in danger, or if you just want to talk. I can help, Amy. Please call.' Louise added her private mobile number before hanging up.

'You think she's in danger?' asked Thomas, once they were back in the car.

Louise shrugged. She thought about the restrained panic she'd heard in Amy's voice as she called in the message. It was conceivable she'd had a change of heart after leaving her friend to be taken by the sea, but the hesitation she'd heard sounded to Louise as if the woman had something else she'd wanted to say.

The station was a different place when she returned. The ghost-town feel of early morning had evaporated and it felt overcrowded as she sat at her desk and checked her messages. Joslyn had sent through a cryptic email to her private account, which effectively said she'd had no luck tracking Paul yet, and there was a note to call Stephen Dempsey at the coroner's office.

'Hi, Louise, thanks for getting back to me,' said Dempsey. 'I decided to start working early on the body discovered this morning. Megan Davies.'

'Slow time of year?'

'No, not really,' said Dempsey, ignoring her attempt at small talk. 'I took a second look once we'd got her back to the mortuary because of the poor light at the scene and I'm glad I did. I'd missed some signs of bruising around the mouth and nose which combined with the blood in her eyes and the high levels of carbon dioxide in her blood suggest she was suffocated. I need to do some more tests but it looks like this wasn't simply another suicide.'

After hanging up, Louise told Thomas about Dempsey's findings.

'So we have a murder case to work alongside the three suicides?' he said.

Louise bit the inside of her cheek. 'I don't think so. Remember, we have a suicide note for Megan. I think we might be looking at four murder cases.'

Louise spent the next two hours preparing the necessary documentation for the Megan Davies case while Thomas re-examined the three previous autopsy reports for details they might have missed. Louise called Dempsey back to confirm he would prioritise the case, and followed up by calling FIU and requesting that hair samples be sent to Dr Everson at the Met. Despite which, she knew the results would take longer than she wanted. Her restlessness was a familiar feeling, and she fought her frustration as she accompanied Thomas to Jay Chappell's bungalow. If Chappell's fingerprints or DNA were found on Megan's body they would be able to make an arrest. Until then, she had to hope that FIU would do as they'd promised and prioritise Megan's case.

'Confession time,' she said to Thomas, as he drove towards Berrow.

Thomas's eyes widened to a comical extreme. She'd enjoyed working with him over the last few days. It was as if the old Thomas was returning. It was now a rarity for him to turn up to work hungover. The bloodshot eyes were gone and the combination of smarter clothes and being clean-shaven had taken a few years off him. At another time, she might have pursued her attraction for him but it was still too complicated, and probably always would be. 'Well?' he said.

'I visited Chappell yesterday. I haven't had time to add it to the report yet.'

Thomas let her words settle. 'Haven't had time?' he said.

'In case you haven't noticed, a few things have been happening of late.'

Thomas returned his attention to the road. He was right, of course. However busy they might have been, she should have added her visit to the report yesterday. If she was being honest with herself, something had held her back. She didn't know if it was the nature of the conversation she'd had with Chappell, the book he'd given her, or the fact that she'd waited around the corner from his house for nearly an hour after meeting him. There was a hint of obsession to her actions, and at the edge of her thoughts was the worry that Chappell had somehow got to her. She recalled the warmth of his rich voice, the almost soothing way he'd spoken to her. All things she didn't wish to share with Thomas, and definitely not on a police report.

Like yesterday, there was no car on the driveway. Thomas knocked on the door, as Louise peered once again through the gaps in his window blinds.

'So what happened when you talked to him yesterday?' asked Thomas. They were back in the car, Louise having left a message for Chappell on her phone.

'I went inside the house and questioned him,' said Louise, hating the defensiveness in her voice. 'I can write it all up for you, Sergeant, if you'd like?'

Thomas didn't react. He pulled out of the driveway, the hint of a smile on his face easing Louise's increased heartbeat, and they headed out of Berrow. 'Apologies,' she said.

'Don't need to apologise to me. You're the boss,' said Thomas.

She let the wind-up go. 'We need to get everyone on to this, Thomas. I want to talk to Chappell as a matter of urgency.'

'He doesn't work, does he?'

'Nothing official, no.'

'Quite a nice place though.'

'From the outside, yes,' said Louise, recalling the desolate interior of the extended bungalow. 'Anything strike you as odd about him when you were processing him?'

'Not really. I guess he wasn't very fazed by it all. He didn't get nervous or tighten up. Nothing seemed to bother him.'

'He doesn't lack confidence,' said Louise, drumming her fingers on the dash of the car. 'I'm going to get someone out there.' She called Simone and told her to arrange for a patrol car to wait close to Chappell's house for his return. In the absence of locating Amy, speaking to Jay Chappell was their logical next step and as he didn't have a work address, using resources to wait for his return made sense to Louise. Not that she needed to defend herself to Simone.

'How's your little niece?' asked Thomas, stopping her internal monologue in its tracks and replacing it with a different kind of worry.

He'd asked her the same question the other day in Nailsea, and her first thought was that he knew about Emily's current situation. 'She's fine,' she said, testing his reaction. She didn't want to lie to Thomas, but the less people knew about Paul's unannounced holiday the easier it would be to manage.

'I know it's a cliché, but they do grow up so fast, don't they? Noah is four now, going on twenty. I see the change in him every time I'm with him. I guess not living with him twenty-four-seven makes the changes that much more apparent.'

Sometimes in her line of work it was hard to remember that other people had their own issues. Here she was worried about her brother and niece, when Thomas was going through a divorce and living away from his only child. 'They change in a blink of an eye. I sometimes go a couple of weeks without seeing Emily, and it's like meeting a new person,' said Louise. 'Sorry, I hope that doesn't—'

'No, no. I know what you mean. It really isn't that bad. As I said, I'm seeing more of him now than before. I'm looking at a two-bedroom flat this weekend as well. I think I'll be skint forever but I'd like somewhere decent for him to stay when I'm with him.'

'That's great, Thomas. I'm pleased for you. Whereabouts?'

'Over in Worle,' said Thomas.

'Oh really?'

'Don't worry,' said Thomas, smiling. 'I'm not stalking you. Worle is quite a big place.'

Louise matched his smile. 'Just don't go expecting any baby-sitting.' She was amazed to find her eyes welling up again at the thought of Thomas alone looking after his son. The parallel to Paul and Emily was obvious but her visceral reaction was surprising. She'd always managed to separate the personal and professional. That she was struggling to do so, coupled with the mistakes she was making, was beginning to concern her.

'Everything okay?' said Thomas, his eyes firmly on the road ahead.

Louise blinked her tears away. 'Yes, just a bit tired,' she said as Thomas turned the corner into the station car park. 'It never ends, does it?' she added, spotting DCI Finch's car in her space.

Chapter Forty-Four

Amy had never seen such an expression on Nicole's face before. Her skin was flushed, and the smile forming on her lips made her look much older. How long had she been talking to Jay? She'd left over ten minutes ago. Had she been with him all this time? Amy wasn't sure if she was jealous or worried. With everything that had happened to Megan, she felt protective of her young friend. Yet, Jay's appearance still had a visceral effect on her. She felt her own face flush red as her heartbeat sped like a giddy schoolgirl's on her first date.

'I found your friend outside,' said Nicole, the movement of her eyes saying, why haven't you told me about him before?

Jay held his hands up. 'I wasn't loitering, I promise,' he said.

Amy dragged her gaze away from his perfect smile towards Nicole. 'Thanks, Nicole. See you tomorrow,' she said, worried she sounded too eager for her to depart.

'Unless you want to join us?' said Jay.

Nicole blushed again. Amy saw the indecision on her face. She knew the effect Jay could have on people so understood her reaction. 'I think Nicole needs to get going, don't you? Don't want to be late for your parents.'

Amy regretted the parent jibe as soon as she'd said it. Subconsciously she was belittling her friend, highlighting her youth. Again she wondered if this was due to jealousy or protectiveness.

If Nicole was hurt by the comment she hid it well. 'Nice to meet you,' she said, head bowed to Jay.

'And it was lovely to meet you, Nicole,' said Jay, taking Nicole's hand.

Nicole's face flushed so red it looked as if she was about to pass out. Her innocent giddiness was so reminiscent of Megan that Amy had to fight the sob rising in her throat.

'Come here,' said Jay, softly, once Nicole had left.

His arms were held out in front of him and Amy slipped hers around his body as if she was coming home. She sunk into his warmth, the smell of citrus on his skin so familiar that she couldn't remember a time without it. He held her, the strength of his body locking her in place. She closed her eyes as she recalled him holding Megan, the way her body shook as he guided her to the next world. Burying herself into his chest, Amy wondered what would happen if he increased the pressure of his grip. Would he be able to squeeze the life out of her? Would she struggle if he tried?

As if in answer, Jay let her go. 'You weren't at work today?' he asked.

The question threw her. She'd never seen him at the café before and wondered why he would choose to visit her there now. 'I didn't feel up to it,' she said, for the first time since he'd arrived noticing the small holdall he must have dropped by the door.

Jay turned to follow her eye line to the bag. When he looked at her, he wore the same innocent expression he always had when he wanted her to do something. 'I was thinking maybe I could stay,' he said. As if it were a question; as if she had a choice.

If he'd appeared there like this yesterday there would have been no hesitation – for so long, it had been all she'd longed for – but now the time had come she was tentative.

Jay moved back towards her, his hands held out in front of him. Amy frowned and reached for them, a surge of power rushing through her as he gripped her hands in his. 'I know you must have your doubts, Amy,' he said. 'Especially after last night. Not everyone understands what we're trying to achieve. Megan understood. She wanted me to be the one to guide her to the next level.'

Amy still didn't know if the police had managed to get to Megan in time. She hadn't dared to look at her phone since she'd switched it off. It was buried beneath a pile of clothes in the corner of the room. What would Jay say if he knew about the phone, about her call last night? What if he already knew? He always seemed to know everything before she did. Maybe that was why he was there, to punish her for trying to spoil his work.

'You do understand, don't you?' said Jay.

Amy tried to control the tremor running through her body. Jay looked so genuine that it was impossible to doubt him. He'd never let her down before, and him being there must mean only one thing. It was her turn.

'Great,' said Jay. 'How about we make some tea?'

All of Amy's resolve disappeared as Jay removed his materials from the bag. She loved the way his face changed when he was working with his medicine. Whether it was the precise measurement of the tea, or the concentration he used when filling the syringe, his face always became other-worldly. She could see this was the most important thing in his life, superseded everything else; everyone else. She'd noticed it that first time, as he'd made the tea in his van, and even then she'd known that was in part what made him special.

'We will make it a bit stronger tonight,' he said. 'In preparation.'

So this was to be it? This was the way it had happened with Megan. Did that mean it would be Amy's turn next?

'Loosen your clothes, lie on the couch,' he said, his voice dropping an octave, resonating against the floorboards and windows, rushing through her bones and already soothing her.

She did as instructed, inhaling and exhaling as he'd taught her, preparing herself for the tea.

'It's ready,' he said. She felt the tension in her body as his hand moved beneath her back, guiding her until she was sitting up straight. If Jay noticed, he didn't mention it. He placed his nose to the brew and waited a heartbeat before handing it to her.

For a moment she was racked with indecision. She'd never felt this way with Jay before. She closed her eyes, picturing Megan struggling beneath Jay's tight grip. He would never purposely harm her, would he?

'Take it, Amy,' said Jay, the bowl of tea still held out in front of him.

He must have noticed her indecision as she took the bowl from him. Her hands were shaking but there was no going back now. She fought the first wave of nausea as she downed the warm drink in one. The shock hit her as the vibrations rushed through her body. She felt it deeper this time than yesterday, Jay true to his word about the strength. Although she remained conscious of her body, she closed her eyes as another world played before her, a place of sharply defined colour and pattern. She was flying through this world of shapes, in and out, between and through the extraordinary geometries. Nothing else mattered, her thoughts and worries extinguished. She pushed through these figures, sensing what lay beyond, what she really wanted to see, while at the same time content to just be there, happy to surrender herself to this eternity of shape drifting.

Jay was gazing at her as she came back, his smile so compassionate she wanted to cry. The vibrations were fading but her skin was hypersensitive, the gentlest draught of air raising pimples on her skin. She couldn't tell how much time had passed when she eventually spoke. 'I'm ready,' she said.

'I know you are,' said Jay, moving towards her and enveloping her once more in his arms.

Chapter Forty-Five

Tension seeped through Louise's body as Thomas parked up. That she couldn't shake her involuntary reaction to Finch's presence angered her. If Thomas had noticed, he was keeping quiet. It wasn't that unusual for someone from Portishead to make an appearance and Finch hadn't shied away from Weston on Louise's account. She knew he revelled in his status, liked to think his position in the MIT set him apart. The cheap trick of parking in her space was nothing new. What troubled her more was Finch turning up again now that the case was growing in importance. She pictured him in the office, worming his way into the investigation, making subtle comments on the current inadequacies of their approach.

She wasn't surprised to see him chatting to Simone in the CID office. Simone struggled to conceal her attraction to him every time he visited. She was stroking her hair now, leaning into Finch as he told her something supposedly hilarious.

Louise heard a greeting from behind her. 'Hey, boss.' Finch looked over as she turned to face the source of the welcome.

'Greg. Nice to see you. Fleeting visit or you back for good?'

Farrell was his usual impeccably dressed self, his hair gelled into a neat parting, the shine on his polished shoes matching the gleam of his teeth. 'Fleeting visit, I'm afraid. I'm here with DCI Finch,' he said, a hint of apology in his voice.

'Everything okay?'

'Yeah, it's all going really well.'

'That's great to hear, Greg, it really is.'

'Louise, how are you?' said Finch, leaving Simone to talk to herself as he joined them.

'Tim,' said Louise, resisting the urge to call him Timothy in front of Farrell.

'Your boy here is doing wonders at HQ. You did well keeping him this long.'

Louise ignored the barely concealed insult both in the patronising way he praised her, and the obviously desultory comparison of her workplace in Weston to MIT; not that she could deny the latter.

'If you've got a second, Robbo would like a word with both of us,' added Finch, after the lingering silence.

I bet he does, thought Louise. 'I'll be there in five,' she said, as Finch returned to Simone.

'Looks like you'll be leaving us then?' Louise said to Farrell.

'He's made a request to transfer me for the next year.'

'I see. Look, I'll be sad to see you go. I'd rather you stayed but I can see the attraction of the big city.'

'Thanks, boss. I appreciate everything you've done for me. And—'

'Just look after yourself, DS Farrell. I think you know what I mean.'

'Ma'am,' said Farrell.

She didn't put up a fight. She'd presumed Farrell would leave for good as soon as he'd accepted the secondment, though she hadn't expected it to come this fast. Farrell was aware of what had gone down between her and Finch, and at the moment she believed he'd yet to fully fall under Finch's spell. She accepted Finch's false gratitude as she signed off on Farrell's transfer, and even stood as Finch departed the office.

'Well, that went smoother than I'd anticipated,' said Robertson, once Finch had left.

The smell of Finch lingered in the office and not for the first time, Louise wondered how she'd ever been intimate with the man. How she'd let him hoodwink her. 'I'm not going to let my personal differences get in the way of Greg's career, Iain. He deserves it and for once I don't think Finch is doing it to get at me.'

Robertson placed his hands together. 'Perhaps I shouldn't mention that Finch has also offered us his help on this possible multiple-murder case then?'

'No, don't mention that, Iain.'

'I anticipated that correctly at least. I told him as much, but we may need to use MIT if things escalate.'

'I can let you know when we get to that stage, sir.'

'Make sure you do.'

Finch and Farrell had left by the time she returned to the outer office. Thomas clicked his fingers. 'Gone like that,' he said.

'You'll probably be next,' said Louise. 'In fact, that should have been you.'

'Not for me, boss. I'm Weston through and through.'

'Good, you keep it that way.'

'Call for you, Louise,' said Simone, from across the office.

'DI Blackwell,' said Louise, picking up the phone from Thomas's desk.

'Louise, it's Alice Everson. We received another hair sample this morning. Sent over by Stephen Dempsey. For a Megan Davies.'

'Stephen's been a busy boy.'

'Yes. So have we, actually. Mark – Dr Forrest – told me you'd called him. So when I saw this come through I took the liberty of rushing through a test. It's come back positive. Like the other three, Megan Davies had significant traces of DMT in her hair.'

'Was the measurement the same?'

'Similar. Obviously the sample came to us immediately so it was a fresher result. I'll email you the details. I hope it aids your investigation.'

'Thank you. Unfortunately, I think it will.'

Louise told Robertson. She could see the energy drain from him as she spoke, his hand moving towards his chin until it rested there, propping him up. 'This all confirms the four women are connected?' he said, through the muffle of his palm.

'Yes and I think we have to treat all four as potential murder victims.'

'At least we'll no longer be known as Suicide by Sea,' said Robertson. 'What do you need from me?'

Louise had already anticipated the question. 'We have a patrol car watching Chappell's place. I think we should apply for a warrant to search the premises.'

'He's not at home?'

'Not since early afternoon.'

Robertson whistled through his teeth. 'I can see how he could be a suspect. Can we link him with anyone other than Sally Kennedy?'

'Not directly, not yet, but he knew about the DMT and was with Sally just before she died. Too much of a coincidence for me – I'm sure we could persuade a judge the same.'

'By "we", you mean me?'

'Sir.'

'And this Amy character?'

'Her I'm not so sure about. She could be in danger, could be in cahoots with Chappell.'

'Let's see if we can locate her, shall we? I'll sort this warrant out. Send Simone in.'

Seconds after Louise instructed Simone to go and see Robertson, another familiar face turned up. 'Tracey?' said Louise.

It was clear Tracey was lacking her usual bonhomie. Louise's first thoughts were that something had happened with Finch, possibly due to Farrell's transfer.

'Let's go somewhere private,' said Tracey.

Louise looked around the office, the prying eyes returning to their work.

'What is it?' she mouthed, as they reached one of the interview rooms.

Tracey squirmed and muttered under her breath. 'It's about Paul.'

Chapter Forty-Six

Louise shut the blinds, the eyes of the office on her. She wondered if this was how suspects felt as they waited to be questioned. Her pulse was rising. She sat, her breathing audible in the small room as numerous scenarios, each more gruesome and devastating than the last, played through her mind. 'What is it, Tracey?' she asked. She wanted to ask so many questions but let Tracey speak.

'I've been digging around. I'm afraid Paul has got himself into a lot more trouble than you may have thought.'

'What sort of trouble?'

'The gambling kind.'

'What does that mean exactly, Trace?'

'I don't know the exact figure but it's significant.'

'Jesus. So I was right. Do you know who he owes the money to?'

'I think the Mannings are only an intermediary but they're taking responsibility for him. Unless he's got the money, Lou, I'm not sure he can safely return to Bristol.'

Louise sat down, the office swirling around her. She wanted to ask herself how he could be so stupid but in truth she wasn't that surprised. It wasn't that which was making her nauseous. What she didn't understand was why he would risk involving Emily. 'Of all the selfish things he's done,' she said, shaking her head.

'I don't know what to suggest, other than try and find him which we're already doing.'

'I'll kill him myself if I find him.'

'Do you want to make it official? If you think Emily is in danger . . .'

Louise knew she had to think about Emily now. If they were reported as missing people and they were found, Paul would be in danger as soon as he left the police station. But escalating it to a missing-person scenario probably wouldn't make much difference. Paul had told Louise and his family he was on holiday. He'd called and sent a postcard. The schools were still on break so he wasn't doing anything wrong on that account. If a civilian had come to her with the same predicament, there wouldn't be much she could have done. The danger posed to Paul from whoever he owed money to was hypothetical at the moment.

'I'll speak to Sergeant Merrick again but I can't see any point escalating it at the moment.'

'I thought not,' said Tracey. 'Listen, I'll do everything I can. Find out who exactly he owes money to. We'll get this sorted.'

'Thanks, Tracey.'

'I know it's the last thing you need at the moment.'

'You can say that again. Did you see Finch when you arrived?'

'I saw him leaving the car park. Don't think he spotted me. What was he doing here?'

'Farrell is going permanent with you guys. At least for the next year.'

'That's good,' said Tracey. 'For us, I mean.'

Louise told her about the developments in the case.

'I've read about that DMT stuff. It's supposedly a bit like dying, isn't it?'

'People are dying at the moment, that's the issue.'

'You think this Chappell is drugging and killing them?'

'There's something about him. If we hadn't spotted him with Sally Kennedy he wouldn't even be on our radar. But that, his knowledge of DMT, and the fact he is currently AWOL makes me think he's involved.'

'Well, look, let me know if I can help in any way. Finch has his golden boy at the moment so he's off my back. In the meantime, I'll focus all my attention on Paul and Emily.'

'Thanks, Tracey. I really appreciate it,' said Louise. They stood and hugged, the smell of nicotine and perfume on Tracey oddly comforting.

'Right, better get back to it. Don't want the minions talking any more than usual,' said Louise, opening the blinds.

Overtime was authorised for a select number of uniformed officers as they waited until the early evening for the warrant to be issued, Louise thankful that Robertson didn't make a comment when she received his signature for permission. She had spent the rest of the afternoon alternating between calling Paul and the woman she now knew as Amy. *If the definition of insanity is doing the same thing over and over again expecting a different result, then madness is close at hand*, she thought.

'This was not cut and dried,' said Robertson, handing her the signed paperwork. 'Judge Boothroyd was reluctant but I persuaded him we had just cause.'

Louise wasn't sure what Robertson wished to achieve by telling her that – as pep talks went, it wasn't the most inspiring – but she didn't respond. 'Thanks, Iain, I'm sure you were very persuasive,' she said, taking the document. 'I'll let you know as soon as we've got something,' she added.

Everyone was primed so they set off immediately. Louise drove alone at the front of the convoy of cars towards Berrow. She didn't know what she hoped to find at Chappell's house, still had no real idea what the man's involvement in the case was beyond knowing Sally Kennedy and his knowledge about DMT. Yes, he was arrogant but that was hardly a unique character flaw among the people she was used to dealing with. The best result would be for Chappell to return home so she could question him again. If he was somehow involved in the women's deaths, she doubted he would be stupid enough to leave anything suspicious at his home. Her only hope was that her earlier visit had somehow spooked him and had led to him making a mistake.

She stopped by the patrol car to confirm Chappell hadn't returned before pulling up on the driveway. Outside, she heard the distant rumble of the sea behind the more pressing noise of the chirping grasshoppers. Thomas arranged the officers around the bungalow before Louise knocked on the door and called through the letterbox. With no answer she instructed the uniformed team to use the enforcer, the force's name for a battering ram.

A faint odour of fish hit her as she stepped through the threshold. She moved to the kitchen as the bungalow was secured, noting the remains of fried salmon in an unwashed frying pan.

'Looks like he may have left in a hurry,' said Thomas. 'Was it this desolate when you visited him?'

'I only saw the living room but that was pretty empty except for the bookcase,' said Louise, moving back into the hallway. Aside from the kitchen and living room, there were three bedrooms and a bathroom, each as sparse as the next with the exception of the smallest bedroom that had been turned into a small office. Books lined the room, on the shelves of two rickety wooden bookcases, and were piled high on the desk.

'Inspiration?' said Thomas, holding up a copy of *Helter Skelter*.

Louise took the book and turned to the blurb at the back, describing in brief the life of the cult leader Charles Manson.

'There's more,' said Thomas, pointing to a line of biographies of other cult leaders including four books on the Jonestown massacre.

'You going to tell Robertson we have the next Jim Jones on our hands?' said Louise, with a sigh. 'Not sure how he'd take that.'

'I'll leave that to you, boss,' said Thomas.

Among the other books were true-crime tomes as well as numerous paperbacks, the majority of which were old science fiction and horror tales. Although she was being flippant, the suggestion that Chappell was heading some sort of cult wasn't as far-fetched as it seemed. It didn't have to be on the scale of Jonestown or Manson, but it was easy enough to imagine Chappell exerting some influence over the four deceased women. They already knew he'd been close to Sally Kennedy, and the images they had of them on the pier suggested she had doted on him. He was certainly charismatic and persuasive enough; couple that with the vulnerability of the four women, and it wasn't beyond reason that he could have had a cult-like sway over them.

She was getting ahead of herself but what if all four women knew not only Chappell but each other? DMT had been found in the hair samples of each. Did he kill them after they took the drug? Was it part of some cult ritual, each taking their turn over the weeks?

Louise placed the Manson book back on the shelf, pleased she hadn't aired her views. There was speculation, and there was jumping to outlandish conclusions with little or no evidence.

'Found this,' said Thomas, jolting Louise from her thoughts as he handed her a framed photograph of Chappell with two women and a man dressed in some sort of ceremonial robe.

Louise took the photograph out of the frame. On the back in small digital ink dots was the date and location. 'Where's Coimbra?' she asked.

Thomas checked on his phone. 'Portugal.'

Louise placed the picture back in its frame. 'Let's search this place from top to bottom. I'd be keen to discover some drugs, in particular DMT.'

'You might have to let the team know what that looks like.'

'Bag anything suspicious. And find out who else is in this picture.'

Chapter Forty-Seven

It was close to midnight before Louise left Chappell's bungalow. Chappell had yet to return and the search had so far proved fruitless. She sat in her living room, holding the photograph they'd recovered from Chappell's home: a younger-looking Chappell with two young women and a man dressed in ceremonial robes. She tried an image search but lacked the necessary skills and equipment to find a match. She'd already sent the image to Coulson and hoped he could somehow work his magic.

She wanted to sleep but her mind was racing so she prepared a bowl of cereal and switched on the television. She wasn't sure where she'd expected to be at thirty-nine but it sure wasn't sitting alone in a retirement bungalow in Weston after midnight, eating cornflakes for dinner.

Collapsing on to the sofa as if her legs had given away, she returned to the articles she'd uploaded on cults. As ludicrous as the thought of Chappell running some form of cult from his home in Berrow sounded, the man matched many of the characteristics associated with cult leaders. Louise couldn't deny his charisma, the intensity with which she'd held his gaze. From what she knew of him he was intelligent and it wasn't a great leap to imagine him manipulating Sally Kennedy and the others.

Not that she could even mention the word 'cult' to Robertson or her other colleagues. The word had connotations that would be misconstrued. At this stage, Louise only had a working theory that Chappell had some form of hold over Sally. The link of the DMT was still unproven and without connecting Chappell to the other three women she knew the line of investigation could go cold. Either way, she wouldn't rest until they'd at least spoken to Chappell again; it could be coincidental that he hadn't returned to his house that night, but if he didn't return tomorrow she would have to consider requesting a warrant for his arrest.

With a sigh she tried Paul's and Amy's phones again before sleeping, regretting it the minute she switched off the light. Her thoughts were bombarded with the very worst scenarios her imagination could muster. She'd seen such terrible things in her time on the force and her mind appeared hell-bent on thrusting Emily into each of those scenarios. Louise tried to convince herself that she was being hysterical – that Emily was with Paul in a remote caravan park, safely tucked up – only to be reminded of her earlier conversation with Tracey about the money Paul owed and the people he was associating with. She could forgive her brother almost anything, had done so on many occasions, but she wasn't sure she would ever forgive herself for putting Emily in such peril. She'd yet to tell her parents but when they finally got Emily back, Louise planned to push for her parents to take custody of her on a permanent basis. At that moment, she couldn't see any other way to bring Paul to his senses.

And if she couldn't, what then? Louise shuddered, imagining Emily years from now in thrall to someone as manipulative as Chappell. It was so conceivable that in Louise's mind it was becoming almost inevitable. With no mother, and a father as irresponsible as Paul was behaving, it was hard to picture a positive future for her niece.

When her phone rang at 6 a.m. she wasn't convinced she'd slept. Surprised to see the name Simon Coulson on the screen, she pressed the answer button and shut her eyes as the IT specialist spoke.

'DI Blackwell, did I wake you? I'm sorry, I thought—'

'It's fine, Simon. What have you got for me?'

'I've been up all night trying to trace that image and I finally got a hit. In fact, I got a hit at three in the morning but I didn't want to disturb you. I was going to call it in—'

Louise forced her eyes open. 'Slow down, Simon. Tell me what you've got.'

'The man in the photo. The one with the robes. Went by the name of Maestro Bianchi. He called himself a shaman. Ran a retreat out of Coimbra in Portugal for people who wanted to experience Ayahuasca.'

Louise didn't like the fact that Coulson was using the past tense. 'What happened?'

'He's dead,' said Coulson. 'So are the two girls in the photo.'

'Don't tell me,' said Louise.

Yet, Coulson did just that. 'Suspected suicide,' he said.

Coulson was waiting with a full printed-out report for her when she reached the station thirty minutes later.

'Did you sleep here or something?' she asked him, accepting the cup of coffee he'd made for her with a smile.

'Haven't slept yet. This is the newspaper report. I hope you don't mind but I've made contact with the Portuguese police team. The investigator named in the report isn't due in for another two hours but they promised he would call you directly when he gets in. An Inspector da Costa.'

Louise took the printout. 'Thanks, Simon. I'm presuming you didn't talk in Portuguese?'

'No, broken English.'

Coulson had printed up two reports he'd found online. Both repeated the same story. A tragedy had hit a retreat in the area of Coimbra. Two young women and the so-called shaman, Maestro Bianchi, had been found dead, hanging from trees in the forest.

'I've been looking into these places. Taking DMT, or this Ayahuasca tea, is obviously illegal here but possession and personal use is legal in Portugal. There are a number of these ceremonial retreats where people can go to take the drug,' said Coulson.

'Saves a trip to the Amazon,' said Louise.

'Exactly.'

'Okay, thanks, Simon. Let's hope this da Costa can shed some light on all of this.'

Louise poured herself another coffee. It was clear Chappell's involvement went beyond mere coincidence and Louise made some notes in preparation for Robertson's arrival. She wanted a full-scale manhunt conducted on Chappell the second her boss arrived at work.

Typically, Robertson chose that morning to be the last in. Like every other number she called, his went straight to answerphone. She couldn't start without his backing so with Coulson, she began updating the rest of the team as they arrived. Despite her tiredness, Louise had to fight her nervous energy as she both waited for Robertson and for her call from Portugal.

Out of what was fast becoming habit she called Paul's phone, the sound of his answerphone message both expected and frustrating. She was about to try her next pointless call to Amy when Robertson arrived.

'Have I missed something?' he growled, as he walked past her desk.

Louise followed him into his office and shut the door. Robertson sat and waited a beat before speaking. 'Tell me,' he said.

The DCI's face was unreadable as Louise updated him. She chose her words carefully, avoiding the words cult, retreat and shaman as best she could. 'I wish I'd stayed in bed,' he said, when she'd finished.

'We need an arrest warrant,' said Louise.

'Do we know when Chappell was in Portugal? Sounds like some sort of bloody kibbutz to me.'

Louise frowned. It was clear Robertson had no idea what a kibbutz was but she wasn't about to contradict him. 'According to the photo we retrieved from his house, it was the same month when these suicides took place. It's beyond circumstantial now, Iain.'

'I agree.' He sighed. 'We had him in custody.'

Louise lowered her eyes. They'd had no way to know when Chappell turned up at the office that he would become the number-one suspect, and even with her suspicions they couldn't have kept him in custody. Yet, wasn't there a hint of accusation in Robertson's words?

'That's hardly our fault, Iain. We had nothing to charge him with.'

Robertson ran his hand over his face. 'Looks like I need another conversation with Judge Boothroyd.'

'I think we should go to the press, Iain,' said Louise.

'Do you?'

'He must know we're on to him by now. We need all the help we can get before he disappears for good.'

'Think about it, Louise. We're already known as Suicide by Sea. We start informing them about bloody retreats and ceremonial drug-taking and they'll have a field day.'

'It's going to come out at some point, Iain.'

'Let's hold off on that for now. They've already run a photo of Chappell. It's not going to look good if we ask them to do it again when they know we questioned him. It hardly makes us look professional, does it?'

Simone knocked on the door before Louise had a chance to answer. 'Call for you, Louise. Inspector da Costa from Portugal.'

'Put it through here, please, Simone.'

Louise placed the call on to speakerphone and introduced Robertson to the Portuguese officer. Louise was ashamed of the officer's fluent English when her Portuguese was non-existent. Da Costa murmured a couple of times as she explained the situation.

'That is very interesting, DI Blackwell,' he said, once she'd finished. 'You think there may be a parallel with what happened here.'

Louise wasn't sure from his tone if this was a question or statement. 'Could you tell me if there was anything suspicious about what happened at the retreat?'

'Beyond four people attempting to take their lives?'

'Four? I thought only three people died.'

'Four attempts, three successes. Apologies. That is the wrong word to use in the circumstances.'

'The deceased were local?' asked Louise.

'No, all four were foreign nationals. The shaman, Bianchi, was resident but originally from Peru. The two women, Greta and Sandra were from Germany. The man who survived was from the United Kingdom. I thought you would have a record of this, no?'

Louise glanced at Robertson. 'Could you tell me the survivor's name?' she asked, an excited tremor to her voice.

'Mr Charlie Barton,' said da Costa.

Robertson seemed to visibly deflate in front of her.

'This isn't the man you're looking for?'

'No, sadly not. Can you tell me in more detail what happened? How Barton survived?'

'Blind luck really. The four bodies were found by another member of the commune.' Da Costa went silent for a second. 'Yes,

Mila Bakker. From the Netherlands. She hadn't seen the shaman or the others and went in search of them. She found the three deceased people hanging from trees. The branch holding Mr Barton in place had snapped. He was unconscious with severe trauma to his neck but he survived.'

Louise thought about the hint of scarring she'd seen on Chappell. 'Was there any sign of drugs?'

'Yes, according to Barton all four had taken the Ayahuasca tea prior to their suicide attempts.'

'Did Barton give an explanation as to why?'

Da Costa's voice changed, his tone taking on a sharper quality that Louise couldn't read. 'He told us that they'd all seen the other side. That they were waiting for them.'

'They?'

'I can send you the transcription. We were of the opinion that the drug was influencing his thinking and obviously that of the three suicides. We sent him for medical treatment but he stopped talking.'

'Was there any hint that he'd coerced the deceased that day?'

'No, no. He couldn't have faked those injuries. I didn't understand him. He appeared distraught to still be alive. In the end he was free to return to the UK.'

'Inspector da Costa, can I take your mobile phone number? I'd like to send you an image.'

'Yes, of course.'

Louise sent him the image she'd recovered from Chappell's house, of Chappell with the shaman and the two women. She showed the image to Robertson as they waited for da Costa to receive the message.

'Yes, that is them,' said da Costa after a brief interval.

'Them?'

'Yes. The three suicides and Mr Barton.'

Chapter Forty-Eight

It had only just gone 8 a.m. but the man standing in front of Amy stank of alcohol. There was a faraway look in his eyes as he ordered a fried breakfast as if he were struggling to comprehend exactly where he was and why he was there. Nicole hadn't shown up for work and Keith was refusing to move from the grill so Amy was running the tables on her own. She thought about Nicole's suggestion that she set up a place and smiled at the memory of the girl's naivety.

Not that it made a difference either way. Neither Nicole's no-show nor Keith's uselessness could dampen the way she felt. Jay had spent the night for the first time ever. Warmth radiated through her as she remembered their night together. To begin with, she couldn't believe what was happening. They'd never slept together before and although Megan had hinted she'd had sex with Jay, Amy hadn't thought it would happen between them. Jay had been kind and gentle, just as she'd imagined on countless times.

In between, they'd talked and talked. They shared their experiences with DMT, marvelling at the similarities: the recollections of shape and sound, the dislocation from the body and the beings that waited to guide them to the next world. It wasn't something either could explain to someone who hadn't tried it. It was easy to dismiss as imagination but Jay knew as she did that what they experienced wasn't simply some trip, some extended illusion of their imagination. There were too many consistencies and similarities of experience, and more than that it simply felt real. It wasn't like dreaming. Amy had no doubt the DMT took her into another reality and because of that she'd long ago stopped fearing death; and because of Jay, she now welcomed it.

And when he'd asked her to write the note, she hadn't hesitated. It was cathartic listing her reasons for moving on, even if she did cry as she wrote about Aiden. She hadn't argued when he'd asked to add the two lines at the end of the note. They made perfect sense to her.

There are other worlds than this. Death is not the end.

Yet maybe this was the reason for her current unease. Not about the DMT, or the existence of something beyond this world, but about Jay and how recent events were changing things. Maybe it was simply last-minute nerves, but Amy sensed an urgency in Jay she hadn't experienced before. It worried her to doubt him. He'd given her so much, and she'd given him so much of herself, that doubt felt like a betrayal. She'd left him sleeping that morning and had been in such a rush that she'd forgotten the phone she'd hidden beneath the pile of clothes. She didn't know what Jay would do if he found out. The phone still had the messages from Megan, and worse, the voicemail from the policewoman. But was it this that was really bothering her?

She went to the bathroom, trying to focus on what was making her so anxious. Jay had summoned everyone together tonight and after writing the note, and spending the night with Jay, she knew what this meant. The last few months had been leading to this moment, so why then was she feeling this way?

'Where the hell have you been?' said Keith, when she returned.

'The toilet if that's okay with you.'

'Table six need their bill.'

Amy stared at the café owner. She could walk away now and not worry about seeing him again. By tomorrow, this job and everything surrounding it wouldn't even be a memory. Memories didn't exist where she was going. Why then didn't she tell Keith where to go and storm out? Was it because she feared she wouldn't be able to go through with it, or was it because she still wasn't sure that Jay would choose her tonight?

She held Keith's gaze for a little longer, his pudgy face scowling under the scrutiny, before moving towards table six with the card reader. If she was lucky, this was the last time she would ever have to do this.

She was home at 1 p.m. Although she hadn't expected to see Jay, it was still disappointing not to find him there. He'd left nothing of his belongings and for a second she wondered if she'd imagined it all. Collapsing on the bed, she lay on the side where Jay had slept last night. She could still feel his heat, the smell of him on the pillows and sheets. She'd been wrong to doubt him. He'd shown her so much. If only he'd been there now, she would have told him all her concerns, how much he meant to her.

In a state of flux – she didn't know where or when they were to meet that night – Amy searched through the pile of clothes where she'd hidden the phone. She panicked when she couldn't find it – a sickness crawling from her stomach into her chest – only to find it in the pocket of her grey jogging bottoms. Her heart returning to something approaching its normal cadence, she tried to switch it on only to be presented with a blank screen.

A second search ensued, this time for the charger Megan had given her. She found it in her bedroom, a sadness creeping over her as she remembered the day her friend had given her the gift.

Yet, although there was sadness that she wouldn't see Megan again – at least not in this form – she was comforted by the knowledge that she was somewhere better now. She'd panicked when she'd called the police, the change in Jay's process, and the brutality of his actions, disorientating her. She understood now. He'd been trying to get the police off his scent. There were still four of them left, five including Jay, and they'd made a pact which she was desperate to honour.

The phone showed twenty-eight missed calls, all from the same number: the policewoman, Louise Blackwell. The woman sounded genuine but she wouldn't understand. She thought Amy was in trouble but she wasn't. Instead of calling her back, she called Nicole to check what had happened to her today only for the phone to beep through to her voicemail.

Amy hesitated before leaving a short message. Chances were she would never see her again. 'Look after yourself,' she said, ending the call.

She was about to switch the phone off again, when it began vibrating in her hands.

Chapter Forty-Nine

'You're sure the man in this photo is called Charlie Barton?' said Louise, glancing at Robertson, who sat wide-eyed and uncustomarily silent.

'He wasn't in such a good state when I saw him, but that is definitely him. Where did you get this photo?'

'What happened to him? After he was taken to the hospital I mean,' said Louise, ignoring da Costa's question.

Da Costa hesitated, as if about to push his own agenda, before answering. 'He was under supervision for three weeks. As I mentioned we questioned him. What is this about, Inspector Blackwell? Are you searching for Mr Barton?'

Louise explained that she believed Barton was an alias for Chappell, or vice versa. 'What happened after his time in hospital?'

'We allowed Mr Barton to return home. The case was concluded. We were satisfied that the three people had died through their own volition. We informed your authorities.'

After reluctantly verifying with da Costa that the Portuguese authorities had fully checked Barton's identification, Louise and Robertson summoned the team together to explain Chappell's alias. If Barton had a police record, or if they had his fingerprints on the database, then they would have shown as a match when they'd taken Chappell's details. Even so, Louise went straight to the Police National Database to double-check.

There was a small file on Barton recording the incident in Portugal, but no personal information – prints or DNA swabs – had been taken after his return. Twenty minutes later they had a driver's licence, National Insurance number, and education record for Charlie Barton. His last address was in Thornbury, south Gloucestershire. Louise cross-referenced this with the details they had for Chappell. Chappell's driving licence was more recent and as da Costa had claimed to have checked Barton's passport, she had to conclude that Chappell was the alias and Barton was the real name of the person they were looking for. She wrote the name Barton next to Chappell on the crime board. 'Let's find out everything we can from this new information. See if we can track down his family and friends. Chances are he's hiding with one of them. Thomas, check the address in Thornbury. See if you can make contact. I'm going to look deeper into these Portuguese cases. Someone over here must have monitored Barton when he returned.'

As the team filtered out, Louise returned to her desk. She checked her phone on the unlikely off chance that Paul or Amy would have called her. She ignored the blank screen and began searching for the names da Costa had given her of the three suicide victims. Beyond a small report in a Portuguese newspaper, there was nothing about the incident at the retreat. She was mildly surprised that a story involving a British citizen hadn't reached the press back in the UK.

The thought made her check the websites of the newspapers Tania Elliot was associated with. She immediately regretted her decision. Tania had written an opinion piece on why young women had been taking their lives in Weston, comparing it to the suicides in Bridgend from the previous decade. If he hadn't already, Robertson would be receiving a call about the press attention and that would only lead to more pressure on her. At least there wasn't any mention of murder, and now they had a credible suspect; even Assistant Chief Constable Morley couldn't argue that Chappell/ Barton was a person of significant interest.

Out of habit she called Paul's phone, only the presence of Simone hovering behind her stopping her from unleashing a torrent of abuse for her brother to hear at some later point.

She almost didn't call Amy – it was beginning to feel like a waste of her time – and couldn't quite believe it when the phone began to ring.

Louise clicked her fingers at Simone. 'Get Robertson and Coulson here now,' she said.

Simone grimaced. 'What am I going to say?'

'Now,' said Louise, raising her voice just as the phone was answered.

'Amy, is that you?' said Louise, her voice low and soft. She waited a beat, her pulse quickening as a murmur came from the other end of the phone.

'Yes.'

'I'm so pleased you've answered, Amy. This is Louise. Louise Blackwell. I left a message for you before.'

'I know,' said Amy.

Although her answers were short, there must be a reason why she'd yet to hang up. 'Amy, are you in any immediate danger?' she asked as Robertson arrived, followed by an agitated-looking Coulson. She couldn't risk putting her on speakerphone but wanted Robertson there to witness the conversation.

'I'm alone. I'm fine,' said Amy.

'That's great. I can only imagine what you must be going through at the moment. I want you to know that you're not in any trouble. We just want to help you. We know it was you who called the emergency services about Megan Davies. Was she your friend?'

Amy sounded as if she was in shock. 'Yes,' came her weak reply. 'Did you . . . Did you find her?'

'We recovered her body. We would never have done so if it hadn't been for you. I would love to meet up with you, Amy. You can tell me what happened?'

'No, I don't think—'

'Do you know Jay Chappell?' asked Louise. She looked up at Robertson as she asked the question. She knew it was a risk but Amy was on the verge of hanging up. Louise heard the intake of breath.

'It's not what you think,' said Amy, sounding unsure of herself.

'He's not who you think he is,' said Louise, not wasting any time. She told Amy as quickly and succinctly as she could about Portugal. 'Jay isn't even his name. His real name is Charlie Barton.'

Louise heard her laboured breathing on the line as Robertson shoved a piece of paper into her hand. 'Let me come to you, Amy,' said Louise, reading Robertson's pointless suggestion to find Amy's location.

'No, I don't think that's necessary. I need to think.'

'Is he making your friends kill themselves?'

Amy hesitated. 'It's not like that. He's . . . We're making our own choices.'

'Let's meet and you can explain it to me. You don't need to come to the police station. We can talk and you can tell me all about it.'

'No, I'm sorry,' said Amy, her voice now raw with emotion.

'Let me help you, Amy,' said Louise, only to realise she was talking to a dead signal.

Chapter Fifty

Amy sat on the sofa, hugging herself. She knew it had been a mistake answering the phone the second the policewoman began to speak but she hadn't been able to hang up. It couldn't be true. Jay would never lie to her – or the others – like that. The officer – Louise – had said Jay's real name was Charlie. Amy closed her eyes, picturing Jay with his kind eyes and smile. He was Jay, her Jay. The policewoman was lying. It was all a trap. It had to be.

She moved to her bedroom and lay on the side of the bed where Jay had stayed last night. It was cold now and she could no longer smell him. She considered what Louise had told her about Portugal, how Jay had tried to take his own life and failed. She'd seen the scarring on his neck and upper chest, his mottled skin that looked raw to the touch. How could Louise have known about that?

The phone was hot in her hand. She didn't even have a number for him so she could call and ask about it. Amy thought about everything that had happened between them since that day he'd found her. The things they'd done together, the secrets they'd shared. If what Louise had told her was true, could she forgive him? Okay, he might have lied about his name but had anything else really changed? He'd obviously changed his name so he could continue his work. He hadn't told the group about Portugal – and it was something she wanted to know about – but what happened there sounded like what was happening now: a group of like-minded people, destroying the binds of their lives.

Louise had said Jay was dangerous but did Amy believe that? He hadn't made anyone do anything they didn't want to do. Had he?

She grimaced as she thought about the way Megan had struggled under his touch that night by the oncoming sea. It had only been a physical reaction, her body's way of fighting to remain in this world, and she'd been so happy at the thought of finally leaving everything behind. She'd struggled but she'd wanted to die, wanted to remain in the new world she'd accessed.

Amy thought about her other friends – Victoria, Claire and Sally. Her recollection suggested they'd gone willingly to their deaths. Yes, Jay had been with them, had eased them into the next world, but there had been no sense that he'd forced them in any way.

Was she trying to convince herself? It hadn't only been Megan who'd struggled. Sally had survived the initial fall in Kewstoke, if only for a few short minutes. Hadn't Amy begun to doubt Jay then? She'd spent the next day on the beach with Megan, waiting for Sally's body to be taken away. She'd tried to share her concerns with Megan but she'd dismissed them out of hand. Of course Jay would never have wanted Sally to suffer, but did he have an ulterior motive in helping them to move on? Were they all moving on through their own will or, as Louise seemed to be suggesting, was Jay somehow coercing them?

After a period of reflection, Amy had to conclude she simply wasn't sure any more. Like everyone in their little group, Jay had his demons. He'd never hidden that fact. He wasn't a messiah, even if some of the group treated him that way. He was simply a flawed individual who'd been given a glimpse of something beyond this world. Amy hadn't fully understood what he'd been going through until now. The policewoman had told her of his aborted suicide attempt in Portugal. He'd never told the group about it but that didn't mean he'd lied or, as the policewoman had suggested, was dangerous. Jay could have taken his life any time after that. Instead he'd dedicated his life to helping others. The lost like Victoria, Claire, Sally and Megan; and yes, like herself.

Amy could only guess at the cost of such responsibility. She'd seen the way he'd looked as he'd held on to Megan as she struggled beneath him. It hadn't given him any pleasure. She'd seen his internal struggle, the pain in his sad eyes as he'd taken Megan's life. Amy had panicked when he'd remained calm. Jay had shown such utter strength to continue when every cell in his body was probably telling him to stop, and Amy had betrayed him.

She wouldn't make the same mistake again. She believed in Jay. Others wouldn't understand – and she didn't blame them for that – but she had nothing left. She'd give everything to him and had to believe he had her best interests at heart.

It was a resolution that was stretched to breaking point as the doorbell rang and Amy peered out the window to see Jay hand in hand with Nicole.

Chapter Fifty-One

Louise slammed her mobile phone on to the desk as in her peripheral vision Simone retreated to the other side of the office. 'I guess we can't find a location from that call,' she said to Coulson, who stood behind Robertson as if he was a shield.

'Let me call the number back and see what I can do. But in short, unless she picks up now, I can't, no. I'll need to speak to the phone operator again.' Coulson dialled in silence only to shake his head after a few seconds.

Amy had sounded conflicted, unsure of herself. Louise had taken a risk telling her about Chappell's former identity. It was possible the man was with her or would see her shortly. When he found out they knew about him being Charlie Barton, there was no telling what he would do.

Robertson wasn't slow in offering his opinion. 'He's going to escalate things now,' he said.

'He already knew we were on to him,' said Louise, annoyed that she felt she had to defend herself.

'If he didn't he will now, but you were right to tell her about Barton. Do you think there's a chance she'll change her mind and help us?'

'She's torn, but he has a hold on her. I think Amy will be next,' she said to Robertson.

'Then we'd better find her as soon as we can,' said Robertson.

Aside from situating police officers by every cliff edge in a ten-mile radius, Louise wasn't sure at that exact moment what else they could do.

Coulson returned with her phone. 'Sorry,' he said, handing it back to her. 'I'll contact the mobile provider now. We might be able to find an approximate location for her even if she's using a burner phone. If she switches the phone on again we'll have an immediate hit.'

'I can't stress how important this is, Simon,' said Louise, jumping as her phone rang again. She shook her head at Robertson and Coulson, who walked away, the phone still chiming in the subdued atmosphere of the CID office. 'Hi, Mum, bit busy,' she said, taking her phone into the conference room. 'Everything okay?'

The sound of sobbing came from the other end of the line.

'Mum, what is it?' said Louise, fighting the multitude of gruesome images taking shape in her mind.

Her mother began to speak then stopped, as if her words had caught in her throat. At moments like this it was best to wait for her mother to find her voice, but Louise was too impatient to wait. 'Mum, what is it?' she asked, trying to keep the urgency and desperation out of her voice. 'Is it Paul? Emily?'

A distant noise filtered through her handset and the next sound she heard was her father speaking. 'It's me, Lou. Your brother called us again,' he said, emphasising the words 'your brother'.

'What did he say, Dad?'

'Well, it was hard to tell, Lou, because he was that pissed. All I know is that he was crying and apologising to your mother which in the normal course of things wouldn't be so bad but when he has our grandchild and it's still the morning then it's a bit worrying.'

Your brother. Our grandchild. Louise ignored the outburst. Her father could get this way when he was worried. She could either be hurt by his words or try to sort it. As always, she chose the latter. 'Did he give an indication of where he was?'

'Cornwall, still, so he says.'

'Did you speak to Emily?'

'No, heaven knows where she was.'

'Okay, Dad. Listen, I'm going to hang up now and speak to a colleague in Cornwall. See if we can find him, okay?'

Louise's earlier tension had manifested into a headache. She placed her hand on her forehead, trying to clear her thoughts. She was being torn in too many directions and the resulting indecision was troubling. From a professional viewpoint, all her focus should be on finding Amy but how could she sit back and ignore her brother's behaviour?

The irony of trying to chase a location for her brother seconds after trying to do the same thing for Chappell was not lost on Louise as she called Joslyn.

'Hang on a sec, DI Blackwell,' said Joslyn, answering. 'That's better,' she said, a few seconds later. 'How are you, Louise?'

'Not great,' said Louise, offering a quick update first on Chappell, then her brother.

'Shit, Louise, I don't know what to say.'

'You've summed it up pretty succinctly. Do you think you could trace Paul's location?'

'You know what that would mean?'

It would become official. To obtain the information, they would have to register Paul and Emily as missing and face the consequences of everything that came with it. Louise couldn't see any other way. In retrospect, she'd let things go too far already. It shamed her that it had reached the extent where her mother was literally lost for words, such was her anguish. 'It's time. I don't want Emily put at risk,' said Louise.

'Okay, I've got the number. You're going to have to leave it with me for the time being. I need to register the case first then try and get the location tracked. Even then . . .'

The tracking couldn't pinpoint location, and Paul could have moved since last using the phone so Louise understood Joslyn couldn't promise anything. 'I know. We're going through the same procedure here. Thanks, Joslyn I definitely owe you one now.'

'No worries, just let your parents know I'm on it.'

Louise called her parents before returning to the office. Coulson was on the phone, hopefully negotiating with the phone companies. The tech guy had proved to be a godsend and she wondered what Finch felt about him spending time with them, only for her paranoid side to suggest that Finch had sent Coulson to them to keep tracks on her.

Returning to her desk, she briefly held her head in her hands, the throbbing pain in her forehead spreading to her eyes, and wondered if there would ever be a time when she could fully trust someone again. As she looked up, Thomas was standing by her desk.

'I've just got off the line to Chappell's mother. Well, Barton's mother. I think you'll want to hear this, boss,' he said.

'I could do with hearing something positive.'

'I wouldn't necessarily call it positive but it might confirm our working theory.'

'Illuminate me,' said Louise, leaning back in her chair.

'His father has passed but his mother still lives in Thornbury. Hasn't seen him since he left home at sixteen. Didn't take her long to tell me about his morbid fascination,' said Thomas, biting his lip.

'Which is?'

'With death. It sounds like a typical teenage thing. Black T-shirt, death metal, that sort of thing. Only his interest was a bit more specific. She told me about one of his English essays which focused on the death of Kurt Cobain.'

'The singer?'

'The singer who shot himself, yes. Seems our young Jay Chappell slash Charlie Barton developed a fascination with suicide. And here's the kicker.'

Louise's mind went blank and she was thankful for the fact. She didn't want to have to imagine why or how a young person could develop such an obsession. Unfortunately her mind betrayed her, creating an image of Paul taking his own life. 'What?' she said, louder than she'd intended, the sound of her voice causing her to wince.

'When he was seventeen, Barton's girlfriend took her own life.'

'How?' said Louise, already knowing the answer.

'She hung herself and Barton was the one who found her.'

Chapter Fifty-Two

Louise stared at Thomas, dumbstruck. She blinked and shook herself out of her surprise, shouting over to Coulson. 'Simon, where are we on a location for Amy?'

'Working on it,' said Coulson, not turning from his screen to look at her.

Louise didn't know if Chappell finding his girlfriend dead was the catalyst for his subsequent behaviour. From Thomas's report it seemed that suicide had been of interest to the young Chappell/ Barton long before his girlfriend died. She didn't know exactly why he killed in this manner – a subconscious way to bring his girlfriend back from the dead, a means of punishing those he felt were responsible for her taking her own life – but she would do everything she possibly could to stop him from doing it again.

'We need to send someone to see Chappell's mother. Find out exactly what happened.'

'I can go,' said Thomas.

Louise hesitated. Chappell was in hiding, that much was for sure. Louise was worried for Amy, and for anyone else in Chappell's radar, and wasn't sure she could risk having Thomas away from the station at such a critical time.

'I'll leave now and be back this evening,' he said.

'Okay. I'll see if I can get Farrell back for a few days,' said Louise.

After informing Robertson of the latest developments, Louise spent a few minutes hovering over Coulson's desk.

'They promised they'd get back to me within the hour,' he said, defensively.

'No, that's fine, Simon. Actually, I wanted to thank you for all your work on this.'

Coulson spun around on his chair. 'Oh, that's okay,' he said. 'Actually . . . '

Louise smiled as Coulson lowered his eyes. 'What is it, Simon?'

Coulson looked around the office. 'My sister. She took her life when she was fifteen.'

'Oh my god, Simon. I'm so sorry, I didn't know.'

'No one here knows. Bullying. You know how kids can be. We didn't read it at the time and then she was gone.'

Louise shook her head. What could she say? The terrible revelation reminded her of the secrets people carried with them at all times, of her own secret she was keeping from the majority of her colleagues.

'I thought. Well, when I heard about these suicides and when you came to Portishead . . .' Coulson looked away. 'I thought maybe I could help. It's silly but I thought if I could somehow help these women it would be a tribute of sorts to Hannah,' he said, looking back at her again, his eyes wide, almost hopeful. 'It's much more common than you would imagine.'

Unfortunately, Louise knew that thousands of people took their lives every year. 'I'm sure Hannah would be very proud of you, Simon.'

Coulson's eyes reddened and he returned to his screen. Louise placed her hand on his shoulder. 'I'm always here, Simon. Whenever you want to talk. I really mean that. Okay?'

'Okay. Thanks, Louise.'

◆ ◆ ◆

They were out of coffee so Louise started a new pot. It probably wasn't the best thing for her headache but she needed a hit of caffeine. She was still thrown by Coulson's revelation. The poor guy must have spent the whole investigation thinking about his sister, yet hadn't said a word to anyone. As the earthy smell of coffee filled the room, she once again considered her own secrets and where they would lead her; and the potential detrimental effect it could have on the case.

She called Dr Forrest, burning her tongue on the first sip of the freshly brewed coffee as she waited for the phone to be answered.

'DI Blackwell, I've been reading updates on your case in the papers,' said Forrest.

'That will make what I have to say easier then, I hope,' said Louise.

'Now you have piqued my interest,' said Forrest.

He listened in silence – interrupting Louise occasionally for clarification – as she updated him on the case, including the latest details of Chappell's alias, and the supposed suicides in Portugal.

'That's one hell of a story,' said the scientist, once Louise had finished.

'Tell me about it. We're treating the four deaths as murder now. Chappell has admitted using DMT. The retreat in Portugal was advertised as a place to take Ayahuasca in a safe environment. The male suicide was a shaman, for what that's worth.'

'Yes, I've come across a lot of these shamans in the UK as well. Can't always separate the sham from shaman, unfortunately.'

'I wouldn't know about that. All I know is that the shaman was advertising the use of this DMT tea.'

'Ayahuasca, yes.'

'I know we discussed this before, about the potential to be manipulated by someone you were with when taking the drug. But could DMT itself make you want to take your life?'

'My short answer to that would be no,' said Forrest, murmuring. 'I think it's certainly possible for someone to have a negative experience from taking DMT but I haven't heard of anyone wishing to take their life after taking it.'

'And the chances of four women each doing so separately?'

'Virtually zero,' said Forrest.

Louise repeated the information Tracey had offered about DMT, that it was like dying.

'Yes, she's right in a basic way. My studies have only been on volunteers in a clinical environment. There are papers of similar studies as well as lots of anecdotal evidence out there. As you can imagine, studying psychedelics has its limitations. My focus is on the potential benefit of the drug in mental-illness cases. We record patients before, during, and after taking the drug. The idea that DMT is akin to dying comes from the feeling of detachment from the body. Some users compare the feeling to a sense of enlightenment, popular in religions such as Buddhism. Stop me if this gets too mystical. I'm all about the hard science but the reports are just that.'

'No, please continue.'

'So when the DMT hits, users often state they feel detached from not only their body but their self too. Hence, the feeling of dying.'

'Is the experience always negative?'

'Far from it.'

'So the users might wish to return to this state.'

'Of course.'

Louise exhaled. 'You mentioned before that users often believe what they experience is real.'

'That's correct.'

'So it's conceivable that they may wish to stay in the state on a permanent basis?'

'As I mentioned before, users of DMT often state that they no longer fear death once taking it. In part, it's what makes DMT so fascinating. Many of the participants, in our experiments and those from past studies, report the desire of not wanting to return from their experience. Many have a certainty of consciousness existing after their death on earth. One of my respondents recently told me that hospice patients should be given DMT as a way of preparing them.'

Louise scratched her head. 'And you?'

'Me?'

'What do you think?'

Forrest chuckled. 'I'm the impartial scientist, I just collect and interpret the data.'

'Okay. So for argument's sake, you take DMT, see heaven. Would it make sense that you would want to return to that state as soon as possible? Could this explain these suicides?'

'I see your angle. What we find is that the respondents who feel this way – that there is an afterlife – have a greater sense of the sanctity of life. They feel free to live life the way they want to.'

'Safe in the knowledge of eternity?'

'Something like that.'

Louise was struggling to cope with the surreal nature of the conversation and was glad no one else was listening. 'So why do you think these women are killing themselves? Could Chappell be coercing them in some way through his use of the drug?'

'Perhaps. Again, it's not something I have come across and clearly it isn't something we've explored clinically. However, the scene and setting of how someone takes psychedelics can't be underestimated as I mentioned previously. We take this very seriously and strive to ensure our participants are relaxed and feel like they are in a safe environment. Also, we would never work with someone with a history of mental illness or depression; we wouldn't, for instance, advise someone to take it alone, or after alcohol, and certainly not in a negative environment or mood. Whether someone could coerce someone into taking their own life . . . I truly couldn't give you a definitive answer. If it was during the trip, my personal opinion is that they wouldn't be responsive enough to take their own lives.'

'They could walk off a cliff though?'

'Possibly, with some assistance.'

'What about hanging themselves?'

'I imagine you would need to look at the technicalities involved but my guess is again, they would almost definitely need some assistance.'

'Could they have taken the drug and then killed themselves immediately after?'

'The onset of DMT can be basically instantaneous, though this would depend on how it is taken, so if they were going to do that they would have to wait until it was over.'

'So Chappell could drug them and suggest they take their own lives?'

'I'm sorry, DI Blackwell, I can't give you a concrete answer. I'm sure you understand the nature of this type of study, at the present at least, makes it very difficult to give a definitive answer to these types of questions. I would say that the scene and setting could make a huge difference to the nature of the experience. So, yes, your Mr Chappell could have a huge influence on the nature of the experience.'

'Thank you, Dr Forrest, you've been very helpful,' said Louise, feeling as if she knew less than when she'd begun the conversation.

She didn't have any time to think further as Coulson knocked on the door.

'Come in, Simon.'

The tech consultant was red, his brow wet with perspiration. 'Everything okay?' asked Louise.

'Yes. We've got a location for Amy's phone.'

Chapter Fifty-Three

Amy stuck her head back inside, and began jumping to some conclusions, none of which she liked. It seemed Jay must have arranged to meet Nicole after leaving Amy that morning. She remembered Nicole's flushed face yesterday when she'd first met Jay. Amy had recognised the adoring look. She'd seen it on the face of Megan and the other members of the group; had seen it in the mirror. She should have realised when Nicole hadn't shown up for work that something was wrong.

With a heavy sigh she picked up her coat, the familiarity of the denim fabric comforting. The phone was on the table, still switched off. It was against the rules to have a phone, let alone take one to a ceremony, but she took it anyway, covering the bulge in her jeans pocket with the length of her grungy black T-shirt.

Nicole ran to her as she left the building, wrapping her arms around her as if they hadn't seen each other in months. It made Amy feel like a grown up. She glanced at Jay, who gave her an enigmatic smile in response; as if Nicole being there was the most natural thing in the world.

Together they walked along the Upper Bristol Road and down through Grove Park towards town. Nicole held her hand as they made the steep descent. Jay, whose hoodie was pulled over his head, walked ahead giving Amy the chance to quiz her friend. 'Is everything okay?' she asked.

'Everything is wonderful. I'm sorry I didn't call into work this morning. Was it busy?'

'Were you with him?' asked Amy. The question sounded more aggressive than she'd intended and Nicole stopped still.

'He said you wouldn't mind,' she said, the happiness slipping from her face.

Amy closed her eyes, the sound of the twittering birds and the smell of the flowers filling her senses. 'I don't mind as such,' she said, opening her eyes into the glare of the sun escaping from behind a cloud. 'I'm worried you don't know what you're doing.'

'I'm not a little girl, you know. You're not that much older than me.'

'I'm not saying that, Nicole.' Amy shook her head. Jay was standing at the foot of the hill. Even from this distance she could see the smile on his face, the confident way he stood. As if he'd planned this little confrontation all along. 'Did he tell you what we do?' she asked.

'He showed me,' said Nicole, the smile returning. 'It's okay, I've done drugs before. I go to uni, for heaven's sake.'

'What did you take?'

'Jay made me a tea. Ayahuasca. He told me what I would see and I did. You wouldn't believe how happy I am now. Or maybe you would,' said Nicole, moving towards her.

She should have been happy for her friend. DMT was a gift. It had changed her life. Before meeting Jay, a shroud had covered her. She would have taken her life earlier but a combination of cowardliness, and a perverse feeling that she would be dishonouring the memory of Aiden, had stopped her. Jay had shown her what was waiting and although she hadn't directly seen him when she'd made the trip, she knew Aiden was there too.

But just because it was right for her, it didn't mean it was right for everyone. Nicole had a full life ahead of her, had no reason to think about moving on. Everyone else Jay had helped – Victoria, Claire, Sally and Megan, and the three others still with them – had a reason to take DMT, to experience the afterlife and one day move on. What would Nicole's story be?

She couldn't deny there was an inkling of jealousy in the way she was feeling. Sometimes it was difficult for her to see Jay sharing himself. But that didn't fully explain her concern. Jay's behaviour was becoming more erratic. The way he'd helped Megan move on coupled with what the policewoman had told her about Jay's other name, was proof enough of that. And now it was clear that he was in hiding. She still believed in him, was sure he had her and the others' best interests in mind, but what if all the pressure was getting to him, was forcing him to take risks and therefore make mistakes?

'You two coming?' he shouted from the foot of the hill.

Amy grabbed Nicole's hands. 'You know what happens, don't you?'

'Yes,' said Nicole, smiling.

'And you know that tonight it will be me?' said Amy.

The flicker of doubt on Nicole's face vanished as quickly as it had appeared. 'Jay told me tonight is going to be very special,' she said, turning and skipping down the hill.

The three of them walked through the town. It was late Sunday afternoon, the bars already doing good business. Outside the Royal Oak, people stood in circles drinking and smoking, oblivious to them as if they were invisible. 'Where are we meeting the others?' Amy asked Jay.

He turned towards her, and even though he wore his hoodie and oversized sunglasses, she still fell for his smile. 'Not far now,' he said. 'You worry too much, Amy.'

Even hearing her name from his lips did something to her. And if that spell was wearing thin, it was still strong enough for her to want to follow him; even with Nicole in tow.

Was it regret or nostalgia she felt as they walked through the row of amusement arcades on Regent Street? Nicole was hand in hand with Jay, and Amy hankered after a simpler time when she'd hung outside these very same arcades. The excitement – never displayed, of course – of such times, smoking cigarettes under the pier, kissing boys, drinking cheap white cider. She'd felt so grown up then, when in reality she'd had few concerns beyond normal teenage angst.

If she could turn back time, would she? She'd been a teenager when she'd had Aiden; and although she'd been a teenager when she'd lost him, she wouldn't give up their time together for anything.

'Come on, slow coach,' said Nicole, waiting for her by the pedestrian crossing opposite the Grand Pier where, it seemed a lifetime ago, she'd seen Jay and Sally hand in hand.

Amy took Nicole's offered hand, the excitement in her eyes unmistakable. Amy knew the DMT all but cleared the system after the initial rush. But Nicole wasn't her usual self. Her pupils didn't seem dilated but Amy would swear the girl was on something. She hated doubting Jay but none of this made any sense.

'May I?' said Jay, taking Amy's hand from Nicole.

Nicole let go and skipped ahead like a child being told her parents needed to talk alone. 'What's happening, Jay?' asked Amy.

'Nicole is very troubled. I could tell from the very first second I met her.'

'What troubles does she have?' said Amy, hating the dismissiveness she heard in her voice.

Jay frowned and it wounded her to know she was responsible for his displeasure. 'I think you, more than anyone, would know not to take outward appearances for granted.'

Amy blinked and looked away. When Jay had met her she'd been the tough singleton. Borderline homeless, she'd had to fight for everything. She'd created a hardened image of her true self and made herself believe it. Jay had seen right through it and that in part was why she'd been able to trust him so quickly. 'It's too soon for her. I don't think she'll understand,' she said.

'Tonight is going to be different,' said Jay, stopping on the promenade to look at her.

'I'm just not sure,' said Amy. She almost called him Charlie, to gauge his response, but that would be a trick and he deserved more than that.

'I do understand, Amy, of course I do.' Jay moved towards her and held her hands in his. 'You do trust me, don't you?' he said, his eyes sadder than she'd ever seen them.

Amy felt tears well up inside of her. She couldn't believe she'd ever doubted him. 'Of course,' she said, whimpering.

'Then trust me for a little bit longer.'

Chapter Fifty-Four

They gathered outside a block of flats on the Upper Bristol Road where the last signal from Amy's mobile had originated. Louise was on the phone to Coulson as Tracey pulled up. 'I brought you some help,' she said, as DS Farrell left the passenger seat.

Louise hung up. 'More the merrier. I think we have a hit on her flat. Flat 12a is rented to a Ms Amy Carlisle.'

She tried the buzzer, pressing multiple buttons until someone buzzed them in through the main door. A musty odour – damp, possibly urine – hit them as they moved towards the staircase. 'Greg, wait here,' said Louise, as Tracey followed her upstairs.

'Eerie place,' said Tracey.

Louise agreed. The dampness in the air was tangible, the wallpaper peeling to reveal patches of mould. It reminded her of Claire Smedley's home in Kewstoke, yet somehow colder, even less inviting.

The pain from her throbbing head had now spread through her body, her limbs heavy and tight as she made her way up the staircase. She should have taken some pills, maybe drunk some water, but there was no time.

Amy's bedsit was on the fourth floor. Louise tried her phone again, knocking on the door when the phone went to answerphone.

When there was no answer, they tried the two neighbouring doors, an elderly lady opening the door of flat 12c.

'Sorry to bother you, ma'am, we are trying to locate your neighbour Amy Carlisle. Can I ask your name?'

'Mrs Harris, if you must know, though Mr Harris is no longer with us. Long gone, you understand.'

'Have you seen Amy today, Mrs Harris?'

The elderly woman shrugged. 'Amy? She ain't in, I don't think.'

'No, I don't believe she is,' said Louise. 'We're a bit worried about her. Could you tell me when you last saw her?'

'Hear her more like. Some handsome fella and a pretty young thing showed up earlier. Ain't seen either of them before.'

'When was this?' asked Louise, scrolling through the photos on her phone.

'About an hour ago.'

'Is this the man?' said Louise, showing her the picture of Chappell.

The woman grinned, revealing red gums and a set of dentures that looked as if they hadn't been cleaned in weeks. 'That's him. Good-looking, ain't he?'

'This was about an hour ago. Do you have any idea where they went?'

'Looked out my window. Ain't no crime. What else am I supposed to do?' said the woman, staring at Louise in defiance.

'No, you've done nothing wrong, Mrs Harris. Did you see which way they went?'

'Down the hill towards town, I suppose,' said the woman.

'Did Amy look okay? And the other woman?'

'Yeah, of course they looked okay. All smiling and holding hands. Up to no good probably.'

'Could you describe what they were wearing?'

Mrs Harris squinted as if she had something in her eye. 'Not really. The man had on one of those blue hood things.'

'A hoodie?' asked Tracey.

'If you say so, love.'

'Thank you, Mrs Harris, you've been very helpful,' said Louise.

The woman didn't respond but kept her eyes on Louise as she slowly shut the door.

'Where have you brought me?' said Tracey, as they headed downstairs.

'God, don't,' said Louise.

When they were outside, she organised the rest of the team to begin searching for Chappell, Amy and the other woman.

'Do you think we have probable cause to gain entry?' said Tracey.

Louise called Robertson for clarification. 'At the moment, we don't even have a workable image for Amy. Nothing beyond this address. If we gain entry we could find something which could lead to saving her life or someone else's.'

Louise could tell Robertson didn't like being put on the spot but she didn't want to risk jeopardising either the investigation or her own career. Finch and Morley were waiting for her to make a mistake. After everything that had happened, an illegal entry could be enough to tip the balance on their side.

'Okay, I think we have enough to justify entering the flat,' said Robertson.

Louise thanked him, still annoyed she had to ask him in the first place. She ordered one of the uniformed officers to get the enforcer. 'I feel like I'm making a habit out of this,' she said to Tracey as they joined Farrell at the top of the stairs. 'You don't have any aspirin or ibuprofen do you?' The headache was now a full-blown migraine and Louise wondered if she was coming down with something.

'You're in luck,' said Tracey, digging a plastic sachet of pills from her jacket pocket. 'You want me to get you some water? You do look a bit peaky now that you mention it.'

'I'm fine,' said Louise, dry-swallowing two of the pills.

Tracey rubbed her hands together. 'I wonder what we'll find,' she said, as the uniformed officer returned with the battering ram.

Louise gritted her teeth. 'Yes, I wonder.'

The door gave way with the first hit, revealing a single room, similar to Claire Smedley's bedsit, with two adjoining rooms – a bathroom and bedroom. The place was as sparsely decorated. She found three photos under the mattress in the bedroom. It was hard to date the pictures. Each showed a young woman who appeared to be in her late teens. In her arms she held a baby with a shock of red hair. Louise looked away from the photo: the similarity to the baby photos she had of Emily were striking. 'Let's see if we can find out who these two are,' she said to one of the uniformed officers.

'Think I've found something,' said Farrell, who was head-deep in a pile of laundry at the corner of the living area. In his hand he held a laptop.

Louise took the machine from him, the throb of her forehead matching the spiked tempo of her pulse, as she thought about the suicide notes she'd read in the last few weeks, hoping she wouldn't find one now.

Like Claire Smedley's, the laptop wasn't password protected. Louise opened the word-processing document and found the note in her recently opened documents. It ended the same way as the others. 'Emily's going to be next,' said Louise, the strength momentarily draining from her as she handed the laptop back to Greg.

Greg looked blank and looked over at Tracey who'd stopped what she was doing. 'You mean Amy?' he said.

Louise lowered her eyes. The pain was everywhere. She felt it in her jawbone as she spoke, her voice raised in an attempt to hide her mistake. 'Just get someone to take this back to Coulson,' she said, ignoring Farrell's question.

Farrell hesitated before walking off.

'Everything okay?' said Tracey, once they were back outside.

'I'm fine,' said Louise. She forwarded the images she'd found under the bed to the officers already searching in the town centre, and told the rest of the team about the note, while trying to convince herself the headache was fading.

'We could be too late?' said Farrell.

'Your joyful insights are what make you such a pleasure to work with,' said Louise. 'I don't think so, not yet. I need to get on to Coulson. It looks like Amy has the phone on her. We need to be ready should she switch it on again.'

Tracey and Farrell lit cigarettes outside as Louise called Coulson. Once again, Louise was forced to confront the thought that Tracey and Farrell had been sent only as a means for Finch to monitor the case. She pictured him pulling up in a car with the assistant chief in tow, ready to take the case from her. She trusted Farrell and Tracey but they would have to follow orders, and knowing Finch she doubted they would even know they were being used.

'Her phone is switched off still,' said Coulson, answering after the first ring. 'The second it's activated again we'll know. It would help if we had the IMEI number.'

Louise passed the information on to the team.

It seemed the success of the case might come down to whether or not they found a phone contract.

Chapter Fifty-Five

Beatrice, Rachael and Lisa were waiting for them at the beach near Birnbeck Pier. Beatrice wrapped her arms around Amy, her red hair spilling over Amy's shoulders, and then repeated the gesture with Jay as the others stood up.

'This is Nicole,' said Jay. 'She'll be joining us tonight.'

'Welcome,' said the three other women, in unison.

'Come sit, we have some food,' said Beatrice.

Amy caught Jay's look, his eyes indicating that everything was fine. They'd never met together in broad daylight, and with the police interest in Jay it felt to Amy as if they were being foolhardy at best.

The old pier loomed out from the mud, the hint of seawater in the distance behind it. Amy had never set foot on the structure, the town's original pier. Such was its dereliction, the public were no longer allowed on it though a man had been murdered there the previous year.

'Tonight is going to be special,' said Jay. 'For Nicole's sake I thought we should meet earlier,' he added, tearing off a strip of focaccia bread from the spread prepared by Beatrice and dipping it in a small plastic tub of olive oil. Nicole was snuggled in close to him, Amy on her right.

Amy couldn't deny the beauty of their spot – if the sea had been in it would have been picture-postcard perfect – and tried to ignore the nagging worry in the pit of her stomach. She ate what she could, trying to share the joy she saw in the eyes of everyone else in the group. They talked like any random group of friends – about everything and nothing – when each knew, as Amy did, that one of them would die that night.

As time slipped by Nicole became more confident, chatting and mingling with the others. Amy was proud of her friend and the knot in her stomach began to loosen. Jay didn't want the risk of a campfire so as darkness descended they pulled on their coats and walked along the beach. The sea was mirror-like as it crept towards the rear of the old pier. Amy felt Jay's hand reach for hers, his skin cool to the touch. 'I used to come here as a child,' he said, to her and her alone.

His attention warmed her. 'The pier?'

Jay nodded. 'The town. I didn't live here as a child. We lived in Gloucestershire. We used to come here and pretend to play families. Once a year until I was sixteen.'

Jay had never talked about his childhood before. 'What happened then?' asked Amy, remembering the tale the policewoman had told her.

'Then I started my journey. I met someone here, someone who opened my eyes to something beyond this world. It was here where it all started,' he said.

He didn't elaborate and Amy didn't question him as he summoned everyone together. Smiling, he pointed to the end of the pier where the remains of the lifeboat jetty pointed into the mud. 'That's our destination for tonight,' he said. 'We better go before the tide gets in.'

Chapter Fifty-Six

Two hours later and they were no closer to finding the phone contract and IMEI number that might lead them to Amy. It was early evening now, the sky already darkening. Farrell had headed into town to coordinate the search for Chappell and Amy. It was Sunday night, the town full of revellers both local and from out of town. They'd gone from bar to bar, and scanned the seafront, but Farrell had nothing to report.

Louise hadn't realised her day could get any worse until a car pulled up outside Amy's block of flats and Tania Elliot stepped out dressed like she was attending a ball. She wore an elegant coat over a black dress, her heels clicking on the pavement as she walked over. 'Inspector,' she said.

'Have we dragged you away from something?' asked Louise.

'Just dinner with a friend. Care to comment on why there is such a big police presence outside this block of flats?'

'Not really.'

'Is this to do with the dead women? A potential suspect?'

'No comment at this time, Tania,' said Louise.

'Come on, Louise, you must be able to give me more than this. I thought we had an agreement.'

Louise couldn't suppress her laugh. It felt good to smile but she feared her laughter would turn to hysteria if she didn't rein it in. Tania stepped back as if startled by such a response. 'Any vague agreement we had evaporated the second you coined the phrase Suicide by Sea.'

'That wasn't me,' said Tania. 'I would never be so crass. Believe it or not, I like this town. And suicide isn't something I would treat so frivolously.'

'If that's the case, I apologise,' said Louise, 'but I have nothing for you.'

Tania looked as equally surprised by the apology as she had by the laughter. It appeared to have stopped her from speaking as she mulled something over in her head. 'I would rather we had a good working relationship, Inspector Blackwell,' she said.

Louise had been on the wrong side of the press too many times for her to consider a proper working relationship with a journalist again. Occasionally the press served a purpose and she didn't want to dismiss Tania out of hand, but she wasn't going to divulge anything about Amy and Chappell at this juncture. 'I appreciate that, Tania, but I'm in the middle of an active investigation.'

'Is Jay Chappell a suspect in the case?' said Tania, undeterred.

'No comment.'

'He's not at his home and I noticed there's also a police presence there.'

'You have been busy, haven't you? No comment, Tania. Now, please let me get on with my work.'

The journalist hesitated as if engaged in some form of internal debate. 'It's come to my attention, Inspector Blackwell, that your brother has got himself into some financial difficulty,' she said eventually.

At least she had the good grace to look sheepish. It took every inch of Louise's willpower not to reach for her. 'You need to be very careful what you say next to me, Tania,' she said.

'I would say it's in the public interest when a leading detective, currently heading a case into four murdered women, has a degenerate gambler for a brother.'

The intensity of adrenaline flooding Louise's system made her nauseous. Tracey's pills had eased the pain in her head, yet every inch of her felt tired and strained. She paused before responding, trying to control the relentless beat of her heart. 'That sounds like a threat, Tania.'

'It's not a threat, it's a reality.'

That Paul's issues could be held against her had not really figured in her thoughts before. She wanted to find him but her main concern at that moment was for Emily. What would happen if Tania found out that he was missing with her niece? She reminded herself to call her parents the second Tania left and warn them not to speak to anyone. 'Are you asking for information on this ongoing investigation in lieu of holding off a story on my brother?'

'That would be blackmail,' said Tania.

Louise shook her head. 'It's good to see you finally reveal your true colours. But something you may not know about me is that I don't bend so easily. Print your story if you wish, I'll take my chances. But remember, everyone will hear about this conversation. Everyone will know you're not to be trusted.'

'That is a shame, Louise.'

'Stick to "Inspector",' said Louise, walking off.

'Lou, a word,' said Tracey, outside the block of flats. She was holding her phone and looked as sheepish as the journalist had.

Louise pinched the bridge of her nose, her heartbeat returning to normal as she heard the journalist drive away. 'What is it?' she said, sounding shorter than she'd intended.

'Sergeant Joslyn Merrick has been trying to contact you. She had my number from the last time.'

Louise looked at the three missed calls from Joslyn, and the six missed calls from her parents, all since she'd been talking to the journalist. 'Did she say what she wanted?'

Tracey's face was blank, which was never a good sign. 'She thinks she may have tracked Paul's location,' she said.

Chapter Fifty-Seven

No one cared that they were trespassing. Although Amy had never been on the old pier before, she knew groups of teenagers had used the place on a regular basis over the years – only last year, a group had to be rescued after becoming stranded on the main part of the pier. Still, there was an illicit thrill to climbing up the stone bank of the jetty in the darkness being guided by the dim light from Jay's torch.

Amy was at the back of the procession, feeling very much like the elder statesman of the group as she helped Nicole keep her balance after she'd slipped on a wet rock. 'Beats working at the café,' said Nicole, looking happier than Amy could ever recall.

With the tide drawing nearer, the sea breeze had picked up and a fine spray of water hit Amy as they congregated by the entrance to the main area of the pier on Birnbeck Island. A pair of battered wooden doors was locked, a thick spiralling chain held together with an oversized padlock. Amy wondered if this was an oversight on Jay's part, only for him to produce a key. 'Fortunately, I've been here before,' he said, clipping the lock open.

The hollow interior felt colder than outside. The six of them shuffled through the opening, Jay locking the door from the inside. 'Through here,' he said, guiding them to a larger, cavernous room. Air leaked through the cracks in the roof and battered walls, but it couldn't mask the various smells of excrement, ammonia, and a deeper more visceral smell of petrol that filled the place.

'They used to maintain the lifeboats here,' said Jay, as he switched on a number of battery-powered lamps he'd arranged in a circle in the centre of the room.

The others were scanning the area. 'Look, you can get to the walkway through here,' said Beatrice, prompting Nicole to skip over to see.

The promenade part of the pier was in disrepair and shut to the public, the wooden boards rotten and unsafe. Beatrice tried the door. 'It's open,' she said, pulling at the crumbling wooden structure. The outside rushed in, the sound of squalling seagulls and the lapping sea obtrusive in its intensity. Jay smiled and Amy saw a hint of impatience in his gesture. 'Come now,' he said. 'We have much work to do.'

Beatrice shut the door and they all took a seat in the circle, Jay's magnetic call irresistible. 'First of all, I'd like to welcome Nicole to our little group,' he said, once they were all together. 'I'm sure you'll make her feel most welcome. She has joined at a very special time for us all.'

The light from the lamps created elongated shadows in the hollow room. Jay's face was only half-lit and Amy wondered why they were here instead of outside like on all the other occasions, in an open setting around the glow of fire.

Jay stood and produced a flask of the Ayahuasca tea from his holdall. The smell of petrol was still rife in the room. As Amy sniffed the air, Jay held her gaze and she saw something she'd never seen in him before: doubt. It vanished as quickly as it had appeared but it threw Amy. She still wanted it over, was desperate to return to that special place where Aiden was waiting for her, but she needed to be sure. Excusing herself – 'Need to pee,' she said – she opened the doors at the front entrance while Jay prepared the tea for everyone.

Door shut behind her, Amy peered along the promenade of the pier that appeared to stretch infinitely into the darkness. The lights from Worlebury blinked towards her through the shadows as if sending her a message. *I don't want to stop what is going to happen*, she told herself, as she switched on the phone and located the policewoman's number. *Just in case*, she promised, placing the phone back in her pocket in the certainty that it would only take one press of the button for the policewoman to know where they were.

Chapter Fifty-Eight

Paul must have called her parents and triggered the tracking software. Louise tried to control her spiking adrenaline as she first called Paul – dead signal – then Joslyn. As the phone rang she received another missed call from her parents.

'Hi, Louise. He activated the phone about twenty minutes ago. I called as soon as I received notification.'

'You have a location for him?'

'A sprawling caravan and camping site on the outskirts of Penzance. Just waiting on your say-so to approach. I'm about thirty minutes away.'

'Thank you, Joslyn. I'll get back to you shortly.'

Her mother was in tears as she answered.

'What did he say, Mum?'

'He wasn't making any sense, Lou. I think he's in trouble.'

'Think, Mum, what did he say?'

'I kept asking him what was happening. I wanted to speak to Emily. He was incoherent, Lou.'

'Okay. Listen, Mum, I need to hang up. I'm working with a team in Cornwall and they think they know where he is.'

'And Emily?'

'Yes, Mum, I'll get back to you as soon as I can.'

Tracey had been watching her and walked over as she hung up. 'You should go. I can take this from here.'

Louise rubbed her forehead. All they had was a last-known location for Paul. He could have left the campsite since calling and could be anywhere by now. But she should be the one who approached him. If Joslyn went in, everything would be on record. What was more, there was no way to know how Paul would react. It sounded like he was in the sort of state where he would be unable to judge his own actions. What if he struck Joslyn or one of her officers? And although she knew he would never intentionally hurt Emily, there was no way to tell what would happen.

'I can't walk out at this juncture of a murder investigation,' she said to Tracey, as if trying to convince herself.

'No one is going to blame you. You're doing this for your family.'

Louise didn't share Tracey's conviction. She'd already made too many mistakes. Finch and Morley were waiting for a final slip-up like this. She could already hear their argument: *if she can't even control her own family, how can she control a CID team?*

But what did it matter? All she could think of now was Emily. Tracey was right, she would never forgive herself if something happened to her niece because of her inactivity.

'I want to be updated every step of the way,' she said, getting into the car.

'I promise, Lou. I'll call as soon as we have any developments.'

If Paul had put Emily in danger, she wouldn't be responsible for her actions. Over the last couple of years she'd forgiven him for almost everything but she wasn't sure if their relationship could ever recover from this. How could she forgive him for treating her parents this way, for taking Emily away? She could accept his addiction was a disease but that didn't excuse the decisions he was making. Taking Emily away was premeditated. He must have been planning it for some time. He'd willingly put her at risk and Louise couldn't see beyond that as she drove along the back streets of town through Worle towards the motorway. She called Joslyn to ask her to monitor the caravan park, but told her not to approach Paul until she got there as she headed down the slip road on to the southbound M5.

She'd only been driving for a mile when Coulson's name flashed on her phone. 'What is it, Simon?'

'Sorry, I know you're busy, Louise, but I thought you'd like to know. Amy has reactivated her phone and we have an exact location for her.'

Chapter Fifty-Nine

The heat of Nicole's body warmed Amy, the other woman's closeness comforting. Jay hadn't drunk anything. He was monitoring the group which was now spread out across the interior of the room, ready to help anyone who needed it. He was sitting on the other side of Nicole. Amy heard him, distant, whispering encouraging words to Nicole. At this dose – and sometimes at the higher dose – it was still possible to converse with the recipient of the drug. Nicole was murmuring something about shapes and numbers, reminding Amy of the first time she'd taken the DMT with Jay. It had been a special time as Jay had guided her, gently increasing the doses until she was able to push through. In a way, she envied Nicole for being at the beginning of the journey, but that was a distant concern now.

Amy downed her tea and lay on her back, her perceptions sharpening as the drug filtered through her bloodstream. The effect seemed immediate. The usual vibrations shook her body and, as she closed her eyes to a world of kaleidoscopic shapes, she briefly wondered if the tea was stronger than normal.

Sometime later, as the initial effects began to wear off, Amy sat up and looked around at the others, who were all sitting up in a kind of stupor. Amy caught a whiff of the petrol in the room once more, carried on the breeze, filtering through the holes in the shell of the pier, and worried if the fumes were somehow contributing to the exaggerated effect of the tea.

It could be that she was tired, or her measure had been stronger than the others, but she couldn't remember the last time she'd felt like this after taking the tea. Jay spoke as Nicole roused herself, his voice thunderous in the hollow space as if a set of speakers had been placed in every corner of the cavernous room. 'Shall we begin?' he said.

As always, the stories were the hardest and the most precious part of their time together. Amy had never been to group counselling before but from watching films and television she knew they followed a similar format. One by one they told the others their reasons for being there. Now that they numbered only six including Nicole, the stories were less wide-ranging. Beatrice told the group how she'd been abused by a close relative as a child, and the terrible life-changing consequences that had brought, whereas Lisa discussed her on-going health concerns: the continuous physical pain she had to endure and how she wanted to experience forever what lay beyond. After Rachael told her tale of being in care since she was born and her feeling that she'd never had any real family, Amy prepared to speak next. Jay had never shared and he never made new recruits speak on their first night.

The tea had heightened Amy's senses. The metallic interior of the pier building was in sharp focus, as were the faces of the group – Nicole in particular – that glowed from the artificial light of the lamps. Jay listened intently as Rachael finished her tale before thanking her for her contribution. Amy felt a rush of love for him as he turned towards her. She was ready to share her story for one last time and to take that final step, yet almost as if it was acting of its own volition, she felt her hand reach into her pocket and rest on the large call button of her phone.

'Everything okay?' said Jay, with such warmth and kindness it almost broke her heart.

'I'm ready,' she said, lifting her hand from her pocket only after she'd hit the green call button.

Chapter Sixty

Louise cursed, louder than intended, Coulson still on the phone. She kept the car on the inside lane of the motorway, knowing it was three miles to the next turn-off. 'How exact?' she asked.

'The signal is coming from the main area on Birnbeck Island.'

'What?' she asked, to herself.

'I thought the place was abandoned?' asked Coulson.

'It is,' said Louise. 'But it doesn't stop people going there.' Security had been upped on the decrepit landmark since the savage murder of one of its caretakers the year before, but Louise imagined it was still accessible for those who wanted to reach it. 'You're a hundred per cent about this, Simon?'

'I'm looking at a flashing red dot now.'

'Her phone is still on?'

'Yes. I know you're . . . otherwise engaged at the moment. Do you want someone from here to call her?'

Louise slowed for the towed caravan in front of her – which seemed to be going at least 30 miles per hour less than the legal speed limit – before pulling out into the middle lane with only a cursory glance. She should be the one to call Amy but still she hesitated. If she called her straight away she might realise her phone was being monitored. She had to give Amy time to make the correct decision herself.

The turning to Burnham-on-Sea was only a mile away and Louise faced a tough decision of her own. She knew if she thought too hard she would see her niece's face and would be unable to make an informed choice. She had to think logically. Joslyn was more than able to approach Paul. If he hadn't been her brother, then Louise would have already sent her in. If he had to be arrested then so be it. Her priority had to be Emily now, and her niece couldn't wait for her to make the three-hour journey down into Cornwall.

But was that really the correct decision, or was she fooling herself? She'd made so many wrong decisions recently that it was becoming hard to trust her own judgement. Emily was a constant worry, probably more than she'd previously accepted. She'd mistakenly called Amy by her niece's name back at the bedsit and she could see now that Paul taking Emily away had impacted her professionalism during the investigation. Surely everyone could see her mind was distracted and if she left for Cornwall now, her career could be over. Yes, the overtime mistake was a forgivable one but the whole investigation had been so sloppy. They'd had Chappell in custody and lost him. She'd been to Chappell's house and not reported it. She wasn't entirely to blame but others wouldn't see it that way, especially if, after they'd just located a chief witness and possible suspect, Louise left for Cornwall.

Switching on the embedded police lights on her car, spooking the vehicle in front of her which almost came to a complete stop, she sped towards the turning. It wasn't only in the investigation that she'd made mistakes. The whole situation with Paul was a mess. Emily had told her she was going away and she'd missed it, and it pained her that her relationship with her brother had soured so much that she hadn't known about his gambling debts. She wanted to scream but her headache was returning.

She was going seventy miles an hour when she swung the car left to take the turning before calling Joslyn.

'I understand, Louise. You're making the right decision,' said Joslyn, after Louise explained the situation. 'I'll find Paul for you and we'll try and make it as smooth as possible. Hopefully we'll get him into custody with no fuss. He can sober up and you can collect him. In the meantime, I'll look after your niece. You get on with your work.'

Louise felt a build-up of emotion threaten to leave her body. She thanked Joslyn, and surprised herself by crying for a full ten seconds before she circled the roundabout and headed back on the opposite side of the motorway towards Weston.

Farrell and Tracey were waiting for her in the car park next to Birnbeck Pier. Louise had been there before, the Pensioner Killer having left his vehicle there last year before his eventual arrest. Throughout the short journey from the motorway, Louise had veered from turning back towards Cornwall and calling Amy. In the end she'd done neither, Coulson having sent a location pin to her phone that still showed the flashing red dot marking Amy's location.

She checked her face in the mirror before leaving the car. Tracey moved towards her as she got out, mouthing the words, 'Everything okay?' for the second time that day.

Louise returned the nod just as Farrell appeared. His eyes darted between Louise and Tracey but he didn't comment. 'The entrance to the pier itself is secured by large metallic doors. We're trying to contact the security providers to get it open but we could cut through the lock if necessary. As you can tell, the sea is in so we don't have any other means of getting to the main section of the pier,' he said.

Louise peered over the concrete wall of the car park. The sea was closing in, swirling beneath the crumbling boards and rusted girders of the pier's walkway. She had first-hand experience of the pier's instability, having walked its broken boards last year.

She had no idea why Amy was here but it wasn't safe and they needed to get to her as soon as they were able. Summoning Tracey and Farrell, she was about to call Amy when her phone rang.

'Amy is that you?' she said, the sound of Amy's breathing audible.

The response was static followed by the distant sound of a man speaking. 'Get on to Coulson,' she instructed Farrell. 'I want to hear this clearly.'

It was muffled but she could make out the man's words. It sounded like Chappell but she couldn't be sure. 'Okay, Amy, when you're ready,' he said.

When Amy did speak, the words were much clearer.

Chapter Sixty-One

Amy had spoken the words so many times before, so why were they so hard to say this time? Was it because Nicole was there and didn't know her history? Or was it because this would be the last time she told the tale? Maybe she was still fuzzy from the tea, but her words felt mangled in her mind and she needed to organise them before speaking. Her reasons for calling the policewoman were muddled but it gave her a strange comfort to know that she might be listening via the phone in her pocket; that there would be a record of what happened.

'Aiden was a beautiful baby. He was so perfect. He had a shock of red hair, this perfect little tuft,' she said.

The group responded, positive and encouraging, and Amy felt Nicole's hand stretch towards her. Her face was tilted in a quizzical look, as if her eyes were saying, I didn't know you had a child?

As Amy told her story, Nicole's grip tightened until it became painful. When Amy reached the part where Aiden died, Nicole was in tears.

'What? What are you saying, Amy?'

'It's okay, Nicole. Little Aiden passed away just before his fourth birthday. He had a heart defect. I didn't know about it.'

'No, no, I can't believe it. I'm so sorry, Amy. You never . . .'

Amy squeezed Nicole's hand and continued. It was wrong that Nicole was here, that she had to hear these stories. Wrong too that she would have to experience what was going to happen to Amy afterwards. But there was nothing Amy could do about it; Nicole was one of the group now as much as anyone else there.

Everyone – apart from Nicole – began clapping. 'Thank you so much, Amy. That was beautiful. Thank you for sharing,' said Jay, wrapping his arms around her again until she struggled to breathe. 'Thank you, all of you,' he said, letting her go. 'You're all so beautiful. Before we continue, let us remember our friends who have moved on. Victoria, Claire, Sally and Megan.'

As everyone bowed their heads, Amy looked at Nicole. She saw the realisation dawn on her friend and wondered if she would get up and leave; and what Jay would do if she did. However, whether in shock or acceptance, she remained where she was sitting.

Jay lifted his head and got to his feet. 'Now, I know things have been strange recently and I appreciate you all sticking by me. Unfortunately, our hand is being forced. We know others would never understand what we are about. It takes a special person to accept DMT, to allow it to guide you to other realms,' he said, pulling out a large leather wallet from his holdall.

The intake of breath was audible as he opened the wallet to reveal six syringes.

'Because of this, I have decided that tonight will be our last together.'

Chapter Sixty-Two

Louise pressed her finger to her ear as Chappell stopped speaking, her energy all but gone.

Despite her resolution to try and separate the personal and professional, she'd found it impossible not to place Emily into Amy's story about Aiden. Emily had already lost one parent and was on course to lose a second if Paul didn't sort his life out soon. If something happened to Louise's parents, or Louise was unable to look after her, it wasn't that much of a stretch to imagine Emily being taken into care or being adopted by another family. What if she moved away? What if Louise had to find out about her death in the same way Amy had found out about Aiden?

She jumped as Tracey placed her hand on her shoulder, glad to be rid of the horrendous fantasy. 'Did we get a recording of that, Simon?' she said, switching into professional mode.

'Yes, ma'am,' said Coulson, over Louise's police radio.

'Where are we on that caretaker?' Louise asked Farrell, still trying to process what she'd just heard. Both Amy's tragic story and Chappell's last sentence: *tonight will be our last together*.

'Should be here in ten,' said Farrell.

'Tell him to get here quicker.'

'Boss. What do you think Chappell meant?'

Louise was exasperated. Half her attention was still focused on Cornwall and she kept glancing at her phone for updates even though it was still connected to Amy. 'I don't know but I need those gates open as soon as possible.' She didn't want to come out with it, but to her mind Chappell's statement meant one of two things. Tonight was going to be the night when he took his own life, or the night when he took Amy's life and the life of whoever else was on the pier with him.

'Come with me, Tracey,' she said, walking to the two inter-locked metallic doors. Louise peered through the gap in the lock, squinting as she made out the crumbling walkway fading into distant shadows. A nervous uniformed officer was standing by the entrance with a set of bolt cutters.

'I'm going to go in,' said Louise, signalling to the officer to break the chain just as she heard Chappell speak again.

'It's your decision as it always has been,' he said, his voice distant. 'Tell me yes or no now.'

For a second Louise thought he was speaking to her. She lifted her finger as she listened for an answer. Almost in unison, a number of voices said, 'Yes.' How many she couldn't be sure, but she'd heard at least three. 'Now,' she said to the officer, who grunted with effort, snapping the chain on his fourth attempt.

Jay started with Beatrice. The group began chanting – 'death is not the end' – but something was amiss in the sound and rhythm, as if each of them were preoccupied with what awaited them. As Beatrice lay on her back, Jay began whispering into her ear before injecting her. Amy saw her body twitch as the DMT entered her bloodstream. 'I'm through,' she said, ninety seconds later.

Jay lay her head down and moved towards Lisa.

'Are you okay?' Amy asked Nicole.

The girl looked in shock. 'Yes . . . Do I . . . ?'

'No, you don't have to do anything you don't want to, Nicole. And why would you? You have your whole life ahead of you. A family who loves you. This is all waiting for you anyway. Why not wait another seventy years?'

'Who wants to live to that age?' said Nicole, smiling, her eyes still red from tears.

'What I mean is there is no rush. You took a full dose with Jay earlier?'

'Yes.'

'So maybe you have an idea of what's there but I wasn't ready after the first time, or the third and fourth time if I'm being honest. It's been a long process. I have a reason to go now, Nicole. You don't. Please don't take it if it's offered to you.'

Jay had already finished injecting Lisa and had moved on to Rachael. Not for the first time recently, everything felt rushed. Jay had said everyone would go tonight, but how? There was no cliff edge so did he intend to go to them one by one, and guide them through like he'd done with Megan? She wasn't sure she could handle that. Her body would tell her to fight and even though it would only last a few seconds, the thought of the air literally being taken from her was unthinkable.

But she didn't have time to dwell any further. Jay was already next to her, appearing like an apparition. 'It's time, Amy,' he cooed, and she lay back on the ground as if she'd been programmed.

'You won't let Nicole go?' she said.

Jay offered her his enigmatic smile and tapped her arm. 'Your earthly worries will be gone now. Make sure you push through and say hello to Aiden for me.'

Amy sighed as Jay injected her, warmth spreading through her body. 'And you?' she managed to ask just before she closed her eyes.

Louise had to leap across the first row of obliterated boards. As she landed, a wooden panel cracked beneath her feet and she grabbed the slimy metal of the pier for balance.

Farrell followed her lead as Tracey watched. It was an absurd time to be thinking it but she regretted not having Thomas with her. It seemed unjust for Farrell to be here and not him. She heard Amy's exchange with a young woman by the name of Nicole and then Chappell. As he said 'It's time, Amy', Louise wanted to sprint the length of the pier to her rescue. Ten steps later she was grateful she hadn't, her foot snagging on a rotten panel of wood that would have broken her ankle had she hit it at speed.

They kept to the side railings, Louise pulling herself forward as fast as she was able. Beneath them, the brown sea was visible between the gaps in the planks.

'Can't see why this isn't open to the general public,' said Farrell, navigating a particularly treacherous hole in the wood.

'Are you sure?' she heard Chappell say in her earpiece.

'I'm sure,' said Nicole, who sounded as if she were crying.

It was a false economy to move faster but Louise couldn't help herself. Chappell's and Nicole's voices were distant and she couldn't hear anyone else. 'Tell Tracey to send the paramedics after us,' she told Farrell, as she jogged along the promenade avoiding the pitfalls and crevices with darting turns and jumps until she was on the tarmac part of the pier, the small piece of land known as Birnbeck Island.

Two steps in and the smell of petrol fumes seared her throat.

'You smell that?' said Farrell, catching up.

'Tracey, not sure how you're going to do it but we need the fire service down here. The place reeks of petrol and I don't think it's an accident,' said Louise down her radio as a flicker of light caught her attention to her left. 'Over there,' she said, pointing to a set of battered wooden doors.

They both took out their batons, Farrell standing to the side as Louise kicked open the door.

'Lovely to see you again, Inspector Blackwell,' said Chappell, as the two officers stepped through the opening.

Louise coughed, the smell of petrol fumes now overwhelming. She wasn't sure how Chappell could bear it. She counted five bodies, all female, lying on the floor. She moved towards the nearest body and bent down and checked the woman's pulse. It was very high, at least 110, but she was alive.

'Care to put that down, sir,' said Farrell, nodding to the petrol can in Chappell's left hand.

'Certainly,' said Chappell, the plastic can bouncing on the tarmac floor, clearly empty.

'What's happening, Jay?' asked Louise.

Chappell grinned, the glow of the lamps distorting his features. 'I want you to know that this is your fault,' he said.

'I'm sorry about that, Jay,' said Louise, trying to humour him.

'You can stand back as well,' said Chappell to Farrell. In his right hand he held a wet rag and with the other he produced a lighter. 'I'm ready to go, are you?'

A distant part of Amy heard the arrival of the police. It was a sound, a feeling that, in her current state, felt like a dream.

She was beyond the physical world now, separated from her body. Many users said DMT was as close as you could come to experiencing death without dying and she agreed. The last few times she'd taken it she hadn't wanted to return. She was separate from her body, could picture it lying on the concrete of the pier; and although she could hear and, if she opened her eyes, see, what was happening at the moment was on the periphery of her experience.

Her reality now was the infinity of space in her mind's eye, the shapes and geometries, and more important, the feeling of being here. The absolute love she experienced at that very second would be explained away in the physical world, but she knew it was real. Why then was she holding back? By now she would normally have completely surrendered to this world, but the sights and smells of the pier were still calling to her. It was only fear stopping her pushing through, but that was what she needed to do if she was to see Aiden again.

But try as she might, she couldn't completely let go and she began crashing back into her body, her lungs tight and filled with a deep and uncomfortable smell. She opened her eyes, gasping for breath, to the sight of her beliefs being destroyed.

Louise would never know for sure how long the impasse lasted for. Her memory told her they stayed that way for an age – the only sound in the hollow shell of the building her increasing heartbeat and the rolling of the sea beneath their feet – Chappell with the lighter held up to the rag, Farrell standing next to her, poised to react.

In reality it must have happened much quicker. Chappell didn't give them the option of trying to negotiate or seek to explain his actions. Farrell ran towards him as Chappell lit the rag and although he reached him in seconds, it was too late.

The fire spread in a mesmerising chain reaction, lighting the lines of spilled fuel in a sprawling inferno. Chappell ran towards the door, shoulders down, crashing into Farrell before he had a chance to defend himself.

'Greg, are you okay?' screamed Louise, who was already moving towards the woman lying five metres from her. She didn't know if it was the noise or the fumes but she was the only one with her eyes open. Louise hauled her to her feet. 'Run,' she said, her stomach flipping as she saw the fire consume the other side of the pier completely, taking with it three of the women.

Farrell was up and moving towards her but by the time she'd reached him, Louise could barely see in front of her face, such was the thickness of the smoke.

'Please, you must get Nicole,' said a voice.

Louise reached out her hand, the woman she'd just pulled up still at her side. 'Get her out, Greg,' said Louise, coughing and spluttering as she moved blindly to where she'd seen another girl.

Acid-like tears ran down Louise's skin and briefly she wondered if the skin was being stripped from her features as she made contact with a limb. She knew there must only be seconds left before the smoke took her so she pulled at the leg. She wasn't sure if her mind was playing tricks on her, but at that moment she was convinced it was Emily she was dragging through the black smoke.

A jet of water rushed through the air and she wondered if she'd accidentally fallen off the pier into the sea below, only for a set of arms to take hold of her and pull her to the relative safety of outside.

Chapter Sixty-Three

The fire service was still working on the pier as Louise came round. She was groggy from the smoke and didn't know if she'd fallen unconscious, or how long it was since she'd been pulled to safety. She was propped up against the rail of the structure, cold air swirling around her. She tried to stand, only for a hand to be placed on her shoulder. 'Emily?' she muttered, before realising where she was.

'Just rest now, Lou,' said Tracey.

Louise blinked, her eyes raging with pain from the black smoke that had covered every inch of her body. Only metres away, the fire was consuming everything in its path and she wondered how long the fire service could keep it from spreading to the main walkway of the pier.

A paramedic sat next to her and placed a foil blanket around her shoulders as Tracey spoke into her radio.

Louise felt as if she were hungover, her brain not quite with it as she tried to recall the last moments of what had happened on the pier. She tried to stand again as the image of Chappell holding the lit rag flashed before her.

'Please sit, ma'am,' said the paramedic.

'Where's Greg?' said Louise, ignoring her.

'He's there, Lou,' said Tracey, dropping to her haunches and pointing further down the pier where Farrell was sitting on the wreckage of a former bench. He lifted his hand and Louise had never been happier to see the wide grin that so often infuriated her.

'I'm okay,' said Louise, brushing off the support of the paramedic and getting to her feet. She took in a deep breath as if the sea air could clear the smoke sitting deep in her lungs. Tracey looked unsure but didn't try to stop her. 'The two women?' she said.

'One has been taken off to hospital. She was unconscious when they took her away but I think she'll be okay. The other one is over there, next to Greg,' said Tracey. 'You should sit,' she added.

'And Chappell?'

'We've got him.'

'Where is he?'

'Back in the van. He escaped unharmed.'

'There's three bodies in there,' said Louise, red flashing before her eyes as she tried to control the dizziness and panic.

'I know, Lou. Farrell told us. It's not safe to go in. They've tried. It's not . . .'

Louise looked away before walking over to the surviving woman, who was sitting on the walkway talking to another paramedic. 'Louise Blackwell,' she said.

'I'm Amy,' said the woman, forcing a smile on to her lips.

'We meet at last,' said Louise, sitting next to her with an inelegant thud. She closed her eyes for a few seconds, the simple motion of sitting draining her energy.

'I'm sorry,' said Amy.

Louise shook her head. She didn't fully understand what had happened but didn't think Amy was to blame. 'You're safe and that's all that matters for now.'

She might have fallen asleep at that point. As Tracey eased her to her feet once more, she felt as if she hadn't spoken for minutes and Amy was no longer by her side. 'Amy?' she said to Tracey.

'She's fine, off to hospital. Just where you need to go.'

'I'm fine,' said Louise.

'I don't like to disobey orders, Lou, but this one time you're going to have to do what I say,' said Tracey, leading her down the pier to the waiting ambulance.

◆　◆　◆

This time she did sleep. One second she was being guided on to the back of an ambulance and reluctantly lying down on the gurney, the next she was awake in a hospital bed. The in between was a haze but she was glad to see she was still wearing the same clothes, even though the smell of smoke made her want to gag.

'Good to see you're back with us,' said Tracey, pulling the curtain aside. 'I have some fresh clothes for you, seeing as you were so insistent not to get changed.'

Louise couldn't remember any discussion of getting changed but didn't comment. 'Anything I should know about in my enforced absence?'

Tracey looked hesitant as if weighing up how much she could tell her.

'I feel fine now,' said Louise. 'The fumes must have knocked me out but I'll be right as rain once I have some new clothes and these have been destroyed forever.' It wasn't a complete lie. She felt better than she had at the pier but the experience had taken its toll. Her mind was still jumbled and she asked Tracey again for verification.

'Amy and the girl you pulled from the fire – Nicole – are both fine. Greg is getting some rest two beds down. Chappell is here. We have two officers by his door. He's suffered minor burns to his face and he won't be going anywhere soon,' said Tracey.

Louise squeezed her eyes shut. There was something she was missing. 'The others?'

'Three bodies have been recovered from the scene.'

'Jesus, my phone,' said Louise, in a panic. Somehow, in all the drama she'd forgotten about her earlier call with Joslyn and her aborted trip to Cornwall.

'Simon still has it.'

'Well, get it back. Have you heard from Cornwall?'

Tracey shook her head.

'Can you call them? I need to speak to Chappell.'

'Do you think that's wise?'

'I told you, I'm fine,' said Louise, with a little more vehemence than intended. 'I need to speak to him now before he can put a story together.'

'You're the boss,' said Tracey, shrugging and closing the curtain as Louise changed into the new clothes.

Louise pulled the curtains open moments later, the blouse Tracey had found for her at least two sizes too big, and was surprised to see Thomas getting to his feet. 'Tracey told me you were getting changed,' he said.

He moved forwards as if he wanted to embrace her and at that moment Louise wanted nothing more; despite which, she felt herself taking a step backwards.

'I wanted to see you were okay?' said Thomas, glancing at the floor as if rebuked.

'Just some smoke inhalation. No different to smoking a thousand cigarettes in a few minutes.'

'That's fine then.' He smiled at her and she regretted stepping back from him. 'Seriously, though, you're okay?'

'I am. Thanks, Thomas. You managed to speak to Chappell's mother?'

'Yes. The second I left her house I found out about all this. You're going to speak to him now?'

'Yes.'

'Then there's something you should know.'

◆ ◆ ◆

'Any news on my phone?' Louise asked Tracey, outside Chappell's door. He was sitting up, both wrists chained to his hospital bed. He looked through the door window at Louise and smiled at her as if she were a long-lost relative come to visit.

'Simon is bringing it over now. You want me to come in with you?'

'Thanks, Tracey. No, Thomas is coming in on this one.'

The concern and trepidation was evident on Tracey's face and Louise was grateful she didn't say anything to stop her. Instead, she placed her hand on Louise's arm and they exchanged a nod.

Chappell didn't react as she opened the door. He sat perfectly calm in his bed, only adjusting his position slightly as Louise took the lone chair next to him.

'We meet again, Jay,' said Louise.

Chappell turned his head towards her and smiled, and this time there was no mask. She saw the malice in the grin, the obvious disdain he had for her. 'Good to see you again, Louise,' he said.

'Shall I call you Jay or would you prefer Charlie?'

A flicker of surprise came and faded in a split second. 'Jay is fine.'

Louise introduced Thomas and went through the preliminaries of explaining that Chappell was under arrest and entitled to legal representation. As she expected, he was too sure of himself to request a solicitor. Probably ascertaining, correctly, that his case was a lost cause. Two officers had witnessed him start the fire on the pier that had led to the deaths of three women. Now all they had to do was make sure he was also convicted for the murders of Victoria, Claire, Sally and Megan.

'How are you feeling, Jay?' asked Louise.

'A bit better than you look.'

'You know how we found you?'

Chappell appeared disgruntled at the question and looked to Thomas, who was standing by the door, silent.

'You were betrayed,' said Louise, choosing her words carefully after what Thomas had told her.

Chappell squinted. 'If you say so.'

Louise took her phone out and played part of the recording from the pier. Chappell's reactions were subtle but she saw the roll of the eyes as he worked out what had happened. 'Amy?'

'Yes. Your friend Amy led us to you.'

Jay frowned, and Louise saw the genuine disappointment in his features. 'You knew she contacted us after you killed Megan?'

Chappell shrugged. 'What is it you want? You want me to confess? I'm not going to confess as I've done nothing wrong.'

'Nothing wrong? You've killed seven women,' said Louise, believing the number was probably higher.

'That's where you're wrong, Inspector. They chose to take their own lives.'

It took every ounce of Louise's strength not to react. Losing her temper would only lead to Chappell not speaking and for now she wanted him to talk. 'You think you're some sort of messiah, is that what it is, Jay? Some type of shaman like your Maestro Bianchi.'

Chappell frowned again, clearly rattled that she knew about Portugal.

'You've been busy, I'll give you that. You killed Bianchi in Portugal, along with those two poor women, Greta and Sandra, then you—'

'No,' screamed Chappell.

Thomas approached, his eyes darting to the chains rattling against the metallic frame of Chappell's bed. Louise held her hand out. 'No?' she asked.

'No. That was a mistake.'

'You didn't mean to kill them, didn't mean to murder your mentor?'

Chappell's front teeth bit down on his lower lip.

'Because he was a man? You meant to kill the others though?'

'You don't understand. You never could.'

'Try me.'

'I could explain everything to you but you would dismiss it.'

'What have you got to lose?' said Thomas. 'It's not as if you're going anywhere.'

'Fine. We were helping them.'

'Helping who? Greta and Sandra?'

'Yes. They had seen the other side. Maestro Bianchi and I planned to help them move to the next level, and then things got out of hand. We took too much Ayahuasca. I guess you know what happened.'

'All three died from hanging and you survived.'

'That was an accident too.'

'You wanted to kill yourself?'

Chappell was incredulous. 'No, but I came close, didn't I?' he said, lifting his head up to reveal the scarring on his neck.

'What do you mean by the next level, Jay?' asked Thomas.

'That I can't tell you about. I could show you but—'

'Oh yes, we know all about your love of DMT. Traces were also found in samples taken from Victoria, Claire, and Megan.'

Chappell looked confused. 'What did Amy tell you?'

It was Louise's turn to smile. 'Back to the betrayal. Amy told us what we already knew. You drugged those poor women and then killed them.'

'I didn't kill them. They took their own lives. I was helping them. You clearly don't understand. I said you wouldn't.'

Chappell was rattled and Louise wanted to push him as hard as she could. 'I've read your book. I understand more than you think.'

'Have you taken it?' he said.

'No.'

'Then you don't know anything about it.'

'I know that it's like dying. That users often believe they have travelled to other worlds or dimensions.'

A half-smile formed on Chappell's lips. 'You read a book and a few articles on the Internet?' he said, chuckling. 'You can't describe what happens, you fucking idiot. You can only experience it.'

Thomas moved towards the prisoner again, stopping short as Louise shook her head. 'You don't really believe it though, do you? You know it's just a drug. Your mind playing tricks on you.'

Chappell's face contorted with rage and he spat at her.

'What the fuck do you think you're doing?' said Thomas, grabbing Chappell by his throat.

Louise wiped her face. 'So you do believe it. That does surprise me. So how did it work? You give those poor women the drug then coerce them to take their own lives?' she said, signalling to Thomas to let go of Chappell.

'I told you, you can't understand. All of them – Victoria, Claire, Sally, Megan, Beatrice, Rachael, Lisa, Nicole, and Amy – especially Amy – wanted it. They wanted to move on. I showed them something special. It was their choice.'

'Their choice to jump from a cliff, to be suffocated to death, to be burned alive, you sick fuck?' said Thomas.

Chappell shrugged and Louise could see Thomas was seconds away from attacking him. 'See, the thing is, Jay, I know you want us to believe that you were helping these women. That you have some higher purpose. But maybe you could help me out with one question.'

'What?'

'Did you sleep with them?'

'What?' said Chappell, colour spreading across his scarred neck and up to his face like a rash.

'We know about your ex-girlfriend – Mabel.'

'I don't want to talk about that.'

'I spoke to your mother tonight, Chappell,' said Thomas, with unhidden glee.

'What? What the fuck is going on?'

'Was she your first, Jay?' asked Louise.

'It wasn't—'

'Do you know what your mum told me? About her precious boy? She said you were in love with Mabel,' said Thomas.

'Look, I don't want to—'

'And she broke your heart, didn't she, Jay?' said Louise.

'Of course, none of this was known during the investigation,' said Thomas. 'You lied and told everyone that she was depressed, taking drugs, but your mum knew and she kept quiet all this time. Until now.'

'So why did you do it, Jay?' asked Louise. 'Was your heart broken that much that you needed revenge?'

Jay breathed through his nose, the fight ebbing away from him. 'We made a pact,' he said.

'A pact?'

'We'd taken some DMT and we agreed that something else, something better was waiting for us. I promised to help her and then to follow.'

'What happened, Jay? You chickened out?' said Thomas.

'When I saw her die I knew she'd gone to a better place. I decided to help others—'

'Did you sleep with her, Jay?' said Louise, interrupting.

'What?'

'Did you sleep with Mabel before you killed her?'

Chappell leant back in his bed, his cuffs clinking. 'You don't know what you're talking about.'

'Did she know that you knew about her cheating?'

The colour on Chappell's face returned and Louise went for broke. After Thomas told her what Chappell's mother had said, a theory had come to her. If she didn't push him now they might never find out the truth.

'No, but what—'

'Did you sleep with Victoria? Claire? Sally? Megan? I know you slept with Amy last night, Jay. Is that how it works? Is it, Jay?' She was inches away from his face now, could taste the sourness of his breath, the smoke still on his skin.

'Yes,' he screamed into her face. 'I slept with them. I slept with them all. Of course you wouldn't understand. I slept with Mabel before she left and she carried me with her. I could see it on her face the second she departed. I saw it on all their faces.'

'You sick fuck,' said Thomas.

Louise pulled her chair back. 'I don't think you're delusional, Jay. You knew what you were doing. I don't think Mabel really hurt you. You were probably pissed off she cheated on you but it gave you an opportunity. You slept with her to get that back and then made sure she could never cheat on you again.'

'Isn't that it, Jay? You're not some kind of messiah. You're an overgrown adolescent who never got over his first girlfriend fucking someone else. That's all you are. Sad and pathetic,' said Thomas.

'You believe whatever you want,' said Chappell.

'But he's not quite right, is he, Jay? It was nothing to do with revenge or sending them to another plane of existence. You used and destroyed these women before killing them. What for? The sport of it?'

Chappell smirked, confirming what Louise had long suspected: that all of it – the DMT ceremonies and the talk of other worlds – had been a fantasy conceived to fit Chappell's twisted desire. They would probably never fully understand his motives beyond the fact that he liked to control and kill young women. No doubt he would stick to his messiah story, but it would be a tale he told for the rest of his life from inside a jail cell. 'Now, if you don't mind, I am a bit sleepy,' he said, turning away.

Louise ran her fingers through her hair, exhaustion rippling through her. She opened the hospital door to see Coulson running down the hallway towards her.

His hand was outstretched. In it, was her phone.

Chapter Sixty-Four

Tracey drove, Thomas in the passenger seat. Louise sat in the back, experiencing the journey in a daze. She'd collapsed to the ground after speaking on the phone, the air knocked so completely from her that she thought she'd never breathe again.

The doctors had told her she couldn't leave the hospital but she'd only had to tell Tracey once that wasn't going to happen. 'I'll drive you,' her friend had said, and here they were slicing through the countryside, the blue lights and wailing siren guiding them to a scene that Louise wasn't ready for.

She could still smell the smoke. It clung to her flesh like a second skin, emanated from the sweat beneath her lips, drifted on her breath as she opened her mouth. A distant part of her was still at the pier, watching the flames spread with terrible alacrity, waking those poor sleeping women for a final few seconds of agonising torment.

Yes, they'd caught Chappell and she'd managed to save Amy and her friend Nicole. *But at what cost*, thought Louise as Tracey took the corner into the caravan park at breakneck speed.

Louise's head snapped against the side of the door and Tracey apologised, slowing the car as the sight of the crime-scene tent – a perfect white to the backdrop of flashing blue lights – got nearer and nearer.

'You don't need to do this,' said Thomas, as Tracey stopped the car, but Louise had already opened the door. She stumbled from the car, her shoes sliding on the dew-covered grass. Her ears were ringing, like she'd just left a particularly loud pop concert. A uniformed officer put his hand out to stop her and Louise looked at him as if she couldn't believe his barefaced cheek.

'She's with me,' came a voice.

'Yes, Sarge,' said the uniformed officer.

'Louise, are you okay? You don't look stable,' said Sergeant Joslyn Merrick, who was dressed in a SOCO uniform.

The woman wrapped her arms around her and Louise closed her eyes, the smell of smoke intensifying. 'I need to see him,' she said.

'I understand,' said Joslyn. 'I'll take her through,' she said to Thomas and Tracey who'd appeared behind her like guardian angels.

'You'll need to change, I'm afraid,' said Joslyn. 'We're not through processing.'

The three of them helped Louise put on the SOCO uniform like parents dressing a child. Her body felt insubstantial like she was elsewhere, as if viewing the scene from another set of eyes.

'Are you sure?' said Joslyn, resigned.

Louise ignored her and stepped through the tent opening, the smell of linoleum mixing with the smoke in her nostrils. The SOCOs moved aside, the photographer letting the camera hang to one side as if he'd been primed that Louise was coming.

'You stupid bastard,' she mouthed, bending – almost falling – to her haunches. Joslyn had hold of her. Even in her mild delirium, Louise knew she couldn't touch her brother. She was glad his eyes were closed. The incisions in his chest and stomach looked too insubstantial to have killed him and she thought maybe this was all a dream. The scene had a dream-like quality to it. She didn't feel like she was here and maybe any second, someone would wake her and she would be back at the hospital in Weston.

Joslyn lifted her to her feet and a wave of blood rushed to Louise's head. She stood that way for a time, trying her best to control her nausea. All she wanted to do was lie down, to block everything from her mind.

'Let's get you some air,' said Joslyn.

'Where is she?' said Louise, tripping through the tent's entrance.

'She's safe, Louise. She's at the hospital with my best officers. I think you need to go there anyway. Come on now,' said Joslyn, leading her to the back of a waiting ambulance.

Epilogue

Three months later

Louise's grief over Paul's death came and went, but the guilt never faded. It didn't matter how many times she was told it wasn't her fault, that it wouldn't have made any difference if she'd continued down to Cornwall instead of heading back to Weston; that Paul had been stabbed earlier that evening, around the same time Louise had helped save Amy and Nicole on the pier.

That she couldn't have reached Paul in time wasn't what bothered her the most. It was the fact that she'd let it reach that stage in the first place. The very first day he'd taken Emily away, all her focus should have been on finding him and getting him back to Bristol. She felt as much to blame as the person – still unknown – who'd sunk the knife seventeen times into her brother's body.

It was the weekend and her parents had brought Emily to see her. It wasn't even lunchtime and her mother was already drinking. She'd never been much of a drinker in the past and seemed to be making up for lost time. Her father looked at Louise as her mother filled her glass with white wine, as if to say, 'Well, what can I do?'

It was hard to ignore the irony of her mother going down the same road as Paul, but what could Louise say? Her parents had never said anything, and she couldn't imagine they ever would, but she was sure they blamed her for not rescuing Paul. They would deny it, might not even know for sure they felt that way, but Louise didn't have any doubts. It was the way she felt, so why shouldn't they?

Louise handed her father a coffee and stood by the glass door in the living room that led to her small paved garden. She waved to Emily, who was playing with numerous garden gnomes left by the previous occupant. Her niece looked up but didn't reciprocate the gesture.

After lunch, Louise drove them into town. They parked in the shopping centre and crossed the road on to the promenade. Now more than ever, Louise felt conspicuous in the small seaside town. She was currently on enforced leave and wouldn't return until after Christmas. Thomas had taken over as interim inspector in her absence. Robertson had said it was to give her time to come to terms with what had happened to Paul, but Louise suspected otherwise. She was still waiting to be summoned before the chiefs and her future was unclear; the fact of Chappell's arrest, prosecution and subsequent three life sentences was the only thing going in her favour. She'd let personal matters affect her work, and depending on who was making the decision that could be unforgivable.

'Can we go on to the pier?' said Emily.

'Of course we can,' said Louise, so pleased to see a hint of happiness on her niece's face.

They still didn't know how much Emily had seen of her father's murder but she'd been by his body when Joslyn found him. Emily had been in counselling ever since and the long-term effect was unclear. She'd been withdrawn over the last three months but that was to be expected. She was going to school and they thought she was getting on well, but Louise could see the change in her and it was the most frightening part of everything that had happened. Every time she had to read about one of Chappell's victims, it was like seeing a glimpse of Emily's future. With the exception of Nicole, Amy's friend who'd been a last-minute addition to Chappell's little group, all of the victims had been parentless or abandoned by their parents at an early age. It was a comparison Louise couldn't yet deal with. She couldn't contemplate Emily being an orphan for more than a few seconds without breaking down. She was her responsibility now, her only real purpose in life ironclad: to make sure her niece didn't end up like one of Chappell's poor victims.

Not that they were seen as victims in all quarters. Chappell had his supporters, despite the verdict and the reopened cases both in Portugal and the UK. So much nonsense was plastered over the Internet that she'd long since stopped looking. To some, Chappell was a messiah-like figure who'd been trying to save those women; a story he'd stuck to at the trial. Louise wondered how many of his sympathisers would have felt the same way if they'd been on the pier that night, if they'd endured the smell of burning flesh.

After Emily had exhausted herself on the rides and machines, they bought ice creams and walked to the back of the pier. It was a clear bright day, reminiscent of the glorious summer the town had experienced. The brown sea was in and lapped at the girders beneath the pier.

Louise gazed out on the Bristol Channel, to the islands of Steep Holm and Flat Holm. To her right, she made out the remains of the old pier. The taste of smoke filled her mouth and she turned back and felt a tug at her hand.

'Thank you for the ice cream, Aunty Lou,' said Emily, slipping her gloved hand into Louise's.

Her mother had witnessed the exchange and turned away, her eyes full of tears.

Louise gripped her niece's hand, fighting her own tears. 'You're very welcome,' she said. From her pocket she produced the toys she'd purchased earlier from the pier shop. Two miniature plastic soldiers, each with a parachute attached to their bodies. 'Your daddy used to love these toys,' she said. 'Shall we?'

Together they launched the toys off the end of the pier, the breeze lifting the tiny men for a time until they dropped slowly towards the muddy abyss.

◆　◆　◆

Amy's pay was at least forty pounds short. She counted it out in front of Keith and glared at him for an explanation.

'What can I tell you, Amy? Times are hard. You know as well as I do that the winter is a bad time for us,' he said.

'I've been here every day this month. Give me what you owe,' said Amy, but there was little conviction in her words. Keith held all the cards. As he was at pains to point out to her on a daily basis, he didn't have to give her the job back. After the night at the pier the police had interviewed her extensively. There had been a huge possibility that she would be charged as an accessory to Jay's crimes. Once, eventually, the possibility of charges had been dropped – the CPS reluctantly accepting that Jay had held an unnatural hold over her – Keith had agreed to give her the job back subject to a twenty-five per cent drop in her hourly wage. 'You think you'll get another job in this town?' he'd said, and she'd had to concede that she wouldn't.

Keith stood, his fat chin thrust out in defiance. 'If you want to come back next week, accept this and get out,' he said.

Amy snatched the pay packet and stepped out into the swirling wind. She was underdressed for the late autumn afternoon, her coat threadbare, her grey jogging bottoms flapping in the wind as she made her way to the high street.

If people recognised her they didn't say anything. It had been big news in the town and still was – the majority of the building on Birnbeck Island had been destroyed, and the case had been national news. But whereas Jay had become famous, a modern-day cult leader, Amy had soon been forgotten, as had all of Jay's other victims.

Amy stepped inside the discount bookstore to get warm. She was glancing at the crime and romance titles when she saw her. Nicole had her back to her. She was looking at the stationery, accompanied by her parents. Amy froze. She hadn't seen her since the court case, and even then they hadn't spoken – Nicole's parents making sure of that.

It was Nicole's mother who spotted her first. It was like she'd seen Jay himself, her face morphing into a mixture of rage and fear as she instinctively placed her arm around her daughter's shoulders.

Nicole turned and Amy was so thankful that she didn't mirror her mother's look of distress. 'Amy, how are you?' she said, shrugging off the arm draped around her.

'Nicole, I don't really think—' began her father, but Nicole cut him off.

'Please wait outside. I'll only be a few moments,' she said. Her parents exchanged worried looks but relented, leaving Amy alone with Nicole.

'I'm sorry about that. They've been a bit overprotective since—'
'Of course, I understand.'
'So how have you been keeping, Amy?'
'So-so. And you? Are you back at uni?'
'I'm taking a year out. They're letting me defer until next September. I'm pretty sure my mum wouldn't let me go even if I wanted to. I'm not sure she'll want me to go next year,' said Nicole, with a smile.

Amy shook her head, her chest tight. 'I'm so sorry I got you involved in all this,' she said. 'I truly am.'

'Amy, you don't have anything to be sorry for. You're just as much a victim as I am. I made my own choices. You didn't introduce us, in fact you tried to keep him away from me.'

'But that day, I should have made you go home.'

'You wouldn't have been able to. You saw me. I was infatuated. Please don't blame yourself.'

'That's enough,' shouted Nicole's dad, causing a number of shoppers to look their way.

Nicole moved towards her and they embraced, the first proper human contact Amy had experienced since that night. 'You look after yourself,' said Nicole.

'You too.'

The journalist was waiting outside her block of flats. 'Amy, how are you?' said Tania Elliot, getting out of the car and taking off the over-large sunglasses that had shielded her heavily made-up eyes.

'I don't want to talk to you,' said Amy.

Tania had started bothering her a few days after the night at the pier. Initially she'd told her she was writing an article on Jay and wanted her viewpoint, but the newspaper articles had come and gone. Now she was writing a book and according to Tania, Amy was the central character.

'I've money for you,' said Tania, removing a wad of fresh-looking notes from her long coat like a magician creating an illusion.

'I told you, I don't want your money.'

Amy had learnt over the last few weeks that Tania didn't like being told no. 'Maybe I should give this to your friend Nicole. I'm sure she would appreciate it.'

Amy laughed. 'You could try.'

'Come on, Amy. Don't you want people to hear your side of the story? You know what the general feeling is about you in the town.'

'The general feeling?'

'You know what I mean. The stories about you and Jay working together; that you recruited Nicole for his little group.'

'If I'm not mistaken, Tania, you're one of the people who spread those rumours.'

'Then let me put that straight. Let me tell the people what really happened.'

Amy moved towards the front door. 'I have to be perfectly honest with you, Tania. I don't think you even care about the truth.'

'That's not true,' said the journalist, but Amy was already walking upstairs, Tania's voice an incoherent noise echoing against the walls of the building.

And if I'd told her my side of the story, what would she have said, thought Amy as she ate her dinner of pasta smothered in ketchup.

Would Tania, and her audience, have liked what she had to say? That she wished she'd died that evening on the pier. That she still believed in Jay, however erratic he'd become in the last few weeks they'd been together; even after she'd discovered most of what he'd told her had been a lie. That his trip to the Amazon was fictitious. That he'd subsequently changed his name and killed his first girlfriend, and three others, in Portugal. How would that play out to Tania's readers?

Yes, Amy appreciated everything the brave policewoman had done for her and was so thankful that she'd saved Nicole. But she couldn't say with any certainty that what had happened to Beatrice, Rachael and Lisa that night was a mistake. They'd wanted to move on as had Megan and the others. The method had been hideous, but it had been what they'd wanted.

Jay had tried to explain at the trial but he was dismissed, both by the authorities and those reporting the case. It wasn't a surprise.

As he'd said, you couldn't understand the effect of DMT – she hated to hear it being called a drug – unless you'd tried it.

And Amy had one stash left, long ago given to her by Jay in case of emergency. Amy had hidden it at work and was glad she had, as twice the police had ransacked her place.

She brewed the tea now, wanting to keep enough connection with her body for her to do what had to be done. She wrote two notes – one for Nicole and one for the policewoman who'd saved her life – before drinking the Ayahuasca.

What did she have left? Jay was in prison, Nicole wasn't allowed to speak to her, and Megan was elsewhere. But this wasn't about them, it was about her. One way or another, everyone in her life had failed her. She could see that clearly now. She understood Jay was a charlatan, but whether by design or mistake he'd introduced to her the one precious thing she had left: a way out.

She let the drug hit her bloodstream and moved her shaking body to the landing outside her front door. She thought about Jay and hoped he would find his own way out soon. She thought about Nicole and wished her a full and happy life.

Finally she thought about her son, Aiden, and, closing her eyes, let herself fall.

ACKNOWLEDGMENTS

Thank you to everyone who has helped me complete this book. My agent, Joanna Swainson, for her comments and advice; Jack Butler and everyone at Thomas & Mercer for their continued support and help in making this series the best it can be; and Russel McLean for his invaluable insights and suggestions that are always so helpful.

Huge thanks also to everyone who has already supported the series, with a particular thanks to the wonderful readers and book bloggers who have taken the time to review it.

Finally, thank you to all my family and friends for their continued enthusiasm and support. Special mention goes to my sister, Claire, for lending me her middle name for Louise Blackwell, and to Alison, Freya and Hamish for being my inspiration and my strongest supporters.

ABOUT THE AUTHOR

Photo © 2019 Lisa Visser

Following his law degree, where he developed an interest in criminal law, Matt Brolly completed his Masters in Creative Writing at Glasgow University.

He is the bestselling author of the DCI Lambert crime novels, *Dead Eyed*, *Dead Lucky*, *Dead Embers*, *Dead Time* and *Dead Water*, and the Lynch and Rose thriller, *The Controller*. In addition he is the author of the acclaimed near-future crime novel *Zero*. The first novel in the Detective Louise Blackwell crime series, *The Crossing*, was published in 2020.

Matt also writes children's books as M. J. Brolly. His first children's book is *The Sleeping Bug*.

Matt lives in London with his wife and their two young children. You can find out more about him at www.mattbrolly.co.uk or by following him on Twitter: @MattBrollyUK.